PRAISE FOR *FROM NOTI*

T0306937

"*From Nothing* is a taut thriller with plenty of soul, action, and percolating dialogue."
- Culture Sonar

"Only a master storyteller could so completely marry two worlds with such intrigue and keep the pace hot, heavy and thrilling!"
- Tome Tender

"A roller-coaster ride of a read that will keep your Kindle lit way into the wee hours."
- Bit Rebels

"Only a Silicon Valley insider with the soul of a classic rock musician could have authored this penetrating story of a man who finds his true identity after suffering the sting of betrayal from the men who promised to help fulfill his dreams. *From Nothing* is the perfect bookend to Ken Goldstein's now-classic novel *This is Rage*—a more personal, yet universal story about one man's struggle to embrace an elusive faith and receive the redemption he may or may not deserve. A book rich with insight and human introspection, *From Nothing* is also a page-turning thriller that will keep you guessing until the very end."
—Stephen Jay Schwartz, *Los Angeles Times* bestselling author of *Boulevard* and *Beat*

"Ken Goldstein has done a masterful job with his latest, *From Nothing*. In this wild ride through the dark side of vulture finance, rock music and Sin City, you'll meet characters that think and speak like real people who find themselves facing tough choices. The plot moves fast and the stakes keep rising. Once you open this book, you won't put it down until you reach the thrilling finish."
—Robert Tercek, bestselling author of *Vaporized*

"I grew up with the music, but the author introduced me to the inner workings of modern tech. A fascinating look at the world of start-ups, innovation, corporate greed, and personal responsibility wrapped up in a gripping, high-stakes thriller."
—Wilson Milam, Tony-nominated stage director

"In his third book, *From Nothing*, I was hooked from the very first page by Ken Goldstein's masterful storytelling. Only he could weave a story of competing vulture capitalists with eyes on a distressed software company with that of a Las Vegas cover band chasing dreams of superstardom—and teach us important lessons about leadership along the way."
—Scott Freiman, Founder, *Deconstructing the Beatles*

"From the boardroom to the bandstand, Goldstein's *From Nothing* doesn't miss a beat, taking readers on a wildly unpredictable but wholly believable tale of 21st century rock n' roll soul redemption. Crackling dialog, tantalizing peeks into the cutthroat world of Silicon Valley, and vibrant scenes of unvanquished rock n' roll dreamers make *From Nothing* a must-read."
—Robert Burke Warren, author of *Perfectly Broken*

"*From Nothing* is a well-crafted, multilayered work of fiction that is all too real. Greedy CEOs. Conniving investment bankers. Spineless board of directors. Powerless employees. But it's deeper than that. It's a brilliant story of life's choices—career or true love, loyalty or betrayal, honesty or dishonesty, morals or money, stagnation or innovation. It's about beliefs in fate or free will, in God or Godlessness. It puts raw talent on a pedestal yet makes it clear that talent can only go as far as luck decides. This isn't just a novel. Goldstein, the artist, has woven a tapestry of life. Read it deep."
—Gene Del Vecchio, author of *Creating Blockbusters*

"*From Nothing* perfectly blends rock n' roll and Silicon Valley with an unforgettable cast of characters. Storytelling at its very best!"
—Fauzia Burke, author of *Online Marketing for Busy Authors*

"*From Nothing* is the most imaginative, fully realized book I've read in a long time. The pacing was superb—rollicking plot, richly detailed landscape, and characters with insights that stayed with me long after I put the book down. I walked into the plot and stayed right there with the characters the entire journey. The combination of high-stakes corporate greed in a software start-up, the pursuit of a rock and roll dream, and a hint of spirituality and philosophy thrown in is a brilliant combination that gives *From Nothing* its own unique voice and resonance. *From Nothing* is everything. I wanted to read it all over again the minute it ended."
—Lisa Hickey, CEO and Publisher, *The Good Men Project*

FROM NOTHING

ALSO BY KEN GOLDSTEIN

This is Rage
Endless Encores

FROM NOTHING

A Novel of Technology, Bar Music, and Redemption

KEN GOLDSTEIN

THE STORY PLANT

From Nothing is a work of fiction. Names, characters, places, and incidents either are the product of the author's imagination or are used fictitiously. Any resemblance to actual events, locales, organizations, or persons living or dead is entirely coincidental and beyond the intent of either the author or the publisher. Where references to existing corporations or known individuals occur, it is for place setting only and not intended to have any further meaning or interpretation. The information and opinions expressed throughout this work are provided for education, entertainment, and informational purposes only, without any express or implied warranty of any kind, including warranties of accuracy, completeness, or fitness for any particular purpose. The information contained in or provided from or through this forum is not intended to be and does not constitute financial advice, investment advice, trading advice, or any other advice.

The Story Plant
Studio Digital CT, LLC
PO Box 4331
Stamford, CT 06907

Author photo by Keith Berson

Story Plant Hardcover ISBN-13: 978-1-61188-254-4
Story Plant Paperback ISBN-13: 978-1-61188-269-8
E-book ISBN-13: 978-1-945839-15-3

Visit our website at www.thestoryplant.com
Visit the author's blog at www.corporateintel.us
Visit the author's website at www.kengoldsteinauthor.com
Follow the author on Twitter @CorporateIntel

First Story Plant Paperback Printing: October 2019

Printed in the United States of America

0 9 8 7 6 5 4 3 2 1

For my Dad

Too early to be a boomer, too smart to miss the beat

You played the game your way

One part Koufax, One part Lenny, One part Sinatra

You showed me how

CONTENTS

Overture 11

Side One: Then
Track 1: Always Fear the Meeting 23
Track 2: You Want Applause With That? 48
Track 3: Meet Thomas Katem 64
Track 4: Your Head Doesn't Look So Good 78
Track 5: On the Road Absent Entourage 94

Side Two: Now
Track 6: Nowhere Man Needed Now 109
Track 7: Play It Again, Victor 134
Track 8: Heraclitus for Dummies 157
Track 9: Original Syn 185
Track 10: The Temple Ascension Beckons 205

Side Three: Evermore
Track 11: End of the Innocent 229
Track 12: That Ain't Working 247
Track 13: What's That Smell? 262
Track 14: Sing or Hit the Curve Ball 279
Track 15: Please Don't Hit Me Again 295

Side Four: EP Bonus Jam Session 311

Acknowledgements & Liner Notes 333
Discography 337
About the Author 341

OVERTURE

We are stardust, we are golden
And we've got to get ourselves back to the garden

Joni Mitchell, "Woodstock"

THE JOB OFFER HAD BEEN A SURPRISE. Five years prior, the notion that Victor Selo was even employable seemed long out of reach. He had gotten one thing right and doors had opened. Reward had emerged when he hadn't been looking for it. Reward, perhaps. A career social worker with enough cases to know had told Victor in high school that his entire life history likely would be determined by a very few choices, hauntingly invisible forks in the road. Too often he wouldn't even know he was at the fork until years after he left it behind. Making the right call was more accident than directive. Luck would always matter but never make sense.

Which social worker had told him that? Maybe it wasn't a social worker. Maybe it was someone in his first band when they broke up the final time. Maybe it wasn't high school. Maybe it was someone from a later band, or some drunk on the dance floor who had to dig deep for the five dollar cover charge but still had a lot to say. It was hard to remember who said it, but that hardly mattered. Victor knew he was there now and only wished he wasn't.

He stared at the offer letter. He had just read it to Claire. The new day job would double his pay, plus bonus, plus stock options, whatever those were. For some reason she wasn't as surprised as he was. She seemed genuinely happy for him. He wasn't sure where to go with her enthusiasm.

"They're requiring relocation," said Victor. "It's not negotiable."

"I know, you follow the work," replied Claire. "How can you say no?"

"You open your mouth and the word no comes out. It's not that hard. I don't want to go without you. It ends there."

"It does not, Victor. You've never gotten an offer like this. If you turn it down, you'll probably never get another one like it. You have to take it."

Victor looked again at the document, shuffling through the three pages of dense legal speak. "Are you trying to get rid of me? Is this the easy way out?"

"I don't think that way. I've said it before. If it's meant to be, it's meant to be." Claire was consistent. She was consistent in her consistence.

"Then come with me. I don't want to do this unless we do it together. We have to do it together."

"My job is here," she countered. "I brought my parents out here so I could look after them. They're getting up there, you know. They need my attention. I want to spend time with them while I can. There may be a time when I can go, but it's not now. We're not exactly on the same page these days."

Her parents? No, that was an excuse. It was his job that messed up everything. It was supposed to be a day job to pay the bills. Software development was supposed to be a sideline to support his music, but it had taken over his life. It had taken over both their lives.

"It's my fault, Claire. I've been distracted. What I'm doing is so different from when I met you. I'm sorry, everything took off so quickly. All of it was an accident."

"It was a good accident, Victor. Yes, you were different when we met, no question about it, but your job didn't ruin things. It changed your life. You found out you were good at something that pays decent money. Two years ago you couldn't put gas in your car. Now an amazing company wants to hire you and put you in charge of product management, the whole studio, everything. That's a gig you have to take."

Claire Mathias was both the smartest and most reserved woman he had ever met. The small Edwardian cross she always wore had been a gift from her grandmother, an understated connection to her past and her heart, etched antique gold with tiny pearls. Her beauty was everyday perfection, the elegant lines defining her contour balanced head to toe, the result of so many morning runs he could never imagine surviving. He knew the entire two years they had been together that she outshined him wherever they appeared as a couple. He liked to eat and she liked to run. He could never compete on looks, a few extra pounds accumulating, no discernable style in his hair or clothing. She won that contrast on every front yet never referenced it. Though they had so little in common, she always seemed to know what he was going to do before he did. She wasn't smug about it, but her certainty made it difficult to move her off a point. Medical equipment sales came easily to her, and while passion for work would never obsess her the way it did Victor, passion for authenticity would always rule her decision tree.

"I don't have to take it," argued Victor. "I miss playing music. I can do that here. I never should have given it up."

"You weren't happy playing music."

"I was happy when I was playing. Everything else was the problem."

"You were born twenty years too late to make it in a bar band. That world doesn't work anymore. I'm not sure it ever did."

"The Beatles broke through at the Cavern Club."

"The Beatles? Really?"

"They played mostly covers when they started out, that ten thousand hour thing means you learn a lot of material."

"Right, and after the ten thousand hours, they had a bit of a following."

"Okay, none of my bands were the Beatles. That was stupid. At my best I never made a nickel more than they got at the Cavern Club. It worked out for them. I thought it would work out for me. At least I tried." Victor went silent. Could he have said anything more lunatic? He could see that Claire knew he was struggling. Sometimes bizarre things came out of his mouth.

"I didn't mean it that way, Victor. I know you tried. You have a gift. God gave you that gift and you tried to put it to work."

A gift, she always called it that. So what, he had a good ear. If he heard a song once he could play it. That had always come naturally to him. He never considered it a blessing, more like a loving demon that bound him to the improbable. It was luck of the draw, an innate skill, hardly the intervention of deity.

"No, you're right. We never came close to breaking through. My bands always fall apart. It's a weird way for adults to live."

"Do you remember the first song I ever heard you sing? When I walked into that dive in North Hollywood where you were playing?" Claire was smiling, the light of her spirit boundless in rejuvenation. That had to be a good sign.

"Eagles, right? 'The Last Resort.' You told me on the break that you liked the lyrics, that you came out here from New England and saw a lot of the same things. 'Across the Great Divide.'"

"Southern California seemed really strange then. I guess I still have a hard time with it, a love-hate thing. Now it's home."

"Los Angeles is different. Most people who grew up here think the rest of the world is what's different, but it's the kind of place someone like you will talk to a guy like me, singing covers in a bar, and not particularly well."

"I hardly ever went to clubs. I just needed to hear some music that night and wandered in. I hadn't met anyone like you. You really wanted that band to work."

"And the one after that. And the one before that."

"That night after you finished your set, the night we met, you told me if you could find something else that you'd be good at you'd do it. Then you did. You made it into something. Now you're being recognized for it. Go with it, before they take it away."

It had happened that fast. He had signed on with a small company to help create a digital database for pop music. What a fluke, people actually paid $1.99 to download what they created, a lot of people. No one had any idea it would catch on, not that kind of viral. The compounding micropayments landed a windfall for a few fortunate angel investors and a halo extended to the inner circle that made it happen. Victor was part of that inner circle. He had newfound believers in distant office parks, and with that came the offer of a lifetime. He could ride the wave as far as it would go.

Victor rolled the contract into a paper tube and looked through it like a telescope, staring at Claire, trying not to be grim. "It's not me. I think about these things a lot. I keep having conversations with myself—long, ponderous dialogues that don't go anywhere."

"I know, you think about things too much. Some things. Other things not at all."

"So I'm hamstrung by consciousness, couldn't that be a good thing?"

Her smile faded. "More like adrift in contemplation. You get angry too often. It's not good for you. It's not good for me. I'm a happy person most of the time. God helps me with that. All I have to do is ask and listen."

"Please, not God, not right now. I respect what you believe, but the idea doesn't work for me. I'm wired for something more concrete."

"God is more than an idea, Victor. Someday I hope you'll discover why I know that. You need to learn to be happy, not empty, not wanting what isn't there."

"Can't I be happy and wanting what isn't there at the same time?"

Claire took the paper tube from him and rolled it out on the coffee table, smoothing out the fresh creases. "I don't think so. You want something, you should go get it. You have to know what it is to find it, and let the anger go."

"I'm never angry at you. You know that, right, Claire? I just can't seem to connect the dots, so I get frustrated. I'm sorry, I can do better."

"None of us can connect the dots, Victor. The dots connect themselves or they don't."

Victor thought about that for a moment. No, she was wrong, but he didn't want this to escalate into a full-on fight, unless it already was. She knew he hadn't come from much, but how could she understand? She hadn't been raised in foster homes. She hadn't been handed off from place to place for the cash subsidies. As a child, Victor got to sleep in someone's house because they were paid to let him stay there—until the hassle wasn't worth it anymore and he was tossed back into the pile. He never knew where he belonged because he didn't belong anywhere. He ended up doing all kinds of stupid things he regretted, but he hadn't crossed the line. He knew that one regret too many would make him an inmate. The best he could do was get out before he was locked in forever.

"There are no dots to connect in the system," he said. "You find a way out or you don't. I found mine, but the fight is forever."

"I know where you came from, Victor. Faith gets us through the hardest times. Think about that once in a while."

"I'll think about it if you come with me. I promise."

"You're not being serious. You're negotiating."

"I am being serious. I will think about it. My mind is wide open to all viable premises. What can I do to convince you to come with me?"

"You're still negotiating, Victor. Not bad, though."

"What's so awful? It's the Bay Area, not Area 51. We'll move your parents there. I'll be making good money, we agree on that. You can do sales anywhere, you're the best."

"Just go do it. If we're meant to find a way, we'll find a way, but don't say no to them, and don't stay here because of me. It won't work."

"This isn't what I'm meant to do, Claire. Anyone can lead a software engineering team. I was in the right place at the right time. That's all."

"You like it better than you think you do, and whether you can admit it or not, you like it better than you like me. I can see that. You can't."

"That's not true. I haven't been myself. I can, you know, get back to where I was."

"We don't go backward, Victor. Neither of us can go backward. Do this and let's see where it goes. I promise to stay open-minded if you do."

"Four hundred miles away?"

"There are flights leaving every hour. Don't be so dramatic."

Again, that impossibly reserved smile. Claire could disarm him with the fewest possible electrons generated from the inner brain. She reached across the coffee table for a pen and handed it to him. She wanted him to sign the offer letter. That would be a life-changer. She was so certain about everything. How could she be so certain?

Victor held the pen loosely between two fingers, dangling it back and forth. "If I do this, we are not breaking up. I want it to be clear that we are not breaking up."

"Who said anything about breaking up? You have an opportunity. It's in another place. Let's find out where that place is. There might even be a place for you to play again. You never know."

"I'm not sure I understand what you're saying."

Claire rose slowly to her feet. "Wishing the eyes of Shakespeare—but were we only playing?"

The words were familiar. It was part of a song he had written for her, but only the lyrics. He never figured out the right music. It must have been a few weeks after they met.

"I remember writing that."

"The words stayed with me."

"You always find the right words, not me."

"Not always, but this time. We all make choices. This is a good choice for you."

"Day jobs like this aren't really day jobs. They take over. They don't leave time for anything but work. You know that."

"Yes, I know that." Claire edged toward the kitchen door.

"The music, I don't know what will happen to me without it."

"You won't lose it, not completely. It's what kept you going from group home to group home, when you were alone. You can't let that stand in the way of your real way out. God gives us freedom but leaves it to us to make sense of our fears and failures. The question is, do you understand what it means to start over?"

She quietly left the room before he could answer. He played back the translation. God let his parents flee from raising a child without a trace of attachment and traded him for a good musical ear. Then God blessed him with a hidden, narrow understanding of technology, and he was supposed to trade his impractical talent for a soft landing—the gift that rescued him for the comfortable ordinary. No, that wasn't a fair trade, not even close. God wouldn't allow such a thing. It wasn't fair at all. The Overseer was absentee, the stuff of elevated words, not tangible, never real. Myth would always be myth, justified by hope, tragically and irresponsibly unexplained. No more stories, no more conjecture. The safety net couldn't be reconciled. It was false determinism, catnip for the easily convinced. All the books he read hiding under the covers in those group homes told him there was no plan, the same books that got him into community college and proved the scientific couldn't be unwound. No wonder he was angry, so deeply troubled by dispassion. He'd been betrayed by nonchalance. Living songs fueled his blood flow, migrating purpose to and from his heart, past the irate harmony, but so damn what? It was another line of business. No wonder he couldn't make it work with her. He had to be alone.

Victor stared at the offer letter for a good two hours before signing it.

Then nine years went by, maybe closer to ten. He didn't see her again.

He would have to answer her question a different way.

SIDE ONE: THEN

You were under the impression
That when you were walking forward
You would end up further onward

The Who, "Quadrophenia"

TRACK 1: ALWAYS FEAR THE MEETING

VICTOR KNEW WALKING INTO THE MEETING THIS WOULDN'T BE AN EASY SELL. He had been at the game long enough to know that being right was nothing more than a good start. What he didn't know was what he didn't know, and like always, that terrified him.

Marin County wasn't just fitted redwood hot tubs and second marriage getaway homes. There was ready cash money for side investments stuffed in every home safe, and tiny software companies bubbling up out of middle age retirement in every guest house. A few of them took condensed space in land-restricted strip malls, and a few of those found a path to going public. Once a company became the province of the NASDAQ, all bets were off. Big dollars could become no dollars in a few bad trading days. Miss a product cycle and the strip mall could be calling anew. Global Harmonics had been one of those moonshots. Landing back on earth amid the medically legal cannabis was proving less gravity defying.

Yeah, Global Harmonics, what an idea that had been! The sometime great notion, an inspired vision from a daring visionary. That's all it was when Victor arrived. He had been somewhat duped, although the founder and CEO of Global Harmonics hadn't seen it that way. Bud Thacker had offered Victor the job of a lifetime to take his brilliant concept and make it into a real product. It was a limitless concept, love at first sight for Victor. He remembered the history vividly, every milestone crystal clear, his mind an archive of the lightning fast second Internet decade's rise and fall. Global Harmonics would create a software engine where anyone anywhere could upload a recorded song in any digital format, frictionless plug and play, and the enterprise model would then real-time generate the sheet music, orchestrations, and licensing platform, all in a nanosecond—instant gratification, instant monetization. Just like that, a song recorded in a garage or banged out on an iPad became globally available for sale, reuse, recording, whatever was possible. When someone uploaded a song, the copyright was instantly filed with the US copyright office, and Global Harmonics issued a contract for twenty-five years of exploitation at 25% of the revenue generated. It was the 25/25 model; that's what they called it, and while it may have seemed steep to many songwriters, where else were they going to get global exposure to hundreds of millions of music aficionados with the chance to monetize their music?

It was all so seamless, so streamlined, a marketplace of musicians buying and selling from each other. The songwriter would keep firm control of the registered work. Any offer to record the song could be accepted or rejected for any reason. If they got a hit, the cash flow would be ceaseless, but the norm likely would be a hundred bucks here, ten bucks there, that sort of thing. For bar bands, that was better money than selling CDs after a gig, and 100% incremental earnings, with the chance to be discovered. It was all upside, no downside, except for the 25% and the twenty-five years, but there was transparency in those numbers and once Global Harmonics hit critical mass there would be nowhere else to go. Global Harmonics had solved the reinvention quandary long since abandoned by the dinosaur MySpace. It would create an online, mobile, social, global, ubiquitous home for music composition with a solid following from starving artists to genre defining stars. The business model made complete sense and there were no holes in the product strategy.

Problem was, the day Victor arrived as head of product management, there was no product to manage. It was all still an idea, mostly stuck in Bud's head. Bud was a big thinker and not a bad engineer, but he might have been the crappiest manager alive. He had hired dozens of software engineers, but had no idea how to organize a team, no idea how to delegate, no idea how to coordinate different styles of code from different coders. It was sheer chaos at Global Harmonics, and the company's burn rate was a perilous bonfire. Bud, a heavy metal enthusiast and sometime bass player, had previously made a cool $10 million at the age of twenty-six, when IdeaGuise—the 3D modeling company where he worked as a coder since dropping out of high school as employee #7—was sold for a billion in cash. He had invested all of that in Global Harmonics, his dream company, to bring his love of headbanger culture to the world. Alongside his $10 million came another $30 million from ThriceBaked Ventures—the same institutional money that backed IdeaGuise—extremely happy with the exit. What Victor hadn't known at the time, with $36 million of the $40 million up in flames, was that ThriceBaked was fed up with Bud's failure to get to market. They had threatened to bring in a new CEO, but Bud begged for one more chance not to lose control, to bring in a strong VP of product management. Bud had seen Victor's band play in LA and liked them. He remembered talking to Victor at the bar after the gig, learning that Victor coded on the side, although his real strength was in organizing teams. He trusted Victor because he was a musician. Victor was his Hail Mary.

The day Victor arrived and saw the disarray, as well as the crippled balance sheet, he called Claire and told her he had made a terrible mistake. There was no company here, no foundation, just a concept and a quickly evaporating bank account. They were practically starting from scratch, one degree above zero, not even. It wasn't a makeover. It was a do-over. The chances of getting from zero to one were formidable beyond belief. They would run out of time. They would run out of money. Morale would implode. They would never get a solid product out the door. Claire told him on phone call after phone call that he hadn't given it enough time, that he needed to tough it out for at least a year before he threw in the towel. If it was a good idea, then make it a good product. Zero to one was the precise formula for winning and she knew he could do it. Truthfully she probably didn't, but she knew Victor would always regret it if he didn't try, if he didn't give it his all before calling it quits. She knew that was who he was. Failing was okay, but not trying was pathetic. Running away would be a container for regret, nothing else. There was inspiration in commitment if he looked for it in the people around him, the people who were counting on him. He had to find the voice, the path. He had to try.

Claire hadn't mentioned God watching over him so Victor presumed she didn't really believe in his chances any more than he did, but her urging turned out to be sound advice. Somehow crawling out of the crater, rallying a team to assemble code from the void, banging out libraries that compiled in the ether, Victor pulled together the pieces and turned the damn thing around. It took seven-day weeks, regular all-nighters, and more high-voltage espresso than any life form could rationalize as safely consumable, but eight months later they delivered a scalable core server. Bud's idea had been good. The talent around them had been good. They just hadn't been sewn together. Victor brought them together and pulled off a miracle. He became a star, most of all in the eyes of the salvaged entrepreneur, Bud Thacker.

With the platform live, Global Harmonics slowly built momentum in the underground indie community. The Seattle alternative crowd jumped in as early adopters, which provided exactly the endorsement the company needed to attract the next wave of aspiring garage bands to establish fan hubs on GH.com. Credibility compounded swiftly as local bands from remote towns began to post their sales figures of original songs distributed across the network, first hundreds of dollars in royalties, then a few breaking into the thousands. Global Harmonics wasn't fully mainstream, far from penetrating the platinum mine of commercial pop, but as membership in the marketplace grew, the cash burn stopped. The company became modestly profitable, and as membership crossed one million, the database of sheet music, samples, and licensing rights found critical mass. It couldn't yet be declared a moonshot, still anticipating a "tipping point," but it was profitable, predictable, and growing.

Victor couldn't pinpoint a defining incident, but it was around this time that he and Claire fell out of communication. With each passing month their phone calls had grown briefer, less frequent, and there no longer seemed like a good time to make a weekend visit. The events seemed unrelated, but as the company gradually took on steam, the distance between them began to widen. When an obscure songwriter uploaded a thin grunge tune called "Motor Runs," the whole world changed. It might have been an accident, who knew how, but Aerosmith put it out as a single and that was all she wrote. "Motor Runs" sold a staggering 100 million downloads. Not only was money flowing to Global Harmonics, the Global Harmonics brand achieved ironclad legitimacy. Within a year, the community on Global Harmonics expanded to 70 million members and

200 million songs. At that pace, even the songs that sold for ten dollars mattered with 25% to the house. Global Harmonics was making it big and making it small. It was the place to go for something new, something untried, something unique.

When the company hit a run rate of $150 million in sales and $17 million in net income, ThriceBaked took the company public at a one billion dollar valuation. Bud was again a superstar. Victor had his retirement in the bank if he wanted it. All was lush within the pastoral hills of Marin.

That was six years ago, a colossal achievement.

Over the next year the stock price quadrupled. That made it a gusher.

It was harvest time. The board cashed in. New marching orders filtered without melody through the art deco corridors. Milk the cow, never feed her. Milk the cow, never feed her.

Victor had a broad, encompassing plan of where to expand next. They would build out a predictive database. They would data mine the patterns of uploads and rent the trends to producers and distributors. All the data they ever needed for a 360 degree vision of popular music economics was stored on their servers. They simply needed to reinvest a small amount of their profits in documenting the framework and expanding their sales force.

"It shan't be so," resolved the company's board of directors. "We're in late stage. The Street loves our profits, but we have to scale into our mammoth multiple. A higher growth rate and new development projects are risky. It's easier to slim down costs. Optimize EBITDA. Generate improved operating income. Pump out cash!"

The myopic board mandated a unified and consistent strategy—manufacture more of the same, only at a higher contribution margin. Lock the platform, let the world's musicians come to us, we're the only game in town and a good one. Victor was instructed to engineer flow through, revenue dollars that drop straight to the bottom line, and while he was at it, keep as few engineers on payroll as necessary. Lower overhead, lower R&D expense, scale into higher returns on reduced investment. Grow the base, ride the horse in the direction it was going, tread water safely in the shallow end of the pool. The quarterly earnings announcements would be gorgeous, exquisite works of art, nothing would please them more. Creativity and innovation could best be expressed on a shining income statement and balance sheet, all legal, impenetrable, absent waste and excess, a one-dimensional cash-flowing wonder! They already had a great product that was proven. Extracting value responsibly was what mattered. Harvesting at this time in a company's lifecycle was the will of Wall Street. The board would hear no argument to the contrary. They were wise. They had been there before. They knew their stuff. Damn it all, they knew their stuff.

Hear the chant. Sing it in your sleep. Milk the cow, never feed her. Milk the cow, never feed her.

CEO Bud tried to push back and conjure up a forward looking vision to partner with Victor, but he was no match for the sage, gutless board. He put up a weak fight for as long as he could keep them listening, but he had sold off too many of his shares over the years. ThriceBaked had gained majority control. ThriceBaked controlled governance. ThriceBaked wanted profits, not risks.

Global Harmonics toed the line and spat out cash quarter after quarter. Monotony, routine, and predictability were lauded as prudent, never scorned. The boardroom suits all seemed to suffer from sameness ailment—delusion. They were under the thumb of the lead investors. Were they idiots? Could they not see that building something new and championing change were the only long-term strategies to feed the Street?

No, they couldn't see the obvious. They absolutely were idiots. Streaming was coming on like a cheetah on the plains. Downloads were on their way to the tar pits. The business model had to change to building artificial intelligence models from complex data sets. Selling product would soon be out. Leasing information was the necessary pivot. The big data in their archives held perpetual value, a sustainable competitive advantage rented to the industry if only they could package it. Victor had to make his case, convince them the company needed to get ahead of the market before it was too late. He had to show them the inarguably foolhardy nature of their thesis. He had to prove to them that they were idiots.

No dice. Victor couldn't make the case any better than Bud. There would be no capital investment with deferred return. He and Bud were directed to secure even greater profits, always more profits. They already owned their fate. They had defined a new product category with a limitless moat to keep attackers at bay. What was the point in driving investment further? Why bother trying to define another category? The chances of succeeding once in the equity markets were incalculable and they had won. Why bother trying again? Feast on the plate before them and savor every bite. There was no need to design a new menu. What was the point in upping the ante, spending unnecessarily when cash was filling landfills? Don't be reckless. Be conservative. Be wise. Excavate the landfills!

The board had been right for a while. The lead investors gloated as they counted their fields of beans. They high-fived as the company's stock price soared to the stratosphere. The partied like a frat with a bottomless keg of premium brew. The party would go on forever.

Four years ago the party had gone on hiatus. Earnings went flat. The company's single product hit market saturation. Every musician and composer who wanted it had it, and since it was a locked feature set, there was nothing new to sell them. It wasn't just their sales. Suddenly, out of nowhere, the moat was breached by engineers in outside provinces. Competitors were abundant, lots of them, mostly copycats, but clever copycats who stayed carefully beyond the bounds of patent infringement and underpriced the offering penny by penny. While Global Harmonics had more than 50% market share, profit margins were being eaten by rising marketing costs to "help the customers find us before they found our sleazy competitors." Now they had to "duke it out with low-cost alternatives" just to hold position. The stock retreated to its IPO price. The ugly had only begun.

Three years ago market share sank to 35%. The company's stock sank 20% below its IPO. Bud was given a year to make something happen. He couldn't. Exploding marketing costs ate him bite by bite, gobbling all the meat on his bones. There were no more monster margins. The company was barely breaking even. Streaming aggregations surpassed transactional purchases, but Global Harmonics was not prepared to ride the new wave of opportunity—those spoils would be claimed by the next wave of innovative start-ups. Bud's spirit seemed broken, his will collapsing without surrounding support. His soundtrack dream was going deaf and mute.

Two years ago market share sank to 20%. Earnings turned negative. With even higher marketing costs, they were losing money to run in place. ThriceBaked and the board fired founder Bud in a press release, which is how he learned about it, when he saw the announcement on the wire. It was no surprise. The same day they brought in a management expert to be the company's new CEO, stealth recruited in a premeditated coup. His name was Maurice Sangstrum. He had been a senior VP of strategic planning at Colgate Palmolive. He had been there for over twenty years following his Harvard MBA and climbed the corporate ladder, but what he always really wanted to do, so he was quoted in his press release, was lead a start-up. What the hell was he doing here? Global Harmonics was a long way from a start-up. The irony leapt from his intentions to his qualifications. Although he was an industry pro in consumer product goods, he knew nothing about music, software, or anything else that couldn't be packed in a box or sealed in a tube.

Sangstrum had been on the job two years, an oddity among the unpolished rank and file, especially the developers who rejected top down authority like immune cells battling infection. He had stuck to the harvest plan, only he doubled down on marketing in an attempted surge at winning back market share. No money for product, just advertising. He bought glitzy TV commercials, direct response snail mail campaigns, the biggest booths on the floor at trade shows large and small. He bought so many search keywords and online display ads, the analysts gave up trying to track them all. Nothing had improved. It had gotten worse, way worse. The company's stock was under seven dollars, heading for five dollars if they didn't make a big move soon. If they broke the two-dollar support level, they would be delisted from the exchange. None of it had to happen, but it didn't seem impossible that Global Harmonics could vaporize. So foolish. So unnecessary.

Why hadn't they listened to Victor? Why the resistance to building on success? Victor had led them to glory and they trusted him. Why stop listening? Why not at least try CPR on a revitalized product strategy? The sky was the limit if only they put a little fuel back into the tank. Not all of it, just some of it.

It was Victor who wasn't listening. Milk the cow, never feed her. Milk the cow, never feed her. Bloody idiots, all of them.

Victor and Sangstrum had clashed almost from day one, but Sangstrum was smart enough to know he had nothing without Victor. Sangstrum owned the mastermind agenda, but Victor owned the hearts and minds of the team. Tragically enough, Victor needed Sangstrum just as much. Victor had taken a fair share of cash off the table over the years selling inflated shares regularly in open executive trading windows, but he was much better at running a team than running his own money. Victor had gotten hooked betting on other tech stocks. He was addicted to the hunt, an amateur equity gambler. He consistently lost more than he made. Trying to come back from his losses, he had placed way too many bets on IPOs. When he did win, he couldn't shake the greed factor and almost always held too long, watching rocket run-ups surprisingly become sunken anchors disappearing into the Sea of Nothingness. Then there were the shorts, those clever bets on intuition anticipating misery. He got those wrong most of the time as well and couldn't resist the leverage offered to him to make a big bet bigger gambling with the house's money, until the house got skittish and asked for the loans to be repaid. His brokerage in downtown San Francisco called often, first to say "hey how's it going," then to remind him they needed cash to cover his bad positions—cash, as in paycheck direct deposit sayonara cash.

Each personal loss for Victor was more disappointing than the next. He had no nest egg, no personal reserves. He was working for the brokerage simply to preserve his credit rating and keep his interest rates low. Now with his stock options underwater, he couldn't quit his job. He had no path to retirement, and with Global Harmonics now a sour offering, his prospects outside the company were limited.

Victor and Sangstrum were stuck with each other. A year ago Sangstrum had stopped the advertising spend and confided in Victor that he was defeated in his current role as CEO. Loser, coward—just a year into his gig, as soon as his stock options had slipped underwater, Sangstrum was shamelessly ready to capitulate. Victor said no, they weren't defeated, they needed to reinvent. The overfed bastard probably learned noble surrender in his prep school when his head was pinned to the floor by a rugby player half his size. He wouldn't have lasted a night in a group home. He couldn't have imagined the survival skills needed to navigate the foster care system. No, they weren't surrendering nobly, summa cum laude or in a threadbare boxing ring. They needed to fight on. Victor wouldn't help Sangstrum sell the company for a quick jolt of cop-out remuneration and a happy descriptor to doctor up the résumé for next dibs, not a chance. Victor insisted over a sullen pale ale he barely sipped that he'd play no part in validating Sangstrum's retreat. After that they pretty much stopped talking.

Victor tried to expand the product portfolio under the radar, but without CEO sponsorship, key new initiatives were a struggle. Victor truly believed there was untapped potential in a knowledge database from the user data they had collected, which they could unlock and sell to the record labels—an entire line of SAAS predictive analytics with very low operating cost once architected. He couldn't prove it because he didn't have the working capital to invest in the model, but he was certain the upside was there. He never gave up. He needed more resources and Sangstrum out of the way.

It didn't happen. Layoffs happened. Demoralizing, lifeblood sucking cost-cutting was ordered everywhere—except of course top management retention pay, travel and entertainment expenses for hanging out at conferences with investment bankers, and incentive bonus compensation for aggressively cutting losses to make bad results slightly less awful. All of the insider packages, especially the deflating "stay bonuses" were negotiated secretively, offstage in confidentiality by Sangstrum alone. Victor had been offered his share but rejected it on principle. He didn't want to be any deeper in Sangstrum's pocket than he was, which further soiled his relationship with his olive-branch offering evil boss. Meanwhile Sangstrum maneuvered in the shadows with ThriceBaked, in silent agreement to offload the beast that was once the great brand Global Harmonics.

It was the circle of life they were all meant to accept as normalcy. For the Global Harmonics originals—the immovable diehards—it was their once happy home being wrecked for a stucco mini-mall. Where they used to play music gloriously in the halls, now they gossiped and fretted and complained about everything—the closed cafeteria they never liked in the first place, the beer bashes with the marginally stale pretzels, the mobile phone bills that no longer got paid for the mobile phones they never wanted. They didn't realize how much they loved everything until it was taken away. Productivity plummeted because it wasn't valued. The rumor mill was an ice storm bringing all useful activity to a frozen standstill.

That brought Victor to the notorious present, where Sangstrum would unveil the showdown. This was the fork in the road. Either Victor would prevail or Sangstrum would have his way. It was all or nothing. Victor knew that with empirical certainty. They needed to listen to him. There were no sensible alternatives. Victor's vision had to make sense. He had to win.

>> <<

Victor looked around the oval conference table and counted how many people sitting there he knew. Seven of seventeen, six of whom he knew to be friendlies. That left one unfriendly and ten coin tosses. The inescapable fact that the one unfriendly was also the CEO was not lost on him. Taking him down in the redwood forest would only be feasible if he grew the friendly count to nine. That meant he needed three. Just three. Three and six were nine and nine of seventeen was a majority vote.

The setting was picturesque. Surrounding the windows were majestic mountain peaks, protected wetlands, the grandeur of Muir Woods—a naturalist's setting for indoor war. Three match sticks to ignite the gathered kindling. Three toothpicks to pluck the bacterial plaque. It didn't seem impossible, except that Victor was flying blind. All he could contemplate were the ten blind bets before him tucked away, bodies seated at a long pressboard slab in this invisible office park.

He had to get three. They couldn't all be owned by Thrice-Baked promising them seats on their next unicorn board. Some of them had to be independent. Three of them had to remain sentient beings. Three had to be possible. The tiny number was daunting.

Sangstrum faked a smile as Victor made his way to the head of the conference room. Did they all know Sangstrum had checked out, that his interest in the company was no longer measurable beyond a countdown clock and a private jet to anywhere but here?

Victor knew it, but not how to say it. The only sensible question remaining was how big a pile of lovely parting gifts Sangstrum was going to take from the prize closet. Victor couldn't have cared less, as long as Sangstrum packed up his carpetbags and made a beeline for the door. The looting would not be up to Victor—he was an employee, not a steward of governance. The assembled, magnanimous minds in the room would decide Sangstrum's payday. All Victor wanted was staying power—a reason to stay, the chance to stay. Sangstrum could live happily ever after in whatever upgraded corner of Hades he had booked with Satan. He just had to go so business could go on. Nothing to it, really. Sanity had to prevail. The Reign of the Deplorable was overdue to end. The Iron Throne that never was would be retired to a bad memory or a drinking song.

Yes, in a few hours, a drinking song. A drinking marathon. Happy hour would be very, very happy with the celebrated slaying of a fleshy, plundering, stinkpot Polo gabardine thug. It would be Aerosmith, and it would be an anthem.

Sing with me, sing for the years
Sing for the laughter, sing for the tears

Victor knew how many people were counting on him. Could he pull it off? He thought he could.

Six friendlies. Three to win. One Demonic Overlord already packed for first class express travel. In fifteen minutes Victor's part would be over. Fifteen minutes to get three votes. Three found votes, one at a time.

"Let's get started, shall we?" commenced Sangstrum. "We have a good deal of confidential business to cover, but before we begin, our music division general manager, Victor Selo, has asked to share a few thoughts with the board. Are we all good to go?"

It began. Slight grins and generally positive muttering surrounded the table. Many of them knew Victor almost back to his starting date, close to a decade ago. They had hired him on a whim and he had exceeded their expectations, adapting the foundation of the simple music database he had developed for his previous employer to an enriched suite of applications that rode the wave of Apple's reemergence in the creativity community. It had been a good ride, a thrill ride of incomparable reward. If only the Cloud hadn't come along and commoditized everything.

"Thank you so much for the opportunity to address you, to share my ideas about the future with you," opened Victor with manufactured confidence. "As you know, I love this company. I really do love this company."

"Your passion is evident," offered Sangstrum, that smug, self-important MBA con artist. Was there no way he could shut up and let Victor talk for fifteen lousy minutes? No, clearly there wasn't. "You wear it on your sleeve. We see it in your performance. You're a good man, Victor. You're a good worker, a smart guy. We're lucky to have you on our team. Please proceed."

Sangstrum was an idealess douchebag, useless to the thinking universe. Sure his PowerPoints were convincing and he could analyze a balance sheet with laser accuracy in nanoseconds, but he lied with such easy abandon it was almost impossible to listen to him without throwing up.

Victor continued with his own forced smile, curving on reflex to a repressed sneer. "Thank you, Maurice. I'd like to begin with a little history, dating back to when I started with this company over nine years ago. Things were a lot different then, as many in this room remember. We were a much smaller company with unlimited promise ahead of us. I moved here to the Bay Area from LA at your gracious request, and not for a day have I been disappointed." Of course he was lying in how he felt about the move, his unresolved regrets, the depth of what he had traded and lost, but that was emotional and they would never know or care.

"That was our previous CEO who invited you, the company's founder, whom I was recruited to replace when earnings and our share price went soft," interjected Sangstrum. "Just offering some additional background for those in the room who may not be familiar with the company's lineage."

Sing with me, sing for the years
Sing for the laughter, sing for the tears

"Yes, I know when you walked in the door twenty some months ago, things looked different to you, Maurice, possibly even bleak. The picture I want to paint today is one that shows those many bad quarters of financial performance were an anomaly, self-imposed, not a norm. All of that can be corrected, reversed for the better, if only we recommit to our greatest asset—creativity."

"That's horseshit." It was a deep, echoing voice from the back of the room. Victor didn't recognize the voice, nor could he see the face of its origin standing behind the summer suits without ties lining the periphery of the table. "Nah, horseshit doesn't smell because it's made of hay. What you're spewing is monkey diarrhea. Thick, mushrooming stench like the soft matter between your ears."

"A colorful description, Devin," noted Sangstrum. "Perhaps you might refrain from comment until Victor has completed his remarks."

Victor recognized the name, Devin, but not the person. Devin McWhorter. He was the rumored buyer of Global Harmonics. Private equity neutron bombing masked as financial reengineering. His airbrushed press mugshot often seen in deals announced online was twenty years junior to his in-person pasty decaying brow. He seldom appeared in public. Victor had never seen him in the flesh, not even at a conference. He was more like a vampire that only came out at night, or in dark rooms like this where juicy blood was about to flow. What was Ghoul-in-Chief McWhorter doing in the room, in a board meeting meant to discuss if an acquisition was even worth exploring? His presence wasn't seen as a conflict of interest. His presence was seen as a done deal.

"May I inquire what the gentleman from the Grey Granite Group is doing at our board meeting?" asked Victor.

"You may ask," replied Sangstrum. "That doesn't mean you're going to get an answer."

"I'm confused," said Victor. "I thought we called a board meeting to discuss the relative merits of combining interests with any number of potential partners, not specifically or exclusively the holdings of Mr. McWhorter. If he's here, I'm not sure how we can have an open, objective discussion of that agenda."

"You are confused," stated Sangstrum in the most direct of tones. "*We* didn't call a board meeting. *I* called a board meeting. You lobbied for an invitation to make a statement and out of respect for your largely successful service, I acquiesced. Let's be clear, you have no board seat, Victor. You are salaried. This is a courtesy."

"You're salaried as well," noted Victor. "You're an employee, same as me, and not a great one, though one with a board vote. This meeting is wrong. This deal is wrong."

"To be clear, Victor, I am the board's chairman as you well know, and at the moment there is no deal. However if you don't adjust your approach, your participation in this conversation will end."

"Oh, cut the corporate crap," belted out McWhorter. "There is a deal. You have no choice. You either sell to me or drown for another year and then file for bankruptcy. Global Harmonics is a train wreck, a lump of tired, local code installations mowed down by cloud computing. I am the only game in town, so get on with the vote and let's get on with life as it's meant to be, sans a good deal of useless expense."

Victor surveyed the table. He had been right. There was going to be a vote. It was closer than he expected, less objective than he expected, and it was certain to be definitive. Sangstrum in his arrogance had made a fatal mistake letting Victor in the room. The board admired Victor. The board understood how much value Victor had created with his deep understanding of music theory and the talented team he had assembled to lead the industry. This was going to happen and it was going to happen now, a once only showdown to dethrone the occupier.

Victor again looked to read the room. Yes, six he knew he could deliver. Six were cognoscente, sympathetic, and credible, for sure. He had helped make them wealthier than they already were, and he had not done badly himself as a result, if only he had hung onto it—if only he hadn't been obsessed by that one bad perpetual trading habit, partial retirement would be an option. Too bad he was leveraged to Saturn, and if he lost this vote, he would be a sorry puke.

>> <<

Bad personal habits. Inside manipulation deals. White collar criminals. Sad drinking songs. Nosferatu with a needy wallet. What happened to the code? The code was what mattered, it was all that mattered. The divine victory of elegant code was no more.

Sing with me, sing for the years

Sing for the laughter, sing for the tears

Victor still needed three votes. He needed them now. His argument was too abstract. Board eyes were blinking and growing red.

He was running out of gas. He had to push uphill and close hard before he lost the floor.

"We are not a train wreck," contended Victor. "This is a magnificent company in a temporary slump, made worse by a visionless CEO who only wants to sell us into oblivion at a fire sale price because his stock options are underwater and there's one year's severance in it for him if we sell."

"That's enough, Victor, you're dismissed," announced Sangstrum.

"I'm not going anywhere. I have a story to tell and I'm going to tell it."

"I was going to keep you on," boasted McWhorter. "I'd heard from a lot of people in this room you used to be good. I thought maybe you could be good again."

"You've been talking to people in this room besides Maurice?" Victor was breathless.

"You are so naïve," shot back the fangless bloodsucker. "Of course I've been talking to people. Why would I be here if I wasn't talking to people? Do you think I'm stupid enough to walk into a hostile room unarmed like you? My presentation was to follow yours, although I was to hear yours and you were not to hear mine. Now it doesn't matter."

"I would like to take a vote," declared Victor. "I would like to know how many of you are in favor of letting this used car salesman sell our beloved company to a toxic predator."

"You're grotesquely out of line, Victor," reprimanded Sangstrum. "You have no authority here, none whatsoever. Beloved? It's a business construct. You need to leave or I'm going to have you removed."

"Removed how?" shouted Victor. "We're not that kind of business construct. Are you going to call the sheriff?"

"What if I told you he was in the parking lot waiting under the pine needles for my call?" threatened Sangstrum. "Get out of this boardroom. We'll settle the remains of your employment agreement later in the day, provided you're not in a jail cell."

"I'm not leaving this room without a vote," demanded Victor. "I know I have six votes at least based on my own recon and that means I only need three to have your ass removed by the sheriff instead of mine. He can escort you and McWhorter to whatever lush island the two of you want to go and you can blow each other happily ever after."

"There's nothing to vote on," refuted Sangstrum. "Only board members can make a motion and no motion has been made. Get out of this room!"

"You put a motion of intent on the table and if I'm wrong, I'll leave, all the way out the door," baited Victor. "If I get nine votes, McWhorter has to leave and I get to finish my presentation on how this company has been great and where we can take it from here."

Victor looked around the room, recounted the six he had in the bag, looked for any kind of expression from the undecided ten. Could he get three? He had to be able to get three. Then he could make his case. Then he would prevail.

"Tell you what," eased Sangstrum, "I'll make you a deal. I'll put the motion of intent on the floor, but if you lose by one vote, you sign your resignation letter right here in front of all the assembled." Sangstrum reached into the thick leather folio of papers in front of him, pulled out a single prepared page, and neatly placed it on the table in front of Victor.

"You already have my resignation drafted? I thought McWhorter said he was planning to keep me." Victor swallowed hard, looked around the table at the endlessly shifting reddened eyes, then directly at Sangstrum, fixed in the sights of McWhorter. Oh yeah, these guys were bad news, the worst. He was absolutely in over his head.

"We don't compare notes, not all of them," replied Sangstrum. "You want to make a deal? My deal is if you lose you willingly leave here without the balance of your contract, forfeit your remaining equity, and walk all the way down the hall into the parking lot, leaving your key on the cement stoop. That's my offer."

Victor tried to push any saliva he could find back into the talking parts of his mouth. "Why don't you just fire me?"

"This might be less paperwork and certainly more fulfilling," answered Sangstrum. "I know you have personal money problems, and I'm not picking up the tab with severance I could redirect to a more helpful soul, not unless I am legally required. Your chance for a soft landing and a bailout is yours to bet. You feeling sure of yourself? Show us what you got."

Victor thought about it for a moment. It was a hell of a risk. If he polled his nine votes the rest would be a cake walk. By the end of the hour, used car seller Sangstrum would be gone. Crypt keeper McWhorter would be gone. Global Harmonics would be on a path to renewal. Camelot would be restored to its glittering majesty. With the tiniest bit of luck, Victor might even be named CEO by the ongoing board, a legitimately landed top spot before the age of forty. If he was wrong, he'd be done, eviscerated without an exit package, a ton of future ownership lit up in flames, his unpaid debts an unsolvable quagmire of legal devastation. It was a tough bet in the fog, empirically too tough even though Victor knew he was right. He needed a hedge.

"Maurice, I'm tempted to take your wager. It will be good for all of us to get the tension out of this debate and move on to something more productive. Before I accept, may I ask Mr. McWhorter one simple question?"

"That's up to Mr. McWhorter."

"For a back office VP you're oodles more trouble than you're worth," sniped McWhorter. "What do you want to stand on your soapbox and ask me?"

"Mr. McWhorter, I happen to be an unlucky investor in several of the public companies you've taken private over the past few years, similar in profile to ours, mostly players in music tech where marketing costs got out of hand. I know their financials up to the time you took them private, and their rough times, same as us. It looks like you're doing some kind of roll-up, so you must have an exit strategy of some sort in mind."

"Hey genius, don't blame me if you buy high and sell low," replied McWhorter. "I'm a pro. You're an amateur. I do my job, which is to optimize. That's why I have a jet, a vineyard, and a golf course, plus innumerable ecstatic limited partners. Is there a question coming?"

Victor let the insults roll off his back. He had no choice but to find the quiet strength to bring down the hammer. "Yes, there's a question coming. Based on our issues at Global Harmonics, trying to help our company dig out, last month I took a stab at projecting a pro forma income statement for the holding company you might be creating for the spinoff."

"Rumor mill send you down a rabbit hole?" groused Sangstrum. "You do find ways to waste time in a crisis."

"With no products to work on, I find ways to keep busy. I'm not a financial whiz, but I know how our business works, and there's no way you could hold revenues on old products if you slashed marketing incentives."

Murmurs ricocheted around the elongated table. Victor had the assembled's attention. Something was amiss in Dracula's coffin factory. The question remained whether they found it troubling or reassuring. Was it reason for concern or entertainment value? Victor saw the path to lowering the boom within reach.

McWhorter was having none of it and attacked. "Are you an amateur bean counter as well, Selo? We have business to conduct. Do you have a question or not?"

"So looking at my imaginary forecast for your rolled up NewCo, I'm guessing in every quarter your operating costs exceed your revenues based on sizeable rebates and refunds, yet you manage to book a bottom line profit without fail by charging off these adjustments as one-time events. You *optimize* by eliminating R&D completely, but your actual recurring costs are hidden at scale. Is that what you're doing, round-tripping revenues and making the whole look better than the individual troubled parts to try to dupe a less tech-savvy acquirer?" Victor choked back a brooding sneer. He had him. He knew he had him.

McWhorter stared at the tip of his Mont Blanc pen for a moment, like Nosferatu contemplating a spike, then put it down on the table and continued without further pause. "You are a punk and that's delusional speculation, but let me answer your question for the sake of transparency. When we make an acquisition, we charge off everything we legally can as one-time expenses. Then we take out the fat, then we enhance the value proposition with proper GAAP channel incentives. Do you have a problem with that? Or perhaps you'd like to accuse me of securities fraud in front of your board."

"Accuse is too strong a word, but thank you for your answer. I want to make sure everyone clearly heard what Mr. McWhorter said, that the entity meant to acquire us, Grey Granite Group, has no sustainable business model in the pile where we'll be dumped.

It is simply a shell acquisition vehicle that buys up down-on-their-luck former cash machines like ours, strips them of earnings, and then aggregates a corpus of corpses, which it someday hopes to off-load on some slumbering strategic and leave the wreckage to burn into ashes."

"I didn't say that," blasted McWhorter. "What kind of a prick are you? This is business, not a symposium in ethics and elocution. You ruined your company and I'm being magnanimous enough to offer to fix it. You should move on before I change my mind."

"And when you buy us at our current fire sale trading price instead of allowing people like me to work hard and drive up that price as a standalone, what does Sangstrum get as a deal sweetener that isn't disclosed?" Victor was as hot as molten steel, searing and unstoppable.

"Everything will be disclosed and your board will compensate your employees as they deem appropriate, not me," shouted McWhorter.

"I believe you fib, Devin. This is an inside deal. You've compromised Sangstrum. You're paying him off, which is the only reason he would recommend it to our board. This board has a fiduciary duty to all its shareholders. They're not selling a going concern for a fraction of what it's worth. You're not going to leverage this historic company into a roll-up you can offload. I can fix it. I can make it worth what it was worth. That will be our legacy, not being added to a scam. All they have to do is bet on me and hit the ejector seat on you and Sangstrum."

"You're going to tell me about leverage, you pissant amateur day-trader?" shouted McWhorter.

The board was squirming, a circle of butts rubbing against thinly padded upholstery. The vehement accusations, the call for fiduciary duty, all of it was getting out of hand. The volume alone was all too discomforting for a Marin County office plaza. Victor looked to Sangstrum to see how he was going to make his final move and rein in the chaos.

"Easy, gentlemen," served up Sangstrum, the beading sweat above his brow not lost on Victor. "A little decorum, a little diplomacy can go a long way in difficult moments like this. We are becoming unnecessarily loud."

"This prick is accusing me of illicit financial engineering he doesn't even understand," yelled McWhorter. "Grey Granite is blue chip. We have acquired seven companies in the last two years and we are welcoming you into that excellent combination. Or maybe we're not. I don't like the energy in this room. Business needs to be kept simple, like making cat food. Mr. Selo doesn't seem to understand that all production efficiency is basically the same. The numbers work or they don't."

Victor took in the mumbling around the table as the board tried to make sense of the discord. The stalemate had to be broken. That would be Sangstrum's gambit. He needed to speak but couldn't seem to find an entry point.

Victor saw the opening and took it. "Maurice, I accept your conditions of engagement. Let's take the vote."

Sangstrum stood silent, the air sucked out of the room with so much speechifying. McWhorter's living dead eyes were bloodshot to the edges, threatening his exit at any moment. Victor wasn't backing down. He knew that getting him out of the room other than voluntarily would require a scene that could stop the deal dead in his tracks.

"You are some piece of work, Selo." Sangstrum got a modest chuckle from the assembled, just what the doctor ordered. Air began to flow again, but McWhorter held no grin, his credibility was in question. Sangstrum continued all-in. "Colleagues, I am not even sure where we are in this meeting, but what I'd like to do is explore whether we have a consensus to hear the balance of Victor's thoughts. That would require a motion to temporarily postpone our discussion with Mr. McWhorter around his very generous, albeit preliminary and non-binding term sheet. I wonder if there is an appetite for such an unusual motion."

"So moved," came an abrupt voice from the far end of the table. It was Howard Tempe, one of Victor's friendlies. Tempe had founded his own software company, taken it public, sold it at top dollar, then seen it stripped down to nothingness. He had been an early angel investor in Global Harmonics, a Marin luminary and part of the recruiting team that brought in Victor. Tempe would support independence and continuity.

Victor smiled, a rarity for him but warranted. This wasn't the board action he had been counting on, but it was another positive indicator. Any defeat to McWhorter would seem to the others predictive. Getting McWhorter out of the room would be a victory itself, a vote of confidence from the board to hear what Victor had to say. How could Sangstrum have been so stupid to open that door? Then again, his stupidity had been evident in every other move he made to date running the company into the ground.

Sangstrum did not look pleased. He looked down at the blank notepad before him and then up again with restraint. "Is there a second?"

"Second," came a voice from one of the ten unknowns, Sandra Wo, also without delay. Again Victor grinned. Wo wasn't even one of the six he knew he had in the bag. She was the president of Marin Community Bank, technically an independent placed on the board for good appearance in the financial community. Victor could see the cavalry was coming to his rescue. His board knew right from wrong. His board understood conflict of interest. His board knew how to push the ejector seat button demanded by their authority. McWhorter had to go, then he would talk, and in an hour Sangstrum would follow him. Justice, fairness, goodness would triumph.

Sangstrum rolled on. "Fine, then. All in favor of asking Mr. McWhorter to leave us for the moment so that Victor can ramble on please raise a hand in the affirmative."

Victor's moment of glory was imminent. The board would not only reject the preliminary offer of intent from the exposed hoodlum, they wouldn't even listen to it. They would listen to him instead. He had needed all of three votes, three votes he couldn't have predicted. Sandra Wo was one of those three. She had even seconded the motion. Two more found votes and glory would rise. Two damn uncertain votes from the mass assembled. Two. Just two.

And that's what he got.

Two votes. Total.

Tempe and Wo raised their hands.

No other hands went up.

"Interesting," smirked Sangstrum. "And those against, who would like Victor to leave and Mr. McWhorter to speak?"

Fifteen hands lifted high into the air, led powerfully by Sangstrum.

Fifteen went the other way. Against Victor.

Had Sangstrum known all along?

Victor had secured six in advance. Only Tempe came through. It was like watching a real-time TV rerun of *Survivor*, victory snuff by blindside.

There would be no vote of confidence in Victor. He would not get to fix Global Harmonics. Cash would change hands, scattered pennies of the once-exultant dollar. The company would die except in name, added to McWhorter's sickening roll-up, soon to be further optimized and dumped on some unsuspecting analog numbskull in search of resurrection and a turnaround head fake press release. Sangstrum would get his, whatever it was that had been illegally promised, maybe banked in Switzerland or the Caymans.

No three votes. No Aerosmith. The gavel shuttered Camelot.

Milk the cow, never feed her. Slain cow en route to butcher.

It was over. Sangstrum was suddenly gleeful. "Thank you, Victor. Your medical benefits will be continued to the end of the month. We'll send along your things."

Victor tried to breathe. He could not. His face turned beet red. Was he having a stroke? Would he collapse on the floor? Sangstrum had him from the outset. Sangstrum outplayed him with promises of distributed liquidity, the safe sideways escape hatch of respectable failure. How had Victor missed it so badly, the triumph of greed over creativity? The board belonged to the CEO. All but two of them. Checkmate.

Sing with me, sing for the years

Sing for the laughter, sing for the tears

Victor gasped, then found his breath. He reached for the laptop in front of him and lowered the cover.

"You won't need that," said Sangstrum. "It contains proprietary information."

"That in a very short time pending perfunctory due diligence will belong to me, you prick," snarled McWhorter.

"Take it now." Victor hurled the laptop across the conference table directly at McWhorter's head.

It was a Frisbee perfect throw, superb thrust and velocity, spiral sailing forward. It landed on McWhorter's right cheek and knocked him out of his chair. Blood flowed from McWhorter's hopefully broken nose. Hmm, maybe he wasn't a vampire after all.

"Milk that, you parasite," whispered Victor.

"You've lost your mind," exclaimed Sangstrum.

"At least I haven't lost my honor." Victor lunged at the table and knocked a half-dozen laptops onto the floor.

"What are you doing?" It was the soft voice of Howard Tempe as he put a reassuring hand on Victor's shoulder. "This is career suicide. You lost one round, that's all."

"I lost everything. I loved this company. I gave up someone I cared about to be part of this mission. You can't take it away from me!"

"You can't survive this," advised Tempe. "Apologize. Tell them you're on meds and mixed up the dosage. It doesn't matter if you're right. This is wrong."

Victor pulled the chair out from under Sangstrum and heaved it at the wall. Sangstrum collapsed to the floor, his dense folio of prepared papers falling from the table and landing next to him. Victor grabbed the folio and began tearing the pages into scraps, tossing them into the air as he bellowed in fury.

"Ten million for legal fees, ten million for severance, ten million for paying off the bankers—watch the shareholders' money dissolve into vapor, you vile manipulators."

"Someone dial 9-1-1," implored McWhorter. "That man is a lunatic. He's dangerous. We're all going to get hurt."

"Tell them I'm a terrorist. That's the buzzword, right. Except you're the terrorist. I'm the good guy. I'm the hero."

A quiet voice spoke directly to Victor. "You need to leave, hero." It was Sandra Wo. Victor couldn't tell for sure, but it looked as though she was crying.

"We can still win this," said Victor, looking for the small tears that were no longer in Sandra Wo's eyes. Had he imagined that?

"No, you can't, not now." She was serious. Fiduciary duty was real. Victor could see she didn't want it to get worse for him.

He had to take the cue. He took a step toward the door.

Sangstrum held up his mobile. "I've got the sheriff on the way in from the parking lot. If you don't want to be escorted, get out of here now."

McWhorter awkwardly found his way to his feet. "I'm pressing charges for assault."

"Good, have me arrested," shrieked Victor. "I'll use my one call from jail to call the SEC."

Victor looked around him: the broken laptop, the disassembled chair, the reams of paper scattered on the floor, McWhorter's horror bloody head. Surely someone had snapped a photo from one of the many devices linked to the outside world. Social media broadcast confession. Damn. Evidence of the breakdown perpetually archived in the cloud. What a mess. What an awful, awful, awful mess.

Victor turned and opened the door. "Hope the rest of your meeting is productive."

Victor exited the boardroom to the sound of arriving sirens. He wondered if he had made his point. They needlessly burned down Camelot in total ignorance for a thankless pouch of pocket change. Had they heard anything he said? Had he made even the slightest of impacts in trying to save Global Harmonics?

He should have been wondering what he was going to do with the rest of his life.

TRACK 2: YOU WANT APPLAUSE WITH THAT?

PROVIDENCE WOULD BE QUIET THIS TIME OF DAY. The earliest happy hour slackers wouldn't arrive until 4:00 p.m. That would be in another hour. Karaoke wouldn't start until 5:00 p.m. The only people inside would be career drunks or the chronically unemployed. Hardly anyone came to Providence for lunch. The place was never about the food. Only in hunger desperation would someone order the Bad Burger or a Wicker Basket of Wings. It was a place to gather around a cold pitcher of beer where sports broadcasts weren't on the wall, an after work haven for geeks and fans of geekdom where music was a family affair.

Here karaoke was cool, especially the rarest of all finds: live band karaoke. It was okay to take a turn at the mic provided you had been downing craft brews well past sunset, more than okay. It was how the tech savvy kept each other honest, each singing out of tune, one worse than the next, but a collective tribe of misfits whose code powered the world and whose passion fueled world change. So they reminded themselves between turns in front of the LCD lyrics.

Blowing off steam was good. It was the stuff of friendship, the stuff of empowerment—but not in the early afternoon when the sun was high and the shadows were thin. That was a time to be productive, or at least contemplative of code to come, procrastination for the overnight scripting frenzy. Afternoon at Providence was purely pathetic.

Victor sat behind the steering wheel of his two-year-old leased Acura RLX, parked between a Ford 150 and a Buick Enclave. To his surprise, there were more than a dozen cars in the parking lot outside Providence. He could only imagine who would be inside. Not him. Not until the reinforcements got there. Some would follow him there, he was sure of that. Well, maybe not sure, but hopeful. Word of the board meeting fiasco had to have leaked by now, through the hallways and down the not-so-grand interior stairs of Global Harmonics. The gossip chain could be counted on for speed as well as efficiency. He would be a forever hero to some for standing up to that asswipe Sangstrum, and a fool of the highest order for taking on the almighty McWhorter with a sardonic audience setting his odds for survival in real time. His loyalists would follow him to Providence.

Where else would he go? Would they come or would they seek cover in their cubicles, keeping their heads low and waiting patiently for currency to change hands? Severance would come to the brave, to those whose talent was in demand and who could take their mind meld elsewhere. The rest would cower and wait for transition offers, sell-out stay bonuses, or elevated roles in a diminished enterprise. What good would it do for any of them to come to him, to drink with him, to sing one last song at the jukebox with a fallen soldier? No, they wouldn't come, and if they did, they wouldn't buy him a beer. No one wanted to sing with him tonight. No one wanted to hear a defeated loser sing in public channeling Steven Tyler.

Victor sat there in the Acura, the interior growing warmer. What would he do now? He wouldn't be employable. No one in tech would hire a madman who tore up a conference room, not unless his code was at the top of the pecking order. Victor was no more than a marketing wonk, he knew that. Tantrums were not permissible for overhead types. Would charges be pressed against him? He wondered why the sheriff had let him walk straight past him as he left the office park. There was the black-and-white with spinning top-lights. The sheriff stared straight at him through impassable Ray-Bans, an easy pick-off. Why hadn't the sheriff stopped him? He let Victor walk straight in front of his car, wordless in the Marin County woods as wordless can get. Victor had been unsure. On top of everything else he didn't want to flee a crime scene. He could see his face hitting the pavement, feel the sheriff's boot making small work of the crawl space between his shoulder blades.

Yet nothing had happened. The sheriff let Victor get into his Acura and drive away. Victor had put it in gear with the kind of wariness a squirrel exhibits body lengths from a raccoon. The Acura climbed over the hill with Victor's eyes more glued to the rearview mirror than the windshield. A half mile over the hill and the spinning top-lights were gone with the horizon. Gone was the sheriff. Gone was Global Harmonics.

Victor was free at face value, yet he wasn't free at all. No escape comes that easily, not from gangland the likes of which he had trashed.

Sunlight poured through the windshield, the sad, interminable sunlight of daylong tedium, sluggish time without goal or deadline. Sweat beaded on Victor's forehead. His felt his forearms perspiring below his short sleeves, worse in the armpits. He touched the pocket on his chest and felt more sweat dripping down from his neckline. He hadn't even rolled down the windows there in the parking lot of Providence. Ahead of him was suburban dry brush, naturally manicured by goats grazing, probably hiding hungry wildlife carnivores of one kind or another stalking the goats. Not far away was the marsh where he sometimes parked and ate his lunch alone, reviewing his hand-scribbled notes over and over for holes and inaccuracies before he brought the wild ideas to his team. He relished those contemplative lunches where he readied his plans for the future, knowing they would only get better when they became shared ideas with everyone's input. Those lunches by the marsh seemed distant now. The minutes were passing in slower motion, too many minutes ahead of him becoming hours, then days. Weeks, damn them. Months. Years. Forever. Screw this parking lot. It was his graveyard.

He thought for a moment of Claire, how he had left her too willingly for the opportunity of a lifetime. No, it was her idea, and she had been right—well, mostly right. It was the opportunity of a lifetime for eight years and two months, the entire stretch before Sangstrum arrived. It had ended as capriciously as it had begun. Victor was alone. Without her. Without anyone. Without a job. Without a mission. It hadn't been worth it. He thought it had been worth it. It wasn't that he needed more. He knew way back then, when he made the decision, he needed something else. He had no idea what he would lose to find it. Claire liked to hear him sing in places like Providence. He liked to look out across the crowd and know he had one true fan. She hadn't come with him. There was a reason.

The oppressive heat in the car interior built to an overpowering crescendo. No air. No breath. Victor was drenched, his dress shirt soaked through, his elbows sticky, his forearms clammy. He could feel the moisture cascading past his knees to his socks. He turned the car key and creaked the window open. Then he killed the engine and closed his eyes, feeling the sweat drip in small streams from his forehead to his chin. If only the morning had been something foul he dreamed, the replay of it in his mind over and over in that daze might have seemed comical.

It wasn't funny, but at least it was sleep.

>> <<

When Victor awoke it was dark. He looked around and the parking lot was filled. He recognized a third of the cars from the office parking lot. Full Stack Max's mustard yellow minivan, dents on three sides. Code Machine Clarence's jacked up Escalade with the shotgun bucket seat usually toting that new kid, QA Juan. Admin Darcy's prized lime green Prius gleaming under security lights as if she had driven through the car wash on the way there. The familiarity was comforting. At least some of them had come. He was head to toe in perspiration but relieved in the dashboard's digital transmission that it was after 7:30. People inside would be singing. There would be friendly faces. Inside Providence it would be safe.

Victor had slept in the car almost six hours. That was odd. He really was drained, more than he had thought. As he mustered the courage to open the car door, a tap came on the half-open window. The face beyond the glass was unfamiliar to him.

"You okay?" It was the voice of a man perhaps a decade older than him. Victor looked at the stranger, his plain grey T-shirt, blue-black lumberjack flannel overshirt, vintage khakis, stubble beard, untrimmed mustache and mutton chops. It was a programmer look, but Victor knew all the programmers at Global Harmonics and they were the only programmers who came to Providence. Who was this guy?

"I'm fine," replied Victor, not yet finding the energy to move.

"Come on inside, you look like you could use a drink," said Mean Master Muttonchops.

"Yeah, I'm coming. Do I know you?"

"You don't. My name is Thomas Katem. I'm an investment banker." He handed Victor his business card through the open window slot. "You're Victor Selo, right?"

Victor eyed the card for familiarity and put it in his damp chest pocket. "Have we met before?"

"It's possible, the circles we travel overlap. Unfortunately your meeting at Global Harmonics was over before I got there. Late to the slaughter, the way I heard it."

"Your loss, we put on a good show. You don't dress like an investment banker."

"It's afterhours. I carry a change in the car. Doesn't everyone around here?"

"You think I need to clean up before we go in?"

"Nah, come on, I'll buy you a drink. I'll bet you have friends inside."

"We'll find out." Victor opened the door and got out of the car. Strangely, the asphalt felt comforting under his feet.

As Victor walked through the doors beside Katem, Providence was in full swing. In all the day's drama, he had forgotten this was Friday, Live Band Karaoke Night. A warm fall weekend was getting under way. Tonight people wouldn't sing with a machine, they would front a cover band. It was what made Fridays special, particularly for anyone who had abandoned a long-ago dream.

At the mic was possibly the worst Elvis impersonator of all time, a grey ponytailer doing his best to belt out "Viva Las Vegas" with more stage drama than musicality. He wasn't an awful singer, he could work his way through a tune with credible intonation. He just didn't sound anything like the King. He didn't look like him either, beyond the tattered white sequined jumpsuit. Elvis recognized Victor from across the room and raised the mic stand to him as he entered. Victor waved briefly, then crossed toward the bar with Katem a half step behind. Elvis found the segue to a low pitch baritone interpretation of "Love Me Tender."

"You know Elvis?" asked Katem.

"His name is Johnny Olano. He lives for this. Friday is his day. Three Elvis tunes, five shots of tequila, and he never goes home alone."

"He must be seventy, maybe seventy-five," observed Katem. "How does he pull off that trick?"

"Welcome to Providence." Victor motioned the bartender with two fingers and was handed a pair of Coronas. Few of his colleagues in the bar were making eye contact with him. A few nodded slightly his way, but his usual warm embrace wasn't to be found.

When Olano-Elvis threw down his ultra-high energy rendering of "Burning Love" and finished his set to a thunderous reception, a poor man's Rod Stewart followed him up. To the crowd's surprise, what the gritty Stewart clone lacked in looks he made up for in energy. The band hit the beat on "Hot Legs" and an 8:00 p.m. star was born.

"You know that guy?" asked Katem.

"I don't," said Victor. "I don't know everyone here. A lot of them know me but don't seem to want to acknowledge it tonight."

It wasn't what Victor had expected. There was palpable distance between him and his peeps from the office. Full Stack Max wasn't coming near him. Admin Darcy noticed him and ducked into the pack. Tonight Victor was on his own.

"So you were late to the meeting," continued Victor. "You hung around Marin a long time."

"The meeting went on a long time," responded Katem. "I tried to insert myself. No luck."

"Is it sold?"

"Yeah, it's sold. I have a client that might have been interested in taking it a different way, but the fix was in. Your guys wanted an exit. That's what they got."

"My guys? Those weren't my guys! Sangstrum is a lowlife carpetbagger. I didn't want the board to sell. I had a plan to keep it alive."

"They didn't hear you," said Katem. "They had other things in mind."

"Cowards, freaking cowards. McWhorter and Sangstrum wired it all for sound. That wasn't a meeting. It was a wake."

"It could have been a meeting with a slightly altered agenda," asserted Katem. "No question Global H was going to sell, but to derail a runaway freight train, you have to know what crowbar to use. Of course they were sure it was a done deal, but changing a pre-charted course requires deft handling."

"Yeah, tact, not my strong suit. I blew it. I guess that's why no one wants to talk to me. I couldn't deliver. How do you know what happened in the meeting?"

"Good network, I know a lot of people. Some believe that secrets are currency and can't help banking a few chips with a text here and there. Makes my work possible."

Victor nodded halfheartedly. Katem spoke truth, ominous but authentic. Rod Stewart made the bridge to "Blondes Have More Fun." The crowd loved him, but Victor wasn't paying attention to the stage. He never much liked Rod Stewart. The guy with the mic was credible. The rhythm was surely there, but how much range did it take if the real deal, a former gravedigger, could pull it off?

Katem signaled the bartender for another round. "Big deals are tough. Not for amateurs."

"Please don't say that. I don't like that word. I'm not an amateur."

"At what you do, no. Playing chicken with warlords, that's something else. If you wanted to take them down you should have called someone like me."

"You seem to know a lot about me, Katem. There are enough people checking up on me. Why would I need you?"

"Guys like you make things work in companies that are healthy. Guys like me make things happen when they aren't as healthy."

"Why are we talking? Why are you talking to me? I don't matter anymore." Victor was annoyed and Rod Stewart twenty feet from him carrying the mic stand onto the dance floor wasn't making it any better.

"Maybe you don't matter. Who knows what happens next? You have my card in case you have an idea. I didn't mean to irritate you."

Katem finished his Corona and got up from the bar. Rod Stewart was surrounded on the dance floor by fantasy fandom that would exceed any karaoke king's expectations. Victor wondered if he had ended the conversation with Katem prematurely, if there was information he needed that he was letting walk out the door.

"You're not hanging around?" asked Victor. "I'm going up in a bit. I'm good at this."

Katem must have been irritated by Rod Stewart as well. He seemed to have had his fill of Providence. "I'll bet you are. I'd say we've had a productive beginning."

Katem grinned and made his way through the crowd. As Victor watched him slip out the door, Ancient Elvis took his seat next to Victor at the bar. The way Johnny Olano dressed in Salvation Army specials, there was little chance he'd notice Victor had been hibernating half the day in a sweltering automobile.

"How was I tonight?" probed Johnny.

"Never better. Especially 'Burning Love.'"

"Buy an old man a drink?"

"Two shots of Patron," said Victor to the bartender.

Johnny let loose an eager smile, gracious for the gift on its way but forever presumptuous. "If you're buying, then make it four."

Victor nodded and the bartender followed through. Both rounds went quickly. Rod Stewart was off the dance floor and back onstage, deep into "Every Picture Tells a Story." For all the dancing women in front of him cared, he might as well have been Rod Stewart. Patron had to be involved there as well, but damn, that Rod Stewart fake was going to have his pick tonight.

"I hate Rod Stewart," said Johnny. "It's like if Elvis took all the soul out of it and had started his career in Vegas, that would be Rod Stewart."

"No, that would be Wayne Newton, but you don't see many Wayne Newton impersonators, because anyone who still likes his act is hitting the buffet on Fremont Street hoping for comps. But I agree, Rod Stewart is overrated, except for his time with Faces."

"I can do Wayne Newton," said Johnny. "Do you think it would get me laid?"

"Johnny, you're Elvis. Everyone loves Elvis. Stick with Elvis. You're the best."

"Yeah, around here I am, but in Vegas, I couldn't get a second look. This dump is as far as I go. Hope it's not the end of the road for you, Brother V."

"Give Providence more credit, Johnny. We have what we have until we don't."

Victor ordered another round. It was gone in sixty seconds. Then another. Soon he and Johnny were weaving. Two more singers got their slots onstage, a thirtysomething Asian diva Victor hadn't seen before doing a near perfect Aretha-Diana mix, and QA Juan dying his way through "Sweet Child of Mine" and "Enter Sandman." Use of the descriptor *unreal* was all-purpose at Providence—it applied equally to the delightful and the impossible.

"Unreal, both of them," mumbled Johnny, motioning for another round on Victor's tab. "You going to sing tonight?"

"I'm going to drink tonight. Then I'm going to sing tonight."

"You are drinking. It doesn't make you sound better, you know? Elvis knew that, but he was Elvis."

"Johnny Olano, there are many things you can teach me, but how liquor impacts our hearing is not in your sweet spot."

"You didn't have a good week, did you, Brother V? I can tell you're not feeling your normal unhappy."

"My normal unhappy?"

"You're not a happy guy, Victor, but once you get the mic you're in a zone of being 25% less sad. I'm not sure if you're getting there with the tequila. Something bad happen to you?"

Victor thought about his normal unhappy, obvious even to Johnny Olano, who knew nothing of the group homes, nothing about Victor growing up in the system. Tonight was unhappy squared, the night following the day he lost everything for nothing. Johnny would never understand what had happened, what he had tried to pull off in the boardroom. To Johnny, Victor was a karaoke singer with a swell car who did computers on the side and made enough money to buy him drinks. Life for Johnny was simple in a way Victor would never know. He ordered one more round. How many was that? It didn't matter. No one but Johnny would talk to him, but they all would listen to him. Sober or not, he was in demand at the mic. Few knew his background, the many bands in his rearview mirror, but he was more than an amateur in a live band karaoke bar. Not much more, but enough to know what he was doing, a ringer who didn't have to reveal his past, only use that talent to stir up the crowd in the present. He knew a lot of material too, which songs would work and when. That deep database was all him.

"Yeah, it was a shitty day, Johnny, a very shitty day. Only one thing left to make it less shitty."

It was time for Victor to sing. He hadn't pulled a number from the dispenser roll, but the house band knew him. All he had to do was make his way to the stage and he would be welcomed. QA Juan had to go. It was good to play behind someone the crowd wanted gone.

On his way to the stage, Victor passed Admin Darcy who was headed in the other direction. She had always been a friend and a confidant in the office. He hoped maybe he could convince her to stay and hear him sing so he had at least one supporter besides Johnny.

"You leaving, Darcy? I'm going to take my turn." The words came out of his mouth more jumbled than he intended.

"I'm not into it tonight, Vic. We heard what happened in the board meeting, the rumor mill at least. I thought I'd come here and shake it off, but I want to go home."

"At least you'll speak to me, which is more than everyone else here."

"You're not a bad guy. You lost a tough battle. People have to digest what it means to them. They'll come around eventually when they know what you tried to do. You know they like it when you sing. Have a good set."

Darcy patted Victor on the shoulder and headed for the front door. He wondered if she was right, if people knew how hard he had tried the save their jobs, if someday they would forgive him for failing. He stumbled across the dance floor to his destination, the one-foot riser under the static spotlight next to the LCD. He didn't know what to expect, but he looked out and Johnny got the welcome applause going. The crowd might have been disappointed in him, but music was music. With Victor at the mic they knew something good was going to happen.

"What are we doing, King Biscuit?" asked Leonard, the lead guitarist who for the next fifteen minutes would be in close physical proximity to Victor's every move.

Victor switched off the LCD monitor. He didn't need the lyrics. "Aerosmith."

"How could it be otherwise?" Leonard didn't need the LCD either. No one in the band did. Every once in a while they'd need sheet, but not for the classic rock library. Leonard had played enough times behind Victor to know what Victor had in mind, but Victor could see him react uncomfortably to the stench he carried onto the riser. "Yo, boss, you shower today?"

Victor had no witty retort, no explicable accounting for his grubby condition. He thought back to the early afternoon, the awful early afternoon, the lyrics piercing his mind. He had to let go of it, all of it. Leonard shrugged it off and played the haunting opening strings for Aerosmith's breakthrough, "Dream On." Then on cue, as if rehearsed, Victor hit the mark:

Sing with me, sing for the years

Sing for the laughter, sing for the tears

Victor brought the room to near silence. They'd heard the song hundreds of times before, thousands of times, but Victor was in it the way Tyler was in it. Every word at the optimal range. Every note at the targeted pitch. Each beat pushed to the accent of resounding emphasis. The crowd sang along, unrehearsed raw harmony like a concert encore, unprompted but making the fills on each reverberating cadence. When the lingering cymbal ended it all, the applause for Victor was heartening, its own form of forgiveness.

Like a pro, Victor was ready to shift the dynamic. "Seger," he quietly said to Leonard.

"'Hollywood Nights'?"

"Yeah, build the full pace, come around twice. I know the cue."

Leonard looked to his guy on the drum kit and they launched. The bass player came in behind them and drove the intro to a steady climb. The digital piano filled the room and Leonard stepped on the floor pedal to distort the chords, extending the opening vamp as Victor requested. That set the tempo for vocals. Victor grabbed the cue precisely where he wanted it, letting him carry the lyrics all the way through, owning the sound end to end:

Night after night, day after day, it went on and on

Then came that morning he woke up alone

His granular layering fit the moment, absolutely solid in his skin. Applause came again, louder, fuller. Then Victor got brave. He would finish the set with a tough one, a track that couldn't be forged. It had put Elton John on the map one unsuspecting night long ago on the air, a BBC radio broadcast that would anchor a live album. It was nothing like the Elton John of today. There was no Caesar's Palace banter. It was the sheer power of voice—raw infused vocal range beyond any mere mortal. Victor knew he could pull it off because he had readied himself to pull it off so many times before. It was "Take Me To the Pilot" and the lyrics glowed:

Through a glass eye your throne
Is the one danger zone
Take me to the pilot for control

Despite the day's catastrophe, despite losing everything so few hours ago, Victor was on his game behind that mic. Leonard knew it, the crowd knew, he knew it. The boardroom bashing he had weathered was no longer relevant, not in this moment. Somewhere in the beer, the tequila, and the draining sweat, that dreary conference room had evaporated. Music could do that for him. The music always did that for him, bouncing off the walls, resonating in the rafters. It never failed him, all the way back to the group homes, the windowless waiting rooms, the government processing centers, the court-appointed guardians routing his future in sealed manila files. He remembered how it had been before he gave it up, his calling, his life's mission to be one with the songs. He never wanted to give that up, but he had to find something else, something better, something safer.

Right, safer, sure. Not even close. It had been all for nothing, but it didn't matter at this shared moment. He was there where he should be, where he needed to be. He was present and alive. He was who he was.

There hadn't been a competition that night, no prizes, no first, second, or third, but Victor had won again with the crowd. That was all he needed, a moment of remembrance, a restatement of self. He stepped off the stage to the vibrant applause, welcomed, appreciated, briefly enriching his soul. He felt the rejuvenation in his limbs more than heard the sound of clapping and hooting, as if he were the real deal instead of a drunken karaoke clown. As he stepped off the stage the approval ceased. The applause stopped completely, Arctic hollow, like a sound sample that had run its course and ended on its mark. The act was over and he was over.

Victor needed a friend. He looked for Johnny Olano, but the night had grown late, and as they say, Elvis had left the building. He tried to throw a few high fives in the aisles following his set, trying to connect with familiar faces, trade quips and tips with acquaintances at least, but there were no takers. They still liked his voice at a distance, but no one wanted to speak to him. A decade invested in Global Harmonics, but not a single colleague approached him. There was safety in separation. They needed to be distant to protect themselves. They needed to secure deniability for self-preservation. He needed to be somewhere else.

>> <<

Victor made his way to the restroom in the back of the club. The booze was weighing on him. He was exhausted, dehydrated. His head wasn't clear. He was even more fatigued than he thought, and he needed some of that alcohol toxin out of him.

As he approached the urinal, everyone at the trough found a way to exit instantaneously. Coincidence? Did he reek that offensively? He wasn't sure. He examined his reflection in the wall mirror, like the Aerosmith lyrics directed. His thinning brown hair was neither parted nor flat, same as always, mussed mop top by default rather than choice, reaching for the neckline, weighed down with sweat. His eyes were so bloodshot he could see no white at the edges. He looked closely at himself, inspected his creased eyelids, his mouth nearing the glass, his breath touching the mirror. He was a portrait of defeat, a decayed vision of someone he never wanted to be. What he saw he despised because he knew it was inescapable. The guy singing was one face of Victor, the stayer who emerged from desertion, but the real Victor had done this to himself. It wasn't purposeful. It was never with poor intention. He had picked the wrong ride, thought he owned the map, and let himself be driven to the wrong destination. Those forks in the road could never be negotiated accurately.

Victor was as close to the mirror as he could get, blocking out all but his own visage in the proximity of the frame. He almost didn't feel the pain as his head slammed into the glass. The mirror shattered on impact. At first he was numb. Was he that drunk, unable to hold his balance and stand on his feet in a public men's room? If he had slipped or his legs had given out, he would have just tumbled over. He couldn't have fallen that hard, so hard that his head broke the mirror into a thousand shards.

He hadn't slipped. He hadn't keeled over. There was a firm hand behind his head. His head had been pushed forward, jammed into the fragmenting obstacle with unforgiving force.

From the grimy tile he looked over his shoulder and saw Thomas Katem. It was the sloppily dressed guy from the parking lot, the investment banker who bought him a consolation drink. Huh?

Blood rolled down Victor's cheeks and soaked his shirt. Victor saw two more threatening guys standing behind Katem between him and the door. There was no path out.

"You don't like something I did?" asked Victor, weakened and perplexed.

"I don't like you." Katem grabbed Victor by the collar and dragged him across the wet floor toward the two others.

Victor looked around for help, but only Katem and his two accomplices remained in the restroom and the door was closed. He shouted out for someone to save him but no one came. He knew more than half the people in that bar. He was a regular there. He worked with most of these people. Even the ones who didn't know him had just celebrated his live karaoke set. Couldn't they hear him shout over the band? Were they intimidatated, afraid, so spineless they wouldn't even intervene in a beating? How alone could he be?

No one would come to his aid. No one at all.

Seconds later Victor was in the alley behind Providence. He had been pulled down a corridor where he was clearly seen struggling. No one had stepped up to help him, not a single friend, not a stranger. Beatings like this didn't happen in Marin, he thought. They were either frozen in fear or apathy. It didn't matter why. He was helpless.

A knee slammed into Victor's gut. Then he felt his left arm pop out of its socket. Then his already wounded head hit the ground.

"What did I do?" cried Victor. "Why are you kicking the crap out of me?"

"You fucked up a deal," explained Katem. "You forced a decision that didn't need to be made. Now it's done and the remaining alternatives have been significantly reduced."

"That wasn't my intention," pleaded Victor.

"I couldn't give a shit about your intention," barked Katem.

Another punch to the back. A kick to the knees. Victor's nose had to be broken. His elbows were frayed skin on the jagged pavement. They kicked him again and again. Why so many times? What had he done that was so bad? Fucked up the deal? Katem wasn't even in the deal. He was trying to insert himself in the deal. Now he was a madman, backed by a pair of vicious thugs who showed no mercy.

"Is this a payback for what I did to McWhorter?" cried out Victor. "Because I hit him with a laptop, he sent you to kill me? I'm sorry I did that, okay? It was stupid."

Katem grabbed Victor by the ripped sleeves of his dress shirt, pulled him within an inch of his brow, and then slammed him back on the cement. "You idiot, you screwed up everything. You made an enormous mess."

"McWhorter is getting what he wants. Sangstrum is getting his package. Why am I on my knees?"

"Did I say I worked for McWhorter or Sangstrum?" Katem couldn't be talked down from his fury. "You couldn't shut up. You couldn't stop yourself. You forced the deal to close before it needed to close."

Victor's shirt was torn from his torso, exposing more scraped skin, bare to his assailants implanting bruise after bruise. He wasn't even fighting back. He should have known how to fight, the system should have taught him that as a kid, but all he had learned was that a lost cause ended sooner without prodding. He was outnumbered and without strength. He had no power to defend himself. He had to wait them out.

"You think everything's so simple, so righteous, so clear!" Katem's foot broke another of Victor's ribs, bringing Victor's lungs to near breathlessness. "You don't understand how an agenda functions. Maybe this time you'll learn."

Victor collapsed, chest to the ground, broken to the core in every way a man can be physically defeated and psychically shamed. As the electrical synapses were interrupted in his brain, he had a thought, the strangest of all thoughts. For no apparent reason, he thought of God. It must have been Claire. She wanted him to think of God. He had never much believed in God, in anything like that, but he had believed in inspiration, that ideas came from somewhere.

If he did believe in God, God would not be vengeful. That was what Claire had taught him. She believed with categorical certainty in God's love. Faith, she called it, the absurdist leap, the protectorate of the unexplainable that gave comfort when none could otherwise be allowed. Claire never tried to bring Victor to her thinking, but she was honest about it. She would talk about God now and again, enough that he would consider the possibility.

God loved us. God loved every one of us.

Inspiration comes from somewhere.

Could that make sense? Could that be resolved with his body being torn apart in an alley behind a Marin County bar by three strangers whose paths had only distantly overlapped with his own, his life in the balance for compromising an agenda he failed to understand?

His life meant nothing to them, only his pain, which they seemed to be enjoying tremendously. They could not be satiated. They kept pounding and kicking and punching him.

Victor tried to conjure an image of a loving God. He tried to listen for God's voice in the music, in any of the songs he had ever sung in front of an audience.

Then a leather boot collided once too forcefully with the left side of his head. His eardrum must have been broken, because he heard nothing but muffled humming in his mind.

Then Victor passed out cold.

TRACK 3: MEET THOMAS KATEM

VICTOR AWOKE IN A HOSPITAL BED. It was a double room with a curtain rack dividing it in two, but the bed next to him was empty. There were no sheets on it, which probably meant he didn't have a roommate. Strange how that was the first thing that crossed his mind. Aloneness again.

Every part of his body hurt. He was conscious but his head was far from clear. There was an IV in his arm. What meds were flowing through him? His arms were wrapped in gauze and fiberglass. He couldn't make a fist. He couldn't see or bend his draped knees. Did he need the oxygen snaking into his nostrils or was that simply hospital procedure? Would he stand again on his feet? This couldn't be permanent. No, not that, not dependency. He craved information, an immediate and accurate assessment of his recovery.

His eyes fixed upon the Latina woman reviewing the chart at the foot of his bed. She wore storage closet issued white. Theresa Gomez RN read the insignia on her coat. Nurse, not doctor—was that good or bad? The rattling of the metal chart on the hook had pierced his sleep. She was about his age, maybe a little older, hard to tell. Not trim, not vastly overweight. She seemed calm, a sign that he might not be in as dismal shape as he thought, but she wasn't smiling, not even a tiny bit.

"What day is it?" he asked.

"Tuesday, all day until tomorrow. Then it will be Wednesday." Quirky sense of humor, or maybe on the side she was a coder.

"I must have come here Friday. Is this Kaiser or Marin General?"

"I don't work for HMOs so that puts you at Marin General. I wasn't on duty when you got here, but the chart does say Friday. I work ICU, not Emergency, another grade up the pay scale and I get to the play the long game. Less messy bleeding, more healing, keep more friends that way. Looks like you slept almost four days."

"Four days isn't sleeping. It's being unconscious."

"Sharp diagnosis. Did you attend medical school, Victor Selo?"

She had his name from the chart. No, she wasn't a coder. She had the seen-it-all attitude of a lifer in the critical care ward. Different mechanism kept her going.

"No medical training but I bet I look awful. Ms. Gomez, is that what I call you?"

"You can read, excellent sign," She made a checkmark on the chart and made a loop around the bed, observing his various wounds up close as she talked. "Call me what you like, but in moderation. We're busy on this floor. Yes, you look awful."

She handed Victor an oversized hand mirror so he could have a look at himself. He looked quickly, shook his head, and set the mirror on the attached table next to him. In one glimpse he had seen enough.

"I don't know what to say. I look like something on the news."

"I don't make value judgements, helps with my optimism. You're alive, give thanks for that. It can always be worse, unless you're not alive. Cognition functioning, stable. Self-identity, promising." She made two more checkmarks on his chart.

Victor tried to lift each of his arms but that brought more discomfort. "Yeah, thanks be to whatever. Tuesday, huh?"

"Tuesday, yes indeed, three more days to the weekend. Hot date this Saturday? It's not going to happen."

"No date, but it's still September right?" Victor's head was slowly clearing. Logic was kicking in. Structured thoughts were reconstituting in his mind.

"Yes, it's September, all the way until Sunday. I think you need a little kicker in the IV." She reached for the almost empty hanging bag and replaced it with a fresh, full one. Kicker? Was she joking? Was that more droll patter or was there something sinister about her?

"If September goes through Sunday, I have insurance until Sunday. I got fired last Friday. My policy is paid through the end of the month, that's it."

"That's what you're thinking about, who's going to pay the bill? You may have lost more blood than that chart says. There's COBRA, you know."

“I can’t afford it. I have serious financial problems and I’m going to be out of work for a long time.”

“We have a special plan for people like you. There are so many these days. Everyone thinks the whole health insurance thing has been solved. So very half ass, dumping the costs wherever they fall. What do I know? I didn’t study business. I could have gone into administration, made a few bucks.”

“How special is the plan? I mean, how bad am I? How much cost are we talking?”

“A few broken ribs, concussion, a lot of stitches, but a lot of the scars will heal up. Doctors here know what they’re doing in the cosmetic realm. It’s Marin after all. Lucky for you, I’d say you were roughed up professionally.”

“Lucky? What do you mean, professionally?”

“Given the beating you took, you should be in much worse shape. Actually, you probably shouldn’t even be . . . well . . . it doesn’t matter. The two of us are talking. That’s what matters.”

“I should be dead?”

“I’m not an expert, but this looks like someone knew what they were doing.”

“I don’t get it.”

“One wrong kick to the head is all it takes. From what I see, whoever did this to you didn’t kill you on purpose. They wanted it to look and feel as bad as it could, but they wanted you to recover. It takes training to do that. You have to understand anatomy.”

A professional beating—did such a thing exist? Victor tried to grasp what she was saying. Would Sangstrum and McWhorter stoop that low for revenge even after they got their way? That didn’t make business sense, yet it began to explain how far he had strayed from an environment of predictability.

No, Nurse Gomez wasn’t evil. She was unnervingly blunt. That was her shield against the daily loss of her calling. She spoke with candor and authority. She wouldn’t rattle off the observation if it wasn’t grounded.

“You know a lot,” said Victor.

“Fifteen years at Oakland General. This place is the Ritz compared to that.”

“When do I get out?”

"I'm not your doctor. Now that your eyes are open, I'll have one come talk to you. Meanwhile, there's a visitor waiting to see you, been here since early yesterday. You want to see him?"

A visitor? Who would come see him in the hospital? He lived alone. Had someone seen him left for dead in the alley behind Providence and taken pity? It had to be someone from the club, someone after the fact hiding from public view. He must have been on a stretcher. Someone followed up on him. He had been unconscious all this time. Had that someone found his ID, discovered he had no family? Gomez had said "him." His visitor was not a "her."

"Did he say his name?"

"Not to me. Like I said, I just came on duty."

"Let him in." Victor was apprehensive, but he needed more information. He couldn't turn away the chance to know what had happened to him. There were too many moving parts, too few clues, and damn, did every muscle and tendon in his body ache.

"I'll let your visitor know the receiving line is open."

Nurse Gomez hung the chart back on the end of the bed and left Victor alone. She left the door open and he saw her wave to someone down the hall. He wasn't up for a visitor, but curiosity had the better of him, plus whatever mixology she had applied to the IV was kicking in. He was starting to like Nurse Gomez in spite of her protective coating. She seemed to understand he wasn't like the other rows of casualties on her rounds.

>> <<

The stranger who walked in the door was a dotted-line cutout from the weekend fashion section of the Wall Street Journal, a well-groomed, fitted torso radiating confidence and spicy male skin lotion. He was trim, handsome, hair in right order, wrapped in dark grey slacks and a pressed blue blazer. He didn't even react to Victor's damaged appearance.

"How are you feeling?" asked his visitor.

"Raring to run a marathon. Who are you?"

"My name is Thomas Katem. I'm an investment banker."

Victor was speechless. He couldn't have heard those words. His IV dosage must have been off, that's why his pain was subsiding while his mind wandered. Terror had arrived. Calling back the nurse was an option, maybe a lifesaving option. Wait, this guy wouldn't hit him, not at Marin General. Besides, he wasn't the guy from the bar who'd assaulted him. There was no resemblance. All he had was the attacker's name. That was creepy, surely more than a coincidence, but it wasn't an immediate threat. Victor still needed information. Let the terrorist talk at least for a few minutes.

"You don't like investment bankers, do you?" said the handsome, creepy visitor with the ultra-strange name.

"You're Thomas Katem? You're not Thomas Katem. Thomas Katem did this to me. He beat me to a pulp, he and the two guys he brought along. What the hell is going on?"

"Victor, I am Thomas Katem. I am *the* Thomas Katem. Do I look like the fellow who harmed you?"

"Not in the slightest. Do you know who I'm talking about?" Victor was feeling pain again, his ligaments inflaming despite the drugging.

"Only in the abstract. We'll get to that. I want you to know that I had nothing to do with what happened to you at that bar or in the boardroom. I hope you'll believe me. I'm only here to check on you as a matter of concern and courtesy."

"What courtesy? We don't know each other. Who was the guy who beat the crap out of me? Why did he tell me he was Thomas Katem? What does any of this have to do with my job at Global Harmonics?"

"Your former job, Victor. You're asking a lot of questions, one on top of the other. I can't answer all of them. I can tell you that I am Thomas Katem and that other fellow is not."

"So there's a guy impersonating you who is prone to violence against me, unless you're lying to me, too. What is this, a bad remake of *To Tell The Truth*? I'm Thomas Katem. No, I'm Thomas Katem. One of us is lying. Go on, win a prize. Choose the correct liar." Ah, the painkillers were swimming upstream, his tongue and temperament unbridled in reaction. Let the juice flow.

"I won't lie to you," said Katem, or whoever this manicured model was. "Maybe I should come back another time."

"No, wait. How did you find me? Why are you here?"

"Do you have any immediate family, Victor? I think the hospital came up short there."

"No, I have no family. I don't want to talk about that. Why did they contact you?"

"My business card was in your pocket, so they called me. When I made the connection between you and Global Harmonics, I decided to pay you a visit."

"Did you want to buy the company, too?"

"No, investment bankers don't buy companies, not for themselves. It's complicated actually. There are many conflicts of interest. We do what we are hired to do without questioning motives and try to stay flexible when friction emerges."

"I'm trying hard to follow you. I'm friction. A thug with your business card beat me senseless and planted your business card on me? That's supposed to make sense?"

"That could make sense. Lots of people have my business card. That's how investment banking works. He obviously wanted to throw a wrench in the deal, see if he could derail it with a sideshow, somehow drag me into it either by association or investigation. Amateur, but not out of the realm of possibility."

"Why does everyone keep saying *amateur*," sighed Victor. "Is that all the world is, professionals and amateurs?"

"I'm not sure where to go with that, Victor. I'm trying to help you sort this out. I thought I'd end run any difficult questions by showing up in person."

"That's crap, Katem. The nurse said I was roughed up by professionals. You know something about that."

"The nurse is your checkpoint for accurate information?" quipped visitor Katem. "Don't you wonder why the first person you're seeing is me instead of the police?"

"The police don't like me, at least the sheriff. My former employer saw to that."

The courteous and concerned GQ prototype pivoted toward the door, angling to depart. "You need some more rest, Victor. You're not seeing this straight. Your head took some heavy blows, I'm sure. It's too soon for you to wrap your thoughts around what's happened. I'll be back in a few days."

"A few days? It won't be September anymore. I can't stay here past the termination of my insurance."

"You're not an easy guy to work with, Victor. I guess that's why Sangstrum had so many issues with you. You're also in a decidedly complicated situation."

"You know Sangstrum? I knew there was more to you than a lost business card."

Katem let that line of inquisition dissipate, then rolled the doctor's stool from under the sink and sat on it at Victor's bedside. This likely would be his gentler side, if he had one.

"Let me give you the part of the story I can tell you. I am indeed Thomas Katem and I am indeed an investment banker. I represent a client that wanted Global Harmonics at a price slightly higher than that pimp McWhorter wanted to pay. Unfortunately that was a poorly kept secret. I was exposed, though not my client. When Sangstrum and McWhorter discovered I was in the wings, they knew someone else wanted in. Time wasn't our friend once the rumor mill put their concoction at risk."

Victor leaned away from Katem, unimpressed with his bedside manner. "The process was cooked. I knew it. There shouldn't have been a process. We could have recovered. Greedy cowards, all of them."

"Yes, that kind of directness got you far, didn't it? Anyway, McWhorter made a fast deal with Sangstrum that included bonus wire payment to Sangstrum's personal account in Jamaica. My client never got to the table. If you had managed to kill the deal on principle, we could have swept in and picked up the pieces—given the fraud, perhaps even at an additional discount. We were rooting for you, Victor."

"Wait, you mean if I had killed the deal it could have been worse?"

"For your company's existing shareholders, yes, but who knows where it could have gone from there. That's not my job. My job is to represent my client."

"How are you representing your client now?"

"The guys who kicked the crap out of you had to have been for hire. Whoever hired them knew you failed, but they knew we wouldn't give up until there were no options remaining. They wanted to tie me to potentially obstructing the close, so they tied me to you as a physical threat that would look bad in court. They also wanted the two of us to meet, and they wanted me to see what they had done to you. I'd say their mission has been accomplished."

"Then it was Sangstrum and McWhorter who had me assaulted?"

Katem swung a half turn on the wheeled stool, avoiding eye contact with Victor. "Can't say for sure, certainly can't prove it. On the surface it seems too obvious, but in the end it hardly matters. We are where we are."

"So they tied your name to something you didn't do, that comes out in the sunlight. Their deal is done. Why are we fighting after the fact?"

Katem rose from the stool, walked to the doorway, looked down the hall, then gently closed the door. He turned back toward Victor, standing across the narrow room, grasping for his own patience. "No deal is ever done until funds change hands and clear. Sangstrum and McWhorter shook hands. So what? Your board approved a binding letter of intent pending due diligence. So what? Due diligence can take weeks or months. The SEC can be active or passive. It all depends on what comes up."

"Your client wants to make another offer?" asked Victor. "They'll have to bid significantly above McWhorter's price. That wasn't your strategy to buy high."

"My problem, not yours. Here's the part you need to understand. There is malfeasance here—absolute, verifiable, inside-the-family fraud. There is also a violent crime committed against you, which your unfriendly sheriff may not care to unravel if Sangstrum is spiffing him. Given the adventures you've experienced the last few days, Sangstrum and McWhorter are hopeful you'll disappear into Neverland. They're also hoping I'll keep my distance for fear of soiling my reputation by my implied association with your assault while trying to shoo-in my client. They are banking on the notion that their fraud will never surface. They want me to know they are serious, that if they do see you again, it will be on my conscience."

"You're an investment banker. You don't have a conscience."

"Funny guy. Perhaps sadly accurate. The thing is, if you can summon some courage, we can help each other."

"I help you expose the fraud, you deliver Global Harmonics to your stealth client. You get a fee, and maybe next time the professionals actually crack my skull all the way through for your trouble. Why would I go near this?"

"A few reasons. First, in the near term, you won't be near it. We're going to get you out of town, so Sangstrum and McWhorter think they've accomplished their mission and gotten rid of you. That lets you heal and get back on your feet."

"There are less dangerous ways to get back on my feet than partnering with you, Katem."

"Second, when we bring you back and you testify, my client would like you to run Global Harmonics. You will be the new CEO."

"You're making me a job offer to be CEO?"

"I'm not, I'm facilitating. But yes, you get to be CEO of the company you love."

"They'll put it in writing?"

"They can't at the moment. The paper trail would be too condemning, largely because the client's name would have to be on paper, which is not something they can risk being publicly known. I assure you there is no securities manipulation at hand, but the SEC can have a kneejerk reaction to information certain inside players consider privileged. You have to trust me. My client will stand by their promise. You will have the offer in writing before you testify."

"Hell of an act of faith on my part. I have a job offer for a company that's been sold, brokered by a guy who may or may not have the name he says he has, from a company that can't be disclosed or put anything in writing. Does it get better?"

"It does, Victor. I understand you have an affinity for music."

Victor was thrown. Where did that come from? How did that matter? Katem stayed quiet, waiting for Victor to absorb it. "I used to, years ago, I gave it up for . . . well, it appears a good, sound thrashing. I found something I was better at, where I could make grocery money."

"You made more than grocery money, Victor. You made a ton of money, at least five million, perhaps twice that. You blew it all trading stocks on the side. That's why you don't have money for health insurance. You've blown almost everything you have. Are you arrogant and greedy in addition to being stupid outside your area of expertise, or are you ready to wise up?"

"Everyone knows a lot about me. I don't want to be under surveillance. Is there any privacy left?"

"Information is all an investment banker has. Digital communications leave breadcrumbs, which makes it easy. I know what I know. I know you had an excellent job that you enjoyed. You were respected in the software industry. You thought you were smarter than you are and gambled your earnings into near nothingness picking stocks. Then you thought you'd bring justice to Global Harmonics all by yourself proving that good would triumph over evil. I also know you used to be in a bar band or two. Covers, mostly. That last part is from YouTube, nothing covert."

"I wasn't much better in the bands than I am at this."

"I dug up some of your tracks. You weren't bad. Bar music is a hard way to make a living, but you played okay. Front man, right?"

"I'm not a great singer. I can sing if I have to. I play guitar mostly. I have a good ear. If I hear something once I can play it."

"Highly adaptable session man. You even tried to write a few originals."

"Are you going to offer me a recording contract?"

"Not exactly, but a gig."

"This is surreal. You're making this up." Victor badly wanted out of the bed, but that wasn't going to get him much of anywhere. Thank God for the meds lubricating his arteries.

"Part three of the deal. First, we get you safely out of town. Second we set you up as CEO in waiting. Third, while you are recovering, we'll set you up with a booking agent. He'll put you on the road. You'll get to play with a working band in front of a live audience. Back to the future for you, right? Have some fun like your old life."

"I'm supposed to believe you know an agent who would be interested in me?"

"Old friend from college, his name is Petrumi. Not high end stuff, but his clients make a living so he makes a living. I gave him your name and he found some old video of you online. He said you were credible, that he could place you. You'll find he's not an ordinary thinker."

"This is a sick joke. I'm not a fool."

"We aren't going to debate that at the moment. Let Petrumi place you somewhere. Get the bandages off, hang out with some musicians, heal your wounds, clear your head. Hide out in plain sight, strum in the background, have yourself the time of your life until we need you back."

"You should leave."

"Think of this as a version of the Witness Protection Program, only the government is not involved so there's a lot less red tape and we will protect you."

"Sure you will. You're the good guys. Witness Protection Program powered by moneychangers, base camp in Hades."

"It's a lot to swallow after almost four days of unconsciousness. Like I said, I'll come back in a few days. We'll talk again."

"I'll be gone in a few days. We have nothing to talk about. I need to get on with my life."

"Don't worry about the hospital bill, Victor. My client has it. Remember this—you're not employable at the moment. You're a disgruntled employee who made a scene in a boardroom. You are scorched earth. You will not work in tech. Best you're going to get is lead barista at Starbucks. We're offering you lead guitar."

"No one gives up lead guitar to an amateur."

"Maybe rhythm guitar. Hell if I know the difference. What else are you going to do?"

"I'm good at what I do. I'll call a headhunter."

"You think investment bankers are bad guys? Headhunters are the sickest leeches on earth. Avoid them like cancer. They are never there when you need them, and when they need you, they'll tell you nuclear waste is a chocolate shake that glows in the dark to get you to drink it."

"Bounty hunters, all of you."

"You need to rest. Let it all sink in. I'll be back in a few days. Whether we work together or not, you'll want to keep this conversation between us. Be careful what you say to the sheriff. He will be here."

Mercifully, Katem left the hospital room. Victor stared at the door for several minutes. Was it possible that anything Katem said was true? Please, he was an investment banker. Truth wasn't even on the table. The motion on the table was whether there was anything of value for Victor in the inescapable breadcrumbs.

Victor closed his eyes. He almost wished he had never opened them.

>> <<

Sleep wasn't on the schedule at the moment. The drip wasn't fully numbing. Extreme pain in every one of Victor's limbs stood between him and more rest, no matter the drugs in his veins. He wanted more meds and used the control switch to call for Nurse Gomez.

Minutes later she returned and changed the bandages on his legs and arms, then his back and chest. The pain remained grueling. He looked across the hospital room and saw something familiar on the counter next to the sink. It was his iPad. It had survived with the well-traveled computer bag that must have been found in his car. He asked the nurse to retrieve it for him as she hung a fresh IV. She brought the electronic tablet to his bedside and left him alone again.

Victor pulled himself upright, feeling the creak in every bone he could isolate, broken or otherwise. An inside deal. Fraud. A professional beating. An offer to be a CEO. An offer to be a road musician. It was more than he could digest.

He snapped the iPad into its keyboard and pulled up the LinkedIn app on the screen. He entered Claire's name in the search box. He hadn't seen her in a decade. They had never come together. No reunion, no long distance relationship, not even an email after the first year they were apart. The last time they spoke on the phone was, what, almost nine years ago? The job had taken over his life. She had to take care of her family. Fade to black.

Victor looked at Claire's online profile like he used to so often, but not for some time, not since the war with Sangstrum took over his being. She and Victor weren't connected on Facebook, not a chance. LinkedIn was a safe zone for both of them, though he wondered if she ever looked at his profile, his well-known workplace all these years, the big promotions along the way as she had predicted for him. He expected she was working in the same job, never needing more, never making waves, no reason to shake the tree. Consistent Claire Mathias.

Oh wait. No, her last name was hyphenated. Claire Mathias-Ancier. Crap, she was married. She was director of sales at another medical equipment company, not a name he knew, but she had been there for six years, since around the time of the GH IPO. She had updated her photo a few years ago and hadn't changed it since. That smile, that even, honest, half-drawn smile. She always looked happy, satisfied, her untouched portrait testimony to the authentic. Her calm was his branch out of reach. Even if they were alone, apart, separated, she would always know the simple joy he never would. Probably had something to do with God.

Married. She was married. Gone. Off the market. No, maybe she hated Mr. Ancier. Maybe she was miserable. Yeah, horribly miserable, wretched. She married the wrong guy. Ha ha ha. She could be saved from that. Saved. But she didn't look miserable. She looked cheerful. Photoshop applied with subtlety, damn it. She was miserable. No, she wasn't. She was gone. He lost her. He never had her. Idiot. Slow moving, useless idiot. Loser. He was the loser.

Victor closed the app with a hard thumb click. No way he could call her. No way he could tell her he had been almost left for dead, that he was wedged in the middle of a corporate war he didn't want to understand. He had tried to save his company, that's all. He had tried to save his friends' jobs because they mattered so much to everyone. He had struck out swinging and had to quickly crawl his way back to health before his insurance ran out or another hired thug made a follow-up run at him.

It was his fault. The anger. The lack of balance. The emptiness. He had never learned to love. The whole of abandonment was endemic, a repeated life cycle, a learned behavior brought on from his first moments of childhood consciousness, when he understood there would be no parents in his life, no brothers and sisters, no grandparents or aunts or uncles. There would be county paperwork and living logistics, that's all. A full plate of food was a luxury item. If he didn't eat it quickly, he might have to fight another kid in the system for the crumbs, if he could somehow learn to raise his fists before he got drubbed. He had gotten used to it and built an impenetrable shell. She had tried to break through it, tried to pry away the armor, but it was fixed to his skeleton, bound with absence and survival. The God thing was too stinking much for him to internalize—he found it ludicrous and she found his judgment insulting. He had driven her away. When she saw a way out, she sent him there. He couldn't blame her for moving on. He had to own it. He had caused it. There was no other argument.

His head rested on the pillow. His body was as uncomfortable as it was unmovable.

He was stuck. Someone named Thomas Katem wanted his soul. That couldn't happen.

He stared out the window at the Marin Highlands. They had put the hospital in a pristine setting for a reason, so patients who might not emerge to their former functional lives could look out and see hope. A fawn nibbling flower petals among the perpetual redwoods might be their final memory. How quaint was that? Those hospital entrepreneurs had thought it all through—efficient humanity, the aggregation of sustenance, mortality leveraged, market pricing a well-examined backdrop for eternity.

Healing wasn't going to be easy. Figuring out his next move, his next step to get past all this, to leave the bankrupt circus to the sideshow freaks—that was all that mattered.

If only he had a plan, or even a friend.

TRACK 4: YOUR HEAD DOESN'T LOOK SO GOOD

Ten days later, on an otherwise ordinary Monday, Victor was released from Marin General. It had taken longer than the doctors anticipated to get Victor back on his feet, maddeningly longer than Victor wanted to be confined to a hospital room with all that was on his mind. Those so-called professionals got awfully close to the line with a number of Victor's vital functions, requiring more tests, stitches, splints, and medications than anyone had hoped.

Nurse Gomez had taken a special interest in Victor, mentioning more than once that she had never met anyone quite as prone to second guessing himself as this patient. He wasn't sure if this was a compliment, but if his constant barrage of contradictory reflections kept her coming by his room and her extra attention accelerated his recovery, he was more than happy to flood her with dialogue. Besides, she laughed at most of his jokes and proved to be a fan of the Beatles, the Stones, and Motown. It was good to have a smart nurse rooting for him.

It was October. Assuming Katem wouldn't come through paying off the bill with Victor's rejection of his Witness Protection offer, Victor knew he would have to pay the balance someday, if they could find him. He couldn't imagine what he owed. He didn't want to look. His goal was to have a new mailing address without forwarding by the time they sent the dreaded explanation of benefits, also known as *the tab insurance ain't picking up.*

Victor had spent most of the past week and a half contemplating where he'd go and what he'd do once he was healthy enough to be released. Katem's offer, if it had been an offer at all, if he had been Katem at all, was never something Victor considered real. It was ludicrous. It would have placed Victor in the control of a stranger with an eerily unknown agenda. The only known part was the hostility, putting Victor in the crosshairs of someone else's money battle. It might have been tempting to take the grand partial-mystery package behind Door Number One, but he couldn't see himself going near it. Katem hadn't returned to the hospital since his first visit. His failure to make good on even that modest promise sealed the no-deal status in Victor's mind. Katem had been there fishing for something. He wanted information, that's all. He either got what he wanted or figured out nothing was there. No hero on a horse. No paid off hospital bill.

Victor had to move on. He would have to get out of town, disappear for a while. If the acquisition of Global Harmonics was going to be contested, then Victor couldn't risk being a pawn in a game of champions. Not champions, well-dressed thugs. He couldn't sustain another physical altercation without permanent damage to his being. He had to go somewhere quiet, invisible, and cheap.

Yosemite seemed desirable. Victor had always loved Yosemite Valley, the summer nature trips arranged through the county by DCFS, the Department of Children and Family Services. He could get a job with the National Park Service, something nondescript, maybe driving supplies around the winding interior roads or helping out visitors at one of the campsites. It would be a good place to heal. If anyone asked about his appearance, he could say he had a mean fall trying to ascend Half Dome. People would buy that or they'd figure him for a whack job mountain man and leave him alone. Yeah, Yosemite, blue skies, fall snow on the way, an isolated winter, long spring walks up and around the melting falls. Done deal.

Then he ruled it out. Yosemite was too close to the Bay Area. High-wealth familiars regularly made the trek to the famed Ahwahnee Hotel, obnoxiously renamed after a legal action The Majestic. He could run into anyone there, important people, competitors who might recognize him, investors who might call him out. What was he thinking? He might bump into a vacationing banker in the Village General Store picking up a pricey loaf of bread or a bag of Chex Mix. No way, Yosemite was a stupid choice, an amateur's choice. He needed to be much farther away.

He thought about becoming an Outward Bound instructor. Outward Bound had been a needed respite for him when he was twelve, the summer he realized he would never be adopted. He had entered the world unwanted and at adolescence became too old for a family to want him permanently, but he wouldn't let that be his ordained demise. DCFS helped arrange for him to get a scholarship for a month at Outward Bound in Joshua Tree, maybe the best month of his youth. He leaned to mountaineer, to repel, to effect the promise of leave-no-trace camping. What goes into nature comes out of nature, no artifacts left behind. That included hygiene, everything got packed out. He loved the outdoors, the smell of a dry brush campfire, and he especially loved the night of his solo in the desert, the night he wrote in his journal that music would be his path to escape. He'd kept that promise to himself and it had led him to Claire. Now he would pay it back. He could get a field assignment in Utah or Colorado. He had a good record with Outward Bound as a young participant. He could easily pass muster as a trainer. They would teach him how to lead the way his outdoor leader had carried him through the arc of awakening. Someone in social services would be a reference for him once they saw in his file how he had worked around his own failings.

Nah, what was he thinking? He was way too old to begin a career at Outward Bound. They would ask too many questions in the interview. When they saw him battered and stitched up, he wouldn't be able to fake his way through the answers. He probably edited the memory too favorably anyway. Outward Bound would always be a safe haven in his past, but the nighttime talks were intense, requiring too much openness, too much sharing. He would inadvertently say the wrong thing to the wrong person and be found out by the wrong people. The risk of being exposed wasn't worth it. Tech guy who lost all his money trading stocks and got beat up by professional criminals playing Tarzan in the wild? Please, they'd laugh him off a quartz monzonite cliff and leave him for a permanent solo in the ravine.

The year after Victor was emancipated from the system, about the time his first band fell apart, he had worked one season as an assistant river guide out of Ashland, white water for day trip warriors, bloat 'em and float 'em. He thought about making the trek to Oregon and signing on as a raft hand along the Rogue River. That sounded like a benign place to duck out, maybe even a little fun.

Ugh, sheer madness. White water navigation was back-breaking work, too physically demanding after his recent pasting. It was dangerous as all hell and one slightly wrong technical hook could easily put him back in the emergency ward. It would be months before his body could take white water. Another stupid idea easily dismissed.

Yosemite may have been wrong, but the national park idea stuck with him. After hours of internal debate and a hundred Internet keyword searches, he set his sights on Yellowstone. It wasn't that far away, but it was far enough. Although he had never been there, it was enough like Yosemite that he could make it work. Simple roads, endless meadows, rustic campsites. He could drive a supply truck or pitch canvas tents. There were plenty of posted job openings. He would have the same solid cover story for his wounds, blame it on falling rocks or a collapsed mega-tree weakened by lightning. Old Faithful would remind him daily of where real power emerged, what mattered in the arc of time and what was temporal. Yeah, it would be Yellowstone, nothing trivial or easily discoverable there. A gig there would at least last him until the Global Harmonics deal was announced as final, maybe longer. He had no idea how long he would stay, but that was where he decided he was going, alone and unknown.

>> <<

As soon as Victor got back to his Mill Valley condo he began packing. He only planned to spend one night there, then hit the road the next morning for Wyoming. He had rented it about two years ago, right before Sangstrum arrived, and now it was month to month. Of course he should have bought a place a long time ago, built some equity for a nest egg, but that bad habit of day trading took the option of purchasing a home off the table. It didn't make sense that he was great with his company's money but abysmal with his own, yet that was hardly unique among his peer group. Spec investing had unlimited upside. It was exciting. It was invigorating. Home buying in bedroom communities was for people with spouses and children. Victor thought someday that might come together for him, maybe even Claire would come to her senses. He'd stop playing the market then and buy a place. Good thing he hadn't. Freedom was key to his exit. He wasn't unburdened by much, but not having a mortgage or a long-term lease was an excellent place to be at the moment.

With the new month, rent was due and Victor couldn't spare the cash. He would leave the next day with a note telling the landlord to keep his security deposit and dump whatever belongings he hadn't taken. He didn't need anything in the condo that didn't depart with him. As he looked around at the piles of accumulated stuff, he realized he never needed almost all of it. Furniture, dishes, appliances—valueless relics of attempted domesticity. It was all so much stuff, just stuff from here and there and this and that. Artisan table lamps and decorative copper kitchenware, glass protected wall hangings, milk crates of trinkets next to unopened trade show swag piled high, shrink-wrapped sample peripherals from vendors, factory-sealed accessories bought from guilt on Kickstarter—it was all baggage. It could all go. None of it mattered. Two rolling travel cases for clothes, shoes, a bathroom kit, done. A duffle for a blanket and sheet so he could sleep in the car, two towels that could double as pillows, his mobile battery chargers, only the essentials, done. Oh yeah, he needed his prized ebony Gibson Les Paul Custom guitar, a small Marshall practice amp, and a couple of spiral notebooks scribbled with old notes in case he was brave enough to try writing songs again. That was it, nothing more. Printed books were heavy and duplicative, easily discarded for electronic versions. His CDs and DVDs were also obsolete. He had his iPhone and iPad. Apple had long ago comped him unlimited online iCloud storage given his standing in the industry. If he couldn't wear it or use it right now and it didn't fit in the car, to hell with it. Junk weighing down his life. Useless garbage, framed pictures most of all.

As Victor pulled and folded from the closet he heard a knock on the door. Just what he needed, a distraction, no thanks. Who could it be? Sheriff? The same sheriff who had visited him at the hospital as Katem predicted and had asked two hours' worth of unanswerable questions? Nothing for him there, a must-avoid unrepeatable moment. Landlord? Already had that planned, to be handled passively without discussion. Jehovah's Witnesses? Way too late to save his dying soul. Nope, no one he wanted to see. Pull, fold, pack, focus. He ignored the knock. The door would stay closed.

Yet it came again. Knock knock knock. Then again. Then the doorbell. Doorbell doorbell doorbell. Relentless, like the scene in *Macbeth* he remembered seeing at the Marin Theater Company up on Tamalpais at a geek retreat years ago. *Who's there in the name of Beelzebub?* Leave him alone, that was all he wanted, a simple sideways escape. Don't ruin it. Pull, fold, pack, quickly. Silence, please silence.

"Vic, I have some stuff for you. You need this."

He heard it. He heard her. He knew the voice. He peaked through the side window of the condo and saw the lime green Prius parked at the curb. Damn, Darcy Alden, the executive admin to his team. She had been there that night at Providence, left early, he remembered that. She was a regular there, a fan of sorts. They had been friends at Global Harmonics for at least five years, maybe more. He had even thought about asking her out, but why blow up a good work friendship for a failed relationship? Plus there was that persistent rumor she wasn't interested in men. That had never been proven, more of an aura she seemed to relish. If that was her preference, his advance would have been awkward. If not, it might be harassment. He was the boss, the department head after all, her sort of de facto supervisor. No, never mind, not worth the risk, too little upside, all downside. He guessed she had left Providence that night because she didn't want to come to terms with his demise following the boardroom fiasco, which would be all their demise when the company was dismantled. Imagine if she had seen him crushed by three guys with a conscienceless vengeance and astonishingly hard shoes.

Victor cautiously approached the front door. "Darcy?"

"No, Ellen DeGeneres. I want you to come on my show and explain tech investing to the masses."

Victor hesitated, stood there. She banged on the door again. Victor thought someone else might see her pounding away, maybe the landlord. That would be a disaster. The landlord would pop his head in the doorway, see the condo half-packed, ask questions, maybe call the sheriff. He couldn't let that happen. Caving to his inner voice, he extended a hand to the doorknob and let her in. "Shhh, come in, quietly." He closed the door behind her.

Darcy looked good, great in fact. She looked friendly. Darcy smiled a lot. She always found a grin somewhere, he had no idea how. At last someone was smiling in his vicinity. He desperately needed to experience a tone other than grim. She looked around at the suitcases, the mess, took it in but didn't overact. She always had an objective style, that composure, the facility to juggle geeky guys and the unknown without unnecessary angst.

"You're head doesn't look so good," she observed. "Are you sure you're okay to be . . . packing?"

"They released me. I must be okay. It's how modern medicine works. If you can walk out, you're better."

"Stops the meter running, huh, Vic?"

"We've come so far. Keeps our priorities straight." Victor must have been feeling better. Darcy looked even better than usual, maybe because they weren't at the office. Her smile reminded him what a smile was, but wait, he was leaving. Don't go anywhere near there. Idiot.

"I'm glad I caught you, Vic. It's good to see you, even, you know, the way you are. Are you in pain?"

"Yeah, I'm in pain, but it's manageable. Need to pause the meds in a while so I can drive, not looking forward to that. You can't be doing that great either."

Darcy shrugged. He had that right, but she wasn't going to say it. Physical pain won out over psychic pain in everyday conversation, even when that psychic pain approached nominal definitions of torture. Victor noticed the thick interoffice envelope in her hands. He couldn't miss it. He wasn't meant to miss it. That's why Darcy was there. She'd brought his separation papers, probably his final paycheck, plus the all-important vacation pay, the legal close-out clause.

"From the office," said Darcy, catching his unrestrained stare on the pack of papers, the recognition of finality. "They thought you'd want to see a familiar face."

"I know the drill. They want a witness that I received it, so I can't sue for their failure to meet their obligations to me as an employee."

"Former employee."

"Right, I was there."

"I wasn't. I heard you were amazing though. Rumor has it you completely stuck it to Sangstrum. Asshole."

"Yeah, he's an asshole, but not half as malicious as the buyer, McWhorter."

"Tell me about it. McWhorter's first talk to the company didn't go well. Every word out of his mouth was a firebomb. You'd think a guy at his level would've heard of public relations."

"I'm sure he adores the nuclear glow. It lets people know what's coming, builds fear leading to the inevitable scream." Victor saw that Darcy kept shifting her weight from one foot to the other, despite her crafted smile. She didn't want to be there. He didn't want to prolong it. "I'll bet my vacation pay is in that pouch, and my COBRA forms."

"Yeah, all that. There's a box of your pictures and stuff from your desk in my car if you want it. You have a nice collection of mousepads from over the years. I like the one with Mickey Mouse talking into the old Motorola flip phone the best. Collector's item, probably worth something on eBay."

"It's yours; all of it's yours. Can't take it with me, got a full car already. Take what you want, dump the rest. Am I supposed to sign for this?"

"Only if you want. They didn't make an issue of it. The visual record was enough, like you said. Besides, I don't think you're going to sue. I don't think you can afford to sue."

"I can't, and I'm not. You know I blew a lot of money trying to make more money. I need to put some distance between myself and all this. And I'm not signing anything."

"I didn't think so. I'd ask you where you were going but I know you won't tell me, because then I'd know and if they asked me I wouldn't be able to honestly say I don't know."

"Good thought pattern. Thanks for understanding. I don't think you'll see me again."

"That kind of makes me sad." Darcy was still shifting her weight, back and forth, forth and back. She handed him the envelope, but he pointed to the coffee table, where she set it to rest. Then that smile, that steadfast grin. "You know, Vic. I always thought when we didn't work for the same company anymore I might ask you out."

"You would ask me out?" He was dumbstruck. He stared at the envelope on the coffee table for a moment, then locked his eyes on her like a school kid. "Seriously?"

"Why is that strange? I know it's not a good idea to date people you work with. You told me that once. Other people told me not to do it, too, especially women, because when it doesn't work out we take the brunt of it. But that's how I knew you wanted to ask me out, because you work through things by saying them, saying what you're thinking, only you're always thinking more than you're saying. I knew you'd never do it. Your work meant more to you than that. You'd never risk your job over something as fleeting as a relationship."

"You're smart, way smarter than me."

"For what it's worth, I thought you were a great boss and a strong leader when we needed one. Everyone at work felt that way about you. Except the people in QA. They thought you were an ignorant task masker who couldn't debug macros, but I think even they miss you."

"I'm touched, Darcy. You're always eloquent. How bad is it there?"

"It's bad. As bad as you look, that's how everyone at work feels. Morale is at bottom. Sangstrum is doing the happy dance, telling everyone how fantastic things are going and how jolly we're all going to be in the McWhorter portfolio. We know McWhorter is going to can most of us and roll up the company into some kind of pump-and-dump scam."

"That's what I said, but proclaiming it aloud wasn't the smartest move of my career. I think it got me beaten up and left in an alley. How can you be so sure?"

"McWhorter gave an interview on CNBC and said that wasn't at all what he intended to do, so of course we know that's what he's going to do. It's all over the Internet that he's a lying snake. The retention bonuses sealed the deal. He's buying time to sift through the payroll and figure out the few people he absolutely has to keep." Darcy stopped shifting her weight. Her feet were oddly planted on the hardwood floor, tentatively holding her ground.

"That's impressive. The whole world knows about the lie and McWhorter thinks the people he needs to retain will be satisfied with stay bonuses."

"Plus the few of us who will keep our jobs will be in a 'leaner, healthier environment.' More cat food like, that's what he said. He's telling us this is an opportunity to learn how business should be done, that it will make us better prepared for the world ahead, instead of this wasteful shitbox we erected making overbuilt products, wasting shareholder dollars."

Darcy remained sure-footed, but started to cry. Victor wasn't sure what to do. He stood there waiting for her to speak again. She couldn't. Her tears were quiet, wordless.

"It was a perfect place for a long time, Darcy. We didn't know how lucky we were, but we were very lucky. We shouldn't have complained about any of it, even though that's what people do in companies no matter what they have, complain about everything until they lose it. Most people never get to work at a place like we did even for a short time. Camelot never lasts."

She still couldn't speak. She choked back her tears. There was something more on her mind, but she couldn't bring herself to say it.

"What is it?" Victor didn't want to push her, but there was something there, something she wanted to let out.

Before Darcy could answer, Victor's mobile rang. He looked at the screen. No way. It was Thomas Katem. His name glowed on the screen, brazenly unblocked caller ID. Victor didn't answer it. He would let Katem evaporate into the ether. He had nothing to say to Katem.

"What do you want to tell me?" asked Victor.

Darcy hesitated. She tried. She couldn't get the words to flow.

Victor's mobile flashed and beeped. Voicemail. Katem had left a message. This was too strange. He never showed up after his first visit to see Victor. He never called. Darcy brought him his release package. Then Katem called. Could she be a part of it? Would she be a part of it? Is that why she was crying? No, not possible, but he had to know for certain.

"Darcy, what do you know about a man named Thomas Katem?"

She answered without pause. "Nothing, never heard the name."

"Really, nothing at all? That's not why you're crying?"

"No, Vic. I'm crying because some of our guys—some of your former guys, the best from the team—they're going to do something horrible tonight. They don't know I know."

"You're the EA. Admin Darcy knows everything."

"Yeah, mostly, but I don't know who Thomas Katem is."

"What are the guys going to do? Which guys?"

Darcy hesitated yet again, but this time she almost got there. "Max, Clarence, Juan, they're going to . . ." She stopped. She didn't want to continue.

"Darcy, what?"

"They were there when you got beat up. They didn't help you. They were too scared. They feel awful."

"Great, so now they're looking to avenge my beating? What are they planning?"

Darcy held it back as long as she could, then let it go. "They're going to trash the code base, the whole system, lights out e-bomb, unrecoverable. They're going to make the company worthless."

"They're going to release a network virus? Do they have any idea how serious that is?"

"They're so pissed off. I've never seen them this angry. When McWhorter compared our work to cans of Little Friskies, they went ballistic. 'Irreversible' is the project code name. I keep seeing it on their mobile screens. It will erase everything. Source code, customer files, historical accounting, tax records. If they pull it off, there's no chance the deal goes through. The company won't be a company. We're talking burnt toast."

"Hacking the assets of the company is a felony. The company is public. That makes it national news, Wall Street fire and brimstone. They will get caught and do prison time. Everyone left will lose their jobs."

"They don't care, Vic. They aren't letting those bastards get richer. I heard them talking in the men's room, on the beer bash porch, in QA. Project Irreversible, that's the legacy they want to leave."

"What were you doing in the men's room?" Victor wasn't sure where those words came from, but his timing succeeded in shifting gears from the grim.

Darcy found a chuckle. "Ladies was full. I had to go. I do that sometimes. Around here, I'm one of the guys, right?"

"No, not really." Victor found a way to share the brief laugh, then quickly brought himself back into reality. "So you volunteered to bring me this package, so you could tell me this in person."

Darcy nodded. Could he believe her? He waited for her to say more, but she had said enough. She was waiting for him to respond. He was going to disappoint her. He knew that. He had no choice.

"Darcy, there's nothing I can do."

"Vic, they respect you. They'll listen to you. If you tell them not to do it, they won't do it. I don't want our friends to go to prison for nothing, for money. I don't want everyone to get fired. What they are doing is wrong. They think it's justice."

"Darcy, these are coders. They don't respect me that much."

"You'd be surprised. They do. Remember what you said before?"

"The EA knows everything?"

"You guys are not that hard to understand. Will you try?"

Victor thought about it for a moment. He had to get out of town, no question about that, especially with Thomas Katem suddenly hounding him again, but if Full Stack Max, Code Machine Clarence, and QA Juan went to prison, it would be on his conscience for not trying to dissuade them. The fallout would be his fault for putting his head in the sand. Darcy had taken a risk and told him the truth. He owed her a try.

"Darcy, I have to leave. I have to get away. I was going to go in the morning, but maybe I'll go tonight. Do you think you can get them to meet me late tonight before I get on the road?"

"Yes, I think I can do that. I'm sure I can do that."

"Okay, get them to the parking lot on the other side of the marsh, on the road that passes Providence. Do you know the place I'm talking about?"

"Where all the programmers get high at lunchtime?"

"Yeah, you know everything. Yes, there. Don't come with them. I don't want you more attached to this than you already are, plus they won't tell the truth if you're there. They'll deny you know what Irreversible means. Big egos, those dev guys. They think they're so clever."

"Yep, headed for the clever corner in prison. Do you think you can change their minds?"

"I'll do what I can, but it's this one meeting. That's it. Then I'm gone."

Darcy shifted her weight again, all to her right foot, then her left. "How long do you think you're going to be gone?"

"A long time. Maybe . . . I don't know. I probably won't come back."

"You never talk about your family, Vic. I mean, your mom, your dad, they've never called at the office. Can't someone in your family help you out?"

"No, they can't." Those were all the words Victor had.

"I'm sorry. I don't mean to stick my nose in your business. Are they, you know, gone?"

Victor thought about that. The right words never seemed to be there. "Yeah, gone."

"I'm sure that's hard. You don't have anyone who can help you at a time like this. I won't pry anymore, I promise."

"It's okay. You're helping me. They were sort of always gone. I learned to live with it. That's how it is."

Darcy shifted her weight back to her right foot and looked squarely at him. "You're complicated, Vic, but you're not hateful. I probably should have asked you out, shouldn't I?"

That surprised him, like it came out of nowhere. "No, I should have asked you out."

"Yeah, but you probably thought I was a lesbian, right?"

"Rumor mills are tough, even in perfect companies like ours."

"Camelot falls. Even Guinevere betrayed her husband."

"No useful metaphor there, but nice try, Darcy. You risked a lot telling me about the virus. You did your part. No regrets."

"No regrets, Vic. Stay in touch with me. If you need anything while you're away, wherever you end up, anything, call my mobile. You can count on me."

Victor walked back toward the door, leading her in that direction, "I know that. I've always known that."

Darcy stopped short of the door. She wasn't quite ready to leave. "Thank you for doing this, Vic. It means a lot. That's why we respect you, because you do stuff like this. Even the QA guys know that. Would I be imposing if I asked you one more favor?"

"Depends. What favor?"

"Stop buying stocks, okay? You really suck at it."

"Admin Darcy knows everything."

Darcy laughed, a hearty laugh, not forced. Victor tried to echo it, but he couldn't laugh in return. He opened the condo door and she was down the stairs in seconds, gone from sight, gone from possibility, an untaken journey he would never get to choose.

>> <<

Victor closed the door behind Darcy and looked around the condo at the disarray, the remnants of his unattached life on display and readied for abandonment. All that stuff was little more than a timeline of despair, special delivery to the junkyard. At least that part of his life's mess would be behind him, trail markers purged from his unhinged chronology.

He stared at his mobile phone. The name Thomas Katem stared back at him in clear bright lettering. Victor couldn't resist. He played back the message:

"Victor, this is Thomas Katem. I'm sorry I haven't been in touch. It doesn't mean I don't care. There have been some complications but the offer is still on the table. You need to take this offer. Call me as soon as you can."

Victor stared at the small screen. Who in the fog of war was this Thomas Katem? What did he want? Why wouldn't he leave Victor alone? Was he for real? What was real?

Victor wanted no part of Katem. Global Harmonics wasn't just dead to him. It was dead to the world. There was no second act in this horror show. It was over. Time to let go. Time to move on. No more fight.

He could have asked Darcy out all those times, all those company parties. She probably would have liked *Macbeth* in the open air theater up on Tamalpais, instead of being there drinking craft beer with a gang of nerds. Lesbian? Really? He never bought that. He was a coward. Self-assessment, check. Victor Selo was a weak runaway nobody who brought on his own misery through ignorance and inaction. Play bad, deserve to lose. Victor absolutely deserved to lose.

Same with Claire. Ten idiotic years. He could have called her back. He could have emailed or texted or allocated a few days off.

How many chances had he blown? How much avoidance could he justify? He'd walked away from her. He'd walked away from a life together to build a database, to build a bank account, and then ditch it on stocks that tricked him. Smart guy? No, a dunce. He was meant to be alone. He could only be alone. Claire said we lived with God's Choices. You had talent or you didn't. You understood love or you didn't. You came from a real family or you didn't. Those were God's Choices. Our job was to make sense of them, to make them work, to learn what we could now and the rest in due time.

Fine then, God wanted him to be alone. That was God's Choice. Who was he to question God's Choices? Who was he to seek what wasn't meant to be his?

This unknowable idea of God would be forever on his mind. With Claire came God. With failure came God. He didn't believe in God. He didn't want to believe in God. He would have enjoyed a conversation with God, but how could he have a conversation with an entity he didn't acknowledge? God was in Yosemite. God was in Joshua Tree. God was in whitewater Oregon. God would be in Yellowstone. Why would God allow one Thomas Katem on the Earth, let alone two—or one who mas masquerading as the other?

Victor was losing it. Sanity, sanctity, both were on the line, some form of sanctuary in the swells of bad decisions. Righteousness had to be in there, too, asylum secured for flesh and soul. God, no God, alone forever and nowhere to go but a national park that couldn't have wanted him. His inveterate colleagues were going to commit a felony and implode. They were going to ruin their lives over nothing. He couldn't let that happen. The escalation had to stop. He had to make it stop this very second. Darcy was right. Claire was right. God was right, if only there were a God.

Victor had to get out of Marin. There was little chance he could stop Geeks R Us from doing themselves in, his friends and former teammates who had turned their heads away when he was left bloody in a back alley. He felt an obligation nonetheless to keep them from blowing up Global Harmonics in a federal crime that would follow them the rest of their days. Darcy had convinced him. He had convinced himself. He at least had to try to stop it all from getting worse.

One last chore, then he'd be long gone for Yellowstone.

No Thomas Katem. No more distractions. Escape. Freedom. Hiding.

Victor had to be gone. Bolt, ditch town, navigate a leave-no-trace exodus from the nearest on-ramp to the thousand-mile-away exit. Nothing could be more certain.

This was his final farewell task, the last act standing between him and the nothing he needed. Was this one of God's Choices? It was another fork in the road that could only be seen in hindsight. He probably wouldn't know for a decade if he was picking the right path. It didn't matter. Max, Clarence, and Juan were idealistic, undisciplined children. They were gifted, brilliant coding stars, someday Hall of Famers, but they were boxed-in victims of naïveté. Darcy had selflessly played her only card on their behalf, a dicey test of obligation and uneasily shared history. They were sheltered from rulings outside the moat, oblivious to the shysters and shrewdly armed ingrates beyond Camelot's influence. They could be slashed into legal oblivion with the stroke of judge's pen. No one could defend them. No one would come to their aide. He was doing it for them, so they didn't have to become him. If that made God happy, then Victor was obliged to serve.

TRACK 5: ON THE ROAD ABSENT ENTOURAGE

At 10:55 p.m., Monday night, Victor pulled off the road into the small parking lot adjacent to Scottsdale Marsh, a half mile down the road from Providence. Before he could put the fully packed Acura in park, his mobile phone rang again. He looked down at the screen. It was Katem once more, the eleventh time in six hours. Katem had stopped leaving messages after the third call, but he kept calling. And calling. Victor stashed his mobile in the pocket of his cargo shorts. He had no interest in talking to Katem, no interest in Katem of any kind.

Ahead in the headlights were Max, Clarence, and Juan. They were passing a joint, silhouette shadows on the brush in the low beams, like high school kids hanging out. They were standing beside Max's minivan, an old Chrysler filled with three generations of monitors, mixers, motherboards, coils of wire, and disassembled chip sets—his silicon storage shed on wheels. He could afford a better ride but didn't want it.

Victor had known Max for ten years, his entire time at Global Harmonics. "Full Stack Max" as he had come to be known with reverence was GH Employee #11, one of the first software engineers on staff with a generous grant of founder's options. He was a first-rate systems architect in that elite class where credentials didn't have to be stated. His elegant code was widely known, in the early days he could deliver the Full Stack on his own when required. He had joined Global Harmonics out of high school. He said he graduated, had a diploma rolled up somewhere, but no one was sure. No one cared. He never missed a deadline, never complained about the enormity of a technical task. Every requested feature set to him was a math problem, the harder the better. That's what he said he liked to do best, solve hard math problems. He compiled to his own beat, a thought wanderer with an elusive muse. Most of all, he loved the company. Where else could he have such a blessed, unquestioned, lucrative young life working on what he wanted, when he wanted, if he wanted? He had been paid well but held onto the majority of his stock option package, perpetually waiting for the comeback that never was. He had thought that a sign of loyalty even when Bud privately nudged him to cash in when he could. Now he was as furious at himself as he was at Sangstrum, but not at Bud and not at the company.

Clarence had come onboard seven years ago, a year before the IPO, when the company began staffing up to drive its hotly anticipated liquidity event. He was the opposite of Max in curriculum vitae, at least on paper, a methodical code machine forever churning out a drill. He had an MS in computer science from the University of Chicago where he had also been a summa cum laude / Phi Beta Kappa electrical engineering undergraduate. He was as brainy as they come, but in any discussion of hacking style with both of them, no one could tell that Clarence had the cap-and-gown degrees Max never would. It wasn't that Max was a great conversationalist. It was that Clarence abhorred petty conversation of any kind. He had tried a stint at McKinsey, but his lack of people skills overshadowed his intellect to the point where he found insulting clients a reflex his chemistry could not reverse. He was offered a job at JPL, but found the pay level absurd for his advanced grasp of science. He knew as much about motherboards as he knew about designing algorithms. Those things he would talk about in soft grunts. His stock options came at a higher strike price than Max's grant, but he sold them in regular tranches and did reasonably well, though not a killing given the crash. He also loved Global Harmonics, and without him the enterprise platform would have been worth a fraction of its former ten-figure asset valuation. In the company's best years, coworkers in the know joked that Max and Clarence *were* the company's balance sheet. Victor never thought of it as a joke.

No one was quite sure where Juan came from. He had been around for about three years, it was hard to pinpoint it. He sort of showed up one day and started working in quality assurance as a teenage temp, about the age Max had been when he joined the company. "Quality Amigo" a.k.a. QA Juan still couldn't be twenty years old. After about a week of bug squashing at large, Clarence snuck him under his wing as his sidecar man, debugging Clarence's code and no one else's. When Max got wind that this new kid was making Clarence look good, he wanted in on Juan's insight. Was Juan an employee or a contractor? He didn't take direct deposit. Did he get paid at all? If he had options, they'd be underwater and worthless, but it seemed to mean nothing to him. He wore the same reddish lumberjack shirt five days a week and the same Carlos Santana T-shirt on the weekends, when the lumberjack shirt was soaking in a sink somewhere. Juan utterly loved the company. It was his whole life. He hardly noticed the business was struggling. He simply immersed himself in the code, happy to be challenged, ecstatic to be accepted on the team. To the best of everyone's knowledge, he had no quantifiable past other than possibly crossing the border as child with some family members from Mexico, but even that was equal parts myth and reality. Juan never talked about the future. He relished the present. The first time Max and Clarence saw a perfect code library he had compiled on his own without so much as telling anyone he did it, they both took credit for teaching him what he knew. That was bluster covering for his quietly discovered talent. He was young, but he would be as good as both of them, especially at network security, which was his gift. QA Juan thought he had found heaven at Global Harmonics and never said a cross word to anyone. He had no complaints of any kind. He was a natural.

The Tres Amigos had become inseparable. They were the Three Musketeers of Geekdom. They were Victor's key to prosperity. Now they were very, very, very angry. This made them very, very, very dangerous—no matter the innocence of their intention.

"Where you headed, Selo?" asked Max. "Darcy says you're blowing town."

"Yeah, I need to get out of here for a lot of reasons."

"You want some of this?" Max extended the joint. It was more than half-consumed and sloppy wet at the end.

"No, thanks, I'm good. I have a long drive ahead of me tonight."

"You going to tell us not to do something?" asked Clarence, not looking Victor in the eye, staring instead into the marsh.

"I'm not your boss anymore, Clarence. I can't tell you anything. In reality I couldn't tell you anything when I was your boss. You'd never listen."

"That's about right," said Clarence. "We made you rich, though."

"We made all the investors rich," added Max, exhaling a lengthy blast of smoke with Marin proficiency. "Now that shithead McWhorter tells us we're cat food."

"That shithead, McWhorter." Juan awkwardly repeated the invective, not his usual cheerful use of language. "He's taking everything. We get nothing. He belongs in this swamp."

Victor tried to change the mood. "I don't think he said we were cat food. He meant what we make is the same as cat food. Get your insults straight."

"Same shit in the bowl whether you're the cat food or you make it," said Max. "Sangstrum takes the money and runs. McWhorter strip-mines what we built and we get wiped. The cat food factory closes up shop."

"You guys made yourselves some money, too," argued Victor. "Come on, we all did well, probably better than Sangstrum."

"Not when it's done with an offshore commission," grunted Clarence, taking the joint from Max. "I did the math on market-rate grease. His exit beats our exit."

"Clarence is dependable with that Chicago math," said Max. "I mean, he would be right, Sangstrum's exit would have beaten our exit, but we're going to adjust the equation, so it's more of a fair split, where he gets zero."

"If you detonate the bomb, you'll get zero, too." Victor ducked the smoke cloud. He didn't like the smell of weed, but in tech culture it was an occupational hazard he'd learned to tolerate.

"Yeah, but we've already taken some off the table," boasted Max, taking another turn on the joint. "I've been here a long time, even longer than you. I got some coin, maybe not a lot. Clarence got some. We'll make sure QA Juan gets some. We'll go do this again somewhere else. Sangstrum can rot in hell. We're buying him a first class ticket."

"It's not that easy," said Victor. "You're committing a federal crime. Destroying a public company is a felony. You might do time, you might not, but you won't work again. This is a small world we're in. Word travels, you know that."

"They'll have to prove it. No chance they can tie it to us." Clarence tried to hand the almost consumed joint to Juan, but Juan wasn't interested. He handed it back to Max, who gladly received the remains.

"We got this, Mr. Victor," said Juan, as politely as his pasted-on defiance would allow. "Believe it."

"You want to be criminals, be criminals," said Victor. "I can't stop you. That makes you no better than Sangstrum. Can you live with that?"

There was silence. It lasted less than a minute, but it seemed like eternity. Dire, untested, unjust eternity.

Max finished the joint and tossed the tiny wet butt in the marsh. "Yeah, I can live with it. I've been here almost since the beginning. That code wouldn't be here without me. If Sangstrum wants to sell it to take his share after doing nothing but wrecking the place, I'm nuking it."

"I'm refining the uranium," added Clarence.

"I'm piloting the missile," said Juan. That sounded funny to three of them, bloodshot eyes and all. They chuckled awkwardly. Programmer humor.

"Hubris will crush you," admonished Victor.

"Eat this hubris, Selo." Max started pacing in front of the van. "They screwed you over royally. We heard about the meeting. You tried to save us. We got that, but they're hanging this on you. You're the one who won't work again. You don't write code. You're just a manager and you're not Steve Jobs, although sometimes you sound like him."

"That doesn't make sense," said Clarence. "Steve Jobs was an awful manager. My dad had a PhD and worked for him twice, got fired three times."

"What does a software manager do?" asked Juan.

"Pay attention, gentlemen," roared Max. "A software manager does what Selo does. I mean, I don't know exactly what he does, but he lets us do what we do, which is way cooler than Sangstrum. I'm sorry, Selo, you're cool, even though we don't think you do anything."

Victor fell silent. They were stoned. They were livid. They were deliberately descending into anarchy. It was a difficult moment and he had to let the conversation go. He still didn't know what to do. He couldn't stop them, not with this argument. He felt the phone buzzing again in his pocket. He changed course.

"Guys, if you wipe out the network code, it's forever. There is no back door. It's a permanent solution to what could be a temporary problem."

"Temporary?" Clarence kicked the dirt next to the van. His gym shoe got stuck in the mud. He pulled hard to release it and his sock came free of his shoe, leaving him with one bare foot. "How the frick is it temporary?"

Victor looked at Clarence's single bare foot and choked back a laugh. These guys really were classic nerds. So smart, but forever frumpy. He forced himself back to gravitas. "This is tech. Things change on a dime. If you ruin the company forever, there will be no company if I ever come back."

"You're coming back?" asked Max, pulling Clarence's shoe from the mud and handing it back to him, no big deal. "To do what?"

"I don't know. Maybe run the place."

That got their attention. The three stooges ran a double take. Victor had the element of surprise, most of all on himself.

"You're going to be CEO of Global Harmonics?" asked Clarence, shaking out his sock and putting his foot back where it belonged.

Max reached in his shirt pocket, found another joint, and lit it up. He spoke as he exhaled. "That's a laugh and a half. They threw you down the elevator shaft, compadre."

"Yeah, maybe I fell. My fault, so what?" Victor was standing his ground, making progress, threading the needle before they could see it. "Like I said, things change all the time."

"Change how?" asked Juan, suddenly interested in taking the new joint from Max.

"You do what you're good at, I do what I'm good at," said Victor. "That's what kept Camelot safe."

"Until we were invaded by barbarians," shouted Max, his face a quarter body length from Victor's. "You got backing, big guy? You making a run at the company before McWhorter closes?"

"It could happen. I'm not at liberty to say." Victor was closing. They were letting emotion consume them. Steve Jobs would be proud.

"That's bullshit," said Clarence. "We're nuking the homeland. Always and forever."

Clarence and Max high-fived, looked to Juan to complete the trio, but Juan pulled back. Whoa. Split interest. Two Amigos. One outlier. Yeah, Steve Jobs would be proud.

"*No mierda*, Mr. Victor?" asked Juan, pulling hard on the joint. "*Cierto*, true words?"

"No bullshit, I have a real story." Victor walked toward them, then looked far down the road toward Providence. "Truth is, I don't know all of it yet, but yeah, I've been offered backing. I have to go away for a while and lay low. When the time comes, I could be back as CEO."

"Could be back?" simpered Max.

Clarence took the remainder of the joint from Juan and finished it. "That's heartening."

Victor leaned against the van. "What do you have to lose? We could save the company we love, lots more good times ahead. Maybe, maybe not. Why not find out?"

"What changed your mind?" asked Max. "You didn't tell Darcy any of this or she would have told us. You either changed your mind or you made it up."

"You're right, I didn't tell Darcy. I was too pissed off, but I didn't make it up." Victor kept staring at Providence.

"Why change your mind?" asked Clarence. "Why not go hide out in Yellowstone?"

Victor turned away from viewing Providence and looked Clarence in the eye. "How the hell do you know about Yellowstone? I haven't told anyone about that."

Clarence laughed derisively in Victor's face and turned his back on him. Juan stared at the ground. Victor looked to Max for the truth. "We all have secrets and none of us have secrets. You were our boss. We like to know what you're thinking. Your mobile phone helps us with that, couple lines of hidden code. You've been googling Yellowstone a lot."

"You assholes spy on me? What trust! See anything else interesting on my mobile?"

Max put it all out there. "Sorry, we're tracking, not spying. Someone named Katem from the 650 area code keeps calling you. We couldn't break the encryption on his message."

"Gee, you're not as good as I thought. Katem is my backing. Want to hear the message?"

"No, we believe you," affirmed Max. "Wanted to hear you say it. So you're going away and maybe you come back as CEO. You want us to wait? Maybe we'll wait."

Victor took a breath. He had them again. He had to make it stick. "Do this for me. Go ahead and plant the network code bomb. Embed it in the kernel, but don't hit the detonator. That can be our ace in the hole. If I'm not back before the close, you can nuke it. If I get into trouble and can't make it back, I'll text you an agreed code to strike."

"Can I pick the code words?" asked Juan.

"Sure, knock yourself out," offered Victor.

"Pendejo Pudding."

Victor nodded his head. It was as good a trigger as any, no possibility for error. "Fine, Pendejo Pudding. If I call or text those words, you detonate the virus."

"You think this Katem is for real?" asked Clarence.

"I don't know, but I don't want you guys to ruin your lives over a dead company. I'm willing to find out."

"What are you going to do between now and then?" asked Max. "Sounds like Yellowstone is off the table."

"Believe it or not, I think I'm going to play some rock and roll."

"Like at Providence?" asked Juan.

"A few clicks up from Providence, but yeah, that's sort of the idea. I'll be invisible for a while. Katem is helping with that."

"The invisible rock star, sure, that's a plan," said Max. "Don't make us wait too long. We're trusting you."

Victor had made the deal. It wasn't what he had come there to do. It certainly wasn't what he wanted to do. He did what he had to do. Max, Clarence, and Juan wouldn't have otherwise budged. He didn't want to see them implode, and he wasn't ready to close the door on Global Harmonics. Not forever, not while there was an option. The words had come out of his mouth. That happened sometimes for better or for worse. Instinct. Stand down, stand tall. Buy time. Make the deal. Had they been negotiating all along? These stooges, these amigos, these musketeers? Did they beat him at his own game? Their game? Did it matter?

Victor stepped away from the van and slowly started walking backward toward his Acura. "No surprises, guys. Patience rules.

I'll see you when I see you, hopefully soon, but maybe not. Do not panic."

Max took a few steps toward him. "Victor, we owe you an apology."

"We're cool. Wait for the code words. Tread water until then."

"No, at the club. We should have helped. We did panic. We weren't there for you the way you're there for us. We never learned how to, you know, fight with our hands. We called the cops. We should have done more."

"We did a little more," added Clarence. "Paramedics were busy that night. Your incident wasn't high in the 9-1-1 queue. We rerouted the task to first position on their system map. Their backend doesn't take much to hack."

"Then you might have saved my life," replied Victor. "I get it. It was scary. There wasn't enough time to think it through. Don't panic again, okay?"

"Sorry, boss," said Juan. "We're the pendejos."

"Not even close. Next time you'll be with me all the way. I'm sure of that."

Victor nodded with certainty, turned, and walked back to his car. He noticed a thin fog forming on the marshland where it connected with the adjoining pond, unusual for late night. There must have been a warm breeze coming from inland, colliding with the cool offshore winds blowing with the Jetstream above. He looked back and saw Max, Clarence, and Juan slipping into the minivan, sliding closed the door and departing the roadside lot. Given their state, he probably should have encouraged them to call Uber, but he had already closed. He learned long ago you can't say anything more once you've closed without ripping open a new negotiation. He knew they didn't have far to drive and hoped they'd get home safely. Once again he was alone.

>> <<

Victor stared at his mobile phone. He knew what he needed to do, his self-assigned mandate. He didn't want to do it, but he had to do it. As reluctantly as anything he had ever done in his life, he hit the callback icon next to Katem's name. It only rang once, not even a full once.

"Victor, it's Thomas Katem."

"Really, what a coincidence. You think you could have dialed me another fifty times? Or shown up again at the hospital like you said you would?"

"You're angry. That's understandable. I should have called back sooner. Your bill at the hospital is paid like I said it would be."

"I didn't know that. No one told me, so maybe you did and maybe you didn't. The thing is, I'm not angry. I wrote you off the minute you left my room."

"But you're calling me back. You must have something in mind."

"I don't know what to make of you, Katem. You lie for a living. I have to figure out if I can live with that."

"Are you taking the offer, Victor?"

"I don't know, Thomas Katem, if that's your name. I'm thinking maybe I'll call myself Thomas Katem. I still have your business card. I can give it to someone and pretend to be you."

"You wouldn't do that, Victor. That's not you."

"What are the complications?"

"The what?"

"The complications. You said in the message you left me that there were complications."

"It's a long story, Victor. This thing is the Exxon Valdez. It's a spiraling shit show."

"It was almost nothing at all. I've intervened on your behalf."

"You're speaking cryptically, Victor. What does that mean?"

"My ass is on the line with people I care about. You have your secrets, Katem, I have mine. I also have a bulletproof insurance policy, so if you screw me on this, I can play all the cards. I'm going to be CEO when the dust clears or there is only going to be dust. We good?"

"We're good."

"What do I do?"

"Can you drive to Las Vegas?"

"It wouldn't be my first choice, but I could. Why?"

"Petrumi—that booking agent I mentioned—he has a gig for you there. That's why I've been calling over and over, opportunity knocks. The agents in Vegas control every room. This is gold. You only got it because I know Petrumi and he trusts me. Gig starts tomorrow."

"I just got out of the hospital, Katem. I need some down time."

"Right, that's why you ditched your apartment, down time."

"The entire world knows everything I'm doing."

"The hospital called to say you were discharged, like I asked them when I was there. I paid the bill. They said you went home. When I didn't get you on the phone, I called your landlord to see if you owed him money. He said you had left and you were whole with the deposit. No spying, okay?"

"No spying, Katem, you just like paying my bills."

"Victor, are you in? I need to know before Petrumi fills the gig with someone else. Like I said, this is gold. You take it or you don't, but I don't have a backup if you turn this down. We can make this a win-win. Witness Protection?"

"You are a scumbag, Katem. Fine, I'll take the gig. What's the gig?"

"Get on the road. Head for the Strip. Petrumi has your mobile. He'll call you in the next hour, tell you where to check in, all of that. The room will be paid for, everything you need to get started will be handled on a house account. You kept a guitar, right?"

"I almost didn't but I did. I have a classic solid body with me in the car. Bud Thacker gave it to me to commemorate our IPO."

"Aren't you the sentimentalist! You're ready to play, that's all I need to know. Wherever Petrumi books you, play the gig until you hear from me. Don't call me. Absolutely do not call Sangstrum or McWhorter. You'll get paid regularly by the band you're with as long as you show up and play. Follow the house rules, no deviation, no gamesmanship, trouble-free interaction. Stay distant. You're a backup musician whose agent placed you there, that's your entire story. If you need anything, call Petrumi. If it's necessary, he'll call me. Don't make it necessary."

"That's it?"

"That's it for now. You do your job, I'll do mine."

"Sure you will. You'll clean up the complicated shit show I can't know about. Make sure there's still a company for me to run when I get back."

"There will be a company. You can trust me on that."

"Sure I can."

"Have some fun, okay? You've earned it."

"Fun, yes. Witness Protection fun. Viva Las Vegas. Do not screw me, you scumbag. I'm telling you, my insurance policy is not something you want to set in motion."

Victor hung up. He was tempted to heave his mobile into the marsh and head for Yellowstone, but he had made a deal. Emotion in real time never made for a good decision. This was logical. He had as much control of the situation as he could hope. Nope, he had turned his back on taking in Ol' Faithful. He was taking Katem up on the offer. In a very short time, he would be playing again in a band.

Victor put the RLX in gear and headed south toward the Golden Gate Bridge. In about nine hours he would be in Las Vegas.

SIDE TWO: NOW

Turn off your mind
Relax and float downstream
It is not dying.

The Beatles, "Tomorrow Never Knows"

TRACK 6: NOWHERE MAN NEEDED NOW

HIGHWAY TRAVEL FROM SAN FRANCISCO TO LAS VEGAS EVOKES LITTLE ROMANCE. It's a sad, long shot down 580 to Interstate 5, hours of nothingness but fast food off ramps through central California, then an eastern hook across the Mohave Desert before the vacuous approach on Interstate 15. That last leg, the federally funded cement pour between Southern California promise and the manufactured Nevada oasis, is entirely without imagination, likely by design—a half hour of nothingness sponsored in signposts by Zappos, now headquartered in the metropolis ahead, how strange is that? The awaiting casinos want consumers on and off the grade, no distractions. Route 66 is barely a memory. Go east, young man, where the endgame forever serves up subsidized booze.

For the driver, it is a stretch of pavement to ponder the roads not taken, the abandoned forks of opportunity. It is less being and more nothingness. It can make a person sad. It can make a person remember. Victor knew that. Everyone who drove it knew that, even if they pretended otherwise, like they were going to the Mad Hatter's Ball with a VIP invitation, an absurdist call to the dumb man's cave of luxury. Party like it's 1999, dude! Vegas antics beckon. It's hard not to laugh before surrendering one's accumulated earnings for a few hours of candy-coated vice where self-deception reigns deniably. Celebrate excess, drink, load up your plate and belly, shop alluring retail, embark with abandon on limitless games of chance. Musicians warmly welcome to fill out the sand city scenery! After the fall, a schmuck is a schmuck. Everyone comes to know that the hard way.

It was a full dark night of driving with mostly light traffic, very little to see in the starless high desert. Thundering multi-axle trucks with masked cargo loads only occasionally cut into the faster left lane. That made for a mostly straight run, eyes forced open no matter the sleep deprivation, heavy foot on the gas to cut minutes off the clock. The tedious haul gave Victor time to think, to let thoughts of the past few weeks enter freely and squat on the present.

Vegas was also a place for shows, glossy stage pageants, adaptations of Broadway productions imported to residence status and extended runs. *Phantom of the Opera. Jersey Boys. The Lion King. We Will Rock You. Rock of Ages.* Victor hadn't seen many of them. Sometimes he would hit a musical with business partners when he was in town for the annual Consumer Electronics Show, but theater wasn't his thing. He remembered one show vividly, not in Vegas and not a musical, a play he had seen as a kid. When he was in the fifth grade, his class made a perfunctory visit to the Music Center in downtown Los Angeles, a field trip to see a stage production at the lavish Ahmanson Theatre. Foster care kids had been invited, though he wasn't sure who paid for the tickets.

They attended a Broadway-bound revival of *Amadeus*. It was a midweek matinee with a full load of elementary school age kids in the house. The room looked like a palace. They sat in the back row orchestra but had decent enough sight lines. Taking his seat, Victor had never heard of *Amadeus*. He didn't even know where the title originated. He had neither been excited nor reluctant to go. A school outing meant at least a half day out of the classroom, which was a welcomed way to mark time. He had never been to a professionally staged play, so that was kind of cool. He had no expectations for what he was about to see, no frame of reference for what it was or might mean. He read in the printed program that the movie star Tim Curry had been a headliner in the original New York cast years ago. That's all he had to go on.

It was a performance that stayed with him the rest of his life. It was plain-spoken poetry like the carefully chosen lyrics in the songs he so loved. Its themes were forever. There in Victor's drifting mind, as he drove Interstate 15, waltzed a mesmerizing actor who reminded him of Tim Curry, bounding across the stage, owning an outlandish interpretation of the composer Wolfgang *Amadeus* Mozart.

Was Wolfie really a rebel? A crazed counter-culture freak? A nonconformist womanizer with no respect for the discipline required of composition, orchestration, and recital? He displayed no deference to the court or the church, none whatsoever. He was a badly behaved genius, an iconoclastic beast refusing to be caged. Most of all, he was a musician. He was Keith Richards. He was Pete Townshend. He was the whole package. Victor sensed the entire story was made up by the playwright, dramatic license as the program notes mentioned, but so what? The story was brilliant. The dialogue was brilliant. Mozart was brilliant.

Mozart defied man, not God. He was one of God's Choices. He pissed off as many humans as he pleased, but he did the work God sent him to do. God's intentions flowed through Mozart's quill, piano, and baton. His mind was fed by the unreachable. He was an instrument of divinity more than a suffering windbag. He made the court's virtuoso climber Salieri mad, reckless, so covetous he had to end Mozart's life. The Requiem would be Mozart's final work and take him to the edge of insanity, but it would be perfect in a way Salieri could never deliver.

Why would Mozart's temporal superior Salieri risk all for this nobody of the day? Salieri would get away with it, a murderous crime recovered only by his confession, so that his tirade against determinism would be preserved in posterity, an argument with deity that transcended human limitation. Inspiration was not up for grabs, it was rationed illogically without appeal. Flesh could be compromised, a pure idea not so much. Why, Salieri, why? Who was more unglued, Salieri or Mozart? Mozart cared not for order, but Salieri cared not for law.

What drove Salieri to the heinous, unrepentant act?

It was fear of mediocrity.

The pain Salieri suffered was corrosive. It became pernicious. In the end it proved debilitating. Mediocrity drove the nobleman to murder.

Salieri wished to serve God, but Mozart got the gig. It wasn't Salieri's call. It wasn't Mozart's call. The decision of who was good and who was great came from somewhere else. The life sentence of mediocrity would be handed down 99.99% of the time. That was how it was. It could be no other way or the alternative case could never be true. Without a sea of ordinary there could be no extraordinary. The sea had to be eternally widened for its corollary to exude value. To be Mozart—mortal rehearsal didn't get to decide that. That choice came from elsewhere, another measuring system, a parallel dimension. God was a tough booking agent.

It was a hard lesson for an eleven-year-old already on his own. It landed that hard. Avoid mediocrity at all costs or your life would mean nothing. No guitar could save you. No computer could save you. You couldn't be saved, not by your own choice. Determination of mediocrity couldn't be avoided without divine intervention. That was all Victor remembered about the theater, about stories on a stage. Salieri was mediocre. Mozart was not. They didn't get to choose. They both suffered but only one mattered. Only one could live on and he would never know it. He would die broken, his life's work for billions of strangers to embrace and rank supremely. Trying wasn't important because it wasn't eternal. Talent was beyond conjecture. It could only be realized if it was meant to be.

Back then Victor was already glued to a Yamaha acoustic he had bought at a garage sale. He played it whenever a moment allowed, usually alone. He was starting to get good at it, getting past the strum and onto the finger pick. He could read the fake charts of pretty much all the Top 40 and knock out the simple songs cleanly, hanging a little on the solos, but getting there. Bands like the Eagles and Wings were mostly done with each other after 1980, but their songbooks were around, plenty of airplay. They didn't yet call it classic rock, it was FM airplay. Victor knew that music might be his redemption, but he didn't want to be mediocre. Abandonment was fate enough. Mediocrity was a life sentence.

He always hated the word *awesome*. Second on the expunge list was the word *amazing*. As descriptors of creative product, they were overused to the point of being meaningless, numb in their application to the ordinary all around him. He would have none of it. He knew he would never be Mozart—that decision had been made for him—but he wouldn't overstate the conventional. No matter his failing, he would only work harder, practice harder, resolve to be better. He couldn't beat fate. He couldn't pretend it wasn't an impenetrable wall, but fate would not stop him from always raising his own bar, never being satisfied, never going with the flow.

There wouldn't be shows like *Amadeus* in Vegas, the pinnacle of commonplace ambitions. Superlatives were rare. Their recognition had to be earned.

Victor's mind had floated to that memory. Interstate 15 was all he saw in the windshield. It was piping to the next node, nothing more. His phone rang and on the LCD dashboard display he saw it was the booking agent, Sandy Petrumi. He knew he needed to answer the call, to get the name of the hotel that would be his destination. He had already talked to Petrumi once an hour ago and instantly didn't like him. It was sort of inevitable. He had to dislike him. Petrumi was loud, impatient, and demanding. He was a conduit, the extended voice of Thomas Katem. Had Petrumi made this whole thing up, invented it for Katem, or was it Katem who made it all up, maybe even Petrumi? Right, how convenient, his friend the agent, the guy who found him the safe-house gig behind marble fountains in the outpost of yuck. A loudmouth, an opportunist, an agent was never supposed to be in the script, certainly not a screamer who said, "Do it my way or the next answer you hear will be no and get lost."

Petrumi may have been tough, but he had nothing on God.

>> <<

Victor pulled off I-15 at the Tropicana exit and merged onto Las Vegas Boulevard. He knew he was getting onto the Strip much too soon, that Petrumi had told him to check into the Golden Nugget downtown, where his room would be covered, but it wouldn't be Vegas without an approach. The sun would come up soon and the city before dawn looked the same as it did all night, almost inviting despite the rampant lights and fountains where they were never meant to be. Las Vegas was almost inviting in the night hours, but in sunlight it gracelessly invaded the timeless desert with a glut of marquee signage and bad taste.

There were worse afterthoughts in America than Las Vegas, but not many, and not by much. The evidence was widely exposed in the mad zoning sprawl. He knew the town reasonably well, the post-modern grid deliberately easy to master. Each January he would make the pilgrimage to the Consumer Electronics Show with some 100,000 other gadget peddling corporate types. He had been going to CES every year since he joined Global Harmonics. He was familiar with trade events at the Disney-like hotels flanking the gateway to the Strip, the Luxor and Excalibur. Nearby towered the indoor-outdoor frolic at Mandalay Bay, where European sun-bathing was allowed and advertised. He usually stayed at the Mirage, the former home of Siegfried and Roy until that one awful incident, but that had brought the Beatles *Love* to town, so somehow light had shined on sorrow. Lennon, McCartney, and Cirque du Soleil—sure, why not? If George Martin hadn't done the mix it might not have worked, but he did and it did, so there. There it was out the car window, the Mirage, adorned at the crown by blown-up images of all four Beatles, a luxury citadel with license to the revolution. Another long block of driving and the lads were behind him.

Onward he crept through the emptying crosswalks. Onward past a child street performer singing on wood crate. Onward alongside the shimmering monorail linking hotel to hotel, as if Uber drivers hadn't put enough taxis out to pasture. Onward beneath Andrew Dice Clay's enlarged visage somehow reborn and relevant on a mural overhead. Onward beyond a smorgasbord of tattoo options and adult video superstores, old school peep shows, easy-money lawyers on billboards, myriad chapels to pray, and pawn shops to buy time in the shadows of the Stratosphere tower and rollercoaster drop. Onward past the looming golden letters T-R-U-M-P and the border zone SLS. Onward to destiny.

Downtown wasn't the downtown of old, but it was half the price of the Strip and reinvented as a friendlier community than the high rent glamor to the south. There were more locals, fewer big money losses by individuals, reasonable prices on food and beverage, and a covered walking mall where Fremont Street was closed to cars. The Greyhound station remained a sound reminder of the sorrow in so many departures, and the homeless were never more than a few blocks from the bronzed glass doors opening into air-conditioning. The Golden Nugget was forever a landmark, remodeled and reborn, its roots the heart of old school nostalgia. It would be a fine place to stay. How could it not be? Petrumi told him not to ask unnecessary questions.

Victor put the Acura in the parking structure and checked into the Golden Nugget just before 7:00 a.m. Petrumi had told him there would be a message waiting for him at registration about what to do once he got there. Victor approached the front desk and silently handed his driver's license to the drowsy clerk on duty, who found him instantly in the system.

"Victor Selo, third party booking, standard queen, staying with us indefinitely." The desk clerk looked at Victor with noticeable caution. Victor's war wounds couldn't be hidden.

"Car accident," said Victor, his appearance inescapable. "I'm going to be fine."

"I'm sure you will be." It was Vegas. He couldn't have cared less. "Your room and occupancy tax are covered, parking included in your rate. I'll need a credit card for incidentals."

Petrumi's check list item one was delivered. One promise kept, a place to sleep without cost. That was a good start, but incidentals like eating, how would he pay for that? Petrumi told him he would get paid by the band. He could use that money to pay his credit card bill online. There would be a time delay between the incidental charges and when the credit card bill was due. He could deposit his pay from the band to his PayPal account and then use that to pay his credit card bill for the hotel's incidental charges. Yes, that would work. The hotel wouldn't boot him as long as Petrumi paid his room rate and his account was current. He could eat. He handed the clerk his Visa card.

The clerk ran the credit card and looked at his screen. "I understand you'll be playing in our lounge."

"Yes, I was told you'd have a message for me at check-in, a contact person."

The clerk handed the Visa back to Victor with a pair of room card keys and pointed behind him. "That's your contact."

A handsome, well-built African American man was standing between the registration desk and the main lobby. He was over six feet and probably under one hundred eighty pounds, part Apollo Creed and part Jimi Hendrix. No one could miss him. He carried himself with an aura of stardom. He was minted to stand out, a head-turner, a magazine cover live in person.

"He just happens to be standing there?" asked Victor.

"I texted him when I saw your name in the log as requested in your file. Good luck with the band, Mr. Selo. Enjoy your extended stay at the Golden Nugget."

Victor stepped back from the counter with his plastic card keys and walked toward his leading man stalker, whose physical presence was a monument Victor had to absorb slowly. This magnetic being, this carved marble Adonis—he knew where he walked eyes fell upon him. Was he famous, a known star Victor should have recognized? He glowed with star quality. He was indescribable. Leather boots, likely handmade, with inscriptions of some sort, Native American artistry. He wore a down vest, bright gold, casino gold, like the sun glowing upon him. He had a half smile, enough that he was approachable, but with measured distance. He was mysterious, far from an open book, fancifully intimidating against Victor's plainness.

"I'm Torch. You the guy the agency sent?"

"Torch?" Of course he was. Illustrated ardor, fire, and ice. Petrumi had mentioned the singer by name, but this wasn't how Victor pictured him. For some reason he was thinking *Rocky Horror*. Must have been Tim Curry stuck in his mind. Petrumi said that Torch would be a good fit for Victor's style, even though Petrumi knew little about Victor's style beyond an ancient YouTube clip.

"Yeah, Torch. It's my band. *From Nothing*. Petrumi send you here to fill the shift?"

"Yes, Petrumi sent me. You make it sound like I'm temp labor."

Torch kept up his trademark smile, fully emitting joy. There was something about him, something beyond words. "What else would you be? We lost our guitarist. We need a substitute, maybe a replacement. They told me you can play. Can you play?"

"I can play. Rhythm backup, right? What do you mean lost?"

"Man, what kind of an amateur stiff are you? He's alive, no one killed him."

Victor knew he struck a nerve. He was off to a bad start, but he was similarly annoyed. "Please don't call me that. I've heard the word amateur too many times for the rest of my life."

"You got a name or should I make one up for you?"

"It's Victor. I mean, I'm Victor. Victor Selo. Didn't Petrumi pass that along in a text?"

"Probably, but that's not going to work around here. Where you from?"

"I'm from nowhere, okay? What does it matter?"

"We're getting somewhere. I got a name for you. You're going to be our Nowhere Man."

"Seriously?"

"I know you're hiding out from something, so I'm guessing you need another name."

"You can't call me Victor?"

"Nope, you're Nowhere Man."

"Fine, I've lived with worse."

"What's your story, Nowhere Man? When did you start playing pro?"

"I went on my own at sixteen. It wasn't working out. Foster parents, not on the same page. I found gigs, I played."

"You make money?"

"Not much, enough to get myself into night classes at a city program. Transferred to UCLA on a grant when I was nineteen, finished at twenty-five. Learned computers, kind of went that way."

"Wow, UCLA computer lab. I studied at the U of Shitsville. No dorms. Classes conducted outdoors. Final exam is finding a place to live without a job or references. Left the system when I was twelve. Got you beat by four years going solo but here I am. I got a good gig. It's a golden gig I conjured from the void—a golden gig at the Golden Nugget in the 24 Karat Lounge, otherwise known as My Room. I own the room and I don't even pay rent."

Victor was stumped. Where was this going? Where did Torch want to take it? He was from the system, too. They had that in common. He needed to break through the defensive line, change the mood. "Torch, I'm sorry if I'm not saying things right. I haven't eaten since yesterday. You want to get some breakfast?"

"Yeah, let's do some breakfast. Get to know one another some. They have a renowned Claim Jumper here, can't beat the selection. I have a feeling you're going to be a regular once you figure out your routine."

Victor followed Torch from the check-in desk across the pinging, binging casino floor. Even at this early hour the slots and tables were half-occupied, the glassy-eyed crowd rolling over to daybreak like the tired overnight clerk.

"You stay at the hotel?" asked Victor.

"No, that's you, man. Hotel rooms are for guys passing through town. I live like a civilian in Summerlin, little house on the prairie. No one there even knows I do this. Most mornings I like to read, even if I'm not university material."

They made their way across the carpeting to the Claim Jumper—coffee shop by day, diner by night—and grabbed a table that peered onto the casino floor. It was an all-purpose Claim Jumper, no different than any in the chain Victor and his coders had frequented—reserved western theme, laminated spiral-bound menu with a hundred choices cutting the same ingredients in different shapes. It could have been anywhere, but this one was in Vegas, enshrined in a downtown hotel. Torch hardly seemed to acknowledge the casino was there. Victor desperately wanted to make a good impression, but connecting with Torch was a task out of his league.

"Mind if I asked what happened to your guitar player?"

"Questions, man, you got questions. I don't always have answers. Be cool with that. His name was Doctor Sludge. He's in county, busted with five grams of the wrong stuff. They took him down Saturday night. Sunday we played with a ringer from Harrah's who knew C, D, and F, not a lot more. I told Petrumi we needed to move along. Now we got you. You don't do the wrong stuff, do you, Nowhere Man?"

"No stuff. I drink a little. That's all."

"Social drinking is okay, part of being a musician, unless you're a twelve-stepper like our drummer, which is cool, as long as you stay in the program. By the way, it's lead, not rhythm."

"What do you mean?" asked Victor.

"Your part, what you play. Actually you play both. We're a one guitar band. Economics matter, we keep the payday a five-way split. Another guitar would be less dough for all, so you play it all. That gonna work?"

Victor nodded, still getting used to Torch's style. He was direct. He was charming. He was in charge. A waitress came by and took their order. Torch ordered English breakfast tea, a fruit cup, and yogurt. Of course he did. That's why he glowed, the brightest energy in the room. Victor ordered the stack of pancakes and scrambled eggs, plus coffee filled to the brim. He badly needed the energy boost—carbs, protein, and caffeine to heal.

"Tell me about the band," said Victor, again trying to build a bridge. This was his new boss. Making a good first impression wasn't optional, yet it wasn't happening.

"Anchor on the electric piano is Synthia Hamada. That's Synthia with an S, like synthesizer, that's how her parent's spelled it. I guess it's a Seattle thing. Parents were both doctors, sisters are doctors, everyone in the family is a doctor. She's the black sheep, probably worse because they think she's sleeping with me, which she's not. I don't mix real business and personal business for all the expected reasons. I like winning, not tension. I met her twelve years ago. We both sang backup one night for Celine when her regulars called in sick, been together ever since. She's the keyboard goddess, grew up with classical lessons in her living room. She holds the whole thing together. Likes this Greek yogurt between sets."

"Got you eating it for breakfast," observed Victor.

"Yeah, she's an influence. Bass player is a local guy named Baker Bagley. That's not his real name but he likes the way it sounds when we announce him in the lineup: Baker Bagley on Bass. We think his name is Joe Smith but who cares? Always call him Baker Bagley, first and last. Says he played minor league baseball a few seasons, loser didn't get past Single A. I can't find mention of him online in any league ever, so who knows his real name or if he even played. Says he played bass in bar mitzvah bands to cover the rent and he has natural perfect pitch, no pun there. We know he can do that, so he stays in the band."

"Perfect pitch is definitely something."

"Dude is dull as a riverbed, but he mostly doesn't bother me, especially when he's not sucking up. On drums is Phil-Phil Tagalo, part Samoan, part Tongan, part Irish, tough dude. He's pissed off a lot. Grew up playing drums in his parents' luau business on an island somewhere. He doesn't talk about it, doesn't have much to say. He had a big break, backup percussion for Elton John at Caesars, blew it when he didn't show up one night, too wasted to remember. Bad behavior like Sludge, but at least he cleaned up, learned his lesson, I think."

"Sounds like a diverse group. And you?"

"I'm The Act. Torch from Oakland. That's what you need to know. You ready for this?"

"I haven't played lead in a while, but I'm guessing I can handle my part. Give me a few days to rest up and you won't be disappointed."

"No guessing and no few days. We play tonight."

"Torch, I got out of the hospital yesterday morning. I drove all night."

"Road trip, we all do it. You're a musician or you're not. Maybe I gotta call back Petrumi."

"Sure, he's going to find you someone before dark who knows more than C, D, and F."

They were sparring. Too much ego at the table, too much posturing. Torch had to be the center of attention, that was clear. Victor had to find a way through Torch's rules of engagement. When the waitress brought their food, Victor speared a whole pancake and devoured it.

"You're a different kind of guy, Nowhere Man. Remember you're playing My Room. Musicians in Vegas are a dime a dozen, got unlimited hacks like you on speed dial if I need one, but the agents control this town, and I can't afford to piss off Petrumi. You want the gig? It's tonight. Sleep all day if you want, not much else to do."

"Except I have to learn the set list. You got a CD?"

"Yeah, I got a CD if that's what you need. You don't know enough songs from the radio when we were kids?"

"I told you, it's been a while. I might be rusty out of the gate. I know the classic rock standards, the core catalogue, and I can follow the keyboard. A little practice time is all I need."

Torch started digging through his canvas shoulder bag, as if no one had asked him for a CD in the last how many years. "You want to play live in Vegas, you gotta know a lot of songs. We play at a different level than the bar bands you know. You're gonna feel that right away and you gotta be there. Be ready for the segue and stay on the beat, zero mistakes. You throw off Phil-Phil, he'll take you for a walk on the break. The drums aren't his only way of letting go. Got a short fuse, breaks the drum heads all the time." Torch found the CD and handed it to Victor.

"If I listen to it once, I can play all the parts that are mine. That's how I work. If I can hear it, I can play it. When's rehearsal?"

"We've been doing the 24 Karat Lounge four hours a night, six nights a week for seven years. I told you this gig was gold. Why would we need to rehearse?"

"Fine, if I have the CD, I don't need to rehearse. How much do you vary the set list?"

"There's two playlists on that CD, Set A and Set B. Tonight is Set A, tomorrow is Set B, then we repeat. We play the songs in the order I call them, that changes depending on how I feel the room, but we don't change the songs in each set and they don't jump from one set to another. We have enough material for two nights without repeating. A lot of people come two nights, so whatever we don't play tonight, we play tomorrow. I keep the room's pulse. That's my job."

"Got it, alternate the sequence, but not the repertoire, Set A and Set B. Sounds a little rigid." As soon as Victor said it, he wished he hadn't. Damn his own mouth.

"Not rigid. Highly polished. We keep the material perfect that way. Glistening."

The more Torch pontificated, the more Victor knew he would have to fight harder to break through. That was the way to go. Let Torch light the way. "You have a formula that works. Anything else I need to know about, what you want from me?"

"It's downtown, Nowhere Man. Small room, usually around a hundred bodies on hand, one fifty at capacity, no real dance floor but they dance in the aisles. Bartender loves us because we make the crowd sweat. Big tabs, big tips, especially the bottle service, we get paid a flat fee from that. No cover charge, people come and go freely. Hotel likes the flow, the casino is never far away. Don't feel bad if they walk out when you're killing it. That's how it's supposed to work."

Victor nodded. "How have you kept the room so long? Seven years is forever in a town like this."

"You know how Mick Jagger thought he was a white man who could sing like a black man? Nice PR, but he never pulled it off. I'm a black man who can sing like a white man and a black man, or a Latino, anything that keeps them in the room for one more round."

"Better than Jagger?"

"Timbre, baby, timbre. You'll be surprised what I can do. My range is without limit. I look for texture, vibrato, substance. Sixties, Seventies, Eighties, Torch is The Act. I hit all the notes. Unforgettable tunes that make people remember—that's the game."

"Got it, as long as I listen to the CD, I'll be fine after the first two shows."

"You be fine at the first show or I'm calling Petrumi and asking why he sent me an amateur."

Victor clenched his teeth. "An amateur with a good ear. You won't be unhappy."

Torch smiled again. "I'm never unhappy. I used to flip greasy steaks at the Sizzler. Now I play live music downtown and get paid for it. Plus this band is on the verge of breaking out."

"You play covers. What's the path to breaking out?" Damn his own mouth again.

"Nowhere Man, don't think of what we do as covers. We do interpretations, panache by Torch. And don't say anything downbeat like that to Phil-Phil. Flunkout twelve-stepper gets mean in the absence of hope. I promised him we'd break out, which is how I got him when he was headed back to luau land. Same for Synthia with an S. We've been doing this a long time together, a lot of years waiting for more to come our way. She's the real deal, blessed talent that turns notes into music. Wait for them to talk to you, not the other way around."

"Any harmony you need me to do? I can sing a little."

"No, you can't, not in this band, real singers do the singing. Synthia and Baker Bagley do the backing vocals. You got two guitar parts to play. It's enough. No mic stand."

"No mic stand, easy breezy. I'll be in my room learning Set A."

"Put some extra shine on Billy Preston's 'Nothing from Nothing.' We play that a few times each night going into the break, closing the set. That's our signature."

"The band's name, clever."

"More than our name. We go around as many times as the crowd hangs with us. If they're on their feet, we're jamming. Sometimes we play through the break, bring the tip jar over the top. You okay playing through the break?"

"You share the tips?"

"We'll see what you earn. How old are you anyway?"

"How old are you?"

"Not as old as you."

"Why does it matter?"

"Style, Brother—what's your style? Who do you play like?"

"I play like me. You mean influences? I don't know, Mark Knopfler in my dreams."

"In your dreams, I get it, I know your sound. Synthia will signal you when it's your solo, gets her hands free to change the settings. Synthia and Doc Sludge had this back and forth thing, she'll show you how to grab the cue, then steal it back."

"When is Sludge due back?"

"Who knows? Court dates are all backed up, no state income tax here. He'll cut a deal soon enough. I'm not sure I want him back."

They pushed away their plates and the waitress cleared the table. Torch looked closely at Victor, as if for the first time he saw the scabs on his forehead, the stitches recently removed. He looked at Victor's marred hands and saw the same. Victor couldn't hide it. He was healing, but he was a wreck.

"One more thing," started Torch.

"You want to know how I got like this?"

"No, that's your business, but I want zero drama. We need this gig to get the next one. We like predictability. We like maturity. We keep control of our lives. That's not the norm in this town. It's my norm and it's absolute."

"This was a one-time thing. I'm not even sure how it happened."

"You got beat up, you got beat up. I don't have a badge. Understand, we are close to breaking through, at least two notches up. I got people coming through all the time to hear us. I have a vision of going to the next level, lead me to my endgame. We could open for someone major, go on tour. That won't happen if anyone thinks we're trouble. We play and we stay out of trouble, not like Sludge. You get it? No drugs on your person. No bad folks invited to hang out. No side deals with the bar or the ladies in the lobby. No mixing it up with the guests unless you're sure it's consensual. Ask three times, then ask again before it actually goes down."

"I understand the rules, Torch."

"Try wearing sunglasses onstage until your face heals up. You'll look cool instead of, well, the way you look. We play 10:00 p.m. to 2:00 a.m. Four sets. Three breaks. Don't be late."

They got up from the table. Torch fixed his gaze on Victor until he was sure the rules had been encoded, then walked away. There would be no more to say until the evening gig.

Victor was exhausted. He went to the parking structure for his clothes, guitar, and practice amp, then made his way up the elevator to his room on the fourth floor. It was standard as advertised: a basic queen bed, a wall unit desk with lamp, a simple chair, paisley patterned wallpaper. He pulled back the blackout curtains and looked directly into the HVAC system. No view, no surprise, but the room was clean and likely no different in appointments than any other room in the entry-level grade. It was fine. It was enough.

He sat on the edge of the bed, wondering if he should sleep, maybe an hour. No, not yet. He found a coffee setup in the bathroom and got it going. Then he restrung his Gibson, put on his headphones, plugged in the CD, and started to listen to the playlist for Set A. The first riff he knew. How could he not? "Wild Cherry." It was easy knowable. Yep, easy breezy. He started to play along into the headphones, the room around him silent. He would sleep later, sometime that afternoon. First he had to learn the set.

>> <<

Victor arrived in the 24 Karat Lounge around 9:00 p.m., an hour early, donning a pair of knockoff Ray-Ban aviators he picked up in the lobby gift shop. He wore clean enough jeans, a plain black T-shirt, and faded sneakers, as nondescript as he could imagine. There were no doors, the lounge was always open, but no one was there yet—no waitress on duty, no bartender behind the counter. There were three blackjack tables along the far wall but no dealers stationed at the moment. Sports scores and video clips appeared on the high-definition monitors around the club, silent nonstop competition, an ongoing invitation to the sports book off the lobby. He grabbed a stool and wondered where he was supposed to stand on stage. He picked a spot behind the mic stand, stage right of the drum kit, and plugged in, opposite the mesh-covered keyboard stage left. He tuned without turning his amp live and ran through the set list in his head.

Around 9:15 a bartender showed and began checking the bottle inventory on the glass-and-mirror shelves. He said nothing to Victor. Five minutes later another bartender arrived and started lining up glasses on the bar. Minutes later an attractive blonde waitress showed, maybe twenty-five years old, soon followed by two brunettes about the same age, all of them wearing tight black cocktail dresses and low white gym shoes. It was a simple, fast routine: wipe down the tables, put out the table tents with the featured drink specials, make sure the chairs were evenly dispersed. It was a better setup than Victor had imagined, cheesy in the casino wraparound, but a well-appointed hotel lounge, way beyond any of the clubs he had played.

By 9:30 a few customers had wandered in. The best seats were commandeered, cigarettes were lit, and drinks were being served. With the customers appeared three blackjack dealers dressed in black and white, one at each table, and from that moment never idle. None of the waitresses or bartenders spoke to Victor, but they didn't ask him to leave either. He wasn't yet part of their routine. They were regulars. He was an outsider on their stage tuning his guitar.

At 9:45 an Asian woman apparently in her early forties approached, slender with long black hair, wearing a stylish purple vest over otherwise clinging dark solids hemmed above low leather boots. Synthia with an S, had to be. She said nothing to him, barely made eye contact, pulled back the zip cover on the keyboard and started fiddling with switches. Victor tried to follow Torch's advice and let her speak first, but it wasn't happening so he broke the ice.

"I'm Victor. I'm sitting in with the band."

"Yeah, I heard. First time in a Vegas lounge."

"First time playing live in ten years, but I sing now and again."

"Right, karaoke, lucky us. Sunglasses indoors, aren't you a rock star?"

"I don't have to wear them. It was Torch's idea. Part of a longer story."

"Torch lights the way. Hope you remember all your chords."

Hmm, not too friendly. Her eyes barely left the keys. That didn't go well. How did she know about karaoke? Of course, Petrumi. Victor had been bottled and sold to Torch, no secrets would stand. Victor played a few more scales, said nothing. A few minutes later Torch made his entrance, looking much the same as he had that morning but in a crisp silver silk shirt, a high five to both bartenders and hugs for all the waitresses. He mingled a bit with the early arrivals, asked for requests and suggested favorites, connected himself intimately to those he knew would be paying his bills before making his way to the minimalist stage.

"Nowhere Man, stage left, near Synthia. You're in the bass player's spot. I told you no mic."

"Sorry, wasn't sure where to stand."

Torch pointed while winking at the early arriving customers near the stage. "Not there, over there."

Victor unplugged and repositioned himself as directed, a few feet from Synthia who had no more to say, carefully positioning her mic stand. He plugged into the stage left stack, not yet switched on. Next to arrive was a guy in a plus-sized tan corduroy button-down carrying a pair of drumsticks—he needed a shave and a diet—obviously Phil-Phil, effortlessly sliding into position in cramped quarters. He said nothing to Victor and Victor didn't bother trying to say hello. Then came a guy in a navy blue no-logo baseball cap with a ZZ Top salt-and-pepper beard carrying an uncased Fender bass by the neck, Baker Bagley. The four returning performers acknowledged each other with nods but barely spoke. It was all routine except for the addition of Victor. No one seemed to care that he was there. He could have been any guitarist sitting in for the night. There wasn't much anyone had to say. Victor wondered if he was being hazed, if they were in some kind of mourning without Doc Sludge, or if this was club normalcy with or without him.

Nearing 10:00 p.m. the club was half-filled, sixty or seventy people in the booths and at the tables. Victor watched the minutes tick away on his watch as each of the musicians checked their equipment but still didn't say much to each other. It must have been the same for them every night. What happened during the day was their own business and hardly mattered. Seven years together, four hours a night, six nights a week, what else was there to say? They exchanged knowing glances—this instrument here, that plug there, Set A tonight, anyone got a cough drop—like locker room buddies, off-the-floor factory workers. It was up to Torch to dial in the add-on, Victor.

"Ready, Nowhere Man?"

"I think so." His voice cracked slightly when he said that. He thought he heard Synthia giggle quietly an arm's length away. He looked back at Phil-Phil behind the kit. Baker Bagley had his bass over his shoulder ready to go behind the stage right mic.

"Real convincing," said Torch. "Hey, you're a college boy. You read books, right?"

"Some, I guess. Why?"

"I like the meaty stuff, big ideas, old dudes. You ever read *The Republic*?"

"You mean by Plato."

"No, by Hunter S. Thompson. Yeah, *The Republic* by Plato. You know it?"

"I think it was in one of my classes. I don't remember it that well. Why?"

"I'm setting expectations for you. When you look at me, I want you to see a Philosopher King. Torch's Law. I keep the vision. I decree how our city state rises and falls. It's not a democracy, but it's a good place to hang, as long as you get it. You get the big idea?"

"I get it. You're The Act."

"He thinks, therefore he is, so he may play. The Philosopher King is The Act. The Act is ready to make some noise. Show me what you know, Nowhere Man."

Victor played the intro lick for "Play That Funky Music" in perfect order, on the beat, a replica off the record. Victor's amplifier wasn't powered up, but Torch could hear the strings.

"He's ready." It was the first encouraging sentence Victor heard from Synthia. That felt better, acceptance of any kind a rare power motivating him.

"Okay, play some funky music, we'll start with that," instructed Torch.

Without warning, Torch turned the PA system live and announced, "Good evening, Las Vegas, Nevada. Gracious thanks for being in our company tonight at the Golden Nugget Hotel. This is the 24 Karat Lounge and we're your downtown party favorites, From Nothing."

There was a modest expression of applause from the early arrivers in attendance. Then Torch raised his arms in the air and the sixty or seventy souls erupted like he was Lionel Ritchie in his heyday. In Torch's mind, he was more than that. He projected enthusiasm. Everyone was in the proper place, no deviation from their norm. The Act smiled in the dark and turned up the stage lights to bigger applause from the tiny audience. The city state was breathing. Baker Bagley pulled a deep E on the bass to set the tuning level. Victor flicked on his amp and matched the low E note. Torch nodded to the audience and then to Victor. It was his cue to launch.

Victor hit the opening riff of "Play That Funky Music." They were live.

Torch hadn't lied. From moment one he was The Act. He had earned the right to say that. He was pure charisma, a vocalist born to perform, in love with every syllable crossing his lips, in love with being loved, his arms around the world:

Hey, once I was a boogie singer

Playing in a rock and roll band

Timbre, baby, timbre. The mood swing was immediate, a comet hurling through the galaxy. With the first notes pouring from Victor's Les Paul, the band's laisse-faire doldrums were transformed into high noon octane. Torch had the crowd instantly where he wanted them, as Victor could tell he had done every playing night for the last seven years. Torch was right, this band was at a different level, sharper than any Victor had ever accompanied. They punched the notes cleaner, filled the gaps with bravado. This was a better game, a platform where poseurs would be exposed. Straight out of the gate, Victor was keeping up, delighted to be holding his own. Every part from the CD was in his head. He didn't miss a note. Torch looked over and winked at him. He had made the first cut.

Music flooded from the lounge onto the casino floor, roulette and craps wall to wall in the backdrop. By the end of the first song, the lounge audience had grown to over a hundred. Like Torch told him, there was no space in the club for an actual dance floor in front of the band, but a dozen were already dancing in the aisles. The waitresses weaved their way through the bodies, trays balanced, not a drop of spilled brew. The preset audio mix was on the mark, the small room's reverb acoustics working in their favor. It was routine, but it was professional routine.

As billed, Torch was The Act. Everyone knew Torch was The Act. Victor knew he would never be anything approaching Torch. That part of divine intervention he understood. Like Mozart, you had the talent or you didn't. Claire would have agreed that kind of decision was reserved for God, and although Victor would dispute it in an argument with her, in his head he would agree. He knew she was right. The talent to own a room with seven notes of the scale was not a human choice. He wondered if Torch envied anyone, whom he thought God shined upon in a mode he wished was his beckoning. There had to be someone. That was how God played the game. It wasn't a lot different than deciding who got to grow up in a permanent family and who got placed in the system. Torch got the system, same as Victor. Maybe he got The Act in trade, the way Victor got his understanding of software systems.

Victor was in awe of Torch, in awe of the ensemble, in awe of his surroundings. He couldn't let that distract him. He had to be present and stay in the sound. He hardly noticed when halfway through the first song the iPhone in his back pocket began to vibrate. He didn't get a lot of calls and there weren't any he was expecting, not this soon. It was probably Petrumi, calling to wish him well in the new endeavor. Victor put it out of his mind and focused on the low action fretboard. Clear head, play the songs, pass the test. He knew this was a real-time audition.

Despite the pressure to win over the band, Victor found the show fun. He hadn't played in front of people in such a long time. With Torch at center stage, the heavy lifting was on The Act, not Victor. All Victor had to do was hit the right notes in the right moments, everything he heard on the recording earlier in the day. Nothing to it. Like a bicycle, back in the seat, boldly surrounded by seasoned pros. Keeping the crowd and the band happy was his only care in the world, most of all the Philosopher King.

Next up, Torch called for "Devil With A Blue Dress On." Synthia played the intro chords on the keyboard, then Phil-Phil and Baker Bagley joined without any visual cue. Victor followed Synthia on the beat, then The Act took over with sorcerous potency:

Fee fee fi fi fo fo fum
Look at Molly now, here she comes

Mitch Ryder & The Detroit Wheels didn't seem like Torch's style, but Torch was a crowd pleaser and this crowd was pleased. Dance. Drink. Return to the casino in a good mood. That was the task. The routine was easy to understand. Once Victor knew the set list, it would be clockwork to stay a part of it.

The mobile in Victor's pocket buzzed again. Who could it be twice in a row? Had to be a wrong number. He couldn't be bothered to check it.

The Mitch Ryder medley ended, but before the last cymbal, Torch twirled back fluidly and mouthed "INXS." He was building on the demon theme, reaching down under for the hit from Australia:

Devil inside, the devil inside

Every single one of us the devil inside

On it went through the hour, song after song, genre after genre. Backbeat rock with AC/DC's "Shook Me All Night Long." R&B with Earth, Wind, & Fire's "September." Latin Blues with Santana's "Oye Como Va." Big hair metal with Motley Crue's "Kickstart My Heart." Torch had not overstated his versatility. There was nothing he couldn't pull off. Victor stayed sharp. As Torch called for each title from Set A, Victor recalled it from memory and held his own. He was where he needed to be on every tune, expectedly on edge but proudly blending into the polished collective. The crowd built to capacity midway through the first set, one hundred fifty revelers loving each selection. Dance. Drink. Return to the casino in a good mood. The party crowd on holiday would dance to anything that came from The Act. No argument, Torch owned the room.

As the first set neared its end, it was Synthia's turn on the mic. She called for Scandal's "Goodbye To You." She sang it flawlessly, like she had written the words herself:

Could I have loved someone like the one I see in you

I remember the good times baby now, and the bad times too

Damn she was good. This time Torch and Baker Bagley sang harmony behind her. Phil-Phil kept the beat, no matter the change in syncopation. Victor found it challenging to play both rhythm and lead, but he picked his parts thoughtfully and got no pushback from the band. He let go and played effortlessly. Absorbed in collaboration, his mind began to wander. Would Max, Clarence, and Juan stick with the plan? Would Claire want to know that he was playing again? Why hadn't he asked Darcy to dinner? Marin was so far away. Beautiful noise filled the brightly lit space around him. Rainbow spotlights covered the stage. Sure it was Vegas, but it was a new enough place for him and that was what he needed. With the music flowing, as long as he could be in the band, the 24 Karat Lounge was a healthy place to be at the moment.

Yeah, the whole thing was okay, everything except the iPhone in his pocket vibrating again. Someone wanted to get him on the phone. That made no sense. Thomas Katem? No way, too soon. Wait, maybe it was the hospital burned for the bill after all? Had Katem lied again? Damn him to hell.

Synthia finished up her part of the set with Lita Ford's "Kiss Me Deadly." Victor closed his eyes. She could have been Lita Ford. He tried not to look at her directly, but the stage area was so small they were practically on top of each other. She was enticing. She was off limits. If she was off limits to Torch, then she was off limits to him. Zero chance she would have anything to do with him. He was a journeyman passing through Dodge. She was on her way with Torch at least two notches up. He was alone but needed to stay focused. He needed to gain the band's trust. Her graceful style, the vitality in her vocal range, her natural ability fine-tuned through all that classical training, she took his breath away. He was on the backing track and yet almost wasn't a part of it. She was art balancing Torch's allure, realizing the playlist. She held her songs with hard-won authority. He needed to stop looking at her and think about something else.

Fifty minutes in, Torch signaled the set finale was coming by calling for Billy Preston's "Will It Go Round in Circles." It was made for keyboard and Synthia carried the introduction. Torch leapt onto the opening lyrics and spun around in a slick pirouette:

I've got a song that ain't got no melody
I'm gonna sing it to my friends

The crowd was in his palm. The Preston bridge meant their signature tune was on deck, the high-output number that carried the band's name. Synthia bridged from song to song, creating a natural connection in the duo that the band had played a thousand times. Victor found her easy to follow. Torch pranced into the audience with his cordless mic and made his way up and down the gyrating aisles:

Nothing from nothing leaves nothing
You gotta have somethin' if you wanna be with me

The Act looked at the champagne bucket nestled at stage center. It was their tip jar and it wasn't filling. Ten minutes into the medley, he reminded the audience that if they were into the party, they needed to show it. There was no movement toward the bucket. They would have danced all night, but they wouldn't pay for the overtime into the break. Torch nodded at Synthia. She played the final chords sixty minutes from the start. Victor felt the phone vibrate yet again.

Torch brought up the house lights to resounding applause. He wasn't impressed and the band slipped offstage behind him, gone in seconds. They had played for the predicted hour. This would be their first break. They would be back in fifteen for another forty-five minutes of Set A, then repeat the cycle two more times. Victor received head nods from Synthia and Baxter Bagley, as much as he could expect from pros on his first outing. They had to get to the restroom, make phone calls, return on time without fail, no spare minutes to chat. Head nods were enough for the moment, even if Phil-Phil hadn't yet looked at him.

Torch was barely sweating, no change in his breathing. This was pure normal for him. The Act was in top condition. He would probably look the same at 2:00 a.m. He obviously wasn't pleased with the cash flow. Victor had sweated through every pore on his body, his dark T-shirt soaked. His breathing was deep and uneven. He was exhausted but he had done his job.

"You got through your first set, Nowhere Man," acknowledged Torch. "You only let Synthia take one lead line from you."

"I was being polite. Do I get to stay?"

"Get yourself a Vodka Gatorade. We go again in thirteen minutes. At the end tonight we do the Preston song again on the finish. I want that bucket overflowing, cash is king. You and Synthia are the keys to that."

"I guess you won't be calling Petrumi."

"Not at the moment. Go get some booze and electrolytes. Long night ahead."

Victor made his way to the bar. He had passed the test. He was a musician reborn. This band was a gift, an ethereal gate to a sense of belonging, recognition of excellence in others and himself. Global Harmonics should have been a lifetime away except for the phone vibrating in his pocket. He ignored it again, no distractions allowable. The only person it could be was Thomas Katem and he didn't want any part of that right now. He wanted to play, to put everything else behind him. There was no way he would he answer that phone. There was no way he wanted to hear Katem's voice.

When the iPhone stopped humming, Victor pulled it from his pocket and looked at the screen. Seven calls over the past hour. There was only one message from the first call, but the same caller was listed seven times. On the screen Victor could not believe the name he saw.

Maurice Sangstrum.

TRACK 7: PLAY IT AGAIN, VICTOR

Victor sat alone in the Claim Jumper off the lobby of the Golden Nugget. It was almost 10:00 the morning after his first gig as a member of a Vegas lounge band. Torch was right. He would become a regular here, the no-frills eatery with Keno available tableside. He had been there an hour, his pancake remains long cold. No one bothered to pick up his plate. Maybe it was a hint. Each time he needed a coffee refill, he waved his arms. Since he wasn't increasing the tip pool, that became harder every passing fifteen minutes. He started getting up and filling his own cup at the drip station. No one told him to stop.

He looked out into the casino. It was quiet at this hour, a few seniors pushing the buttons on what used to be mechanical slot machines, now numeric displays, rollicking video repositories affixed to credit card readers, coins no longer required. Progress, he thought, innovation everywhere. A few other couples in the restaurant stared distantly into each other's eyes, blank zombie stares of the sleepless trying to reboot hope. Had they lost everything playing hand after hand, roll after roll, spin after spin the night before, clawing through the hours for a comeback? Were they now passing time waiting for the Greyhound scheduled pickup back to anywhere but here?

It had been a glorious night for Victor, a seismic boost in self-confidence being back on a stage, no matter the size. He could still play, keep up for the full four-hour gig and that felt good—more than good, it was an injection of brain nutrients, unfiltered uplift, soulfully reassuring. The Philosopher King was pleased with his performance and no one else in the band had a bad thing to say. Phil-Phil hadn't acknowledged his existence, but he guessed that Phil-Phil and Doc Sludge were friends and Phil-Phil saw Victor as foreign matter infecting the organism. At least Phil-Phil hadn't said anything at all, so Victor took that as a positive sign. Maybe he could stay here in Vegas for a while, just be in the band until his body recovered. It wasn't that bad a place to be, despite the past tugging away at his spirit, always tugging, never fully in the rear-view mirror. He couldn't let that overwhelm him. He had to stay in control of his destiny any way he could, determinism be damned. He had survived being fired and beaten. He couldn't survive being played or conned. He couldn't allow himself to break.

He stared at his iPhone. The seventeen times Sangstrum had called after the original message were sequenced about twenty minutes apart. The calls had started around 10:00 p.m. and stopped around 4:00 a.m. Sangstrum must have given up and gone to sleep. Would he call again this morning? He probably would. Victor played back the message for the fifth time:

"Victor, it's Maurice Sangstrum. Please call me as soon as you get this. We need to talk. I know you don't want to, but do it. I don't know where you are, but there are things you don't know. It's important that you call me. I have something for you."

Victor continued to stare at the iPhone, lost in the message, lost in the crossfire of a tired hotel morning, the splendor of mild pain in his fingertips from four hours of playing and an afternoon of practice, protective calluses soon to form anew, and a sordid trail behind him he would rather let go. Letting go, that was unlikely. A familiar voice from over his shoulder called out from the marble floor and grabbed his attention. It came from the entrance to the Claim Jumper, the hostess stand abutting the casino carpets. It was Torch, dressed in tapered sweats, star quality gleaming even in his workout clothes.

"Nowhere Man, you a morning person?" Torch was smiling. Victor noticed that Torch was often smiling, even when he seemed perturbed. "Join you for a glass of water?"

"I thought you lived in Summerlin," called out Victor.

"I like the gym here, it's a perk." Torch entered the restaurant and planted himself at Victor's table beside the food remains.

Victor gently turned his iPhone face down and put it on the table, then covered it with a napkin, hoping Torch wouldn't notice. "Not my kind of perk. I like breakfast."

"Yeah, I got that yesterday. You better take care of yourself, find a routine if you want to do this. Healthy living is part of winning. I do my weights, then I run, then I eat. You can't just eat if you want to play the long game." Torch took the glass of ice water Victor hadn't touched.

"We all have our routines. You run in the desert heat?"

"I like it outside in the morning before it gets too hot. Dry air is good for the heart. This is the last window of the day before the streets become hell."

"You don't sweat much."

"Look like Jupiter, be Jupiter. You made me look good last night. Synthia, too. You get it, how we work it. I didn't miss Sludge. You got better each set. Smooth, no unnecessary movement, low friction. Tucked in where you need to be, like you've been doing it all your life. The Nowhere Man is on the job."

"I serve at the pleasure of the Philosopher King."

"That you do. When we break out of here, you could be part of the reason."

"Count me in, as many notches up as The Act will go. Does that kind of thing still happen?"

"We're making it happen. I talked to Petrumi this morning. He and I got a lot in common, considerable shared interests. He's working to get us a private Beach Party gig over at Mandalay Bay."

"You're booked here. How do you do that?"

"Night off is Monday. All we need is an open Monday slot at Mandalay. They get name acts over there, premier talent. We get seen, Petrumi moves us up, gets us out of downtown after seven years waiting. Unrealistic expectations are building blocks. We build until the levee breaks."

"You have big dreams. I'm kind of blown away to be a part of it."

"I told Petrumi you could cut it. Tonight is Set B, what we didn't play last night, mostly for the people who come two nights in a row before they head out. Switching it up is good for the tip jar, plus it keeps us from going insane."

"I'm all over it. Set B, I'll learn it this afternoon. What else am I going to do?"

"That's tonight's hymnal. Then tomorrow back to Set A. That's our routine."

Victor said nothing but kept his eyes on the napkin over the iPhone, hoping it wouldn't ring. Torch could see he was pensive.

"Something on your mind, Nowhere Man?"

"Not really. It doesn't bother you playing the same material every forty-eight hours?"

"You think what we have isn't working?"

"Of course it's working, but what's it going to take to go beyond Mandalay?"

"One real show on your résumé and you got ideas of your own. Damn, am I wrong about you?"

"No, you make the calls. Like you said, I get it. I was just thinking at some point I could help you with the set list, explore some new sounds, stretch a little. You know I have a music database background, right?"

"A database is a pail of slop, Mr. Roboto. I'm looking for polish. That's the sound you hear from this band, the sound of perfection. Stretch for perfection, not for slop."

Victor could see that Torch was getting irritated but couldn't help himself. "You ever try an original?"

"Seriously, you want to change The Act?" Torch finished the glass of water in a gulp, dumbfounded, incredulous.

"Not change. Evolve. Follow the sound where it goes. At some point is there a Set C?"

"We do this for money, champ. This isn't an experiment. We built those set lists carefully over time. The laboratory is locked. We don't change just to change."

Torch rose from his seat, more agitated than Victor expected. Victor knew he needed to back down.

"I'm sorry if I'm out of line. I guess I'm a little ahead of myself. Thinking freeform is kind of my . . ."

"You're way ahead of yourself. This is day two. You're not anointed. You had a decent night. Don't bank too much on that. The Act changes when The Act wants it to change, which I do not."

"I was just trying to help you brainstorm . . ."

"Help me? You don't even back down when you're unarmed. One night under the spot and the computer geek thinks he's Bruce Springsteen serving up new lists and originals. Stay to the side, impresario, where there is no mic for a reason. Find the chords, pick the leads, don't piss me off!"

"I'll be polished tonight for Set B, Torch. You have my word."

Torch recovered his calm and pushed his chair back into place under the table. "I gotta go, got an appointment on the Strip. Phil-Phil asked me if you're smart enough to hang with us. He doesn't say much, you know. I told him so far so good. Don't make me wrong."

"I hear you. Follow The Act."

Torch darted past the hostess stand, then looked back. "You want me to handle that iPhone so whoever's harassing you can move on into memory?"

"No, I'm good. No drama, I heard you on that."

"No drama and no freeform. And stay out of the casino. Worse than crack."

Torch jogged off down the hall. Victor was relieved their conversation was over, but knew he would be unlikely to survive many more of these tense exchanges. He wondered at some point if Torch might understand that innovating had to be part of their roadmap. Victor had come on too strong, but he would look for another opening. He would find a way to get Torch to embrace change. The downside would be a repeat of what he just suffered, and that hardly seemed like a good idea in readying the band for the breakthrough they were seeking.

>> <<

Victor waited until Torch was out of sight, then pulled back the napkin covering his iPhone. He had to get ahead of this. He hesitated, then pushed the callback icon that dialed Sangstrum.

"Victor, is that you?" There was that voice—that grating, strident, fetid voice. He hated it even more. He hated Sangstrum even more, an impossibility.

"It's me, Maurice. What do you want?"

"I called a bunch of times. Was my urgency not apparent?"

"I'm on the phone now. That could end in an instant. What do you want?"

There was a pause. Sangstrum must have been caught by surprise when Victor redialed him. He must have needed a moment to conjure his words, craft his lies.

"It goes like this, Victor. I might have treated you unfairly."

"Seriously, Maurice? A bullshit apology from you? Where's this going?"

"Maybe I did call to apologize, Victor. Maybe I was unnecessarily abrupt."

"Are you having trouble closing with McWhorter? Something go sideways in your deal? It doesn't make sense for you to call me. You're not the kind of guy of who apologizes except as a negotiation tactic."

At that moment a bullhorn sounded in the aisle beyond the restaurant. At first Victor thought it was a fire alarm, but it was the brash trumpeting of an enormous slot machine centered on the casino floor. Sirens blew, red-and-blue lights circled like the Nevada Highway Patrol on the hunt. Someone had won the house jackpot. A really old guy in a wheel chair had a hundred grand cash money more than he had three seconds ago on a dollar wager. Vegas winning came any time of day or night. It had to happen periodically to break up the incessant losing and paint a picture of hope, prove the dream always alive that paid for the chlorine-clean fountains and subsidized prime rib.

"What's that sound?" asked Sangstrum. "Where are you, Victor?"

"I'm not telling you anything, Maurice, except I'm seconds away from telling you to go to hell. Last chance, what do you want?"

"I was reviewing the exit package Darcy delivered to you and I noticed it was, shall I say, light?"

"It was what you owed me, nothing more or less. It was what I expected. Are we done?"

"I think we owe you a debt of gratitude, Victor. It's only now that we are in due diligence that I fully understand how much you contributed to this company. Without you, Global Harmonics wouldn't be what it is. Quite frankly, we wouldn't have anything worth selling."

"You didn't need to sell. You needed to rebuild. I told you that over and over. You didn't want to listen to me. You never wanted to listen to me."

"I'm not perfect, Victor. You were a pain in the ass, but you did good work here. I want to offer you a performance bonus."

"A performance bonus, just like that? Out of the blue, you want to send me money? This is really something. I can hardly wait to hear it. Why and how much?"

"Let's start with how much. One point five million dollars wired today wherever you want it."

Victor was aghast, his heartbeat quickening, his pulse pounding in his chest. It took a few moments for him to respond. This was a negotiation and he couldn't show his cards. "A million and a half dollars after the fact for services rendered, ain't that something! And the why?"

"It's complicated, but I need you to sign some paperwork."

"Ha, there you have it. You need something from me and now I'm worth a million and a half dollars. Can't imagine what it could be. My letter agreement with Global Harmonics was uncontested work-for-hire. You own, or I should say, the company owns everything I did, patents and all. What is it you want me to sign?"

"A simple non-disparagement agreement and a binding release of liability."

"A gag order? You want to buy my silence and promise not to sue? You are a peach, Maurice. Why do you need those?"

"I don't, but for purposes of due diligence, they will be good to have on file. They'll help the deal close more quickly."

"Facing obstacles, Maurice? Do tell."

"Fine, I'll be completely honest with you, Victor. You are likely to get a call soon from some people who may ask you some questions about the deal, about me, about who knows what. I want you motivated not to talk."

"Possibly the Justice Department?" Victor was grinning ear to ear.

"No, not the Justice Department. No release could stop you from talking to them. Other people who have different thoughts about the deal, who want to know some information."

"That you're not providing them in due diligence, you scumbag carpetbagger?"

"Again, nothing like that, but there is a possible conflict of interest at play, and we want you aligned with us for an expedited close."

"You said the money would be wired today. How does my signature get you to a close? I could go off the ranch any time after I have the money. What are your remedies if I open my mouth and fly the coop?"

"If you were to speak after the close, *you* would have the Justice Department issues, they would shift onto you. All you have to do is sign the acknowledgement of your willing commitment to be silent and non-litigious and you get the money. It's that simple."

"A million and a half dollars never to mention Global Harmonics again? I have to tell you, it's tempting, but I'm going to take what's behind Door Number Two."

"There is no Door Number Two, you asshole. One point five million is the offer."

"I'll take nothing and my right to free speech. Thanks for playing, Maurice. I hope the deal implodes and you end up in litigation for years—for the rest of your life, paying your last dime to an Ivy League lawyer who despises you as much as I do."

"Fine, Door Number Two: Two million dollars."

"Nope, not interested."

"I can't go above two million, Victor. That's what the board authorized. At the end of the day I am an employee, just like you used to be. Take the deal."

"No deal. Die in hell." For the first time in his life, Victor was enjoying a dialogue with Sangstrum.

"Okay, I will try to get more. I have to go back to the board. What's your number to seal your mouth? Four million? Five million? We have to get this done."

"No million, Maurice. No money, no deal, no silence. I'm not you."

Victor clicked off the phone. The day was young. He had already had a fight with his new employer, been bribed by his old employer, and it wasn't even time for the lunch buffet. There was only one thing left to do before brushing up for his second night in the lounge. He needed to call back Max, Clarence, and Juan and make sure they kept the digital bomb loaded. He had known that was going to be useful. As long as there was a nuclear virus to release, Sangstrum couldn't harm him. Despite his rough morning, Victor held all the cards.

>> <<

Victor was in his hotel room practicing Set B. It was excellent material on par with Set A—solid, relatable, well-chosen hits connected dot to dot. J. Geils Band. Robert Palmer. Rolling Stones. Ohio

Players. What struck Victor as extraordinary was the range of material, the brand promise that Torch had first shared with him and from which he never retreated. Timbre. Tapestry. Youthful memories made real again if only for a drunken moment. No ordinary cover band could pull off a playlist that diverse, that wide ranging. Torch knew what he was doing. He was in touch with what worked. The Act was in ideal form—if only he knew how good he was and would be willing to stretch slightly beyond his comfort zone into the present, Victor was sure he could help catapult the band into the stratosphere. If he could get them to try an original, that really would be something.

There were plenty of opportunities for Victor to shine in both sets and he liked that. The counterpoint of songs night to night would definitely bring back the crowd for a second night. Not too much to learn, most of these he had played as a kid or mimicked at Providence. Yeah, he knew a lot of songs. Karaoke was good for something. Hear it once and he had it. It was going to be a good Wednesday night, between now and then maybe room service. Burger, fries, Vodka Gatorade. Make that a double. A triple. And an ice cream float. All charged to Petrumi's account. He would play on a full night's sleep, half of it in the morning. The road was the right place to be.

Victor had jacked his headphones into the practice amp and was making his way through the Bangles with so much zeal he hardly heard the knock at the door. It was a surprise interruption. Maid service had already been through their rounds. Other than Petrumi and the band, no one knew he was at the Golden Nugget, unless Petrumi told Katem. Wait, was this what Sangstrum had called about? Was this the conversation Sangstrum had offered millions to shut down? Yeah, this was it. This was going to be good, really good. He wasn't sure if he would talk, but he was going to have a blast listening.

Victor shed the headphones and opened the hotel room door. There was the real surprise of the day: Synthia with an S. What was she doing there? How easy had it been for her to find his room? Suddenly he didn't feel as safe as he wanted. That was going to be a problem. Security. Staying invisible. Fine, he would deal with that later. Right now he needed to deal with Synthia. That was enough stress for the moment.

"You learning the rest of the material?" she asked.

"Yeah, getting through it, Set B. You want to come in?"

"For a minute, okay." Synthia was beautiful, perfect skin, perfect hair, but there was a wall around here, a perpetual force field, impenetrable. She was a single woman playing live in Vegas, probably hit on hourly. Maybe she was single. Why did he assume that? It didn't matter, she had to protect herself. She wasn't accessible. She was a musician, not a person. She would never want anything to do with him. What did she want?

He closed the door and she sat on the floor near the window. "I saw Torch this morning. He said you guys were pretty happy with me last night."

"You were okay. You got through it. You didn't step on any of us too badly."

"That's good to hear from you. I tried to keep up. I'm doing my best to follow your lead. Sometimes you're way ahead of me."

"You're fine, a little out of practice. Don't reach too hard. And take it easy on Torch. He's the leader here."

"You talked to him this morning, too?"

"Yeah, we're tight. Don't get on his nerves. The show is about Torch. It's his vision. We call it a band but it's his show. We're backup players. He owns the room. That's the way it works."

"I think it's about you, too. He can't take all the limelight. Did he send you here to reprimand me?"

"No, Vic, Torch doesn't send me. He's The Act but I carry the weight as music director. It's him with the audience. It's me otherwise."

That was cool, she'd said his name. Yes, he heard her distinctly. She said *Vic*. That was progress, plus she told him she was the band's music director. That meant she had power of her own. She had to be telling him for a reason. This wasn't a random drop by. There was more to it. He needed to say something witty in response, something worthy of her reconnaissance.

"You pick the songs?"

"We do it together, but I work out the arrangements. I know his voice and how to put the right tracks behind it. Same for me, I know what I like to play and I want to play somewhere else, somewhere better. This Vegas thing is hard. It gets to you. It's work for a musician, but it's not what we want to do. It's not what I want to do."

Confide in her, thought Victor. Build a common bridge, but don't look at her too much, not with that hair, not with those eyes. Don't give away the weakness. "I spent a lot of my life thinking the same thing. I always thought I wanted to do something else, something bigger. Then I got it. It wasn't so great."

"What wasn't so great? Petrumi says you made a ton of dough."

"I did and lost every penny. Buying stocks is not the same as gambling, but it's close enough and it's addicting. Then you're working for that, to pay for the stocks you thought you wanted to own but keep finding out you were wrong."

"I don't get it. Why guess at wealth when you know you always lose?"

"Ego, greed, stupidity. I never really wanted to buy stuff I didn't have. I wanted the freedom to do stuff I hadn't done, like what you're talking about with a different gig."

"It's not the same. You had other options, Vic." Damn, she really was beautiful, especially in the afternoon light, the falling shadows through the open blinds, even more so in a Vegas hotel room with blackout curtains one day after a gig. And she'd said his name again, no accident there. Zero chance that was an accident. Wait, stop. She was a bandmate. No messes. He had promised Torch no drama. No bloody chance. She wouldn't be interested anyway.

"Have you ever been married?" she asked.

Weird question. Why was she asking? Where was this going? No drama. Zero drama.

"No, almost once," he answered.

"What does almost mean?"

"It means I screwed it up badly. I chased other dreams. Got 'em, too."

"You might have made the right decision."

"I doubt it. There was this God thing that got in the way."

"God, yeah, that's a thing. I'm still working through that."

"Me, too." Victor stopped. He didn't want to go there. "What about you, ever married?"

"Every musician over the age of thirty has been married at least once. Lucky for me, just once. I sucked at it, but at least I was loyal."

"He cheated?"

"Maybe. I never asked. Sex wasn't the problem. We had nothing to talk about. No kids either. I would have really sucked at that."

"Yeah, me too, not much of a role model, no lessons to pass along. Why did you get married?"

"He had a thing for musicians. I had a thing for consistency. Both got solved in different ways. He was a dealer at the Bellagio, but he gave back all his money to the house playing after hours. I got this gig around the time he went bust so I pay alimony. I share an apartment off Paradise with two roommates and write him checks. He hands them over to the pit boss to pay down his debt. Two more years and I'm free. Bad choices follow you a long time."

"Sounds like the judge got it wrong."

"That's what my parents said. They offered to help me if I went back to medical school. I told them that's not me. I need to play music no matter what. Sometimes I wonder if they have it right, if all of this is a dead end."

"At least you know they're there if you need a fallback position."

"We haven't talked much since the divorce. We were never very close."

She went silent. Victor could see she didn't want to talk about it anymore. She had gone looking for information and given up too much. They needed to move on. Maybe there was something there. How could he know?

"Torch says he wants to play Mandalay Bay," said Victor. He had to break the thread. She needed to go so he could finish learning Set B and not make a mess of things on Vegas adventure day two. She was staring at him silently, probably seeing through what was there, figuring out where this was going before he could. He had to let her speak next.

"You get in a DUI?" she asked.

It was his face, the artifacts of recovery. No matter the work at the hospital, he would carry the battle scars of his beating for life.

"No, not a DUI, something else. Don't worry, I told Torch it wouldn't happen again. It was a one-time thing."

"I'm not worried. You're the one who got hurt. Are you still in pain?"

"They told me when I checked out of the hospital I would have headaches for a while. They were right. Some days my equilibrium is off, but it's not debilitating. I work through it."

"Healing never comes fast enough. Then we find a way to get pummeled again."

"Maybe I deserved it. My other life in business got complicated. Software stuff."

"You write?" she asked, another surprising tangent.

"Software, no. I'm overhead, a manager."

"No, I mean songs. You ever write songs?"

"Not really, not for a long time. You?"

"Dabble. Music better than lyrics. Torch said you asked about originals."

Torch was listening to him. That was strange. He had batted it away hard. Then he told Synthia. Now she was here. There had to be a reason. Of course there was a reason. She didn't want him. Not Synthia with an S. What had he been thinking? He was an idiot. Thank God he hadn't tried to make a move. No move. No drama. Retreat to safety. The subject was originals.

"You're a cover band, I mean, an interpretive cover band. That's what the crowd likes, right, the familiar?" Victor wasn't sure where to go. He had to go somewhere. Back to rehearsing. Quickly. Clear the mind.

"Covers get you in front of people, but you can't make a name playing what anyone else can. What label signs a cover band? How do you headline when your competition is the real deal? Torch is better than that. We're better than that."

Victor was thrown, flattered, mystified, all at once. He picked up his guitar and played a few unamplified chords. "Getting beyond the known is a risk. New stuff is never perfect."

"We've tried a few things over the years," said Synthia. "Nothing's worked. They want me to figure it out, but I'm not that good at it. I don't have the whole package for a hit, definitely not the courage to fall flat. It's hard to make something emerge out of nowhere."

"I know, I've had that experience with my company. It has to come from somewhere. You fill the emptiness and then it's there, but it doesn't just happen. Maybe we can work on it together?" Victor thought he had the full message and an exit all in one idea.

"Might be a good idea. Who knows?" She got up from the floor and headed for the door.

Victor heard her loud and clear. Word from Torch had been delivered. "I'll see if I can dig up some lyrics," he said. "I'm sure you have some melodies you can make work."

"Big opportunity if we get Mandalay. Could get us to the next level if we pull it off. Maybe together we can figure out something that works. Good thing Petrumi found you."

Suddenly it hit Victor, how he got there. It was no accident, no coincidence. Sludge had left them high and dry. Petrumi could have put anyone in that slot. Any session musician would have wanted the Vegas night pay. It was Global Harmonics. Victor knew music. They needed a writing partner. That was how he got the gig.

"Petrumi made a good choice sending me here. I'll see what I have in my notebooks."

Unlike Torch, Synthia never smiled. She might have been incapable of smiling. She opened the hotel room door and then turned back. "One more thing—the set list, leave that to me and Torch. I'm sure you like to change things up but that part we know. Don't push."

Torch and Synthia were of a single mind. Any word to one was a straight line to the other. *Make a note of that in your mind*, Victor told himself. *They are one and the same.* Consistent, ambitious, hungry, talented, coordinated.

"Got it, low gear on the change. Let me get back to polishing the second set. See you onstage."

"Follow us, Vic. We've been doing this a while. Just play the songs."

Vic again, she'd said it once more. No act of chance here. Their intersection was directed, deliberate, guided with intention, steered with purpose. Something miraculous was in the making, if only he could stay ahead of the logic.

Synthia left with no more fanfare than she'd arrived. Tonight was going to be another good show. Maybe later they would write a song together that would work. Yeah, maybe. His path had been charted. It would be on him to deliver.

>> <<

Five minutes before show time, Torch was absent, nowhere to be seen in the lounge or adjacent casino. Synthia stood at her keyboards without a care, ready to go on with or without him. Baker Bagley in his blue baseball cap was at the bar chatting it up with some customers, equally indifferent to Torch's nonappearance. Victor approached Phil-Phil at the drum kit, who still had said nothing to him. Was this going to be awkward? What was going on with him? Victor took his best shot.

"Phil-Phil, just checking in. Am I doing what I need to do for you?"

"You're a guy from somewhere else temping on our stage."

"I'm here to do a job. Tell me what I can do to be better."

"Don't talk to me, don't miss a note, and don't think this is permanent." Phil-Phil wouldn't look him in the eye. He spun his drumsticks and tapped each of the cymbals for tone.

Victor stepped down from the platform and onto the floor. Baker Bagley left his attractive new friends at the bar and approached Victor. "That's him. It's what he does."

"Torch said I shouldn't talk to him."

"He was tight with Sludge. He's hoping Petrumi can get him out of the pen on a plea."

"I guess I'll be here until then."

"Maybe you will. We need to be perfect every night no matter what. You were off tempo a little last night on the first Preston go-around, better on the second."

"Coming up to speed as fast as I can. I'll be on it tonight." Victor's eyes couldn't escape Baker Bagley's unkempt Karl Marx beard. He wondered why he kept it so long, if it was a tribute to his baseball days.

"Polish, that's Torch's Law. That's why we don't mix up the material much."

"Doesn't it get stale doing the same songs every other show?"

"No, stale is waiting tables, serving pasta shells and meatballs when you tell your friends you're a musician. Stale is being stuck playing Single A ballparks with a per diem that buys you two hot dogs to carry you through nine innings in front of a few hundred pensioners. This isn't stale. This is pro. Torch only works with pros."

"He's late. Do we start without him?"

"Sometimes. He does a lot of side gigs. When it's time to go on, we go on. He usually makes it, but if he doesn't we have Synthia and in a pinch I can sing lead."

"Did you like playing baseball?"

"I do this better. Outfielders who can't hit a curveball don't get called up to The Show. This is easier and lasts longer even if it doesn't pay much better than the minors. You got Set B locked down?"

"I made my way through the CD Torch gave me. I think I've got it all."

"I heard, you hear it once, you can play it. Very cool. And you want to try an original."

"Word travels fast."

"We're a small band with a lot of time on our hands. Torch wants us to break out. We like that idea."

"Something more than a cover band?"

"Maybe. Not here. They'd toss us. But at some point. We need to be ready."

It was almost time to go on and Torch still hadn't arrived. Baker Bagley advanced to his position opposite Synthia on stage and glared at Victor's Gibson.

"Spiffy axe for a guy who hasn't played in a while."

"It has a little dust on it. It was a gift from an old friend."

"Dust or rust?" Baker Bagley grinned.

Victor took that as the bassist's approval, a touch sardonic but that was fine. He wedged himself into place between Synthia and Phil-Phil, plugged in, and waited for direction on the kickoff tune. With seconds to spare, Torch entered the lounge and hurriedly made his way to his center stage mic stand. His hair was done up like Elvis.

"You going on like that?" asked Synthia.

"Sorry I'm late. I'll lose the pompadour on the first break."

Torch loved to make an entrance. He adored his entrances almost as much as his finale. Victor looked at him in his Elvis hairdo. He didn't know what to say.

"No words, Nowhere Man. We had enough this morning. I do the Elvis Chapel of Love a few days a week, moonlight on wedding ceremonies, make a few bucks."

"The Act has no limits." Victor was so caught off guard he didn't know what else to say. His words came out more skeptically than he intended.

"You don't think a black man can do Elvis?"

"That's not what I meant. I assumed this show was your whole world."

"Music is my whole world. I make six figures at the chapel. Four weddings an hour, four-hour shift, two half songs each and a photo. On the renewal vows I officiate the ceremony. Yeah, I'm the African American Elvis, how about that?"

"Sounds like easy money."

"It's why Mandalay matters. We need a breakout gig so I can fund my nest egg. I'm going to own that Chapel of Love. That's my way out. Easy money forever."

The Elvis Chapel of Love—that was Torch's endgame, his life plan. He was going to buy the Elvis wedding business, his own personal gold mine into retirement and beyond.

"Peace, Love, and the King, I'd invest if I had any money left."

"Laugh at me and you're fired. That holy love shack is my dream. You laugh at a man's dream, you violate his soul. Where are your dark shades?"

Victor knew he needed to shut up. He reached in the pocket of his flowered rayon shirt and affixed his cheap aviators in place. Phil-Phil was already stepping on the bass pedal, pumping the room's energy. Synthia was vamping on the keyboard, feeling the room for presence. Baker Bagley was improvising, waiting for direction from The Act.

Torch abruptly grabbed the mic and kicked off the evening: "Hey, everyone, gracious thanks for being in our company tonight at the 24 Karat Lounge. We're your downtown party favorites, From Nothing."

Without prompting, Phil-Phil mightily slammed into the snare and hi-hat. Set B was rollickingly underway, no need for the routine to be telegraphed. Victor knew instantly from the beat they were opening with Led Zeppelin. He followed on the power chords and Baker Bagley came in strong beside him. Torch brought up the stage lights and in seconds was in his zone:

It's been a long time since I rock and rolled

It's been a long time since I did the stroll

Like the night before, the band was flawless and the tourists were rowdy. Torch owned the room on impact. Seconds before they finished the opener, he turned to the band and mouthed the words "Freeze Frame." That was his version of spontaneity—never letting them know what was coming but expecting everyone to play his choice on demand. They segued into the J. Geils Band hit, followed up with Robert Palmer's "Addicted to Love." The Act was polished and perfect.

Polished and perfect, that was the big idea, each song making more sense to Victor, each song pushing him to his best. Then the set got more interesting. Torch swung another unannounced transition, this time to the Rolling Stones. He wasn't Mick Jagger. He was as advertised better than Mick Jagger. Soul Brother Mick Jagger, the Mick Jagger Mick could never be except in his satanic prayers. That was something to behold:

Please allow me to introduce myself

I'm a man of wealth and taste

That was bold. That was intrepid. That was out there in front of the boomers, coming through one part Altamont, one part Hammersmith Odeon, all reduced to a tiny showroom with echoes banging off the back wall. The distortion filter kept Victor on the mark. If Torch was Mick, then he was . . . never mind. No chance he could go there, but it was fun to think it. It was a grand spectacle in a limited space, and as long as he could keep up his dreams were attainable. He played through and then they segued naturally to another Stone's standard:

Oh, a storm is threatening my very life today

If I don't get some shelter, oh yeah I'm gonna fade away

Right behind Torch, precisely where she needed to be, there was Synthia on the backing vocals. Torch's range was her range, beauteous and unlimited. She had the keyboards under a spell, two hands dancing in overlapping directions. She could lead and fill simultaneously. Wow, no-mic Victor was out of his class by a long shot. He stepped back and played his part. Mostly he listened. Eerie, tactile, screaming power. The crowd flowed with the beat, literally dancing in the aisles. Crazy, bloody crazy. The Act knew how to satisfy and soar. How he next moved the band a decade ahead from "Gimme Shelter" to "Miss You" was anyone's guess:

I've been walking Central Park
Singing after dark, people think I'm crazy

Torch made it look effortless, but it was so refined, so rigorously implemented. That's how he owned the room. That's how he owned every moment in their presence. The art was in the detail, and the detail was their calling. They followed the Stones trio with "Love Rollercoaster" by the Ohio Players. How did Torch make that change? Then "Surrender" by Cheap Trick, another non-sequitur magically made organic. Victor got half the spotlight on that one and didn't disappoint on the progression. Torch gave him a nod and shifted the lights to Synthia, who drowned the room in her turn on vocals:

Time Time Time
See what's become of me

Victor knew his next lead was coming. Phil-Phil marked time with his drumsticks: one two three four. Victor hit the intro on "Hazy Shade of Winter." It was Paul Simon's song, but it was the Bangles version the crowd wanted. Victor attacked the intro riff with vigor. Baker Bagley nodded, letting him know he nailed it, tempo and all. Synthia sang it with a darkness he couldn't have anticipated. The harmony from Torch was chaste and haunting.

As Synthia wrapped up her solo, Torch took the mic back and nudged Victor. "You a shredder, Nowhere?"

"What do you have in mind?"

"Derringer, crowd favorite, but you gotta land every lick."

"Count on me."

"Kick it off. Timbre, baby, timbre."

Victor blasted his way into "Rock & Roll Hoochie Koo" and delivered as promised. The band came in immediately behind him, recognizing the tune from the first chord. They didn't need to talk. All they needed to do was listen and react. Torch sang it his way, unmistakable but perfect, and the aisles were filled with bopping middle-agers rekindling yearbook memories.

Torch read the crowd as blazing and had the band skip their first break, save for two minutes to down the round of hard drinks Baker Bagley's latest friendlies sent to the stage. Victor was wiped after putting his all into the Rick Derringer tune and had been expecting fifteen minutes to recover. No way was he going to tell

Torch he needed rest, but he would have to pace himself for the next hour or risk exhaustion.

The band opened their blended second set with "What I Like About You" by The Romantics. They followed that with "Let the Good Times Roll" by The Cars, another romp that kept the aisles full. Midway through Foreigner's "Juke Box Hero," the champagne bucket was seeing a healthy flow of dollar bills with a few fives and tens tossed in for good measure. Following a knockout switch to Grand Funk Railroad's "We're An American Band," the mic came back to Synthia for Heart's "Crazy on You," giving Victor another workout at her side, doing his best to play both the rhythm and lead parts without an acoustic backup. Synthia's vocal track would have made Ann Wilson bow in awe:

But I tell myself that I'm doing alright

There's nothing left to do tonight but go crazy on you

It wasn't just her singing. Her intuition for knowing when to cover rhythm for Victor on the keys was mind-blowing. When he took the lead lines, she held the chords as if they had played the song together a thousand times. She wouldn't let him struggle. Her steady structure held him in place and let him go where he needed. No one in the club would know they were a guitar short or improvising the division of labor.

Victor was getting more than his share of solo time, feeling the strain, but no way was he going to ask for a break. His bandmates were pros and he had to remain on par. There was tightness to the band, an expert flow. They could roll here or there, back each other, come out of nowhere or make it seem that way. They were versatile. They were fluid. They were in their element. His expectations of himself were never greater. He had to be one of them.

It was already a great night, an excellent night. Set B proved even more fun than Set A. It was or it wasn't. It didn't matter. Every song flowed. Victor was in the moment, equal to his bandmates, like he had been with them forever. Torch turned the beat to Stevie Wonder:

Very superstitious, writings on the wall

Very superstitious, ladders 'bout to fall

It was all good, their performance escalating weightlessly until Victor looked into the crowd and saw . . . No, it couldn't be. Claire?

What was Claire doing there? Was that her husband dancing next to her? She didn't dance. She hated Vegas. She hated clubs. Did she hate him now?

Victor felt dizzy. His feet weren't firm. It was an easy guitar part for him to play with Synthia and Baker Bagley doing the heavy lifting and Torch out swaying with the audience, living Stevie in the beat. Wait, that wasn't Claire. What was Victor thinking? What was wrong with his brain? His mind wasn't stable. He couldn't focus. He was fading.

Victor held onto his composure and played through. He fought to find his footing. That one drink couldn't be taking him down, not that kind of knockout, but he was in a daze. What was wrong with him? Too much of it all. Katem. Sangstrum. McWhorter. Max. Clarence. Juan. Darcy. Hold the virus. Release the virus. Desert highways. Elvis chapels. Les Paul. Mick and Keith. Vegas e-slots. Claire. Synthia in his standard queen hotel room. Fixed set lists. Original songs. Hold the input, please. Drunken crowds. Phil-Phil who wouldn't talk to him. Baker Bagley in the minor leagues or maybe not. Little Stevie Wonder. Rockin' Billy Preston. Torch The Act, the Philosopher King. Timbre, baby, timbre.

Damn it all, he was falling apart! Stop the noise. Repress the drama. Stay hidden in plain sight. Don't lose the gig! Not over Claire. Not over Sangstrum. Victor kneeled while he played and tried to shake it off, but he had lost the rhythm. Clear! He needed to get his head clear.

Synthia could see something was wrong. "Vic, you got this? Segue to the finale. Big tipping crowd. Lots of go-arounds on deck."

Vic, she said his name, he heard her say it. It wasn't enough to ground him. He thought back to the hospital. He was vanishing into the haze, relapsing out of consciousness. The beating was more severe than he thought. His concussion hadn't mended. It was too soon for him to be onstage. It was too hard to be playing rhythm and lead on the same fretboard. What was he thinking? He wasn't well at all. He needed to get off the platform before he collapsed in front of the partygoers. Torch could not see him implode. That couldn't happen.

"Nowhere Man, get back on the beat," ordered Torch.

The glistening was off. No anointment, no made-man. Victor's participation was unacceptable to The Act. He wasn't okay as advertised, the pitch was oversold, but that wasn't Torch's problem. He had to pull out of the dive. Spiraling toward a collision course from the clouds to the gravel riverbed, he had to level off or lose everything again.

No, he couldn't start over again. He needed a breath, a deep guttural breath. With the last strength he could summon, he forced himself to inhale, no matter the thick cigarette smoke in the air. There, his heartbeat was even again. He felt it normalizing. No idea how, but he was recovering in real time. He was coming back, finding the beat as Torch had ordered, but was he too late? Had he blown it? What was Torch thinking? What was Synthia hearing? Was he soft? Was he unable to be one of them? Did he have too much of what they thought they wanted, too many chances, too many forfeited rewards? Did they envy him, his way out, his way back? Could he fly or only glide? He would leave them at some point. Did they know that? Were they better off without him?

Of course they didn't need him. They could get some other hack on speed dial. They would dump him as soon as Sludge was released. They would let him go as soon as the lights went down. They didn't like his ideas. He couldn't write a song for them and he threatened their playlists. Music database guy from the Bay Area. *Domo arigato*, jerk. He saw people who weren't there, dizzied himself with illusions, crackpot delusions of love lost returning to haunt him. Dreams lost returning to taunt him. They were a much better band without him. No question, they were pros. He was an amateur, worse than an amateur, a poseur. Dump Victor. Dump him now. He was damaged goods forever.

Victor came back to his feet, battled himself back to his playing stance. He found the frets, looked to Synthia, nodded that he was good to go. Synthia played the intro for Preston. There was no medley this time, just the eponymous tune. Victor's fingers held down the chords, making the switches on instinct. Torch took the mic. It was routine again, safely back to routine:

Nothing from nothing leaves nothing
You gotta have somethin' if you wanna be with me

This time the dollar bills were flying into the champagne bucket. It was going to be a long one. Synthia took her initial solo, then handed it off to Victor. He found her last note, turned a variation on the theme, then gave her back the lead. Synthia riffed again and it went back to Victor. On the next exchange Synthia pointed to Torch, who pulled a harmonica from his pocket and wailed the blues, nearly busting though the platform under them keeping time with his boot. Synthia and Victor took another turn. Phil-Phil got a quick drum solo, leading the run up to "Baker Bagley on Bass." It was round and round of revolving loops between Synthia and Victor, surging another fifteen minutes after playing through their break. Victor recommitted himself on every handoff, breaking through his own ceiling and minutes later surpassing that. Would he have a few minutes to recover when it was done? That was Torch's call. The tip jar runneth over.

Torch at last signaled to end the set and Phil-Phil crashed the closing cymbals. The stage lights faded and the band stepped away unfazed, everyone except Victor. He had no energy to move. Torch brought up the house lights and the sweat pouring from Victor's forehead formed a puddle on the stage. He didn't need vodka, just Gatorade, a gallon of Gatorade—and an excuse, at least an explanation. At the moment he had neither. First he would have to explain the meltdown to himself.

TRACK 8: HERACLITUS FOR DUMMIES

THE PANIC ATTACK—OR WHATEVER IT WAS—THAT NEARLY TOOK DOWN VICTOR ON HIS SECOND PLAYDATE AT THE GOLDEN NUGGET APPEARED TO BE AN ISOLATED OCCURRENCE. That didn't mean another wouldn't come, but so far so good. He had no interest in seeing another doctor. His medical insurance had lapsed, he had little cash to spare, and any dire diagnosis would likely cost him the guitar gig.

Victor convinced himself the incident had been a relapse from the beating he took at Providence, lack of recovery time after leaving the hospital and immediately joining the band. He came clean with Torch about the professionally delivered concussion he'd suffered, suggesting that he was like a retired NFL player released into civilization. Residual relapse was bound to happen. Torch made it clear that it could only happen once and that was behind them. He liked the way Victor played, but Victor had to be a pro. He could never allow it to happen again. Right, like Victor had a say in it. Of course he agreed to Torch's Law. What other choice did he have? If it happened it happened.

Equally unpredictable, the grand inquisition prophesied by Sangstrum never occurred. No one ever came by the hotel to approach Victor or inquire about anything related to the Global Harmonics deal. No offers, no shakedown. He kept waiting, but it never came. At times Victor felt really stupid about it. He should have taken the money, all of it, signed the heinous papers, and skipped off debt free. That would have been the ultimate way to screw over Sangstrum. Hindsight, the tangible chance for revenge, always so clear in the abstract. Damn Sangstrum. Damn the whole of Global Harmonics.

This band—that was where he wanted to be. It was all about excellence, musicianship, not about infighting or desperation. The artistry surrounding him was a matter of honor, a higher calling of fulfillment, not a conduit to someone else's agenda. He didn't have to lead. He only had to play. He didn't have to pretend to care about an abstract goal or allow his passion to be compromised. He just had to hold his own with consistency. They were going somewhere better on the groundswell of merit, he knew that. He had to make sure he didn't destroy it—if only he could wean himself from contemplating the few changes he knew Torch didn't want to hear.

Two months had gone by and Victor no longer needed the sunglasses onstage. Each week, three alternating nights, they played Set A, four sets each show, varying the order but not the playlist. The other three nights they played Set B, also four sets. All shows began at 10:00 p.m. and finished at 2:00 a.m. It was clockwork, four hours each night with three breaks, unless the signature tune ate into the break. Tuesday, Thursday, Saturday was Set A. Wednesday, Friday, Sunday was Set B. Mondays were dark. Smooth as spun silk. There were no surprises, precisely the way the Philosopher King demanded. Some nights the tips were better than others. Some nights they would jam on the finale until 2:30 a.m. As long as they were selling drinks, the bartenders and waitresses were game to serve on. It was all up to Torch. He called the shots. He charted their path. Torch would look at Synthia if he wanted to keep going, she would look at Victor, then they'd go around again. That was the only real variation from night to night. It would stop when Torch called time, "Nothing from Nothing" improvised endlessly as Billy Preston never imagined it.

Torch had been clear. He demanded a routine. He demanded perfection, predictability, and loyalty in equal measures. He held himself to the same standard. If Torch was into you, he was into you without exception. He took and gave in equal doses. If Victor gave him reason to worry he couldn't follow the routine, he would be out. Routine was a requirement of the gig. Soon enough, Victor's entire life would be part of the routine.

Predictability was sacred. Repetition was exalted. Playing that many tight sets that many nights in a row was an endurance contest only pros could handle, but the stacked hours of precision showmanship weren't the hard part. For Victor, some nights began to feel monotonous. What had started out not long ago as new and different had become mechanical, each show more of the same. Victor found it ironic that something as vital as live music could be machine driven, but that was at the heart of the performing arts. *You go back, Jack, do it again*—the same, only better. He talked to other musicians around town and discovered the Broadway musicals were exactly like that. Everyone had a mark to hit, taped landing spots on the wooden floor for the lights to find. Of course it seemed fresh and original to an audience seeing it the first time, but it was a product. Learn it, rehearse it, play it, do it again, only tighter. That was how Torch wanted it so that was how it was. Set A or Set B, impossibly rigid, no deviations except for song order each night and a touch of extempore in the solos. Get it right, keep it right. Grow the following. Don't question what works. Forget change. Don't bother stirring the pot or it will boil over.

Milk the cow, never feed her. Milk the cow, never feed her.

Soon it was autopilot gnawing at Victor in the band the same as it had unsettled him at Global Harmonics. No change, no risk, no discovery, just getting the proven to market. They were filling orders to make the bottom line, not pushing themselves to break new ground before it was needed. Routine was stale. Sameness was stale. No, it wasn't the Sizzler or nine tedious innings of Single A baseball on a half-empty stomach without a crowd, but change had to come. He could never leave well enough alone. He had been accused throughout his life of not being able to go with the flow, upsetting the flow, repeatedly bringing change for change's sake. That wasn't fair criticism in his mind. Yes, he was a disruptor, but to make things better to stay ahead. That was always his intention. Sure he was wrong some of the time, but he only needed to be right when it mattered most.

There would come a time when he would try again with Torch. He knew Torch would resist. Torch was about finding the target and staying on the target, getting it right and keeping it right. Victor was about finding a new target to stay interested, to stay alive in his mind. At some point they would clash, hopefully to a productive resolution, but Victor had to wait for the proper moment. The door had to open on its own. This wasn't his band. Victor knew that. After two months he remained an invited guest. He knew change would be good for Torch, to take the band to a higher ground, but the how of change was as difficult to introduce as the what. No more scenes, no more anger, ease off the conflict. Polish to perfection, prove dependable, strap in for the ride. Torch was driving the bus and there was no shotgun seat. A route-skirting routine would come in its own time or Victor would break everything, most of all trust. Change, balance, trust, they all mattered. Innovation was a ravenous beast bucking to roam free in open terrain. The cage door kept the peace but couldn't contain the inevitable release.

Though Victor hadn't come close to collapsing again, his headaches remained viciously chronic. He learned to manage the pain, ignored it mostly, and never openly acknowledged it again. Yeah, his head hurt a lot, but it wasn't going to be a game ender. He couldn't give Torch a reason to doubt him. He couldn't allow doubt to exist with anyone in the band. He played on.

As the autumn weather tempered the desert heat, Victor would go for long walks on the Strip during the daylight hours, leaving downtown and venturing toward the gaudy fountains and towering marquee billboards. Since there weren't any new songs to learn there wasn't much else to do during the day. Gambling, drugs, hookers, no thanks. Shopping wasn't of interest and eating in restaurants alone wasn't appealing. He found some inexpensive deli counters he liked and would eat quickly or get a sandwich in a sports bar in the late afternoon when most people were gambling or at the pool. No kale or quinoa; that was Torch and Synthia chow, clean fuel for the vocal chords. He surfaced limitless Vegas varieties of shrimp cocktail and fanciful pizza by the slice. He would catch a movie here and there, mostly for the air conditioning, way too much comic book fare for his taste, but occasionally a tale of human intrigue that didn't rely on superhero powers would sneak onto the screen. He would wander by the Elvis Chapel of Love and wonder if Torch was on duty, never daring to look inside and get caught watching his boss moonlighting in white sequins. Victor overheard side conversations from club patrons all the time that Torch was one of the most popular wedding Elvises in town, but it wasn't something Torch wanted to talk about. It was a side gig for cash and he wanted it left at that until he had his down payment and financing.

The silence from Global Harmonics was perplexing. Not only hadn't Sangstrum called again, Victor had yet to hear from Thomas

Katem since the day he left for Vegas. He hadn't called back Max, Clarence, and Juan since the first time Sangstrum called. There wasn't a need. That whole tech world seemed behind him and Vegas was becoming home. Well, maybe not home, but a familiar enough encampment. It may not have been the apocalypse he imagined, but a town built on odds-making would never be a comfort zone. He liked playing the gigs. He really liked being in the band, but he didn't want to be in Vegas forever. Neither did Torch, so one way or another change was coming.

The idea of an original song was lodged in Victor's mind, waiting for the chance to emerge. He would try to write at the lunch stops or staring at the ceiling from his standard queen bed in his increasingly claustrophobic room, but that wasn't getting him far. One afternoon, while he was paging through one of his old notebooks, the phone in his room gave an unexpected ring. It was Synthia. She seemed to like to do that, surprise him when he least expected it, always guarded and detached but much less predictable than Torch. He wasn't sure if they were friends, but her talent blew his mind, especially when they traded off solos. She lifted his performance to his very best.

"Can I come to your room?" she asked in the kindest voice he had ever heard from her.

It was an offer he couldn't refuse. An hour later, when he opened the door for her, it was all business.

"I want to play something for you." She was carrying a small portable keyboard under her arm and instantly unfolded the stand. The blackout curtains were pulled back so the afternoon light beamed dazzlingly on her face. She sat on the right edge of the bed in front of the keyboard and plugged it into the nearest wall socket three feet away. He sat on the far left edge of the bed, as far away as he could. Where else could he sit? No big deal, right?

Synthia played the refrain of a song that reminded him of "Band on the Run," only the slow intro was more romantic and the tempo change in the middle erratically more fierce. It was like McCartney breaking out on his own but holding onto his roots, a catchy tune that grabbed people intuitively and held them with bombshell complexity. Paul, Lady Linda, attempted dynasty resurrection, harkening a renaissance in texture. The rhythm sat under the melody line and didn't take over. It wasn't a dance song but it wasn't a ballad. It wasn't like anything the band had played together, yet it was foundational, composed as if they had played it a thousand times. It was a sound all its own, the kind of unique sound a band needed to break out and distinguish itself from the pack. Every band that charted fought to carve out its own sound and this song got there. It made his toe tap. It made him want to move and listen at the same time, like Carole King or Stevie Nicks or Alicia Keyes. She had been holding back on him. This wasn't a fluke. She had written before. She knew what she was doing.

"Try adding some fills," she said.

Victor slid out his guitar from under the bed, plugged it into his practice amp, and joined her on the refrain. He found the treble notes blending in naturally, expert but effortless, the way winning music was meant to sound and be played. The song was already working. They were collaborating. The duet felt right, building with balanced tension, resonating and quickly evolving. Was there something more to it, more than an evolving composition? No, of course not, not for her, not for Synthia with an S. She was a working musician, his bandmate, the band's venerated music director who happened to be sitting on his bed. He was a dork loser barely keeping up.

Minutes after they got going, they heard a pounding on the wall. Oops. Vegas, daytime, people sleeping, wasting the day to get to the night. Victor usually played with headphones, but in the moment he was playing full volume. So was she. With the wall pounding they had no choice but to stop or expect security. No security. No thanks.

"What do you think of it?" she asked.

"It's really good. I'd say amazing, but I don't like that word."

"Awesome?"

"Sure, I'll give you one awesome this time. Have you played it for Torch?"

"No, it's not ready, needs some lyrics. Got any?"

"Haven't come up with anything that doesn't embarrass me yet, but what you've got starts me thinking in a different way. Let me dig a little harder."

"That would be cool. Do you want me to burn a CD for you?"

"Nah, it's in my head forever. Let me see what I can do. If I figure out something you like, we can pitch it to Torch together."

"Sounds good, Vic." Synthia nodded without readable expression. There it was, his name again, the way she said it unlike any other person on the earth. She folded up the portable keyboard and started making her way to the door.

Victor maneuvered off the bed to power down his amp, trying to reestablish eye contact with her. "We could get coffee if you want and talk about it some more, or go down to the lounge and work on it. I doubt anyone will be there."

"Sure they will. We got a lot going on at the moment. I just wanted to get your brain in motion, see what you might come up with. You excited about the new gig?"

He had no idea what she was talking about. "What new gig?"

"Torch didn't tell you? Petrumi got us a private party at Mandalay Bay. Some band cancelled last minute. There's a big shot hosting the event but he can't tell us who it is, or who may or may not be there. Anyway we're playing the fake beach with the wave machine. Stage is four times the size of ours with a dedicated sound and light guy."

"I had no idea."

"Weird, we have rehearsal this afternoon at 4:00 p.m."

"We're rehearsing? We never rehearse. Is that why you came over?"

"Yeah, plus I wanted you to hear this without Torch casting his shadow too early in the process. He left me a message a few hours ago. You didn't get one?"

Victor looked at his iPhone. The battery was dead, everything incoming silently relegated to voicemail. That must have been why Synthia called on his room phone. Damn, how stupid of him. He plugged it in and there was a message waiting from Torch: "Nowhere Man, surprise rehearsal today, 4:00, the lounge, don't be late. We got Mandalay. You need to answer the phone when I call." Click.

Thank God, thank God Synthia called his room or he would have missed showing up for the rehearsal. Fate again or freakish good luck? It didn't matter. He got the message in time. The Mandalay beach party was on and they were halfway to an original song.

"Watch yourself with Torch this afternoon," said Synthia. "This is our transition gig. He worked hard to get it. He will protect it."

"I understand."

Synthia put down the keyboard in the small hallway near the door. Victor looked at his watch. It was just past 3:30. They still had a little time if she wanted to talk. She was easy to follow during the show, impossible otherwise.

"Torch says you came out of the system, same as him."

"Is that a coincidence?"

"You tell me. I don't think Petrumi would have looked that up on your sheet."

"No, probably not."

"So what's that like, coming out of the system?"

"Hard to explain. You have parents, right?"

"We all have parents. I mean, I don't know, maybe not the same way. I guess my parents don't think much of me, given all my mistakes."

"They may think more of you than you're aware. They know you have talent. You can call them. I don't have that option. I don't understand what having that option means."

Synthia stared at her keyboard case, ducking eye contact with Victor. "I want them to be proud of me. I want to have something to say to them that they want to hear."

"When you have foster parents, you don't say much to them at all. The less you say the better. You keep your head down so they don't throw you back sooner than usual, but you can't control that. You can't control anything."

"Are you mad at them?"

"My foster parents? Which ones? There were dozens."

"No, your real parents, your birth parents?"

"Yeah, pretty much all the time, every single day. You never know if the bed you slept in last night will be your bed the next night. You hope it will, but you can't make it happen. The government is paying them for that bed, paying your way. When it's not worth it to them anymore, they move on. You move on."

"I probably should call my parents. Maybe after Mandalay I'll have something to say."

"We're going to the next level, right? That could be a big deal. Let's go rehearse. We don't want to piss off Torch."

"I don't piss off Torch, you do. Remember, whatever he wants to do, that's what we do. Whatever he wants to play, we play."

"Not too hard to figure out. Set A or Set B, both polished and ready to shine."

Victor grabbed his guitar, put it in the case, and followed Synthia down the hall to the elevator. He knew Torch called all the shots. That was never clearer, but now they had Synthia's original up their sleeve. The gig at Mandalay might be a launching pad. Victor wondered if he could help make the launch even higher.

>> <<

At 3:55 Victor and Synthia walked into the mostly uninhabited 24 Karat Lounge. In the back of his mind, Victor knew he wanted to propose some new ideas for the Mandalay gig, fresh material to ignite the band's spark, stretch everyone's performance. It was a shame the original song Synthia played for him wasn't ready. An original in front of the touring circuit scouts could change their perception of From Nothing. Torch would have been good with that. It was the direction they needed to go, but the song wasn't finished so Victor had to go a different way. It would be a risk to open his mouth, but he couldn't help himself. He would look for an opening with Torch. He knew Torch would make the call, but how could he forgive himself if he had a game-changing idea and stayed silent? He didn't tell Synthia what he had in mind. He was going to take his best shot with the Philosopher King. God Help Him.

Torch was already in the room sitting on a cocktail table when Victor and Synthia arrived. He was anxious, antsy, not showing off his normal smile. "You don't answer the phone when I call, Nowhere Man? You got something more important going on?"

"Working on our music, Torch. That's what we do. I was trying out some new stuff with Synthia."

"New stuff? I'll bet you were. The two of you getting tight, huh? Gonna destroy our band with drama before we get a shot at something better."

"There's nothing going on with me and Synthia, Torch. I'm not an idiot."

"Do I get a vote?" asked Torch.

Victor wondered why Torch was in such a foul mood when he should have been elated. Did he really think that Victor had hooked up with Synthia? The words "new stuff" had come out his throat with a callous tinge, cutting off Victor's prospects before the proposal was out there. Victor knew he had to play his approach carefully, but he was convinced he had to get Torch to think about some different songs—younger, more contemporary material to light up that beach. They needed spontaneity. Their performance needed to be unforgettable.

"Torch, let's talk about something else?" said Synthia.

"You bet, Lady Piano. What do you want to talk about?"

Before she could answer, Baker Bagley and Phil-Phil entered the lounge. All conversation in the room stopped. Phil-Phil said nothing as usual, went straight to the kit and started tapping the snare. Baker Bagley seemed to sense their entrance had interrupted a tense moment and tried to make light of it.

"Why so glum?" said Baker Bagley, straightening his baseball cap. "No more Single A ball. We're playing the beach at Mandalay Bay. We've waited seven years to seize our castle. Is someone upset about the contract terms?"

"Nowhere Man and Synthia have been working on new stuff," cackled Torch. "Guess they don't like our old stuff. Musty ancient crap. Maybe we should try out some new material, risk everything on a whim."

"Mandalay is a door opener," said Baker Bagley. "We need to pick our material carefully, the songs we do best. We have one chance to get this right and be seen."

"Exactly, which is why I called this meeting, to decide *together* if we go with Set A or Set B. I want to discuss it with the band. Your vote comes last, Mr. Database Genius."

Torch wasn't being rational. He must have been nervous about the gig. It was the band's first audition in ages. Everyone knew that. It had taken forever to get it and now they had it, but the pressure weighed heavily on Torch. He kept looking back and forth at Victor and then Synthia. He couldn't be jealous. There was no reason for him to be jealous. There was no reason for him to suspect anything. Pressure never meant much to Torch, but he wasn't himself.

"Torch, no one said anything about new material," said Synthia. "I don't know where you're getting that."

"New stuff. I heard him say it. The two of you were trying out new stuff instead of thinking through our polished playlist. Too busy to call me back. Right, I want us to play songs we never played before, because that's why we've been making the material we have perfect for seven years, so we could change everything as soon as we got our shot."

"The Act is good, Torch," praised Victor. "Your material is good. You're good."

"*Our* material is good," corrected Synthia. "*We're* good, but like all musicians, we can be better."

"Except I'm The Act. You questioning that after all we've done? You figured it all out, but when the lights shine hot, I'm holding the bag."

The room went quiet again. Synthia shook her head and walked over to the keyboards onstage. Baker Bagley followed her and reached for his bass. They were walking on eggshells, fighting back the sting of Torch's fractured ego. Phil-Phil remained silent, spinning his drumsticks forward and back.

"Torch, which set do you think we should go with?" Victor knew he had to try to ease things over. "You know that place better than any of us."

"How do I know that place better than the rest of you? I haven't played there any more than you have. Don't play office politics with me."

Victor made his way to his amp and plugged in as he spoke. "Tell us what you want to do. I'm going to tune up."

Torch stepped between Victor and the amp. "New stuff like what, Nowhere Man?"

Victor realized what was going on. For the first time, Torch was unsure of the band's material. He had waited all this time and now he had Mandalay Bay, but like Baker Bagley said, what if they blew their one chance? Torch's anger was summoned. The Act was faking an act. He needed a way to hear what Victor had to say without making it look like he needed Victor's input. It was a clever ruse on Torch's part, unless Victor had it wrong and The Act was genuinely pissed off. Should he put it out there and risk getting clobbered or let Torch settle it with the others? Victor chose to go fishing. Once again, God Help Him.

"If you're honestly asking for my opinion, I have some ideas. I think if we reach a little we can get some serious attention. This is a chance to show we're a different kind of cover band, flexible in ways the audience doesn't expect, show off your interpretive skills, give us an edge."

Synthia looked at Victor like he was out of his mind. He knew that vexing look. It was the look that asked what the hell was he doing? Was he suicidal? Was testing his theory worth the wrath of Torch? Uh-oh, he'd read it wrong. He needed to end the fishing expedition before Torch torpedoed the boat.

"Too many words, Nowhere Man," enunciated Torch. "What songs are you proposing?"

Too late. The boat had left the dock. Victor had to fish. "Okay, don't get mad at me. This is going to sound weird, but how about Tupac?"

"Tupac Shakur who got clipped in this town? Have you lost your mind? Have you been paying attention to what we do up there?"

Victor took a breath and doubled down. "Open with 'California Love.' No one will see it coming. It will blow their minds and fill the dance floor. You can sell it."

"Why, because I'm a black man, you asshole?"

"No, because you have range. It's a younger crowd. We have to win them over in the first five seconds. Start with contemporary, then work our way back to nostalgia."

"I don't rap. This is not a hip-hop band. That's not our thing. Plenty of others do Tupac, none of them worthy. Any other bright ideas?"

Victor went silent. He needed to protect himself, but Torch wasn't letting go.

"I asked if you had any more bright ideas."

"You really want to hear what I have to say or is this . . . ?"

"What else?" blasted Torch.

"Bruno Mars. 'Uptown Funk.'"

"He owns that song. I'd be a laughing stock. What else?"

"Gaga, 'Born This Way.'"

"Me sing that?"

"No, Synthia, you do the harmony."

"Synthia open for the band, are you popping pills? What else?"

"I was going to say Katy Perry, but that won't solve the problem if Synthia can't open."

"What else?"

"Okay, let me try a different idea. We'll go backward then forward. Black Eyed Peas, 'I Gotta Feeling.' Dance line on the sand, get people moving right out of the gate."

"You got a death wish going on? That song is formula plastic, a corporate cartoon."

"Interpret it, make it your own. You'd be surprised what you can do."

"I don't want to be surprised. I want a predictable standing-O."

Baker Bagley unexpectedly tapped out the song's lead line with two fingers on Synthia's keyboard. "I kind of like Will-I-Am," said the bass player. "He gets people moving."

"It's not us," roared Torch. "We don't play artificial. We play who we are."

"Fine, then I'm wrong," grumbled Victor. "My mistake."

"What else?"

"Nothing else. I should have kept my mouth shut. I'm sorry I upset you. Happy to stick with Set A or Set B."

"Happy?" Torch looked behind Victor's amp at a rumpled stack of papers stashed against the wall. "You obviously got more ideas. Those your notebooks?"

That wasn't an accident. Torch must have found the fake charts Victor had been collecting before the meeting started, who knew how long ago. Victor tried to stand in front of Torch and block him from reaching for the paperwork. "Nothing there, more ideas that suck."

Torch blew past Victor and grabbed the stack of papers. "Couldn't help yourself. You wrote it all down."

Torch clearly didn't see the bravery in Victor's initiative. He started paging through Victor's notes and peered at the playlist on the first page. "'Happy,' 'Blurred Lines,' 'Moves Like Jagger,' 'Raise Your Glass.' This isn't who we are. This material would kill us forever."

"You can do it, Torch. I know you can if you want."

"You don't want to build on what we've perfected. You want wholesale change right before the biggest gig we ever played. Oh, this is classic, Cee Lo Green. He wants me to do Cee Lo Green."

"I don't love a lot of the new songs either, but we have to win over the crowd to play what we want, to be who we are," begged Victor.

Torch started to tear that page into shreds, then stopped in mid-motion, gazed at it again in disbelief and threw the pile of papers into the air, scattering them around the stage and across the club floor.

"You're not a Nowhere Man. You're a Freak of Nature Man, a bad mutation in evolution. I became The Act with a delicate touch. I read Malcolm Gladwell. I did my ten thousand hours and now we got two perfect nights. We choose from that because we paid our dues."

"Change is how we get better. The Beatles weren't the same in Hamburg as they were at Abbey Road."

"We ain't the Beatles, Nowhereville. Don't be playing the Heraclitus card on me."

"Don't know Heraclitus, sorry. Big hair band?"

"What, you illiterate? Heraclitus, pre-Socratic philosopher of change. You can't step in the same river twice—ancient and does not apply. We step in the same river perfectly every time we play. The Greeks got a lot right but they got a lot wrong. Do yourself a favor and read up."

"I thought you might be open to going down some new roads to make us better."

"Do I look like a flunkout from *The Voice* who'll sing any crap to be asked back? Do not break my band. Do not shuffle the deck of my dreams. I got this right because we know what to play and how to play it. You know how to get the shit beat out of you."

Milk the cow, never feed her. Milk the cow, never feed her.

Victor heard the playback loop in his head. Torch was guilty of spreading the same disease as the flunkout executives at Global Harmonics. He had no idea of the constraints he was putting on the band forever demanding more of the same.

"I'm not saying anything to the contrary," argued Victor. "Think about bending a little to let in some air, open the hatch to a breeze.

Make the whole thing vibrant again, not routine, not preset, something more, exactly what we want to bring us to a place that's new."

"You want to change everything. Who do you think you are? Stuff change up your ass. You think we couldn't have gotten this gig without you? You are a footnote in From Nothing history, nothing more. You are a Nowhere Man. You are nothing else. And don't be tossing out the Beatles to make a point. It proves you're a know-nothing."

Synthia looked for a way to break the tension and stopped Torch mid-rant. "Maybe we are too comfortable, Torch. We want to sound polished, not canned. Victor wants our sound to be its own thing, different, that's all."

"We don't need to be different. We need to do what we do because that's what we do."

Torch looked to the others for support.

"You're The Act," said Baker Bagley. "What you want, that's the sound. Torch's Law."

"Set A or Set B?" asked Phil-Phil without intonation.

"I thought I called a meeting to discuss that, but Mr. Nowhere Man Database Genius Freak of Nature Mutation thinks we should try some contemporary tunes to get the attention we deserve. What do you say to that?"

"Play the gig without him," said Phil-Phil.

"No guitar at the beach party, are you insane?" clamored Baker Bagley.

"Call another hack," said Phil-Phil. "I know ten guys who want it. Or Lady Treble Clef can record an overdub track and hit playback. Who gives a shit?"

"No, he's gonna play," said Torch. "He's gonna play what we always play."

"Fine, Set A or Set B?" repeated Phil-Phil.

Synthia picked up some of the strewn papers from the floor. "Maybe we should at least try the new material. We could test it out now, see if we can pull it off."

Once again, stunned silence filled the half-darkened lounge. Synthia was no more her predictable self than Torch. She had broken their Vulcan mind meld in public, pure defiance to his musical authority.

"Seriously, Synthia, you like this brainless idea?" yelled Torch. "Afternoon delight must have been something to twist you into that realm of misunderstanding."

"Seriously," said Synthia as quietly as she could.

That stopped Torch in his tracks. He must have known he had gone too far. After all those years, they had their own vocabulary and he had crossed the line. He never saw it coming, never saw Synthia breaking ranks. The venom was flowing from his lips. He changed course on a dime, but not his tone. "Fine, everyone on stage. Nowhere Man, hand out the syllabus."

Victor waited warily, like making a left turn on a green light turned red in LA. Was Torch really stopping or coming through the intersection to annihilate him if he followed through? He joined Synthia in picking up all the papers he had drawn up for the new songs and held them tightly in his hands, a school kid with his homework afraid of the teacher. Torch tapped his foot impatiently and pointed his index finger at Victor, in effect ordering him to do it. Victor handed out the music packages one at a time.

"I'm game for some Black Eyed Peas," said Baker Bagley, looking at one of the sheets.

"Shut up, you bearded Joe Smith bat boy or whatever your name is. We might as well play 'Dancing Queen' if we want to please. 'Mamma Mia,' we can play the whole Abba catalogue. But let's find out how clever our Nowhere Man is—like Synthia said, see if we can pull off something new. You want to try a fresh tune, call me Will-I-Am."

"Faster to fire him and get a new guy," said Phil-Phil.

"Nah, let's try a little Heraclitus." Torch made his way to the center mic stand and fired up the practice amp. "Synthia with an S, come in with the piano line."

Victor stood motionless. All eyes were upon him and he hadn't picked up his guitar.

"You need more of an invitation, Nowhere?" belted Torch. "We're playing your tune."

Victor strapped on his guitar, flicked on his amp, and readied himself to come in behind Synthia on the chord progression for "I Gotta Feeling." He knew Synthia didn't need the fake charts. She could play anything hearing it in her head, same as the rest of them. They were top-of-their-game pros and could play anything they wanted after all those years in countless clubs lighting up every genre imaginable. No request ever stumped a club professional. Baker Bagley found the bass line instantly and Phil-Phil had the intro rhythm.

The band was on it, boom. Unfortunately Victor had never played it and hadn't listened to it in a while. He played in the wrong key and the others stopped. The room went silent again.

"Sorry, my bad, this one's new to me." Victor looked over Synthia's shoulder at the page from his notebook on top of her keyboard.

"See where to come in," she said. "You take the steady chords so I can go up. Let's try it again."

"Oh goodie, the music director is gonna conduct, sister feels the beat." Torch continued snapping his fingers with the kickoff. "Five six seven eight . . ."

Victor led in on the chord progression and Synthia came in over him as promised. Phil-Phil and Baker Bagley were again on the money. Torch stared at the lyric sheet and tried to find the rhythm as he spoke more than sang the opening lyrics:

I gotta feeling that tonight's gonna be a good night

That tonight's gonna be a good night

Torch wasn't close to singing on tune. Victor had never heard him that off, not even in the vicinity of that far off. Torch's heart wasn't in it. He was hardly trying. He stopped speak-singing and the room was quiet again.

"That was shit," said Torch. "Run it again!"

Victor began in earnest, then Synthia and the others with easy flow, but Torch was a full beat behind them:

I gotta feeling that tonight's gonna be a good night

That tonight's gonna be a good night

It sounded worse on this go than the previous play. Was Torch blowing it on purpose? This time he couldn't or wouldn't match their rhythm. He stopped the band by throwing up his arms.

"Shit. Do it again."

"Let's get everyone on the same beat," said Synthia. "Phil-Phil, give us the . . ."

"No more directions," shouted Torch. "Again."

"Maybe let's try Cee Lo," snickered Baker Bagley.

Torch grabbed the mic from the stand. "You think this is funny? I'm making a point. I said again." Then he sang it even worse, more off beat and further drifting off key, like he couldn't do it at all:

I gotta feeling that tonight's gonna be a good night

That tonight's gonna be a good night

"Screw this." Phil-Phil broke a drumstick slamming it into the back wall.

"I'm making a damn point," bellowed Torch. "Again!"

"Don't try to sing it like Will-I-Am, sing it your way," said Victor.

"I'm gonna sing it like a monkey wrench up your asshole, you asshole. Now you're gonna tell me how to sing as well as what to sing? Play your part, I know mine!"

Victor played. Synthia followed. Phil-Phil and Baker Bagley had it down. This time Torch screeched it:

I gotta feeling that tonight's gonna be a good night

That tonight's gonna be a good night

Torch tried to interpret it, but his rendition thudded into disaster.

"You sound like James Brown doing Wayne Newton," said Baker Bagley. "It sucks."

"This whole thing sucks," echoed Phil-Phil, throwing another drumstick at the wall.

Synthia played a few refrains of an alternate beat, trying to salvage it, then turned to Torch. "Can we try . . . ?"

"No, we cannot!" Torch dropped the live mic on the platform, blasting feedback through the amps, everyone in the band covering their ears. "Who made you music director?"

"I am the music director."

"Right, and who made you the music director?"

Victor was shocked that Torch couldn't do it. The band might have been able to pull it off, but Torch was stuck in what he knew. The material was too new for him, too different. Either it had been too long since he'd tackled a new song or he had no will to try anything new. He had no will for change, no desire for risk. Victor had exposed him and Torch didn't appreciate the exposure. Nope, Torch didn't like change. It wasn't his thing. Victor should have known that.

Torch grabbed the mic from the floor and slammed it back in the stand. "I know what works. This doesn't work. We're doing Set A. Any more suggested changes and I make lineup changes."

Torch switched off the mic and walked out the lounge door. Phil-Phil strutted out behind him, tossing the cheat sheets onto the floor behind his kit. Baker Bagley followed the two of them, leaving his stack on the music stand. No one needed souvenirs of the failed rehearsal. That left Synthia alone in the club with Victor.

"I thought we were getting closer," she said. "He should have stayed with it."

"Phil-Phil and Baker Bagley had it," said Victor. "They sounded good even though they threw me under the bus."

"Yeah, I heard it. Torch heard it, too. He could do it. He didn't want to."

"We have to make this gig work. I didn't do us any favors."

"We'll be okay," said Synthia. "Torch will cool off, especially if Mandalay goes well. He'll be on as soon as the lights come up. This won't matter."

"I'll see you over there. I guess I have one more night with the band."

Victor left the lounge in silence. He looked back and saw Synthia picking up the song sheets from the floor. As he made his way down the hall, he heard her on the keyboard playing "I Gotta Feeling." He had no idea if she had ever played it before, but she played it blissfully with an added hint of her own flare. Maybe he wasn't completely wrong, not that it mattered.

>> <<

The crowd at Mandalay Bay was much younger and drunker than the regular types at the Golden Nugget. They dressed better and their waistlines were trimmer, more self-conscious, a prove-it-to-me gathering. Downtown was friendlier, more of an easy-going local crowd, people showed up for the music and to let go. At Mandalay people were looking for something beyond the songs, falsely casual. It was glamor seeking, at least at this private party, plenty of boomers in attendance mixing freely with the Gen X and Millennial set. There were suits among them as Torch had anticipated. The band had moved upmarket, two notches at least, whoever's party it was. Petrumi had delivered.

The beach party was as strange a fiasco as they come, but this was Vegas, so nothing was really strange. The outdoor stage overlooked the wave pool, periodic machine pumps rolling over the trucked-in sand, a simulated ocean-side dance floor ready for the taking. The lights overhead were bright, varied in hue, casting an endless spread of shadows across the pool deck and palms. The drinks were prepaid, the bar hosted by the mystery sponsor. Whatever was being pitched in the cabanas was nobody's business except buyer and seller. This was not the Nugget.

The band stood off to the side of the stage, waiting for their cue from the sound and light guy. The sound system surrounded the pool, more wattage than they had ever played. Synthia stood beside Victor, observing the sea of populated lounge chairs.

"You ready for this?" he asked.

"It's Set A, how ready do I need to be? We've played it a trillion times."

Victor surveyed the pool crowd in an endless loop. "Do you think we belong here? A classic cover band doesn't seem like the best fit for this place. Do the Mandalay people know who we are?"

"I don't think the management has a clue what we're doing here," said Synthia. "It's a private party and Petrumi shoehorned us in. Retro always works if you ease people into it. We've been at it long enough to make it work."

"Yeah, you seem to know what you're doing," replied Victor. "The original you played for me this afternoon, I've never heard anything like it. It's . . . what's the word I'm looking for? I guess, spectacular."

"Oh come on, it's a chord progression with a bridge, might be something there when it's a full package. But thanks, I accept the compliment. You're the database genius, right?"

"I think I found some lyrics that might work."

"No way, you came up with something that fast?"

"Maybe. I dug through some of my old stuff after our rehearsal broke up, remembered something that seems to fit. I could be wrong. I'm getting a lot wrong these days."

Victor pulled a folded page of lyrics from his pocket and handed it to Synthia. Her eyes locked onto the page like scripture at a holiday service.

"This is wild. Did you write this, Vic?"

"Most of it a long time ago. You reminded me of it. A friend helped me with the idea. I reworked it around your rhythm."

Synthia stared at the words in print. "It's . . . I don't know . . . reflective."

"Is that good? I mean, on par with spectacular?"

"Let me work on it tonight after the gig. I'll let you know. We have an important show to play first."

"Let's hope we're celebrating. This crowd looks different, way more than I imagined."

"Don't be nervous, Vic. We can play this crowd. Torch knows how to do it."

The stage went to dark preset, which was their cue. Synthia refolded the sheet of lyrics and stuffed it in her back pocket, then took her place behind the keyboard. The others followed her onstage and took their places. It needed to be a good night. It needed to be a good gig. It needed to move the band to the next level, wherever that was, however that was.

"Roll with the Changes," instructed Torch.

"REO Chuckwagon?" questioned Phil-Phil.

Victor could hear in Phil-Phil's voice that he was unusually anxious. He couldn't remember Phil-Phil ever second-guessing Torch. It was a standard from Set A that always worked, but did it fit the audience, especially to open?

Baker Bagley sounded even more uncertain. "You sure, boss? A lot of youth out there to start with an oldie like that."

"What I said is what we play," said Torch, never more certain in attitude. The Philosopher King had spoken the law.

Seconds later the PA announced: "Welcome to the beach at Mandalay Bay. On the main stage tonight, from downtown Las Vegas, From Nothing."

That was different. They were introduced by someone other than Torch, an omniscient voice from the booth. The stage lights came up hot and full. Synthia and Phil-Phil kicked it off together as they had so many times before. Right behind them were Baker

Bagley and Victor, 100% on key and together. The stage came alive as Torch took the mic under his command, solid in his skin, pouncing on the words:

As soon as you are able, woman I am willing

To make the break that we are on the brink of

Victor looked out on the beach. No one moved to the sand. There was no dancing. The crowd hardly noticed there was a band onstage. Torch was struggling to inject radiance into a lifeless interpretation of the failed opener.

Fine, that one didn't land. No worries, it was early, not enough drinks making their way from the bar. Torch called for Starship, still doing the show his way:

Find your way back.

Find your way back to her heart

Nothing. No reaction. Crickets would have chirped a more uplifting response. Stay cool, nix any panic, maintain presence. Next they tried "Twilight Zone" from Golden Earring, always a winner for them, an undulating beat that Torch made his own every time they played it:

Soon you will come to know

When the bullet hits the bone

No observable connection. People chatted politely but couldn't be moved from their schmoozing. Whatever conversation they were having with each other was more interesting than anything coming from the stage. It was death on the beach. If this had been *The Gong Show*, the gong would have been struck with a mangling swing of the mallet.

From Nothing held onto nothing. They had been onstage a half hour and no feet were moving on the sand. Not one tune was clicking. Wild Cherry died. Mitch Ryder was DOA. Santana was nada. INXS was flatter than the desert floor.

The band's material left the crowd cold. No one would dance. No one would listen. As Victor predicted, they were too canned, too staid, too forced, too predictable, too manufactured, TOO OLD SCHOOL! Autopilot wouldn't work with this crowd. It may not even have been the songs, just that they were coming out too rehearsed, like a Vegas standard, not a wake-up surprise. This crowd needed something spontaneous, something to talk about later. They needed their own version of fresh. Victor had never seen Torch struggle. The Act had nowhere to go. The worst of his fears had emerged. He was singing to stone cold silence. The hook had to be coming soon. The event promoter would fire the band on its first break and revert to a DJ with a hard drive.

It was time for Synthia to take the spotlight with Scandal. The evening so far hadn't even brought polite applause. They were background noise, easily ignored for chit chat or snide remarks. Victor knew there was no way Synthia wanted to sing to an ambivalent audience.

"We're dying," he whispered to her.

"Astute observation, Vic. I don't want my turn. I want out of here."

Victor stared at the lapping pool waves on the combed sand. "We can't abandon the stage. That's all people will remember, that we walked off. It will kill the band."

"You think we could try the new stuff?" Her words were uttered with an exhausted sigh.

"We don't know the new stuff."

"We can wing it. You'd be surprised what desperate musicians can do."

"Like this afternoon at rehearsal? Is that a good idea?"

"This band can play anything. I went through the cheat sheets after you left. I can carry the backbone on all that material if anyone strays. Ask Torch if he's up for it."

"Me ask Torch? He already wants to kill me."

"No, Phil-Phil wants to kill you. Never mind, I'll ask Torch."

In the silence, Synthia wandered over to Torch and whispered in his ear. He looked directly at Victor, then back at her. She sauntered toward Baker Bagley, who tipped his cap and nodded. She next went to Phil-Phil who twirled his drumsticks. Synthia was right. They could do it if they wanted. It was up to Torch.

Torch went back to Synthia and whispered in her ear. This time he wouldn't even look at Victor. She crossed back to Victor. "Torch says Peas."

"He can't sing it," said Victor.

"He can sing it. He didn't try before. Now he needs it. Come in straightaway and don't let it lag."

"You sure that's what Torch wants?"

"Or we could end our career here in front of a fake beach."

Victor saw Torch scowling at him as he returned to the microphone, then he turned to the crowd with that magazine cover smile.

"Gracious thanks for being in our company tonight. I'm Torch and we're your downtown party favorites, From Nothing. We're all warmed up and gonna shift gears a bit, try something new for us."

"Good call, Torch," said Victor softly.

"You better be right, Nowhere Prick."

Synthia led with the intro chords. In came Victor, Baker Bagley, and Phil-Phil. The crowd recognized it instantly. Younger energy. Stronger connection. Heads turned to the stage and slowly started nodding to the riff. The band was getting people's attention and the partygoers were headed to the sand. Torch pulled the mic from the stand with a sonic eruption:

I gotta feeling that tonight's gonna be a good night

That tonight's gonna be a good night

The tipping point tipped. Feet flocked to the water's edge. The dance shore was full. The crowd kicked up sand like a desert storm. Lights flooded onto the waterline and human movement was fluid. There would be a Mandalay party after all, with a downtown cover band in full force and acceptance.

Victor was in awe at the turnaround. He had never seen change take effect that quickly. The musicians beside him pulled off a world class rebound, no comparison to any of his prior bar bands when they died and tried to recover. Torch had scored with no time left on the clock. The audience was his and that was all he cared about. Torch turned to the band and mouthed "Tupac." Ignited anew, he stepped off the stage wireless and free-roaming, like so many nights at the Golden Nugget, only out on the sand and out on a limb with all-new material:

Let me welcome everybody to the wild, wild west

A state that's untouchable like Elliot Ness

Torch banked the memory of Tupac and shifted back to the familiar. He guided the band to merge from "California Love" into Marvin Gaye's "Heard It Through the Grapevine." Synthia and Baker Bagley vamped a full three minutes on the opening with Victor improvising on the fills. They were stealing back a classic. Torch was back on known terrain:

I bet you're wonderin' how I knew

'Bout your plans to make me blue

Victor wasn't sure what high note Torch had hit, but The Act went up an octave and took his audience with him. This dance beat was squarely in the Torch zone and the crowd loved him for it. The Act was alive and well, marching on the sand at Mandalay Bay. The cabanas emptied. The beach was full and the party was rotating into higher gear. Even Phil-Phil seemed exultant, stronger, more inventive than Victor had heard him keep the steady beat.

"Timbre, baby, timbre," said Torch as the song ended. He didn't have to hard sell anymore. He had managed to meet the crowd on its turf and swiftly they were his. The Act could sing anything. He was on a desert high. His voice was filled with vibrancy, expanding their surroundings into a pure concert experience.

They played Bruno Mars. They played Drake. They played Seal. They played Usher and Rihanna. They played John Legend and John Mayer. They played Imagine Dragons, Coldplay, and Green Day. They played Lady Gaga, Katy Perry, and Beyoncé. Late in the show they took a turn on Adele.

Sure the band was winging it, but no one knew that except them. Miraculously raw and untried, it all worked. Victor had never been part of anything like it.

Mixed in with the new material, they played Springsteen, Supertramp, and the Supremes. They played Patti Smith, Tom Petty, Tina Turner, Steve Miller, Joan Jett, George Thorogood, and Janis Joplin. They played Queen, Journey, Chicago, Temptations, Kiss, Clash, Sweet, Styx, Triumph, Police, and Pretenders. They played Fleetwood Mac, Steely Dan, Doobie Brothers, Bad Company, Three Dog Night, Bachman-Turner Overdrive, KC & The Sunshine Band, Electric Light Orchestra, and Traveling Wilburys.

Medleys and mashups, full songs and half songs; Set A and Set B were end to end, enshrined and expanded. They jammed. They soloed. They traded off. They reveled. Torch called out the titles freely one after another, nonstop scintillating without a break. Once he owned the space, everything was possible.

Toward the end of the celebration, Torch tossed Victor a bone, the Beatles' "While My Guitar Gently Weeps." It was his way of saying thank you, a familiar pick from Set A, a showcase for the guitarist. Victor appreciated the gift, but at that moment his head started ringing. He looked into the audience. No, make it go away. It can't be. Not now. He couldn't go dark in front of the beach crowd. He looked into the audience and was sure he saw Thomas Katem. Come on, no, this wasn't fair. Was God making another choice? Was the fork in the road a people mover off a cliff. No, No, No! Victor had saved the gig. There was no Thomas Katem there, just like there had been no Claire there.

Victor had to hold on. He breathed deeply and almost missed the transition to his moment, the opening solo enchantingly composed by George Harrison. Katem had to be cleared from his mind, but there he was on the sand. It was Katem. It wasn't Katem. Victor's mind was going blank, but he wasn't going to let it shut down. He found the lead line and saw George Harrison playing in his mind. Torch's voice held Victor in place like it did every night:

I don't know how someone controlled you
They bought and sold you

Do not black out. Stay with the band. Focus on the frets. This is too good to blow it. Don't blow this. He made this happen. He had to stay with it all the way.

This was no longer a private party. It was a tour de force exhibition, a masterpiece audition for whatever could elevate them to the next level. If someone important was out there—the secret host, the promotor, super-agents who controlled the A-list—the band was going to launch. Torch was certain they were out there and the band had proven itself. There was one more piece of business to deliver and they would be ready to ascend. They needed to play the finale.

Victor cleared his head. No Thomas Katem. No blackouts. He forced himself to stay in the moment. They had to finish the show strong. It had to happen. For Synthia. For Torch. Yes, for Baker Bagley and Phil-Phil. He owed them. He had to stay focused. Ignore the pain. Deny the pain. No collapsing. No seeing things. Global Harmonics was in a distant universe. Maurice Sangstrum, that scumbag, was in a distant universe. The hospital beating, McWhorter, Max, Clarence, Juan, Claire—they were all in a distant universe.

Stay in the moment. Stay in the beat. Head clear. Focus. Play like never before.

They had played it a thousand times before, ten thousand hours and all, but this time would be different. It was the first time the Mandalay crowd heard it and it had to sound like the first time anyone played it. Synthia came in from a different angle. Phil-Phil changed the fills on the tom-toms. Baker Bagley was punching the bassline in ways Victor had never heard him do it. Victor audaciously stood beside Torch and dared to share the spotlight with him. It may have been this time alone, but Torch was okay with that. He let the magical, soulful lyrics run:

Nothing from nothing leaves nothing

You gotta have somethin' if you wanna be with me

Then came the go-arounds, twenty minutes of skillful spontaneity. Synthia and Victor led off the improv as usual. Baker Bagley took an extra thirty-two bars. Phil-Phil lingered on an extended percussion run, durable footwork on the bass drum. Victor back to Synthia. Synthia back to Victor. Back and forth, forth and back. Torch took the wireless mic and harmonica to the pool's edge where he splash-danced with the crowd, boots kicked off, his bare feet in the lapping waves. They played the refrain over and over with the crowd sweating enough to replenish an aqueduct.

From Nothing couldn't have been better. They played a full five hours without taking a break. They had never sweated so much, individually or collectively, no one could tell if that was pool water, humidity, or sweat puddling on the stage. It didn't matter. It was a rout. Finally the lights came down. The playdate was done. They would play no encore despite the standing ovation. Professionals knew to go out on that high—to get the game-changing call—they had to leave the party wanting more. All that was left was to hear from Petrumi.

Suddenly Victor wondered if he had taken too many solos, more than his share. Was this a transient moment meant to end? Had he forced too much change? Was he taking too much credit? Would Torch hate him forever for being right?

The band had taken a step forward, but there was no way Victor could know if he had taken a step forward. The crowd stormed the stage. As the band made its way down the steps to mingle, each of them knew they had done their job. It was a perfect gig.

Victor felt his mobile vibrating. Could that be Petrumi? No, not possible, not that fast. He wouldn't have called Victor. He would have called Torch.

Victor pulled his mobile out and looked at the screen. It was a text from Thomas Katem. "Solid gig, Victor. Need to be in touch with you now. Important. Will work out the details ASAP."

It was the only thing that could have ruined it. He couldn't have imagined it, not an abdomen-cleaving dagger on that cue. It would have been better if he had blacked out and collapsed into the wave pool. Katem was there. His past was back to dispose of him. At that very moment of glory, it was already over, unless Victor found a way to duck it.

If Claire had been right about God, and she probably was, human roadmaps were meaningless. He wondered if Claire organically understood what an oddball, disarming, ironic sense of humor God chose to wield on demand. Artists could act on whim to alter any short-term fate. Creativity was choice, an easy dodge out of the way of implosion. God's choices were deliberate, never spontaneous, all invisible and big picture. No one could compete with the high-impact divine.

Oh yeah, it had been a *good, good night*. A big night. The biggest! The band had rescued itself from oblivion. Then the curtain call yanked Victor back to a reinvented oblivion. It was Oblivion: The Sequel. Purgatory was naturally resilient, abundant in the innovation of setbacks. Dylan had been prescient: *Knock, knock, knockin' on heaven's door.* A few years later the upshot: *You're gonna have to serve somebody.* Claire would call it purpose, destiny, eternally a reason we could never understand. There was no humor there, none at all. The lessons were His to determine, ours to learn. She would never find that funny. That was why she would always be happier than him.

TRACK 9: ORIGINAL SYN

Victor had been right about Mandalay Bay. He knew the audience would be different. They needed something different. He connected the dots with a star DJ's vision and a sly bartender's mastery of mixology. His intuition—the sum of all his life's input and learning—miraculously served him well with everything on the line. Performing elegantly across a blind arc was a matter of deconstructing data, internalizing the full environment, normalizing its intricacies, and only then determining the path to an experience.

He had bought himself another day, but he wasn't sure how far he could ride that goodwill. He led Torch to make the right song choices, but his relationship with Torch remained incomplete. Neither of them had healed from a life of abandonment. Neither would ever fully trust the other. They were becoming useful to each other, creatively codependent, but Torch was a wizard who cast spells, Victor a seer who sourced their components. Torch could do what Victor could portend, and that put Torch miles up the food chain. Victor marveled at how nimble the band's performance became as soon as Torch committed to it. They could play anything, rehearsed or unrehearsed, from any canon of memory that could be translated into seven notes arranged in endless variation. Victor dissected compositions, but his bandmates were artists. The best he could do was keep up, excavating craftsmanship that extended outward to listening souls and lit up fragile lives.

An audience was built of aura, alive in its listening habits populated over time. How strange it was that the music people favored defined them in so many ways—what they liked, what they rejected, what stuck with them from their school years, what they kept, what they burned into memory, what they let go. How was it that what they heard in a single decade—for most, their second on the planet—encoded a set of remembrances that stayed with them forever? It was simply commercial output, a business after all, nothing more than that—song factories a few years removed from Tin Pan Alley. It wasn't Beethoven or Mozart, but it was glue—happy and sad, lived and imagined, the soundtrack of youth became the soundtrack of peoples' lives. How outrageously peculiar and powerful a force these random songs became. These manufactured bits of the ephemeral, of sound become thing, became permanent in personal histories. Resonant memories could be made to work to unlimited advantage.

Victor couldn't let that go. He was sitting again at breakfast in the Claim Jumper, back at the Golden Nugget after the band's incredible night at Mandalay Bay. He was entranced not so much with their actual stage performance but with its impact, its visceral connection with all those feet dancing in the rolling waves. The band was hot. Torch had delivered. Synthia held them together. The broadened set list made it happen. The database in Victor's mind was the database in the crowd's collective mind. Not genius, but insight, mindfully curated awareness. They relived those long ago days. A few drinks, a few joints, and boom, spontaneous celebration. What was better than being young with an entire life of hope ahead of you?

Nothing was more powerful than hope. That was Claire's ideal, what she saw in God, what God saw in us—joyous potential. Nothing was more motivating than an unconstrained future. That was what the music held for anyone who touched it, anyone who sweated it. That was the hard drive of memories left behind, making possible the hope for memories to be made.

The songs in Victor's head were not unique, but the mix was meant to be shared. These were his songs, the songs he had made his own by selecting them and applying context. The gift he discovered was something else, the same something that had put Global Harmonics on the map. The points of connection were not the same for everyone, but everyone could latch onto points of connection. Everyone could feel something if they let themselves feel it. It might be hip hop. It might be metal. It might be a bubblegum ballad. Each moment mattered. The dots could be connected and connection could be earned in the collective beat. The mashup of adolescence in anyone could be awakened from dormancy if the words were sung to them in the proper moment. The listener's foot would begin to tap the ground rhythmically, forcing them to remember and relive those awkward teenage blues.

How else could you explain Elvis impersonators? Beatles tribute bands? Rod Stewart wannabees? Motown revivals? All those covers, all that cheese? It wasn't cheese if you treated the material with respect, if you bypassed mockery in deference to authentic passion. You never made fun of what you copied. You rendered it as your own to rekindle its emotional center, its origin in time, the context that empowered it with authority. Heraclitus offered a provocative point of view, but so did Torch. Everyone needed to belong, and the best place to belong was the years from which taste and preference emerged.

Get back, get back to where you once belonged.

Billy Preston played on that track, too—with the Beatles, the actual Beatles, all four of them barely thirty years old. A half century later, Beatles facsimiles were ubiquitous. Self-trained copycats with silly mop-top wigs that looked nothing like the Fab Four were easily forgiven for tearful nostalgia. Mick Jagger was still on the road acting like he was twenty at seventy. The Stones had been touring the same material for five decades, an impossible attraction that always sold tickets. Genuine or tribute, they all sold mountains of souvenirs from the gift shop 365 days each year. Childhood was childhood for life, no one could steal that hard drive. It followed everyone. It was renewed with every generation, every half generation. Its power could not be underestimated. Its influence and potential to unlock dreams could never be denied.

From Nothing now had a runway, a gift of the collective embrace. All the moving parts weren't in perfect order, but they were unpacked and out of the box, a puzzle to assemble under the spotlight. All the band needed was a single unrealized something to become current and join the perpetual canon. Victor knew he could help. He wanted to help. He had to help.

This time no one onstage noticed his near meltdown. Their weak start at the beach party was forgotten as quickly as they turned the corner. They had been consumed in the moment. The reaction to the beach party gig was beyond Torch's expectations. As he predicted, the right people had been there and heard them. The band's range, its combustion, the capabilities of each musician were all on display. Musicality was in broad evidence, Tupac and Marvin Gaye to Katy Perry and the Preston finale. It had been a wild night.

When Petrumi called late that night with the offer, Torch confessed for the first time in his life he had been made speechless. The secret sponsor throwing the party was Joe Walsh. He had been hidden away somewhere listening, hanging out with the all-star band he had assembled for a gig next Monday. From Nothing had been offered a slot to open for Walsh's band in Los Angeles at The Greek.

NFW. Joe Walsh at The Greek. Up at the top of the world, abutting the Griffith Park Observatory where James Dean would forever be an apparition.

It was incomprehensible. It was supernatural. Walsh got the idea a classic cover band would set the proper mood for his show and added it to the card, just like that. It was a miracle, except that it wasn't. Guys like Walsh could make that kind of thing happen without a second thought. Torch had called Victor with the news an hour ago and said he wanted to meet with him. He would be along anytime now. Victor wasn't sure if he would be gleeful, envious, or evasive. He would be Torch, but with that brief phone call and the words "Walsh at The Greek," Victor surmised he was still in the band.

Victor looked up from his breakfast and surveyed the casino floor around him. As usual, even at this hour there were players. They were low-stakes players, but they were as hypnotized as the big-money night players. Maybe they would come to the show tonight for Set A. Maybe they would file for bankruptcy on their way home. He never played the tables in Vegas. It reminded him too much of his problem with trading stocks. Sometimes he wondered if he could sit at a table and play one hand, win or lose, to convince himself he didn't need to play the risk game anymore, that he could live with what he had. No, that would be a mistake. Stocks had no more upside for him, especially since he had no more income to squander. A hand of blackjack, what would that prove? It would turn him, a borderline exile coercing himself to redemption, into one of them, again a victim. The Greek Theatre was there for the taking. Walsh had asked them to the meat-eater's ball. Getting that right was risk enough. He had to clear all the obstacles from his path, clear his head, not let the weakness of his past sway him from the trail.

The reality of success was clear. The reality of no-value risk was equally clear. The reality of distraction was to be avoided. Every treasure chest of thrills was punctured with holes by design. The casino was a reality, an existential threat to the naïve. Torch had warned him against it. So far so good. No blackjack, no stocks, no coming off the rails. Not this far along the tracks. Back to his coffee. Back to envisioning The Greek.

Standing in Victor's way at the moment was the unwanted appearance of Thomas Katem. There he was in plain sight. Reality emerged out of the ether and invited himself to the breakfast table. That wasn't good. That was the kind of drama that Torch told Victor to steer past. Victor would have to work rapidly to escape Katem before Torch arrived.

Katem didn't ask for permission to join Victor. He sat down beside him with the privilege of oligarchy. Manners meant little to the ruling class. He already had secured a cup of coffee.

"Nice surprise seeing you in Las Vegas," said Victor.

"You look good, Victor. Last time we were together you looked a bit scary, like the Elephant Man. You've healed considerably."

"You think?"

"You sounded terrific last night. Looked like you were having fun."

"Beats the hell out of getting beaten up in a karaoke bar. You've been silent and out of my life a long time. I figured the deal was dead."

"No, not dead. Sometimes these things take longer than you think they will. Nothing in business happens fast enough." "My exit came fast."

"Yes, that's true. Getting close to your return though. I think you'll agree our version of the Witness Protection Program has been a success, exactly as promised."

"What if I don't want to come back?"

"Come on, you want to do this for the rest of your life?"

"Do this, as in play music? Maybe." Victor took a sip of his coffee. It was cold and he wished he had a new cup, but there wasn't much opportunity to step away cleanly at the moment.

"I hear you have a new gig on the horizon, something phenomenal."

"You're obviously dialed in."

"Yeah, remember, Petrumi was my college roommate. You do recall how all this came together, right?"

"Someone pulling all the strings. You know Joe Walsh, too."

"Nah, that's Petrumi. You earned that. It will be a fitting swan song for you."

"A going away present, even if I don't want to go away."

"This isn't your life, Victor. Global Harmonics is your life. Two months ago you knew that. Have you forgotten?"

"Maybe I've changed. It happens."

"I don't think so. I think you're caught up in the moment. Here's the deal. We have a settlement conference planned in LA next Tuesday. You play the gig Monday night, then you make an appearance at our meeting Tuesday."

"Tuesday I have to be back here to play Set A."

"I don't think that will be necessary. Petrumi is working on your replacement. You play the gig, then you make a surprise appearance at our settlement conference."

"What is a settlement conference as it pertains to Global Harmonics?"

"You're going to testify in front of a mediator that Sangstrum and McWhorter colluded to defraud their shareholders. Sangstrum tried to sell the company below fair market price. We have a shareholder class action pending against the transaction. A judge saw merit enough to grant an injunction and the principals opted for a chance to work it out. Once you expose them and reveal that you're also willing to testify in court, they'll sell the company to a private equity fund that I represent. They will make you CEO like I promised."

"This is what you had in mind?"

"Yes, this is what we had in mind. A full-fledged class action would ruin both Sangstrum and McWhorter. Sadly if we went through with it, it would also ruin the company. This way Sangstrum and McWhorter take home a little dough for their trouble, we withdraw the lawsuit, and you get to be the man. Legal, quiet, and simple."

"What if I don't want to do it anymore?"

"I guess all your friends at the company will lose their jobs and the company will be broken up into pieces. Your code won't mean much in an asset sale."

"You're sure the company is still worth buying?"

"At a fire sale price falling out of deal collapse? Absolutely! And we're confident you know how to fix it. My client takes it private, you shore it up, and in a year we flip it at a monster premium. Home run, including for you."

"I want to stay in the band."

"Not an option. This was temporary. I parked you here. You don't seem to be remembering things well. Are you having medical complications?"

"Let's not go there. I want to play music, not go back to business."

"I'm delighted you enjoyed your respite. Problem is, whether you join with us in this action or not, your gig at The Greek is going to be your last."

"You're calling all the shots, huh?"

"I don't think of it that way. I'm thinking of it more as guiding you to the right decision. Incidentally, have you heard anything from Sangstrum?"

"Not for several weeks, maybe longer. He called once. Then I never heard from him."

"Offered you a bunch of money in exchange for your silence?"

"You do have your finger on the pulse."

"Don't let it phase you, Victor. When we unload Global Harmonics in a year, you'll make many times what Sangstrum offered you. I am pretty certain of that."

Victor was silent a moment. He knew Torch was on his way and he should walk away from Katem, but he couldn't resist the chance to get some clarity. "May I ask a question?"

"Sure, you can ask. Not sure I can answer, but I'll do my best." The sound of Katem's voice was infinitely stoic.

"I'm sure you will. Who beat the crap out of me and said they were you?"

"Right, that. As you were informed, they were professionals. Hired hands, nothing more."

"Who hired them?"

"Is this necessary, Victor?"

"If you want my help, it's necessary."

Katem took a breath. He remained emotionless, but he was having a hard time maintaining eye contact with Victor. That didn't necessarily mean he was lying, more that he was trying to appease Victor while avoiding unneeded conflict. "Victor, are you familiar with a company called MSE?"

"MusicSense Enterprise? Of course. They're the biggest competitor to Global Harmonics, international rollup of music tech platforms. They're ten times our size, only we're bigger in the US."

Katem now looked at Victor directly. "They wanted to buy Global Harmonics. They wanted a seat at the table, to be part of the auction."

"An auction would have been in Sangstrum's interest. It would have driven up the company's value. If they pushed it above Sangstrum's strike price, he would have made money on the exit."

"Yes, an auction would have been in Sangstrum's interest, except for the kickback that he was getting from McWhorter, cash to be placed in an offshore account, far more valuable than his stock options, which he had incentive to leave underwater."

"So they were being frozen out by an inside deal. What did that have to do with me?"

"McWhorter was going to buy Global Harmonics at a manufactured discount and then turn around and sell it to MSE at a premium. It didn't have to be a distressed asset, they painted it that way and set themselves up as a temporary middleman, adding no value but controlling the transaction. MSE was trying to get in the room to bypass the layer, but Sangstrum wouldn't allow it. McWhorter was Sangstrum's exit strategy, not the company's best path. You didn't hear it from me and you could never trace it, but MSE hired some guys to rough you up. They wanted to make it look like McWhorter had done it for sticking your nose in his business, to stop the deal in its tracks when your beating was investigated."

"But you told me to leave town, that I'd come back later as CEO."

"Yes, that's what happened, because MSE told their thugs to drop my name, because my firm had failed to get them to the table, and it was our job to deliver you to them. We had a better idea. Put together a class action against Global Harmonics, utilize you as our star witness, have one of our PE clients buy up the remains of Global Harmonics, fix it, and then sell it to MSE at a monster payday."

"Don't you have a fiduciary duty to your original client, MSE?"

"Sort of, until they find the edge of the law. Then it's a negotiation. We knew what MSE had done where you were concerned and told them some distance might be in their best interest."

"You mean a single deal fee wasn't enough for you, even though the whole point was for you to get them back to the table."

"This is the way it had to be, Victor. They had no choice when we explained the facts. So here we are."

"Is there anything you won't do to make a deal happen?"

"It's a mighty big payday, Victor, including for you, and you get to help us stiff both McWhorter and Sangstrum. All you have to do is tell the truth."

"About Sangstrum? Not MusicSense? Not about getting beaten to a pulp?"

"Ancient history, pal. That's a big part of why we had to get you out of town for a while, so you could look presentable and not put any stink on MSE for their unfortunate misdeed. Sangstrum and McWhorter don't know that you got beat up, just that you disappeared and that you know they colluded. You are their worst fear in this lawsuit. As soon as they see you on our side, their deal is dead, ours proceeds, and you're the new boss."

"Until the next sale, and you get the fee for brokering that as well."

"Yes, until the next sale to the guys that had you roughed up. You'll sell to them and be gone, so no bad blood. You'll never meet them."

"Two bites of the apple for you."

"Something like that, but who's counting?"

Victor sat stunned, staring into his cold coffee. How much of this was true? How far could he be manipulated? Could anyone in this food chain be trusted? What happened after he sold to MSE—was he back where he started, with nothing to show for it but a quick run as a puppet CEO and a bank account filled with heartless cash? He didn't want it. He didn't want any of it. He wanted to be free of it. He wanted to be in the band, but that wasn't his either.

That had been manufactured as well, to give his wounds enough time to heal so he could appear at a settlement conference without fresh bruises.

Victor wasn't sure what to say, what to do. He was outgunned, outmaneuvered, less than a pawn in this chess match. He badly needed air. It was a blessing when Torch showed up in his running sweats, the Philosopher King arriving majestically beside the chain restaurant table.

"Am I interrupting something?" asked Torch, unsuspecting any element of the negotiation in front of him over waffle scraps.

Katem rose from the table. "No, I was leaving. Victor, I'll be in touch in LA."

"Of course you will," responded Victor.

"Heck of a show, friend. You have talent." Katem never made eye contact with Torch as he trailed his way into the casino. Torch watched him make his way through the small morning crowd, waiting for an explanation from Victor, but none came without prodding.

"Who was that, Nowhere Man?"

"A guy from my prior life. Don't worry, it doesn't matter."

"Drama? You know what Aristotle said in *Poetics* about drama? He said it's all fake, so don't waste your time on it. It's an imitation of what matters, so don't be getting beaten down by a bad copy of reality."

"No drama," avowed Victor.

"You bet no drama. You stick with the Philosopher King, this city state stays strong, repels the bad guys. You're listening, right? The Act knows the stage."

"I am crystal clear on that, boss. Can we get out of here?"

"Sure thing, let's go for a walk. Focus our consciousness on items that matter."

Victor got up from the table and looked around to see if Katem was lurking nearby, listening in on their conversation, further plotting his exploitation and demise. His neck nearly snapped in reflex, startled by the sound of the automated slots clanging out a new winner. Katem was long gone.

>> <<

Victor followed Torch out of the Claim Jumper and across the casino floor, toward the exit doors of the Golden Nugget. They stepped out onto the Fremont Street Experience, one of the oddest indoor-outdoor malls of all time, a covered plaza, which had replaced most of the original downtown Fremont Street with a perpetual pedestrian party zone. An archway covered the promenade with locals and tourists zip-lining the length of the Experience above them. The first time Victor walked beneath fee-for-flight humans soaring above the twenty-four hour carnival of cocktails he found it unnatural. Now it was normal. That was Vegas. The otherworldly rapidly normalized into everyday occurrence. Vegas got under your skin and altered preconceived notions of weirdness. Nothing in Vegas was weird. The mitigating variable was price.

At the end of the Fremont Street Experience they reached the remaining vestiges of the old Fremont Street still in decay, then turned onto Las Vegas Boulevard. A few miles to the south, it would become the Strip. Here the pawn shop roadway was the opening artery to downtown. Victor felt it unusually warm for this time of morning, this late in the year, or was it? He immediately began sweating. Torch showed no signs of sweat. He seldom did. Their marathon performance the night before was a rarity in that regard.

Victor wiped his brow with the half sleeve of his lavender polo shirt, a leftover from some trade show he couldn't remember. "We headed anywhere in particular?"

"Going to the Chapel of Love. You can escort me to my moonlighting gig." Torch saw that Victor was dripping, distracted, almost in a daze. "You okay, Nowhere? You got no color in your face, not like that kitschy shirt. That debonair dude shake you down for some dough?"

Victor wiped his forehead again and forced out a response. "I'm alright. You're not going to make me run, are you? I didn't eat much."

"Whatever you want, Nowhere Man. I'm okay with walking."

They walked for half a mile, both uncharacteristically silent. Victor knew he needed to start the conversation. He wasn't sure he had the energy, but he needed to move forward.

"You're mad at me, right?"

"For having all the answers? A little. I'll get over it. The Walsh gig is a healthy healing mechanism."

"Why did you want to see me this morning?"

"I was thinking about change, Nowhere. What comes next? What do we do next?"

"You mean what do we play at The Greek?"

"You got a knack for curation. The floor is open to ideas. Got something in mind?"

Victor slowed their walking pace to a crawl. He was perspiring heavily and knew he needed to proceed with caution. "You ever do Prince?"

"Wanted to be Prince my whole life, never had the guts to sing him. I guess after Tupac anything is possible."

Victor caught his breath. That was unexpected, much too easy. Was Torch coming to trust him? Maybe this was a breakthrough. He needed to ride the wave, build their rapport. "Your Beyoncé wasn't bad either. I thought you'd leave that one for Synthia but you nailed it."

"Here's the thing, Guitar Hero: we gotta get our signals straight. I think you like it in this band, but this is my band. You can't be making me less than I am or it's not going to hold together."

"I thought you were happy getting the gig at The Greek."

"Outcome is cool. Process is shit. We gotta fix that. Plus Petrumi got us the gig, not you. You helped, I'll give you that, but you gotta get your head on straighter. I saw you struggling up there toward the end. You going dizzy again?"

"I kept it together. I didn't miss a note."

"You almost did." Torch paused, then struck deadly. "You and Synthia, that's a thing?"

"No, I told you before. We're working on a song together. That's all of it."

"Yeah, she told me. She wants to put it in the show."

"What do you think?" Victor was as hopeful as he had ever been.

"I'm thinking about it. It's a big move. If it works, we're the real deal, might lock in Walsh's attention. If it craps out, we're a cover band that embarrassed itself in front of an LA crowd. Not my idea of a launching pad."

"Have you heard it?"

"Not yet. Is it done?"

"No, she's still working on it."

"I hope she puts it in my range."

"It wasn't written for you, Torch. It was written for her."

"That's a problem. If we're gonna do an original at The Greek, I should sing it. I don't care who writes it, but I should sing it."

It occurred to Victor why they were out walking. Torch wanted the original for himself. He knew they needed an original to break out beyond cover band status, a hit they could ride to celebrity, but he wasn't willing to lose the spotlight to Synthia if it rocketed. Nothing with Torch was straightforward, but his message became clear when he wanted it to be clear. They were most of the way there, but not complete.

"Is Synthia cool with that?" asked Victor.

"I haven't told her yet. It's gonna be your idea. That's how you get right with me. You get her to see the light, and then you fix it so it works for me. Timbre, baby, timbre."

"I'm not right with you even after The Greek?"

"You want her? This is how you make it right with me." Torch was still not being straightforward, but at least he was being clear.

"I told you, Torch, we're not . . ."

"Words, Nowhere Man, a copy of a copy. Don't try to fake me. I get the song, I cut you a break. Everyone has what they want. She'll get over it. She knows how The Act works."

There was no sense arguing with Torch. He had made up his mind. "I get it, Torch. We'll make the song work for you."

"It's going to sound just right next Monday at The Greek. That's gonna be something. Opening for Joe Walsh. The Greek, my friend, the Temple of LA Almighty. We are called to rise. The Philosopher King ascends."

They arrived at the nondescript driveway for the Elvis Chapel of Love. It didn't look like it started out life as a church, but an A-frame of white shingles and a contoured aluminum steeple had been grafted above the roofline of the single-story, standalone stucco cabin structure. It had to be fifty or sixty years old, maybe older, all two thousand square feet of it, but it wore a recent coat of bright pink paint, none of it peeling. Beside the stained glass door—The King in multi-color silhouette, no less—was a friendly welcoming plaque with the hours of operation, 10:00 a.m. to 10:00 p.m., off-hours booking also available for special engagements. A faux wood-paneled station wagon and a shiny red Ford F-150 pickup adorned in white tissue paper were parked in the small chained lot behind. There were also two mid-sized limos parked there, one white, one black, both prom night ten-seaters with the chapel's logo magnet mounted on the driver's side doors. Their drivers must have been waiting inside.

"You make the big money here?" asked Victor without any hint of judgment.

"This is my 401k. We get a road tour, we come off the road with that money plus what I've saved, I'm going to buy this place in few years. I'll be singing "Can't Help Falling in Love" into my nineties, training a generation of newbies to fill in around me, but instead of getting paid per wedding certificate, I'm gonna keep it all."

That was Torch's plan. That was his long envisioned endgame. He wasn't looking to score going to the next level on tour. He was looking to raise capital to invest, to make enough money to buy his nest egg and do Elvis forever—or employ Elvises forever. The revelation was unmistakable. It was Torch as only Torch could see building on The Act.

"I guess Elvis is as close as we get to eternity," said Victor. "We all crave memories."

"Only if you know the secret, Nowhere Man. The secret is authenticity. We never mock The King. We become The King. People travel here from all over the world because Elvis is as much in their heart as the person they want to marry or the love they want to marry again. The voice of The King resonates in their imagination, his image emblazoned beside their image. A love song of long ago, a photo made permanent today, that's love transformed to the enchanted. Come on in, I'll show you how that which is genuine creates cash every fifteen minutes."

Torch opened the glass door to a festive high five from a fellow about his same build, ten or so years his senior, white dude with Elvis pompadour slicked, another wedding officiant, possibly the current establishment owner. Victor was about to follow Torch into the few rows of pews ahead when he felt his mobile vibrating in his pocket. He needed to see who was calling him. Could it be Katem again so soon? Petrumi telling him he was about to be canned like

Katem had said? Synthia telling him she had finished the song but what did it matter now?

"I gotta get dressed and work up my hair for the first ceremony," conveyed Torch. "You coming?"

Victor reached for his phone. No, this call wasn't an ordinary surprise. It was beyond expectation. Victor's heart rate felt like it doubled, his chest muscles pulling away from his ribcage. On the caller ID screen in clear text appeared the name Devin McWhorter.

"I'll catch up with you in a few minutes, Torch."

"In a few minutes I'll be up a hundred bucks. Be quiet when you come in, especially on "Love Me Tender." Gratuities are generated by tears. That's my specialty. If you change your mind and need to work on that song for me, no worries, I understand."

Torch slipped into the humble chapel. The elder Elvis who greeted Torch saluted Victor and closed the stained glass door behind them. On closer inspection Victor saw in the etching a composite of Graceland, Priscilla, scenes from *Jailhouse Rock* and *Blue Hawaii*, all framed by flower leis and a ring of gold records. Rapt in the ancestry, he stood to the side of the driveway and answered his phone.

"McWhorter, really?"

"Victor, you remember me. That's a good thing."

"I broke your jaw with my laptop. It's a pleasant image I've permanently encoded. What do you want?"

"Victor, we won't ever be friends, but that doesn't mean we can't do business so I'll get to the point. I understand you may be invited to a meeting next Tuesday with Maurice Sangstrum and myself. I would like for you not to be at that meeting."

"Have you discussed this with Sangstrum?"

"No, we're not talking to each other at the moment on the advice of counsel. I know he offered you a small sum to sign an NDA and you refused. I respect that. I need you to do three things: not show up for the meeting, not speak about your relationship with Global Harmonics in any capacity, and after your performance at The Greek, stay out of California for a year while the dust settles."

"You know about The Greek?"

"We know about a lot of things. In exchange for your compliance, I am willing to pay you $10 million. Stay with the band, follow their fate, have a ball. You also can't discuss this with Sangstrum as that would be collusion, an argument we are currently working hard to counter. Do you have all that?"

Victor's eyes became fixed on the minuscule engraving of The King on a Harley. He had no idea what to say. Ten million dollars to stay with the band and separate himself once and for all from these scumbags, leaving his former co-workers to fend for themselves at the mercy of these scumbags. Did he have all that? "Yes, I have all that."

"And . . . ?"

"I'll think about it."

"That's all I can ask. Thank you, Victor. I know you're smart and it looks like you're onto a fine new career in the arts. This should accelerate your trajectory to independence."

"You'll hear from me before the meeting if we have a deal. I suppose I can dial back this number and give you an account number for the wire transfer. If we do this I want full payment in advance."

"How will I know that you won't show up at the meeting after I transfer the money?"

"There will be lawyers there. I will leave the money in the account and if I burn you then you can tell them I hacked you and stole it. I'm guessing that would freeze the account on the spot, assuming I lied to you."

"You are a smart man, Victor. I look forward to your call."

"I said I would think about it. I'm not there yet."

Victor disconnected the line, releasing the hyena back to his hunt. He was sweating again heavily, even more than after his meeting with Katem. He heard the beauty of Torch's voice bleeding through the pink walls over a karaoke song bed of "Love Me Tender." Timbre, baby, timbre.

He thought about entering the Elvis Chapel of Love to observe affection still alive, life vows exchanged in harmony, decade old renewals creating "a forever moment" as advertised on the chapel entry sign. He considered going inside to pray, taking Claire at her word and seeking higher guidance with all earthly logic escaping him. The material world was failing him. The voice of Elvis was as sincere and authentic as any sound he could imagine.

He changed his mind. Torch had been gallant, inviting him to his sacred refuge, but Victor would have to take a rain check. He headed north again on Las Vegas Boulevard, back toward the Fremont Experience and the Golden Nugget. He had a lot of work to do, especially with Synthia on the song.

>> <<

It was a roasting, sweaty walk back to downtown. When Victor arrived at the Golden Nugget, he sat outside by the pool for a long time where the midday sun grew brutally hotter with each passing minute. Hamstrung by consciousness. Adrift in contemplation. He knew that calling Claire was probably the worst idea in the world, but he had to tell her about The Greek. If there was any chance she might come see him play, that would be a healing moment. He couldn't leave it alone.

When she picked up the phone, he knew instantly he had made a huge mistake. She recognized his voice in the first spoken syllable.

"Victor, why are you calling me?"

"I'm sorry, I thought you might want to hear my voice."

"It's been a lifetime, Victor. I'm married."

"I know. I saw that on LinkedIn. You changed your name. I wanted to tell someone, to tell you . . . I'm with a band. I'm playing The Greek."

"You're playing music again? That's wonderful."

"Yeah, I lost my job and then connected with this Vegas cover band. They're incredible, big time rising stars, gargantuan bit of luck. We're actually opening for Joe Walsh if you can believe that. It's a long story. I'd love to tell you the whole thing."

Victor heard the call waiting prompt on his phone. He looked at the screen. It was Synthia. She must have been ready to play the finished song for him. He let her go to voicemail.

"Victor, it's not a great idea for you to call me."

"I know. I wanted to tell you about the gig. I mean, it's a big gig. I was thinking . . ." He paused. He didn't know if he should say it, if he should ask it. She was married. It would be a problem for her to come, but why should it be? It was her marriage. If she was happily married, surely she could come to see him play. She could bring her husband. Of course she could. No, that wouldn't work. Not at all.

"You were thinking . . . ?" Claire broke the silence. He had to ask or hang up.

"I don't know, I was thinking I could give you my VIP tickets. I only get two. I have to give them to someone. Or sell them, which would be funky."

Victor was lying. There had been no mention of VIP tickets. He would have to buy them, probably cost him the whole take from the gig. So what? It was worth it completely.

"You want me to come to The Greek?"

"Yeah, I mean, it's right there in LA. Wouldn't be a big deal."

"It would be a very big deal. I told my husband about our relationship. It's in the past. It has to stay in the past."

Victor's call waiting interrupted him again. He hoped Claire couldn't hear it. Why would Synthia call him twice in two minutes? Strange, but he let it go to voicemail again.

"I understand." Victor was looking for something better to say but didn't know what that would be. "You're right, it probably wouldn't work. It would be complicated."

"It would be extremely complicated. I'm glad you understand."

"No worries. I'll sell off the tickets or give them to groupies. I'm overdue for groupies, don't you think?"

"You're too old for groupies. Give them to someone who loves music. You know a lot of people who'd want to be there."

Victor was silent. Even if he did have a pair of VIP tickets, he didn't know anyone who would want to be there other than for the headliner. He felt that aloneness—desert island dreary aloneness headed into The Greek Theatre of all places. He pictured her on the other end of the line, healthy and effervescent in her happy new life, the timeless Edwardian cross forever grounding her in calm. He had lost some weight, but not enough. At least he didn't look as hideous as he had two months ago.

"Are you okay, Victor? I didn't mean to hurt your feelings."

"No, it's fine. It's good to hear your voice, really good. You still doing that, I don't know, thinking a lot about God?"

"I do all the time. Did any of it rub off on you?"

"You'd be surprised. Happily surprised."

"That's good to hear. God will protect you, same as He protects me. We all make choices, but God loves us the same whether we're right or wrong."

"Yeah, choices. I've thought about that a lot. Sometimes you don't even know you're making one that matters. You don't see the fork in the road until years after you've picked a path. Then it's too late. You already decided."

"It's never too late to pick a new path. Every day you can start over if you want. You have to decide to do it. Make a new choice, and that's a new fork in the road, no matter where it leads you."

"But it's too late for some things, right? That happens no matter what you choose."

"Sometimes, but make it a good thing, not a bad thing. You can always change courses if you want. If you're supposed to make a change, you'll do it. God wants what's best for us and already knows what we don't, how it's going to turn out." She waited for Victor to talk, but he had no response. "Good luck with your show, Victor. Good luck with the new band."

"They're a good group. I'm having fun. I'm sorry if I bothered you."

"You didn't bother me. I'll tell a few old friends about the gig. They'll go. People will be there. You won't be alone. Goodbye, Victor."

"Goodbye, Claire." There was something about her words that were final. He had to find a way to accept that goodbye as their last.

As soon as Victor disconnected his mobile beeped. He looked at the screen. Two messages, both from Synthia. He took a breath and hit playback.

"Vic, hey, hope everything is okay with Torch. I've been working on the song, the words you gave me. I switched around some of the lyrics, but it's coming together. Let me play it for you. Call this final cut one." The phone went dead. She must have lost him and called back.

Victor played back the second message and heard Synthia play the familiar song intro on her electronic keyboard. She had laid down a telecom recording of her song, which now was their song. Damn, she had pulled it off, his lyrics brought to life:

Joys from a balcony, sitting on a ledge
Together we are silent, wary of the edge
Overhearing echoes, the many words we've said
But were we only playing?
Waiting for a lifetime, no childhood to leave
The veranda set before us, please no longer grieve
This hideout is forever, we chose here to believe
But were we only playing?
I greeted you, I say goodbye
Our dreams and memories lift high
I pray for more, you only cry
But were we only playing?
Leaving soon, I sit and stare
Not moving up or being there
Wishing the eyes of Shakespeare
But were we only playing?

Simply enough he titled it "Playing." Claire would never hear the song, though it had long ago been her idea. Victor hit the save button for voicemail on his mobile. He thought back to his call with Claire. He thought of Synthia the first time he met her in his standard queen hotel room with the blackout curtains open. He thought of The Greek. He had some work to do with Torch. There was no way Torch was going to sing that. It wasn't for him.

"Playing" would be the band's first original song if only it didn't die before it was born. His head filled with that daunting old adage: You want to make God laugh? Tell him your plans.

TRACK 10: THE TEMPLE ASCENSION BECKONS

THE FIRST TIME VICTOR PLAYED IN PUBLIC WAS ON THE STREET. He knew he was invisible. He wasn't homeless but you couldn't tell that to passersby. He was busking in Westwood, as safe a place as he could imagine, to see if anyone would listen when he played. The acoustics were awful with endless cars motoring by, dodging pedestrians in the crosswalks. Every unplugged chord he played was muffled by the pavement. There was no echo, no reverb, just plain flat sound.

He was twenty at the time, still working through his extended freshman year at UCLA on generous loans and grants, gratefully applying the government investment that saved his life. A few people did stop and listen, but what he found most disturbing was that no one would look him in the eye. Even the people who did toss a few coins into his open guitar case wouldn't make eye contact with him. There was safety in keeping distance from a vagrant, a street musician who might or might not be aspiring to higher elevation. As long as people didn't make eye contact with him, he would never be human.

Victor figured if he could hold an audience of any kind on a public street, everything after that would be an improvement in the profession. He was mostly right. He thought of that whenever he walked by someone homeless or who looked to be homeless. He would force himself to make eye contact, to ensure himself that someone asking for a handout was human no matter how ragged they appeared, no matter how long it had been since they'd bathed. The streets of Las Vegas were filled with the homeless during daylight hours. At night, they somehow disappeared. The classy hookers took their place, or the guys handing out coupons for less classy strip clubs. The homeless could only hang out as long as the sun loomed overhead. He guessed the police had decided that was how it would be. Some were musicians like him, less fortunate perhaps, others were folks who had lost everything. To Victor they would always be that same person he had been, busking on the streets of Westwood among the premiere movie houses and fellow college students, though this peer group was not on its way to a diploma, not bound for a software company IPO, not someday going to join a promising cover band.

It didn't matter to him. Human was human. He was a kid who'd survived the system, forever homeless with or without four walls around him. He understood privilege, the presumed normalcy of safeguards, what others thought and why, who was at fault and who was in judgment. He thought of the words sung by Roger Waters: *I recognize myself in every stranger's eyes*. Each day walking past the homeless was a forever moment. It could have been Victor, a kid spat out by the courts who got lucky enough not to live on the street. It probably should have been Victor, but it wasn't. It was humbling. It reminded him why sharing trumped greed, no matter the personal cost.

Getting out of Vegas was a good thing. He couldn't leave all the town's debris behind him, but he could block out the prism blemishing his self-image. He would never escape the homeless. He would always be one bad decision from swapping places with them. He could never forget that. No one paying attention could forget that. Deniers, the cruel ignorant, what did they know? In their minds they would never be homeless, but even the least suspecting might end up on the street. Welfare, public assistance, no one ever thinks they will need it until they do. It's so easy to cast stones, to judge, to shame. Then one day it's you. The safety net is a bridge back that no one should ever need, but when the fallen seek shelter, how gracious is thy bounty.

Humility, the great leveler. No, those *comfortably numb* bystanders weren't outputs of the system like Victor. None had absconded becoming a statistic the way he had. They were normal. They were severely taxed citizens burdened by overreach. They were respected consumers, self-assured and self-reliant. Their lives were meaningful, independent, coherent. Yet no matter their arrogance, no matter their self-importance, 99.99% of them would never do what he was about to do. They would not walk onto a grand stage like the one he was about to take. He was playing for them as he had so many times before. This time he was appearing at The Greek Theatre in Los Angeles, California.

Why was he thinking about the homeless? It was the guitar in his hands, the warm up acoustic, the Yamaha he'd played on the street in Westwood. It had traveled with him to the future, to the green room under the temple dome. Same guitar, same Victor, a change in scenery and time, that's all. He knew this one wasn't his. That first guitar was long lost, except in his mind. This one probably belonged to someone in Walsh's crew who'd left it sitting on a stand. Crazy how much it looked and felt the same, a chance replica embodying transferal. He would always be homeless in his heart—the group homes, the shelters, the dislocating foster care, he would never release their memory. He would dance and sing and play forever among the mirrored destitute.

Torch and the others had flown in on the promoter's charge card, but Victor had wanted to drive. He hadn't had much use for his car the past few months and there was something therapeutic about driving out of Vegas on the same road that brought him there. He thought about asking Synthia with an S to come along with him, but he was afraid she might take it the wrong way, or worse, Torch would take it the wrong way. He needed the time to think, to clear his head, take in the barren roadside, let the sounds and smells of casino hell die in the rearview mirror, even if it was only for the night, driving through the dark after his final Set B on Sunday. They were going back after the Walsh gig, until the next big thing came their way, but he was going to the settlement conference Tuesday morning and that would end his music career. He held little doubt that was the necessary decision, that Katem owned his soul and taking McWhorter's money would cause him to be crucified, but he needed time to bridge the self-betrayal. Maybe Synthia would have lunch with him at the Sunset Grill after the meeting, before they said goodbye and she flew back to do Set A on Tuesday night. Yeah, maybe.

Opening for Joe Walsh at The Greek was impossible to digest, wildly beyond the scope of the possible. Petrumi told Victor this was Walsh's warm-up show for a full tour he was about to commence with the Eagles, another cash-in reunion that would undoubtedly sell out, but first Walsh wanted the spotlight to himself at one of his favorite local venues. His all-star band was even more outrageous. He would be playing with veterans of Toto, Argent, Procol Harum, Average White Band, Men at Work, and who knew what special guest might show up for a hit or two. Rumors were rampant. Retirees from Mott the Hoople? Emerson, Lake, and Palmer? The Kinks? Sure, most of them were has-beens in need of a payday, but they were legendary stars of a mythic age, no one could take that from them. More than that, they were musicians, pros who'd made it into the club. At least for tonight, they were peers.

The only thing that made it tangible was actually seeing Joe Walsh backstage at The Greek. There he was in the wings, kicking the tires on this and that detail. He wouldn't talk to Victor, not a chance. He wouldn't talk to Torch or anyone else in the band, but it was him. Joe Walsh was there. The gig was theirs.

When the stage lights came up fully, they would be blinding. That was what the stagehands told them in sound check earlier that day, when the sun was still out. Victor had slept a few hours on the benches when he arrived, and awoke to the afternoon heat. The heat, always be ready to feel the heat. He had learned that in Vegas. Tonight he would be playing outdoors under the searing star struck lighting. Don't let your knees buckle, the stagehands told him, or it would be lights out. Flex your knees. Take in the crowd. Forget they were there. Play like it was a dive club. Ignore the full house, more than five thousand who'd paid serious money for Walsh. First would come their unrequested bonus, From Nothing.

As the band walked onstage in darkness in front of the meandering crowd, Torch turned to Victor and handed him four small scraps of paper. "Here's the set list, Nowhere Man. Hand it out. Everyone already knows the new open you picked and the regular close. Only surprise is we're gonna do the new song tonight."

"'Playing,' the original? No, not tonight."

"I like it. Lyrics are a little LSD zone but that never hurt Ziggy Stardust. You and Syn made it work and I appreciate that. The Act is ready to innovate. You taught me a new game."

Ziggy Stardust? Victor felt something in the back of his neck, a sharp stinging jolt throbbing into his skull, numbing his brow and forehead. No, not again, not now. Were his knees going to buckle? Was he going to black out onstage?

"Does Synthia know?"

"I thought I'd let you tell her."

"When would you like me to tell her?"

"In the next thirty seconds, before the blazing luminosity starts cooking us. We'll hit it on our sixth tune. I can feel it's gonna work with this crowd."

"This crowd is going to be ambivalent toward an opening act. We only get eight songs, including the finale. You want to risk one on our first original? We haven't rehearsed it."

"I gave Baker Bagley and Phil-Phil the sheet. You and Syn know it. No rehearsal required. Keep it fresh, spontaneous. That's your story, Brother. For the love of God, stick to it. It's a risk, but it's how we break through. Hand out the set list!"

Victor looked at the digital countdown clock beside the reference amps. Twenty-five seconds left to lights up.

The Philosopher King made his way to the mic in the shadows. Was he crazy? Was he suicidal? Did he want to implode onstage, destroy the band, all to show Victor who was boss? He couldn't be that stupid, that vindictive. It made no sense. This was not in his interest. Victor felt ill, dizzy, drifting from the long drive and lack of sleep. He quickly handed the set list to Baker Bagley and Phil-Phil. He wanted off the grand stage badly.

Twenty seconds left.

He made his way to Synthia and handed her the set list.

"You okay, Vic?" she asked. "It's dark and you look white."

"Torch says we're going to do the original sixth up."

"He's insane. We've never played it together. Have you even heard him sing it?"

"Not me. It's yours. He stole it. He could die with it."

"He dies, we die. What's he thinking?"

Fifteen seconds.

"He's thinking spontaneous. He gave everyone the sheet. Maybe we can pull it off."

Synthia noticed the ready lights were saturating, signaling they were about to come up full. "Crap, I gotta roll the opening dub tracks. We're going live. The Greek, baby." She couldn't hide her glee, her excitement, her pride. That smile was new to her. Oh, that auspicious, stunning smile.

"This is it, the big time." Victor gave her a high five. Her palm was dry. His was not. Hers felt fantastic.

Ten seconds.

Compared to their home base, the stage was enormous. Torch was way out front, taking in the verve from the mosh pit in front of him where select members of the audience would remain on their feet and dance the entire show. Phil-Phil was upstage spinning his drumsticks in the near blackout, sky high and commanding on the eight foot elevated platform. Baker Bagley took a fixed stance behind his mic at far stage right. Synthia rolled the recorded opening background chords farther away at stage left, for the first time leaving plenty of elbow room for Victor. He wanted to puke. His knees were weak. He couldn't let them buckle. The heat was coming. Do not let them buckle.

Five seconds.

The opening live chords flowed from Synthia's fingertips to the amps stacked above and beside them. Full bass. Subwoofer vibrations. The sound board at the center of the house levered up to full power. The crowd rumbled with unexpected acceptance, a kind welcome in the making. Where was the ambivalence? Had Victor called the opening correctly? Was this going to work?

No seconds.

The words came slowly from Torch's lips in the dry ice fog, over the keyboard chords from Synthia, playing into dimly lit shadows:

Dearly beloved, we are gathered here today, to get through this thing called life.

Lights up. Phil-Phil clicked the four count. Play now. Be part of it. Hit it. The Philosopher King was not Prince. Victor was Prince. His knees were solid. His guitar exploded. *Oh no let's go*

It was the perfect choice. The band pulled off the powerful opener better than Victor anticipated. The spirit of Prince was forever beloved, the combination of Torch's melodic elegance and Victor's studied guitar work bringing him to life with luring fervor. "Let's Go Crazy" built on the crowd's enthusiasm and fed their appetite for revelry.

The show was off to a brilliant start. One down, seven to go, clock ticking against glory. The a capella from Torch, Synthia, and Baker Bagley that followed was another unexpected move, "Nowhere Man" by the Beatles. Torch must have picked it to say thank you to Victor:

Nowhere Man, please listen
You don't know what you're missing

The Beatles at mid-career from *Rubber Soul*, what a pick. Not the early Beatles, not the studio Beatles. The thinking Beatles! The psychedelic don't-think-you-can-pin-us-down Beatles. The band's meticulous tribute grabbed the crowd. Two songs in and they were completely at home in the amphitheater. They played with joy, as comfortable as they ever were at the 24 Karat Lounge, no matter the additional 4900 people cheering them on.

Victor took in the moment. If only he hadn't looked beyond the nearly blinding lights into the mosh pit. There was Katem, exactly like he said he would be. Then he looked out into the center house seats. Was that Sangstrum? Damn it all, it was. How did he know about the show? What happened to the Witness Protection Program? There had to be a leak, or maybe this was a setup. Did they know each other were there? Either Katem was lying or their secret had been compromised. There was no easy way out. Victor had to shut them out of his mind. He had to stay focused on the gig, this gig of a lifetime. In a half hour he could sort it out. He owed the band complete concentration for that next half hour. Don't think, play!

Katem and Sangstrum were both at the show, both unwelcome, both unavoidable, yet there was no sign of Claire. If only she had come to the show, he could have dealt with the rest. That would have changed everything. He hadn't given up on her. She'd taught him to hang onto hope. No, that wasn't happening, what a dunderhead idea. She wasn't going to be there. She told him that. She never bluffed. She always said what she meant. No, stop it! He had to focus on the gig, the immediacy of their performance. Torch was counting on him. Synthia was counting on him. Baker Bagley and Phil-Phil were counting on him. Forget Katem, Sangstrum, Claire. He needed to play. Play from the heart. Play like never before.

Third up was another monumental gamble. Phil-Phil had walked out of the room when Victor had suggested "Sugar Sugar" by The Archies. Now they were playing it and the raucous pit before them was a sea of smiles:

Sugar, honey, honey
You are my candy girl

Impossibly it also worked. It sparkled. It was pure saccharine bubblegum nostalgia. The crowd ate every ounce of sap and sweetness. How did Victor know?

Three for three. They were on a roll. Victor regained his focus. Fourth in the set was U2's "Elevation." That was the contrast moment showcasing Torch's range. His drive was incalculable:

High, higher than the sun
You shoot me from a gun

It was another hit with the exuberant crowd. That was four behind them, half the show in the history book and they were unstoppable! Torch owned the place, no different from any other night, the scale expanding in his favor. The Act forever owned the room, no matter the size, no matter what was at stake.

Fifth tune in the lineup was "LA Woman." It was a regular pulled from Set B, but tonight it carried undiscovered punch, a souped-up delivery of story legend and setting. Torch channeled Jim Morrison with veracity, gravitas, a dose of illumination Victor had never imagined:

Are you a lucky lady in the city of light
Or just another lost angel, City of Night

They played for a hometown crowd of Morrison fanatics. The Doors were practically LA's house band. Five in a row solid. The time had come for mystic number six.

Over the roar of the crowd, Torch walked downstage center and put the wireless mic in the stand. "Gracious thanks for being in our company tonight. We're From Nothing, from downtown Las Vegas. Mostly we do covers like the ones we've been playing, the songs we love, but we've been working on something special we want to share with you tonight. This is our first original and the first time we're playing it in public. It was written by our music director, Synthia Hamada, and our guitarist, who joined us not long ago, Victor Selo."

That was nice of him, the shout-out for writing it. He used his real name, too, that was polite. Now he could steal the song in good conscience, presuming he didn't crash and burn.

"I'm gonna turn the mic over to Syn on this one. I think you'll like her voice. We all do. This is 'Playing.'"

Torch backed away from center stage and cued the sound and light crew to pick up Synthia instead of him. Victor was astonished. Torch had done the right thing. He had been playing Victor all along. Synthia looked at Torch, perplexed, then nodded to Victor and went into professional mode with the song's opening chords.

The lyrics came out of her mouth borrowing the voice of Christine McVie. She couldn't have been better. Torch was equally flawless on harmony, standing to the side of the stage, giving Synthia the spotlight alone for the entire song.

"Playing" brought down the house, fortifying its impression with each subsequent verse. It blew Victor's mind that they could pull it off, never having played it before, but this was a once-in-a-lifetime band. Maybe it was the gazillion hours night after night in the small clubs, maybe they were unnaturally gifted, or maybe it was meant to be, somehow celestial, omnisciently ordained. They did it, the absolute impossible. The reception was on par with the delivery, impeccable. The audience rose to its feet. It was an arena standing ovation with mobile phones flickering. The original was an instant hit. There was no doubt in Victor's mind it would chart.

Amid the applause, Torch walked up to Victor. "Seven up. Ready to show off your stuff?"

"I think so," said Victor.

"You told me once you could do Knopfler in your dreams. Still got it in you, Brother Nowhere?" Then to his drummer: "Double four time, Phil-Phil."

Phil-Phil clicked his drumsticks on a fast four-four count and the lights exploded. Victor had no time to react. He grabbed the lead line from heaven.

They blasted through a raw, turbocharged version of Dire Straits' "Sultans of Swing," a sequence of guitar licks and extended solos for Victor. He was feeling something he hadn't felt in over a decade, the pure bliss of playing, the otherworldly power of music flowing from his being, flowing into the audience, emanating from the band. Moments like this were brief, but at this second he felt happy in a way he could never describe. It was unexplainable when music took on soul and lifted it to spiritual gain. So rare, so immediate. Maybe this was what Claire had been talking about. How could she know? This was what Mozart knew, what Salieri could never know, the intangible love of sound. Why couldn't it happen more, be made to resonate on demand? Enjoy the sound, enjoy the music. Play, just play.

Then they played song eight, the finale. They would have gone around forever on "Nothing from Nothing" but the stage manager pulled them after ten minutes, which was five minutes over the line. Walsh must have been getting irritated at the ongoing standing ovation.

The gig was over in what felt like a microsecond. It came and went so fast. It was impossible to believe it had even happened. They had played the set of their lives. Victor knew they had exceeded all expectations for an opening act. Not only were they perfect, the audience loved the original. They weren't just a cover band anymore. They were musicians who had entered the club. They'd played The Greek in LA. They had opened for a star and now they had their own star power.

Victor would remember it forever. He expected Torch only saw it as a launching point.

>> <<

Petrumi phoned the band backstage before they got to the green room. They gathered around Torch's mobile, Petrumi still no more than an eerie voice from the cloud. They could barely hear him over the crowd, but his voice was vibrant.

"Walsh's people called me after 'Playing,'" said Petrumi. "You got a big star who thinks you're good."

"Yeah, why wouldn't he talk to us? Asshole." Torch was posturing. It was a paper thin objection. Victor knew that. He wondered if the others did.

"What does it matter?" snapped Petrumi. "He's a name, not an asshole, and he wants you."

"Wants us what?" interrogated Torch.

"On the road with him, with the Eagles, to open for them on the final reunion tour."

Silence. It couldn't be. None of them could believe it.

Torch blasted back at the agent, much to the Victor's surprise. "Petrumi, you playing a joke on us? Why are you phoning this in? This is a big night for you not to be here."

"No joke. Sorry to miss the show. Had to be in New York to strike if you scored. You did your thing, I did mine. You're coming here for opening night at Madison Square Garden."

"Gigs like this don't land on folks," protested Torch. "What's the real story?"

"The real story is they never liked the opening act the label stuck on the card, but they couldn't agree on an alternative. Walsh recorded your original and streamed it to the others, who agreed to give you a chance. They put the other opener on ice and you have one night to win the rest of the tour. Satisfied or do you want me to try to get Henley on the line?"

"Damn, we're really in." All of the bravado in Torch's voice had evaporated.

"I gotta go, need to find you a backup for the Nugget. Don't party too hard. Biggest show of your lives is this Saturday. Travel docs coming your way. The promoter will get you here ASAP so you have time to rest up and rehearse."

Torch clicked off the phone and stared into Victor's eyes. Victor stared into Synthia eyes. Phil-Phil and Baker Bagley stared at each other. It happened that fast. Years of waiting and the big break at last fell upon them. It was the miracle all bands anticipate will never come. This time it had.

Victor didn't know what to say. He tried to find words of gratitude, words of anticipation, words of any kind, when out of the corner of his eye he saw Katem making his way toward him backstage. There he was, Petrumi's evil frat brother headed toward Victor, undoubtedly about to dredge up calamity. Was Sangstrum on his way backstage as well? Did Katem have a clue? The onslaught of drama was inevitable and inescapable. Victor had no choice but to deal with it. He could not let Torch hear any of it. He intercepted Katem and led him aside, deep into the wings, before Torch saw him.

"That was some show," said Katem. "Prince Victor rocks."

"I'm glad you were entertained. Do you know who's here?"

"Everyone's here! It was an exceptional performance, couldn't have been better. It's the right way to go out."

"I don't want to go out."

"I know that, but once you're back at the office, you'll settle in. You'll be the boss soon. It's good to be the boss."

"I'd rather play in the band."

"It's not a choice."

"Does your buddy Petrumi know?"

Katem said nothing. Stupid Victor, what was he thinking? Of course Petrumi knew. He was in on the whole thing. He'd concocted the whole thing.

"Do you want to tell Torch or do you want Petrumi to do it?"

"On that I get a choice? Lucky me. I'll tell him. He's not going to like it."

"No, he's not going to like it, but Petrumi will find them another fit, just like he found you. Everything's going to be fine."

"Right, everything's going to be fine."

"Tomorrow morning we'll send a car for you. We're going to prep you before the settlement meeting. It's similar to a deposition, a bit less formal but the opposition will be present. We need to be sure you say all the right things in the afternoon. You okay with that?"

"On that I'm sure I don't have a choice," answered Victor.

"No, not really. Say your goodbyes tonight, get a full night's sleep, and in twenty-four hours my client should be wrapping it up with Global Harmonics. Your CEO announcement could come as soon as next week."

Victor looked offstage and saw Walsh getting ready to walk on. Beyond him, advancing toward Victor at full stride was Maurice Sangstrum. How did he get a backstage pass? Oh, right, money.

"You know who that is?" asked Victor.

"Joe Walsh? Petrumi has known him for years. How do you think you got booked at The Greek, a coincidence?"

"No, that guy behind him, Maurice Sangstrum. I started to ask you before if you knew he was here."

"Yes, I know who that is. I was a little surprised to see him in the audience, but not really. Obstinate twit probably had you under surveillance. Good reason for me to be leaving."

"Should I talk to him?"

"Do you have anything to say to him?"

"No, but I don't want to run. I want to hang out and hear Walsh, kind of a one time thing after opening for him."

"Do what you need to do. What I need to do is not be in the vicinity of Sangstrum until tomorrow. I'll see you in the morning. Don't forget your chat with Torch—and the full night's sleep. Seriously, we need you to be sharp tomorrow in front of those criminals."

Those criminals, not easily distinguished from *these criminals* who currently owned his ass. The whole thing was unflushed sewage Victor wanted to hose off, but more than that, he wanted to listen to Walsh who was about to start singing thirty feet from him on the stage where his former band just became Something.

Katem darted back down the side stairs. Was he headed back to the VIP seats? Was he going to enjoy the rest of the concert as Victor squirmed? He seemed to have no worries that Sangstrum could turn Victor against him—or maybe that was part of his strategy. The whole damn thing was so sick, so manipulated, so convoluted. There was no way Victor could know who was in control.

Joe Walsh was introduced to a standing ovation. Tracking behind him like a morose shadow was Maurice Sangstrum. The band Victor helped put on the map had been invited to go on the road, opening for the Eagles. Instead, Victor was about to face the Sith Lord who'd fired him, whom he could unseat if he stayed true to his word and showed up in the morning. Choices, more choices. God's choices or woefully mortal?

Walsh opened predictably with "Life's Been Good." He was magnificent. His stardom had been earned, a virtuoso's career built from obscurity one track at a time. He played like it was his first time in front of an audience, with all of the passion his audience expected. He would never take an audience for granted. He knew the rules. He relished the expectations.

Sangstrum was not listening to the magnificence in their presence. He was fixed on flipping Victor, lowbrow salesman to the end with a cheap opening line. "Victor, I had no idea you were that talented."

"No, you never did," replied Victor, eyes transfixed on Walsh playing under the same spotlight that had flickered on his own fretboard.

The band? Where was the band? Where was Synthia with an S, who had killed it on the original? Where was Torch, who had brought down the house, eight for eight and angelic on harmony for the original? Why was Victor alone again?

Walsh changed it up and played "In The City." Victor remembered the first time he had heard it blasting in stereo, sitting in the front row of a movie theater ten feet from the screen, watching hyperbole gangland ripped from Greek mythology in *The Warriors*. Recalling the imagery of Riffs and Rogues in combat, the ruby lips of the DJ summoning the Lizzies and the Baseball Furies to street war, Victor forced himself to ignore Sangstrum and listened carefully to the lyrics as Walsh let go of them one syllable at a time:

Somewhere out on that horizon

Out beyond the neon lights

Sangstrum didn't belong there. This was a holy place, a shrine commemorating talent. Victor didn't belong there either. He belonged with Claire, or with Synthia, but not Sangstrum. Anyone but this puke Sangstrum. No, not his choice. God's choice. Fine, if God wanted him to negotiate instead of finding love, so be it, bring on the lies.

"Victor, I know we've had our differences . . ."

"How did you find me?"

"That's what's bothering you? Simple matter. We discovered a few lines of server code used to locate your mobile phone. It was parked in the archive, a little sloppiness on the part of your former team."

"My guys aren't sloppy. You dug it out."

"It's company intellectual property, Victor, ours to excavate. Let it go, let's move on."

"I don't want to talk to you."

"I know you don't, but I can help you. I saw you talking to Thomas Katem a moment ago. If you think I'm a bad man, you have no idea what you're dealing with there. If I'm Satan, he's Satan's creator."

"That would make him God. Rotten analogy. I had a girlfriend who taught me this stuff."

"Fine, religion is not our topic. I'm sure Katem is promising you the world, but I can get you what you want. If you don't take me down tomorrow, I can make sure you stay in this band."

"You're lying, Sangstrum. You're always lying."

"No, I'm not. McWhorter wants the company. He's willing to pay. He doesn't want it going to Katem's private equity client. We will pay Petrumi a king's ransom to keep you in the band, to hell with his friend, Katem. You disappear with From Nothing and we sort out the rest."

They'd dump money on Petrumi so they could shred the company? How did that make economic sense? It was more of the same, only with a cash kicker for green mail. Nothing ever changed with these manipulators.

Milk the cow, never feed her. Poison the milk, let the cow die.

Victor saw their strategy, but not the logic in their lying to each other.

"You think Petrumi will stab his college buddy Katem in the back for me?"

"No, for money. I'm sure he will. We've shaken hands."

Milk the cow, never feed her. Strangle the cow for kicks, laugh your ass off.

"It won't happen, Sangstrum. You're making up this crap because you want an exit package. Your greed has swept away your judgment."

"It's not about the exit package anymore, Victor. It's about my dignity. It's about my reputation. I didn't make enough to retire on this deal. I have bad habits like you. If this thing melts down, the next decade of my life is shit. I don't deserve that. You don't either. You don't want to be CEO of Global Harmonics. It's a stripped down operation. That's all it is. Do it my way and you can play music. McWhorter gets Global Harmonics. I get a press release headline that sets me up for the next thing. Will you consider it?"

Sangstrum would have made the worst infomercial host in history. Each promise sounded like third-rate advertising copy coughed up with a 1-800 phone number. Each pledge sounded like a deposed dictator begging for his life. Sleazy lines from a heartless con man. Victor looked into the wings and saw his bandmates. Torch looked at him peculiarly, like what the hell was he doing backstage with a stiff suit? Synthia was still smiling, still glowing. Baker Bagley was pouring champagne down his throat like his team had won the Pennant. Phil-Phil was onstage playing bongos behind Walsh, who was playing "All Night Long."

Victor continued to look at his friends, not Sangstrum, as he spoke. "A while back you offered me $5 million for my silence. McWhorter offered me $10 million. Are those offers still on the table?"

"That's where we are, negotiating price?"

"Not necessarily. I want to understand my options."

"Fine, we'll take care of Petrumi and we'll take care of you. All $15 million to you and you stay in the band. We never see or hear from you again, 100% full release of liability and a perpetual gag order. The young lady at the piano might even take you seriously. Who knows where it might lead if you helped her out of debt."

These guys knew everything that mortals could know. Information was its own currency. Victor let that comment go by. He was too smart to react to that at this point in the negotiation. He turned his head and looked straight at Sangstrum. "It's a generous offer. Enticing for sure."

"Do we have a deal?"

Victor lowered his eyes and walked a few steps toward the stage, closer to Walsh, still well out of sight of the audience. "I have to go. I'm supposed to get a full night's sleep."

"Will you think about it, my friend?"

Victor turned back toward Sangstrum and walked straight past him as he spoke, heading toward the exit stairwell where he stopped. "I'm not your friend. You can't keep me in this band. You can't protect me. It's only about you. It's always about you."

"I can protect you if it means protecting me. Katem is small time. Petrumi thinks he's useless and burned out. Trust me on this. This kind of money talks."

"Trust you, sure."

"You'll think about it?"

"I'll think about it."

"That's all I can ask. I hope I don't see you tomorrow. You have my number. Call me in the morning and tell me where you want the money wired. I can have it transferred in thirty minutes' time."

"I'll bet you're already in touch with Petrumi."

"Pending your cooperation, of course we are. Celebrate tonight. You've earned it."

Sangstrum sauntered down the same back stairs Katem had crawled. There was little chance that he was going back into the house seats. He couldn't give a shit about Joe Walsh, serenading the hills of Griffith Park with "Funk #49." He couldn't give a shit about anyone but Maurice Sangstrum.

Next up was Torch. Victor had to tell him he was leaving the band. Or not.

Celebrate at The Greek. Party on, Nowhere Dude. Damn, did all of this suck.

>> <<

Victor sat alone in the green room behind The Greek. Celebrate, you betcha. After three Vodka Gatorades he had graduated to a tequila sunrise, ostensibly in honor of the musician onstage, nonsense because he joined the Eagles years after the song broke. Then another, no excuse necessary. Less nonsense, more drinking, an array of indulgences on the house. Walsh's all-stars played live on the green room monitor. Everyone else was in the wings listening, while the stage hands smoking cigarettes out on the loading dock waited for their cue to break it all down following the final bows.

No, Claire hadn't come to the show. This shouldn't have been a crushing blow to Victor, but it was. Something had to go right tonight besides the performance. How could a band open for Joe Walsh, play perfectly, launch an original, and still life was a mound of manure? That was Victor's life. That had always been Victor's life.

Walsh was hammering his way through "Life in the Fast Lane." It was his signature riff from *Hotel California*, the Eagles' concept album so iconic it had no peer, a multi-platinum record incomparable in composition, equally majestic in performance almost forty years beyond its origin. That kind of landmark record was Hall of Fame material, as good as it could get for a rock band wanting to leave a legacy. Victor was invited to become part of its ongoing history and instead had to let it go. He had to let all of it go to become CEO of a dying company. More idiocy.

Victor had passed Synthia on the way to green room. She could not stop beaming, maybe the happiest day of her life. She expected the same from him, but he was somewhere else.

"Vic, our song worked. I mean, hello, they loved it. Standing O!"

"You were great. Torch surprised both of us."

"I wasn't that surprised. He can get a little nuts, wander into the war zone, but he's not a bad guy. He never learned to trust anyone, same as you, but he isn't one to repeat the past."

"Yeah, me either. Can we talk later?"

"Sure, whatever you want. Smile a little, would you? This is a forever moment."

A forever moment, why did she have to call it that? Victor couldn't find any such moment. She reluctantly left the green room as he requested. He found the surrounding shelves amply stocked with numbing potions, bottle after bottle, copious brands and spirits.

A half hour later Torch found him behind a small wall of clear plastic cups and melting ice. They could hear "Rocky Mountain Way" on the monitor. Walsh would soon take his bow. Victor turned the sound as low as it would go. The two of them were alone.

"What's up, Nowhere Man? Why are you down? We killed."

"You killed. For me, unmet expectations." Victor had devolved to straight vodka.

"Unmet expectations, yeah, we all got 'em, but now we got Walsh." Torch poured himself a vodka on ice. "Hey, I owe you an apology, hard as that may seem. You pushed us to go fresh. That got us here."

Victor topped off his plastic cup with the bottle closest to him. "You got you here."

"Of course I had something to do with it, but you got us the next one. Petrumi called me back, didn't want to say with everyone on the line in case it irked me, but Walsh told him you're a natural. He thinks your guitar work would open strong for them. Don't worry, I'm fine with it. I'll take the next step any way we can get it. That third party endorsement makes you one of us. You are absolutely one of us."

"Torch, this is impossible for me."

"What's impossible, college boy? For you, nothing. Say it."

"I don't think I can go with you."

That certainly was not what Torch expected. He dropped his drink. The vodka and ice splattered on the tile floor.

"What do you mean, you don't think you can go? Walsh loves you. I'm The Act, but you're The Love."

"No, I'm the goat. It's not the right thing for me to go."

"Is your brain clogged up again with that post-traumatic thrashing? This is Walsh, champ. He gets sick one night and you could be sitting in with the Eagles. You're the understudy. He's got Phil-Phil out there now on maracas. You gonna let that chance go?"

"Phil-Phil played with Elton John. He's a known entity. Walsh won't miss a show. Walsh would never let me in."

"You don't know that. Walsh is a wild man. He could go AWOL anytime. Plus we need you. I hate saying that but it's the way it is. I apologized, you heard me say the words. Here are some more words, simple ones: You must be on the tour, period."

"Torch, you don't know how good that sounds, but . . ."

"Nowhere Man, damaged kid from foster care, listen to another guy who beat the system. You don't go, we don't go. You get that?"

"I have prior responsibilities. I can't walk away from that."

"You can walk away from us?"

"It's not my call. I wish it were my call, but I'm not the decision-maker. Not here."

"You are always your own decision-maker! Damn you, I knew this would happen. I never should have let you in. We prop up a new act and you abandon it for something better. Silicon Valley money, right? Going back dust to dawn?"

"It's not that. My life would be better staying on with you. It's complicated, but this is yours. You built it. Maybe I helped wake you up a little, but you're The Act and I'm not. I have to be somewhere else or a lot of people get hurt."

"You're killing me, Brother. They may get hurt, but I'm getting assassinated. You listen to Torch. You find a way to go with us! You hear me? You find a way to go."

"I'm sure Petrumi already has a backup for me. He hasn't told you everything. He knows it could go either way. He wins either way. Agent, you know?"

"You know what? You don't know the whole story. Yeah, Petrumi thought you might be out. That was the drill, he told me that. He said we come here, we play, then probably you leave, but then something else happened."

"You knew I was out after the gig?"

"You keep thinking you're the only smart guy in the room. You're not. You know what else? Things change. I learned that from a computer dude I know."

"What changed?"

"Walsh. Petrumi told him you were out, that you were a stand in for Doc Sludge who was coming back, but Walsh nixed that plan. You're his pick. No Nowhere Man, no opening for the Eagles."

"This is bullshit."

"This is reality check. You leave, you screw us, most of all Synthia. Think about it hard, Nowhere Man. The world is at your command."

"I can make it up to you, Torch. When I get through this, I can back your Elvis Chapel. I'll have the resources to help you realize your dream."

"I don't want your charity, money grubber. I back myself or it doesn't happen. That's law one of the Philosopher King." Torch kicked the plastic cup from the drink he dropped across the floor.

Victor stared at the wet tile. "Trust me, it's not my call. I don't want to make it worse."

"Yeah? Law two is don't trust pricks like you. You only make it worse. Rehearsal is Thursday in the Big Apple, some studio on Sixth Avenue, they texted us the info. Don't even think about missing it or I'm gonna make that pissant in the sports jacket seem like your guardian angel." Torch turned abruptly and left Victor alone in the green room.

Victor was dumfounded. He had no idea who to believe. Could Sangstrum deliver? Could he really deliver? Could he really stay with the band if he screwed over Katem? Could he duck another beating, stay alive, and really open for the Eagles? Did he have the sheer force of will to survive as CEO of the ravaged company with Katem's venomous buyer in the driver seat? Did he even have the talent to reinvigorate Global Harmonics, save his friends' jobs, and rebuild Camelot?

No, they were all liars. No one told the truth. No one could be trusted. He was going to end up with Nothing. No CEO. No band. No Claire. No Synthia. No God. Nothing from Nothing.

There was only one way Victor could escape. He had to stay with the band. He would donate all the blood money to a support fund for his former employees. He had to defy Katem. He had to undermine Sangstrum and McWhorter. All of it had to happen in a single move.

His anger was back, returned in full force, unrestrained fury, justified by their unyielding manipulation, malice, and greed. They had brought it on again. They were without values, without grounding, acquiring money and only money at any human cost, avarice unbound. He could not hold himself back. He could not impose self-control. His breathing was uneven. He could see no sane path, no compromise, nothing but savage resolve. Wrath. Pain offered traded for pain processed, the infliction of permanent regret. It was their fault, not his, a decision made as no important decision should ever be, without emotional clarity. Not stoic. Vengeful.

In his head he heard the steady rhythm of the Talking Heads: *One two three four, Burning down the house.*

He had to do it. He had no choice. He had to release the virus. There was no other option. Global Harmonics had to cease to exist.

He was going on the road with a Vegas cover band to open for the Eagles. He had fought too hard to be reborn. Modern faith be damned.

He had found his way again, fought his way back. He had a path recast, hope never before seen. He had crafted it from humiliation, from loss, a new day he had won and had to hold, however trite the onstage gig. He liked playing guitar. He liked the sound of Torch's voice telling him to go around again. He was not losing this creation, this place before an audience, this song beside Synthia driving home The Act.

Claire was wrong, but she had taught him well. Being alone was a lousy choice, but its modest upside had to be avenged. Rebirth meant death. Salvation meant courage, conviction, transparent honesty no matter the decibel level. Not another false start, no matter the cost. Transformation required a slaying of the chains. It was okay to scream. They made him scream. Not him. Them. No more the victim, not again, not still.

Victor pulled out his mobile and texted Juan the code words: "Pendejo Pudding."

An unrecallable virus thread into the neural network and it was done. With Victor's command, the impact would be immediate.

Juan instantly texted back: "Gracias, señor. Adios pendejos. *Don't believe me just watch.*"

Bruno Mars, perfect trigger play. It was as appropriate a soundtrack as any.

It was done, the meltdown order sealed with a text. The role of Judas in tonight's performance had been played by everyone.

The world would never be fair, but it would always be filled with possibility. Victor's bounty would be his soul, his life's treasure found in free will. Those were the terms of his separation. For that generous severance, he had to kill the company forever.

SIDE THREE: EVERMORE

Since my friend you have revealed your deepest fear
I sentence you to be exposed before your peers.

Pink Floyd, "The Wall"

TRACK 11: END OF THE INNOCENT

"There is no proof of God. That's how faith got its name. Faith is as inarguable a platform as ever devised. Duly impenetrable. Purposefully inextinguishable. If you choose to believe, bully for you. It's pointless for anyone to tell you you're wrong, and pointless to think anyone who doesn't believe should care. God is the not the delusion. The search for measured evidence in a vacuum is the delusion. No one has proven it. No one can prove it.

Plato couldn't prove it.

Aristotle couldn't prove it.

St. Thomas couldn't prove it.

St. Francis couldn't prove it.

Descartes couldn't prove it.

Leibniz couldn't prove it.

Kant couldn't prove it.

Hegel couldn't prove it.

Kierkegaard never bothered trying. He was fine with the absurdity of faith.

Pascal formulated a pragmatic wager weighing heavily in favor of God, but left evidential proof beyond the argument of intellectual choice.

Darwin could argue proof of natural selection and still believe in God, but he couldn't prove God.

Nietzsche turned the proposition on its head and few understood what he was saying. He was an ally to believers but they attacked him for redefining the problem.

Sartre denied it entirely until fear overcame him on his death bed. Then he flip-flopped, making a mess of his own denial.

Anne Frank tried to reconcile the traditional healing power of belief with historical horror, but never emerged from youth to finish her thoughts and testify with unreserved conviction.

Einstein figured out how to blow up the world, but couldn't offer a clue to the ultimate origin of the Big Bang.

The epic discovery of DNA unlocked the gate to the remaining mysteries of biological life, but produced no definitive evidence to substantiate the divine.

It's as simple a point as the premise is incredulous. No matter what we can prove, no one can prove or disprove God. No impeachable case can be made either way, for or against. Existential quarrel is no more decisive than the unanswerable is a compelling treatise. There is no applicable science, no relevant algorithm, no enduring theorem. Both sides can stomp their feet and walk away self-righteous, but neither can win the argument. It is an unwinnable debate, empirically inarguable and bad for friendships.

The Genesis creation myth, that grandiose yarn, was that for real? Could any life bypass the dysfunction of Original Sin? Seriously? Prophets and saviors? Balderdash! Psalms are poems, no more. Seas don't part. No one walks on water. Facts require substantiation. Make it real or leave it in the storybook. Stop fixating on intangibles and get on with matters you can quantify and act upon."

That was a hell of a soliloquy. Coming from an agent awakened before dawn three hours ahead in another time zone, it was even more stupefying. Who would have figured Sandy Petrumi the bearer of didactic inquiry, deliverer of an iron-fisted monologue in response to a simple drunken question from Victor, "How do I get proof there's a God?"

He only had the one confused question to ask and he meant to ask The Act. He asked it before he saw who was on the screen, only to have the answer drilled into his cortex with uncanny recall.

It was a fair question. If there was a loving God charting a course for the world, why had Victor's parents abandoned him so soon after he was born? Why would he never know them? Why was he raised in foster care, in a system run by overburdened bureaucrats whose own lives often seemed as troubled as his own? It was unfair. It was cruel. Deterioration was a norm. Love wasn't abundant. Pain was abundant. Personal confusion was abundant. Conflict and injustice were abundant. War, disease, starvation, malnutrition, homelessness, drug addiction, alcoholism, homicide, suicide, neglect, abuse, spiritual despondency—where was the overriding love? Rising above it all had taken every ounce of strength Victor could summon and still his head would never be clear. If clarity couldn't be omniscient, then it had to be material. God had to be provable.

Talking God with a godless agent—what a concept! That was Victor's first face-to-face encounter with Petrumi. No longer was he an omnipotent, disembodied voice. He was an annoyed, impatient, hassled, ambitious, thin-haired, tan-face-painted, late middle age street reptile wrapped in a white cotton terrycloth robe. He was a dry-aged steak-eating lifetime frat boy in an expensed hotel room woken at dawn by a wasted client. Victor hadn't meant to call Petrumi. He had intended to call Torch. His head was foggy and he pushed the wrong button somewhere around 3:00 a.m. and connected live, delivering Petrumi as real as they come.

Petrumi had definite opinions about things. He had one question of his own for Victor: "Are you in or are you out?"

"The band?"

"Yes, you drunk moron, From Nothing. If you're not in, I have to put that on the table with Walsh and the boys."

Victor had no good answer, but the fact that Petrumi was leaving it to him to answer meant he had options he didn't think he had. He needed to think about that, pleading that his own free will was back on the table. "I'll have to get back to you on that," he muttered.

He reached for the screen and closed the Skype call. His body was shutting down. At the end of Petrumi's rant, Victor still wanted to reach out to Torch, but he didn't have the energy. He wondered instead all night—would Torch agree with Petrumi? Did Torch share Victor's obsession with refuting fate? The Philosopher King was a product of the same cynical system, but he saw escape as triumph, evidence enough of divine intervention if that proved reinforcing. Torch read the great thinkers. Torch didn't need proof of God. He could cleverly frame the juxtaposition if he wanted. What about music? Where did that come from? Was anything meant to be?

Victor considered inspiration the missing link, the Big Bang of ideas. Art couldn't be all luck. Talent couldn't be all happenstance.

There was some randomness to it, entropy was irrefutable, but to cordon off darkness there would always come light in one form or another. Chords weren't an accident—they were mathematically exact, exquisitely precise, flawless in numeric design century after century. How did that happen? Where was the hand that made it sound right? Code came from somewhere, not fingers typing, the metaphysics behind typing. Determinism, where was that? Winning and losing? Justice and poetry? They were even less tangible. They could never be explained, but they were too complex to go unguided.

"Alchemy," Torch would tell him when he asked the unanswerable. "Be cool with it."

Smart guy, Torch. Was there ever a doubt?

Had Claire won her point? Was she right after all?

Was Victor the one who had it all wrong, demanding the tangible where the ephemeral was so much stronger? Who was deceived and who could see?

He already regretted his decision to release the virus. It was a decision made in anger, an intoxicated muddle, swirling emotion over logic. A drunken stupor, was that an excuse? Would judge and jury cut him some slack? That didn't sound even a little bit right. He had annihilated the remains of the company, exorcised its demonic soul, but had he given up his negotiation leverage? He had been irresponsible, acted impetuously. He needed to retreat from the error, but what was his fallback? How could he start his life over and stay with the band? How could he answer Petrumi's much simpler question? He had nothing to offer anyone. What, he wondered, was less than nothing?

He looked at the digital flip clock beside his hotel room bed. It was 11:45. The hangover hurt. His mouth was dry, his body craving clean fuel. Damn it, he had missed the prep meeting with Katem. That was going to cost him. Katem would think it had been intentional. Maybe it was intentional. Did it still make sense for him to attend the settlement conference? What would he say unprepared, having blindsided Katem and his adversaries in a unified unrecoverable act? His head hurt from the inside, yet here he was in another hotel bed arguing again with himself in abstraction—arguing with Petrumi online, arguing with Torch *in absentia*, arguing eternally with the long-escaped Claire over free will and fate.

Hamstrung by consciousness. Adrift in contemplation. He felt sick, weak, inept, uselessly drained and dehydrated. Night sweat had soaked him. He was debilitated by colliding cohorts, one part repentance, one part self-loathing, two parts apathy. Morning-after binge reboots were never his thing, but he knew he had to make it to his feet. It was an important day. He had business pending, critical business. Coffee wouldn't help, but he had some anyway, from the drip pot on the bathroom counter. It wouldn't hide much, but he brushed his teeth twice. He could still smell the alcohol in his pores. He needed a shave, more than a shave, a makeover, a facial peel, a body repeal, a soul recall, and quickly.

He showered, remembering last night, the perfect show. Joe Walsh in the flesh. Then the awful conversations with Katem and Sangstrum. Then the worse conversation with Torch. No conversation with Synthia, their bonding song released as a living entity into the world. She probably wouldn't want to talk with him again. The threats, all the threats.

He had ordered the virus deployed. *Release the Kraken!*

The drinks, the vodka and tequila, so much alcohol, his night sweat worse than any other. Trashed to the core, even then all he wanted was proof of God. With proof he could surrender to fate. Free will was a joke. Let fate take its course. Let his birth parents face him with the truth of their abdication, hear the stories of how he clawed his way through the brawls, the loneliness, the humiliation, the judgment. Give him proof and faith would be declared the almighty and forever champion. Yes, a fallback to faith, prove it out.

Impossible. Couldn't be done. So there was faith. That was where he and Claire parted.

He was truly an idiot to ever think he could be loved. He wasn't worthy of love. He could have anything but that. How could he have what he could never understand?

He managed his way out of the shower. He would go to the settlement conference and make a guest appearance, blame the missed morning on booze. He was a musician. Why not?

He looked at his iPhone. More than a dozen messages from Katem since 9:00 a.m. This wasn't going to be pleasant. He got dressed in what he could find in his suitcase with the fewest wrinkles, then made his way to the street to find an Uber.

He was en route, still contemplating, still sweating fermented commodities. Nauseous, disgusting, weak, humiliated. Had he lost? Was it over?

In the back seat of the small Ford whatever it was, finding air where so little was available, Victor wondered back to how he had arrived, how that same illusiveness had worked for him rather than against him. He had never been sure why he had been so successful at Global Harmonics, why a music guy could make it as a software guy, but one thread in his career had been consistent. Early on Victor had figured out that software engineers—coders, programmers, whatever you wanted to call them—were more like musicians than they were like technicians.

There was something about software people that allowed an easy connection for Victor. When they weren't defensive, they were sensitive. They were quiet. They were thoughtful. They fashioned themselves as creatives. They were too often passive aggressive. They liked feedback but hated criticism. They liked collaborating intensely but abhorred petty conflict. They liked to party when they weren't working. They had subtle, wry senses of humor. They could tune out background noise, ignore distractions, focus. They wanted to find the next big thing. They grew restless with sameness. They could be very mean spirited when under attack. *Schadenfreude* was universal but a despised contest of wills, a sabre fight fought for position but never a trophy awarded. They needed a safe place to test out their theories and fail without finality, a playground more than a fight arena, a referee who explained the rules and loved the game.

Just like musicians.

Did the icy-hearted money swine know that? Did the venture pukes know where their money came from? Did they have a clue or were they completely assured that destroying souls created value? They were nothing without coders. Coders were nothing without inspiration. Victor had been inspiration. Now he was dying in the back seat of an Uber Ford generic, stench dripping from his skin, septic synapses dizzying his brainwaves, masking thought with anger.

It was anything but a coincidence to Victor that so many of the coders he managed were off-hours musicians. They liked to sing karaoke at Providence. At house parties they played guitar, piano, flute, and saxophone. They admired musicians, classical to contemporary, hung album covers in their cubicles beside vintage concert posters and talked about whether Eric Clapton was the best of all time, or Jeff Beck, or Jimmy Page in his prime, and for the outliers like him maybe Knopfler. They would learn their solos and play them back. They would dissect sheet music and overlay the music theory metrics of chord construction and harmonic progression. They would look for repeating patterns in their code. They would dig for cyphers and point out code structures embedded in musical composition. They did it all the time.

It taught Victor to be a conductor first, a boss second. His job was to bring the orchestra together as a whole, not dictate an agenda. He was there as a leader to protect a spark, not as a manager to draw up task lists and stack wood. He treated his teams as creative partners, the way he always wanted to be treated. It was a great fit that took him to the highest level of authority at Global Harmonics, as deep into executive management as anyone could go who wasn't a founder or an MBA ball buster. It always worked for him. He consistently delivered. He was trusted by those who did the real work so he could sign up for tough deadlines and deliver on demand. The people above him never understood it, but until Sangstrum, they hadn't wanted to know the how, only the what. It all snapped together.

Was this God's doing? Was this what God wanted of him? How could he know?

Victor always understood the mean-spirited part when under attack and embraced it as a stealth advantage. He had the soldiers in his camp no matter what the generals thought, he just never told anyone. His power base was in the people who propped him up, not the people who put him in power. He had the ticking bomb in the talent pool's loyalty. It was his secret, his strength, his confidence armada. He threatened to unleash it all the time in silent dialogues in his mind, but never pulled the trigger. He never even talked about the trigger. He only used it once. This was the once.

It had been a solid, comprehensive, end-to-end plan. The dormant virus implanted in the Global Harmonics core was a plan to keep him safe like no other. It had not even been his idea, only his spin. His restraint made the trigger all the more lethal. Now he had put the company out of its misery. It was a silent massacre, justifiable to the knowing, but it was a crime. He had to confess. It hardly mattered. That decision made him free.

No, there would be no confession. That wasn't what Claire would have told him was ordained. To hell with Petrumi and his covetous rambling. To hell with the Philosopher King and his prima donna anointment. To hell with the all-purpose cover band. Victor was not a musician. He did not belong onstage with Synthia, Baker Bagley, and Phil-Phil. He was a fraud. So what if he could play by ear? He had to cut them lose. They had to be gone. From Nothing was over for him.

So what of the promises he'd made to Torch? He couldn't guarantee that he was coming back. The Act would figure it out. The Act always figured it out.

Remorse without the possibility of renunciation? No, that wouldn't fly. Try harder. Dig deep and come at it from their point of view. It couldn't be that dire. There had to be a fix.

Wait, there had to be a data backup. Max, Clarence, or Juan must have kept a backup. They weren't amateurs. Even an old backup would do, any version stashed anywhere. If he could identify the existence of a network backup, he could still negotiate with both threats, either as salvage or a remaining peril.

Sangstrum had to face justice. McWhorter had to be stuffed in a box. Katem was evil and using Victor as a tool, but so what, there was possibility in compromise. Katem didn't know what he had done, the drunken act of betrayal. There would be no trace, no one could tie it to anyone. He would twist Katem's trap into compliance and beat all of them at their wicked contest. He would bluff his way through it and hope he could restore the inner workings with the salvaged remaining bits hopefully stashed somewhere on a compact hard drive in a Felix the Cat lunchbox. Global Harmonics would find continuity.

Finally he was clear. He had the path. No rhythm, no lead. Maybe God was involved, maybe not. It didn't matter. It was decided and he didn't make the call. He answered the call. This was a new day, a different day no one saw on the horizon. The corner office was his. He had to take it. Victor Selo would become CEO.

>> <<

The Uber driver unloaded Victor in downtown Los Angeles. It had been years since he had been downtown and he had forgotten how crowded the streets were with cars stuck trying to change single-direction lanes to make a right or left turn from block to block. The connecting monoliths cast shadows on skid row, high-rise glass containers of complex word games boomeranging the ceaseless sunshine. It was nothing like the City by the Bay in form or style. Architecture in LA was an afterthought. Sprawl trumped beauty in every tradeoff.

Victor entered the appointed tower on Flower Street designated for his arrival by Katem in a desperate text. He took the elevator thirtysomething stories upward, rising above the smog line, and fumbled his way into the chrome-trimmed conference room. It little bothered him that he was interrupting the assembled two dozen bodies mid-meeting. There they were in process, all of them: Katem, Sangstrum, McWhorter, legions of lawyer and accountant types in the same boring blue suits. They probably once listened to music, too. Maybe they still did, but the lyrics would be dead to them. They were idealists no more.

Katem rose from the table as if on a stage cue to intercept Victor. He seemed emotionless but wary. The others around him were not nearly as angry as he thought they would be. Where was their usual ire? Had they been expecting him even though he missed the pre-show? Didn't they know of the corporate assassination?

"You left the car I sent waiting for you," whispered Katem. "You didn't answer when I called your room multiple times and you missed our prep meeting. That wasn't wise." He looked for a reaction from Victor, anticipating what he would say or do, looking for a sign.

Shouldn't Katem be relieved he was there? Shouldn't he have altered his welcoming remarks? Of course he should have, but he didn't know it yet. The reveal was minutes away. Victor had silently played his wild card offstage and they could never tie him to it. He would be their sole remedy, the man who could dig out a backup. He was almost enjoying it.

Almost, but something wasn't right. The others were too calm, too accepting. He had blown up their company, melted it down into random bits of data, withdrawn the deeply discounted prize. Pendejos, all of them! They should have pounced. They had to know he had destroyed them. Maybe they didn't have complete information. Or maybe they did have complete information. Which of them had the currency? Who had the upper hand?

Milk the cow, never feed her.

Pay the price, you self-serving bastards.

"I have something to tell all of you." Victor felt awkward, unbalanced, not the normal head clouding, instead the lingering alcohol impairment fighting against his logic. He didn't look or smell like someone who belonged in a corporate conference room at cloud-level altitude. So what? It was about to become his meeting. If he smelled of last night's binge, so be it. That was more their problem than his. He wasn't going to be judged for his appearance, only his resolve.

"Enlighten the unknowing," taunted McWhorter, calm beyond calm.

That wasn't the right way for him to say it. Why the grin? Why wasn't he throwing a laptop?

"I know I'm only a pawn in all of this, but I have a sense of where we go from here, where I lead it from here. There's no reason for me to play games with you. In case you haven't heard, the company is dead. A virus killed it."

The room laughed out loud, everyone except Katem, who appeared stunned. They must already have known. Of course they did. The axe had already fallen, but they were rolling with it. How could that be? They knew they had lost it all. Why were they laughing?

Then Victor remembered how they won, how they always won. If you weren't in the room, you don't know what happened, and even if you were in the room you may not know exactly what happened because there was always another room and you weren't in it. Decisions are made in private, offstage. If you don't see them happen, you're speculating, same as an outsider. If you thought you heard one thing and another happened, there probably was another meeting you missed. You didn't miss it accidentally. You weren't invited. Gossip and speculation were a waste of cycles in corporate life. Only real information, indisputable accurate data, was currency.

Everything Victor knew about surviving corporate politics was embedded in that thought. It was one of the few things he had learned about business from his group home parents. They would get screwed over all the time by their contracts, believing them to be bankable when they could be retracted with a stroke of a pen in the state capital. Lease up more space, take on more wards, sorry, bad tax quarter, no checks for you. Yeah, they could dump the kids, but not the overhead. No one told them everything could change without warning, but it did all the time. Victor had been screwed over by the state budget so many times, losing one bed and being kicked to another, all because of a meeting somewhere that involved his life but didn't include his participation. He took that with him in business, knowing the one meeting behind his back could immobilize his career. High-stakes screwing was the art of the blindside. The guys at the top mastered it in ways that made them invisible no matter the spotlight.

"Have you monitored the server core today?" Victor was fishing for insight.

"Your virus was amateur," chuckled Sangstrum. "We located it in vitro and knocked it down minutes after your bobble heads popped the cork."

No, not possible. They knew it was coming? They saw it ahead of time and intercepted it? That couldn't happen. There had to be an inside player. Did someone confess? Yes, someone told them. How could they block the virus? His guys were too good. Unveiling it wasn't possible. Not Max and Clarence on the hosting side. Not Juan at the neural code interface. No way, not a chance. None of the three of them would talk.

"My virus? No, not my virus."

"Victor, this wasn't anything we ever discussed." Katem was breathless, silently imploding before his very eyes.

"No, of course not. There was nothing to discuss. Sangstrum pissed off some coders and they did what coders do. I found out this morning. That's why I'm late. I was trying to help with damage control."

He was the worst liar ever. At least bluffing was off the table. The invented backup would no longer need to be faked. So who broke down and gave up the plan? Did Max or Clarence take a payoff? Juan didn't even care about money, his pride was all that mattered to him. No one else knew. Wait, could it have been Darcy? Had Darcy become Judas? Sangstrum had bought off someone. He couldn't run the company, but he could always dig into the how and the what. Somehow the data bomb had been defused. The damn company was cursed to permanence. It just wouldn't die.

"We have it traced to your team," said Sangstrum. "They're loyal to you and wouldn't do anything like try to kill their own company without you in the loop. We expected it. We have reproducible evidence in their pithy source code comments. We hired an upmarket security firm to assist us with the transition and ensure continuity of operations. They told us this was a top ten tactic so all they had to do was find it. We took the core offline two days after you left and we've been running a redundant clean core. Your guys touched nothing and didn't even know it. Our hired gun Ivy League guys are way smarter than your self-taught guys. Your guys are fools. You're a bigger fool for not knowing that."

His guys hadn't been bought off. They revealed themselves when they let the monster out of the cage, only it didn't matter because there was another cage—just like there was always another meeting in another room. The only thing Sangstrum knew how to do was hire. That's why he kept Victor even though he despised him. He had working capital, he had stockpiled resources, he knew how to procure war room materiel. He had no humility other than to know what he didn't know. He sniffed shit while it was still food. Well played, Satan.

"Is there anything else you'd like to share with Mr. Sangstrum and Mr. McWhorter?" prodded Katem. "Victor and I have met. We have an arrangement that predates the virus. Since the company is still functioning, I believe we can proceed. "

Whoa, talk about rebounds, what a ricochet shot! Katem was lightning fast on his feet and undaunted, a human rubber band instantly past irritation.

"White knight strategy?" belted out McWhorter. "Your arrangement is DOA." He wasn't laughing anymore.

Sangstrum wasn't laughing either as he stood up slowly. "Sadly, Victor, being party to an attack on your own company is a violation of your NDA, which as an officer transcends your active time of service. You compromised fiduciary duty when you tried to set off that virus. What was that text, pendejo something? You left the breadcrumb in open cyberspace with astute timing. You've also been violating securities law by intervening in a public market transaction colluding with Mr. Katem."

"Violating securities law? You made a backroom deal." Damn it all. Victor had left a gaping hole. If they could tie the virus to Victor, he would never be CEO. He had no idea how a ruling would go if it went before a judge, but it didn't look to be in his favor.

"Silly fiction from a disgruntled scoundrel," said Sangstrum. "You should have taken our conversation last night to heart. Instead of seeking consensus and walking away a winner, you went off the ranch. Now you're in a heap of trouble."

Katem could see that Victor's shirt was sweated through. Would Katem let it go to court? Could he get a judge who was another frat buddy and slip him an envelope of cash? He must have been wondering why Victor missed the briefing. Victor didn't know the right words to say, but he had a good enough idea. He could still bring it to an end. He could still crush Sangstrum and hand the company to Katem's client, MSE. He could become CEO of Global Harmonics and fix everything if his fingerprints on the virus were wiped. All he had to do was throw Sangstrum and McWhorter under the bus in front of all these witnesses, get it on the record unambiguously how they had frozen out the free market from creating a fairly valued transaction.

Do it. Do it now. Why the hell not? Because if he did it, that was the end of the band. Katem couldn't get him a clean out. He would spend the next year in legal proceedings with suits and countersuits, endless depositions and ugly *Wall Street Journal* headlines. No opening for the Eagles. Torch The Act and Synthia with an S would be screwed over. Could he do that to them? Could he do that to himself? Did he still want to be CEO? Was Global Harmonics even worth saving?

Do it. Say it now. Trash the sycophants. Take the reins. Do what's right, not what's wrong. For Darcy. For Max and Clarence and Juan who had risked everything for this. There had to be vengeance. There had to be justice.

That NDA was epoxy. Victor had violated his promise, broken his contract. They would come after him hard. He hadn't seen it coming. He had put himself at risk. Game changer. Logic changer. Pivot now. He would never be CEO. He might go to prison. He would get nothing. No CEO gig, no band, no money, no jobs, nothing. He couldn't risk it. Sangstrum had him. Sangstrum knew he had him.

"Victor, when we last talked, you told me you had something to say to these gentlemen. This would be an excellent time." Katem was dead serious. This was Victor's final chance.

Trust Katem? Not possible. Take down Sangstrum and McWhorter and triumph? Not possible. Victor knew he was outplayed. Katem was a mouthy manipulator in combat, not a titan who mattered in truce. There was no way he could protect Victor. That virus was on Victor, failure or no failure.

No, Sangstrum was a war criminal. McWhorter was a war criminal. They were irrelevant to human advancement but complicit in sedition. Katem wanted the company more than they did and he was smarter. He had something up his sleeve. That's why he wanted to brief Victor. He shouldn't have missed the briefing. That left him flying blind.

This was emotion, not reason. Where was God? Where was Claire? Save the company or save the band? Pick one, the one he could deliver. Did he want justice, fairness, or righteous truth? They weren't a package deal. No bundles to compare. Something had to give.

"Victor, walk out of here in silence and you have my word we are done," said Sangstrum. "Your life is your life. Mine is mine. Let's separate cleanly. I have a release to that effect if you'd like to read it." Sangstrum was way ahead of Katem. That was news to Victor. That was his get-out-of-jail card. It had already been drafted. Victor looked at the release. He could walk away unsullied. The company would die but he was safe. Petrumi would leave him in the band because the gig was a done deal. Joe Walsh was on his side. Petrumi had trumped Katem the same way Sangstrum had trumped Katem.

"Victor, things are never as straightforward as they seem," countered Katem. "That's why we have laws. The truth has to be told. Would you care to tell the truth now?"

Katem, that festering leech, how dare he? He lied as badly as the others. His subversion of civilization was small-time treason, lazy three card monte, not the high rollers bunker.

Victor took the release, two copies of a single page, skimmed it, signed both, then handed the pages back to Sangstrum.

"Sign it in front of all these people, you piece of shit."

Sangstrum signed it without reaction and handed one copy back to Victor. He put the other in an envelope, sealed it methodically, and slipped it into his briefcase.

"It's meaningless," said Katem. "You can still tell the truth."

"I have nothing else to say," concluded Victor. "I've given up too much of my life to this godawful company. I don't want to run it. It's done."

"It's not done," said Katem.

"Yes, it's done," repeated McWhorter.

Victor stood and turned to leave.

"You think it's that easy?" said Katem. "Go strum your guitar."

"Nothing about this is easy," howled Victor.

"You don't know the least of it," said Katem.

Victor left the room in silence. He had made his decision and had autographed documentation making it final. The negotiation was over, winners and losers to be declared, though he wasn't sure which outcome described his status. He would stay a musician. There was one last thing he needed to do before rejoining the band on tour.

>> <<

Plans are idealistic constructs, unnatural machinations drawn from the minds of optimistic intenders. They often have little to do with real world activity. "A plan is something you have," said Mike Tyson, "until you get hit."

Had he fought in a different ring, he might have added: "Or until your code fails."

Even a self-perpetuating virus could die of its own bug-infested coding. Victor had given the Pendejo Order unleashing Project Irreversible, thrown the almighty sucker punch when backed all the way into a corner, but the power blow was without thrust. The virus had not executed. That was all Victor knew. There had to be more to it.

Victor made his way down the elevator from the cloud-perched conference room to the first-floor lobby. He ducked into a marble restroom, hid himself in a fabulously clean toilet stall, closed the metal door, and used his mobile to Skype ringleader Max. He didn't care if anyone heard them. He was humiliated, but their plan was destroyed. He had to know what happened.

Max promptly picked up the other end of the video call. In the background Victor could see Clarence. They were incomprehensible, babbling, their faces contorted in a way Victor had never seen them. Victor wasn't sure where they were. It wasn't the office. It wasn't the parking lot near Providence. It looked like a tiny apartment with an unmade bed and cheap male clothing strewn about the floor. It could have been a tenement except for the stacks of computer equipment and LCD monitors.

"Where are you?" asked Victor.

"Juan's apartment," answered Max.

"Why does Juan live in a dump?" asked Victor. "He makes decent money."

"He sends it all to his family in Mexico," said Max. "That's what he does with his money, hoping someday they can come here."

Max was having a hard time getting out the words. Clarence kept interrupting him, asking inaudible questions, tearing through the apartment as if he was looking to discover evidence before someone else did.

"Why is the Global Harmonics server core still up?" pressed Victor, trying to wrestle a sensible explanation.

"It shouldn't be, but I guess our virus was thin," explained Max through the din. "Juan's trigger code drew a blank. Their minions deflected the path. We have no idea how they did it. PhD's or something, maybe CIA alums, who knows?"

CIA alums? Why would they risk their reputation on a corporate crime? Max wasn't making sense. Clarence wasn't saying anything coherent at all. And where was Juan? Why were they in his apartment? Victor couldn't make out any more of the story from their mayhem, but he could sense there was something more to the incident, something worse he didn't yet know. Clarence stared at Max, then both of them directly into the camera lens at Victor. They were frozen solid. Victor saw his loyal brothers-in-arms gazing back into the video picture without a clue. They had been disarmed. They no longer had a threat to deploy. They had been defeated.

"What do we do now?" asked Max, a tear streaming down his cheek.

"Write another virus and get one of the idiots there to click on it in an email," said Victor. "Make it worse, way worse."

"We don't have time," shouted Max. "The shareholder meeting is tomorrow morning. We can't kill the code base by tomorrow morning."

"Yes, you can," demanded Victor. "You can erase it. A simple command structure for erase all, that's easy enough. Use an outside DNS attack. Reformat the drives. You know how to do it. Hell, I can barely cobble together HTML and I know how to do it. Do you want me to get an underground hacker to do it for you?"

"Our fingerprints are already all over it," screeched Clarence, finally enunciating something understandable. "You want us go to prison for a felony, maybe accessory to something worse?"

"We were willing to do it before," said Victor.

"We weren't going to get caught before," yelled Max. "And that was before, oh God, that was before . . ."

Clarence was rocking back and forth in front of the screen, whimpering erratically. "Victor, what should we do? They're going to sell the company to McWhorter at the shareholder meeting. Once they call it to order, it won't last ten minutes."

"Shutting up would be a good start," said Victor, failing to apply the delicacy that long ago had secured their trust. "Calm down and let's think this through. What happened?"

"Can you make it back here by the meeting?" asked Max.

"I'm in LA. I doubt I could make it in time. There's nothing I could do anyway. What's going on?"

"Juan couldn't believe his part of the code failed," said Max. "He couldn't stomach losing it, what was happening to everyone. This is the only company he ever wanted to work for. He didn't think anyone else would hire him."

Clarence picked up the thread. "Juan took a bunch of pills and swam into the marsh. We found him this morning face down in the mud. He killed himself over this stupid company. He was nineteen."

Victor couldn't believe it. No, not that. Juan was a kid. It was a failed virus launched on a failed company. It wasn't even the trigger code that had failed. Sangstrum had been way ahead of them and they never knew it. Juan had blamed himself for nothing.

"He's dead? Juan's dead?"

"He was our friend. He tried so hard. He thought he let us down. He couldn't live with that. He couldn't face us. We had no idea he would take his own life."

"Guys, I'm on my way. See if you can find his family. Have Darcy connect you with one of the lawyers in my contact file. She'll know which one. Do not talk to the police without a lawyer. Don't talk to anyone. I'll be there in less than eight hours."

Max and Clarence continued crying softly. Victor ended the Skype session and made his way back to the street to call an Uber. He needed to get back to the hotel and retrieve his car. He wasn't sweating anymore. There was no more sweat in him. He had a long day and night of driving ahead of him and hoped the adrenaline would carry him back to the Bay.

TRACK 12: THAT AIN'T WORKING

Victor drove the rest of the day and through most of the night from Los Angeles to Marin. He wasn't sure what he would do when he got there. Juan was dead. He couldn't change that. Global Harmonics was all but dead. He would never be the company's CEO. He had left Katem at the altar, betrayed the soulless betrayer, saved his own skin in another rash decision. The final stroke of the company's demise was singed on his back. Juan's suicide was his fault, at least in part because he hadn't contemplated something like that. How could he have seen that coming? It didn't matter. It was on his watch, collateral damage born of sloppy strategy. Now Victor had to face his friends, his former employees, help them find whatever was next, a safe haven. He probably couldn't help, but he couldn't hide from them no matter his shame.

Throughout the night Torch kept calling him, first every fifteen minutes, then every thirty, then once an hour. It was a familiar scenario, the endlessly unanswered calls in declining intervals, the impatience of expectation, digital fulfillment demanding immediacy. It had been almost an hour since his last call. Maybe he had given up. No, not likely. Torch was certain that without Victor there was no gig opening for the Eagles reunion tour. From Nothing was depending on Victor and he was AWOL. Torch had to be fuming. He had been reluctant to trust an outsider like Victor from the start, and as he must have imagined, Victor let him down. Why couldn't Torch understand? It wasn't about the band. It wasn't even about the company. He simply couldn't handle the pressure. When put to the test he couldn't face it, couldn't stare down the devil. Again he got the high-stakes answer wrong, charted the wrong course, picked the wrong fork. He handled difficult people wrong. He was no good in the big leagues. He was responsible for a kid taking his own life. How could he think about playing guitar?

He had chosen not to be CEO of Global Harmonics, not to be owned by Katem, but leaving the band behind was a choice beyond his control. Juan made it different. He molded Victor's perspective into something less self-serving. Torch would be crushed, but he would find a way out of the trough. Torch was the survivor Victor wished he could be. Torch knew how to find a smooth path through the worst of terrain. He was a model for Victor but well out of reach. The band would be fine in his hands. Synthia would remain his copilot no matter the storm. She had her song. She was on her way. She didn't need Victor anymore. She never did. The band never did. Petrumi would work his magic and slip Doc Sludge back into his slot, warts stripped from his biography with the darkest clouds clearing, open road ahead for the daring maestros. Victor would convince himself of all that and live with his own version of reality.

He couldn't do the same with losing Juan. That was too much for him. After eight hours on the road, long past midnight, he pulled off 101 onto the frontage road, passed Providence, and parked his Acura next to the marsh, a familiar space though no longer safe. That was the last place he had seen Juan, when Max and Clarence had signed onto Victor's backdoor plan. It was the place Juan ended his life, where they found his self-drugged body floating in the muck. It was no way for a promising young life to end. Victor hadn't thought it all the way through. He hadn't projected where his plotting could lead. He had no idea of the inglorious splinters that cracked the glass of shattered plans. He was clueless.

He stared into the marsh until dawn. A few birds came and went with the early morning light, but little else moved, least of all him. Staring, just staring. Wrong, so wrong, so many times wrong. He waited for Torch to call again. Another call would come any minute or maybe it wouldn't. Maybe Torch was the smartest guy of all. Maybe he finally went to sleep and when he woke up he would start over and move on. Torch's dreams were alive and real. Victor's were dead, same as Juan.

Victor sat motionless as the sun broke the horizon. The sun had returned to view as certainly as anything in the universe. It was fully a new day, Wednesday, the data was irrefutable. He hardly noticed when the banged up lime green Prius pulled up next to him. He recognized the car from work. It belonged to Darcy, the office admin, the lost date, the friend who had brought him his exit papers and wished him farewell on his journey months ago. That seemed longer ago than it was. So much had happened in that window of time, yet here he was, the same sad sack, still the guy who couldn't chart a proper course that steered around hell.

He looked out the car window at her and forced a half grin. It was good to see her. It also wasn't a surprise. When he called her last night from the road and told her he would be there, he knew she would come. Darcy was dependable that way, so very dependable in ways he could never be. She got out of her car, opened the door to his, and sat in the passenger seat.

"Thanks for coming," said Victor. "I needed to see a friendly face."

"You look spent, Vic. Are you okay?"

"Better than the last time you saw me."

"That's not saying much. Did you sleep at all?"

"Not last night or the night before. It doesn't matter."

"It matters. You need to clear your head. The shareholder meeting is in a few hours. The company will be sold."

"I know. I could go, but what's the point?"

She must have known he was right. There was nothing he could do to stop the sale. He had signed Sangstrum's release. She didn't know that, but fate was committed to ink.

"It's not your fault, Vic. He was a kid. He let it get to him. He thought the company meant more than it did."

"I should have seen something like this coming. I didn't handle the whole thing right. I planted a bomb and didn't understand what it meant."

"You tried to help us save the company. You took a risk. It didn't work out. You couldn't have seen this coming."

"It's not the first time, Darcy. I always see the problem, but I can't find the solution. I decide I'm right and that's all that matters. Being right doesn't matter if you can't make it right."

"I'm not sure that's true. We do the best we can. We can't see the future. We try to figure out what's right and mostly we botch it. It's what you meant to do that counts."

"No, intentions are meaningless. If you want to go to war, you have to know how to win. I always want to go to war and only think I know how to win. I was wrong when I tried to block the deal between Sangstrum and McWhorter. That wasn't my place. I was out of my league. Then I threw a laptop at the guy's head, like that helped."

"It made you a legend." She smiled. He couldn't help but laugh slightly.

"A legendary doofus," he said.

"Better than a forgotten doofus. Sangstrum will be a forgotten doofus. McWhorter will only be remembered because your laptop collided with his head. You won."

Victor dropped the grin. "No, I lost my temper and I lost the game. Then I did it again when I told the guys to plant the virus. I did it for the wrong reasons. It wasn't thoughtful. It was desperation. It was for me, not you guys."

"I doubt that. If it had worked, we'd be having a different conversation."

"If it had worked the company would be dead. We'd be having no conversation."

"The company was already dead, Vic. There's nothing left. We have to move on. It started as an idea. It ends as an idea. Nothingness returns. It doesn't matter."

"No, the virus would have killed the company and I'd be playing a gig opening for the Eagles. It was all about me."

"And we'd be proud of you. We'd be cheering for you. Your good is our good. We're connected that way. It's beyond us. It's something we can't control. It's forever."

"You sound like someone I used to know."

"That girl you left ten years ago in LA—you aren't over that, I know."

"I don't think I left her. I'm over it mostly, just not the parts where she talked about God. I have to get that out of my head. This won't help."

"Juan is with God. I think he'll be fine. Maybe that was what God wanted."

"Not you, too? Not now, okay. Not now."

"Juan is dead. You can think it's on you, Vic, but it's not. He made a bad choice. You have to learn to look ahead, to see what's next."

"He was such a good guy, so committed. He taught himself the game. The whole world was ahead of him. He didn't have the perspective to put it in context. When's the service?"

"Not sure, a few days at least. Remember we don't know where he came from. We have to find some family, someone who knows him besides us. It's weird."

They were silent again. Victor stared at his smartphone. Torch hadn't called. Maybe God was whispering in his ear. Maybe he could hear Darcy. Maybe Torch was moving on.

"Do you know what's happening with the company, Vic?"

"It's at a stalemate. Sangstrum was in a war with another company that wants to buy it. I was supposed to deliver the sale to his competitor and become the CEO, but I didn't help them close. I didn't want to help them close. I wanted to stay with the band. I didn't want to be under their thumb. I wanted to get away."

"The band was good for you, huh?"

"Not perfect, but better than this. I couldn't do it forever. I'm not wired the way Torch and Synthia are. They're in the band, plus these other two guys who don't like me much. Everyone likes the way we play. We had an unbelievable night at The Greek opening for Joe Walsh with a song I helped write."

"Opening for Joe Walsh a few months after getting fired—how many people can say that?"

"He asked us to go on the road with him."

"Yeah, you said the Eagles reunion. That's impossible to turn down. Wish I could be there to see it in person."

"I'm not going. I have to fix the situation here. Maybe I can get McWhorter to hire me and piece the team back together."

"Vic, you have to go. You can't fix this. McWhorter is going to strip it down to the studs. We'll all be getting termination notices tomorrow."

"I'll talk to him. There could be a way he comes out better if he listens to me."

"What's wrong with you? Is your head still recovering from being bashed in?"

"No, I'm clear. I've got to help find Juan's family, then get with McWhorter and work a deal."

"There's no deal with McWhorter. That deal is done and will sort itself out. We'll find Juan's family. You have to go on the road with your band. You can't let them down."

"I've already let them down. I disappeared on them yesterday to come here. They've probably replaced me already."

"Where are you supposed to be?"

"Tomorrow in New York for rehearsal, some hall on Sixth Avenue. Saturday night we're supposed to kickoff at Madison Square Garden."

"If you don't show up, that will be an even worse choice than throwing the laptop."

"I don't think so. This time I've thought it through. This time I have to get it right. I have to help wind down Global Harmonics and clean up the last mess I made in Los Angeles walking out of their meeting."

"You can't change anything here. If you don't go with the band, that's where the next mistake happens. That's something you can control. This isn't."

"I need to see where Max and Clarence are. They were freaking out when I talked to them yesterday. I feel responsible for them. Let me talk to them and see where it goes, see if they're on the same page as you. No one else can get hurt because of me. I need to know that." Victor's phone rang. Finally. He looked at the screen. There was the name he expected flashing on display.

"Are you going to answer it?" asked Darcy.

"It's him. He hasn't given up."

"Have you?"

He stared at the phone, then at the marsh, then at Darcy. It had been hours since Torch tried to reach him. The widening intervals told him this might be his last chance. Darcy's eyes were fixed on him, determined to cause him to choose the right fork in the road.

Victor clicked the answer button.

>> <<

A few hours later Victor pulled into the parking lot at Providence. The last time he had been there was the day he had been beaten. Thomas Katem Day. Some version of Thomas Katem. It was 9:45 a.m. and he had some time to kill before he saw Max and Clarence.

They were at the shareholder meeting two miles away. They had to see it happen. The meeting would commence at 10:00 a.m., and the substance of it would complete by 10:10 following the merger vote, when all the proxies of the institutional shareholders would be reported and recorded. The retail tally and vote of those present would follow, as if that meant anything beyond a formality. Victor couldn't stand the idea of watching it happen. That vote was ten minutes of memory he didn't need to encode.

Providence wouldn't open for lunch until 11:30 a.m. but the door was open for the few employees loading in supplies. He crept in and caught a glimpse of the familiar karaoke stage with its surrounding cocktail tables. No customers were there, just two waitresses setting up for the day and the bartender taking inventory. Victor wondered if they would remember him. Of course they did. They were friendly, invited him in, offered him coffee. He had been onstage for open mic more than enough times to be remembered, good nights and bad. They told him a friend of his was there too, another regular who sometimes came in early, not necessarily for breakfast, which they didn't serve. A friend of his? What friend?

Sitting at the bar was Johnny Olano of Elvis impression fame. He was in street clothes and didn't look much better than Victor. He had a coffee cup of something in front of him, no steam off the brim. Victor couldn't tell what it was, but as he approached Johnny, he could smell the familiar alcohol of the pores. That was sad. He knew old man Johnny as a club rat who loved the stage, who loved playing The King. He didn't know him as a drunk. Maybe he had a bad night. Maybe this wasn't his regular routine.

"Johnny Olano, Elvis of Marin, how are you doing? Remember me? Victor Selo. I used to go on after you."

"Teen idol, sings 'Dream On,' I know you." Johnny took a swig from the porcelain cup, smiled at the bartender for a refill. He got it with the bartender shaking his head to say don't expect more. "Where you been, Brother V? You've been away awhile."

"Did you miss me, Johnny? That would make me happy, that someone of your talent missed me."

"Of course I didn't miss you. I hate losing out to you on those twenty-five dollar gift certificates on competition nights, but it's good to see you. You don't look great."

"I'm okay. Haven't been singing as much. Got back into my guitar with a paying gig."

"You had the best paying gig ever at that software company. Walked away I heard, around the time you got beat up here. You should see a doc about some of those marks on your face. The med tech these days is something. Shouldn't you be at the shareholder meeting?"

"Johnny, what do you know about shareholder meetings?"

"It's over at the Wyndham, isn't it? You could still make it if you run. More going on there than here."

"I've had my fill of Global Harmonics. We took it as far as it could go."

"I don't think so. It was doing great. Then it stopped. Something bad happened after you left. Your friends don't come around much anymore. This place is hurting. Sometimes it's just me and one or two others on the karaoke machine."

"I didn't know you were that up on Global Harmonics, Johnny. I never knew you that way. Do you know a lot about the software community?"

"Would you believe me if I told you I used to be a UNIX programmer?"

"I would, but you're probably lying."

"I'm not lying. They didn't pay us as much in my day, before all the IPO madness, but I coded. Sang on the side. Now there's no 'on the side.' I just sing, better than you I might add."

"You want to open for the Eagles?" asked Victor. "I know a cover band that needs a decent guitarist."

"You walked out on that, huh? That takes balls, or you're an idiot. Nah, I'm too old, I like it here, even with the small audiences, as long as they don't close. I win the gift certificates most nights now, but they cut them to ten bucks."

"Times are hard, you adjust."

"You should go over to the shareholder meeting. Make a stink. Go on the record that those crooks screwed everyone. We need the people back here after work, not more layoffs."

"I said my piece with them, Johnny. Did nothing. Believe me, I was in the thick of it. Make a scene there? I don't think so. I may go see the new owner afterward, see if I can help him get things moving again. I haven't decided yet."

"Choices are hard," acknowledged Johnny. "Forks in the road, we don't see them when we're standing there, only when we look back, and then we've long decided."

"Too many hard choices. I get them all wrong. Most of them. You ever get married?"

"Yeah, sure. Twice. Three times sort of, but it doesn't count if you don't get a legal marriage certificate, so call it two."

"It didn't work out?"

"It worked out fine. Why do you think I did it again?"

"I don't get it. If you get married again, it means you failed."

Johnny signaled the bartender for a top-off. He was downing them fast. The bartender told him no more until that night. He offered one to Victor on the house. Victor stayed with coffee.

"My first wife died on me. We were married eleven years, five months, four days. We got married young. We were finally ready to have a child, but she got a cold that became pneumonia. Her heart stopped in her sleep. It crushed me."

"I'm sorry. I didn't mean to upset you."

"It was over forty years ago, I'm good. That's why I got married again a few years later. That was the 'sort of,' another UNIX programmer, lasted six years. She was a free spirit like me and left one day without warning. That was okay, it was a fine six years, a bad day, then some healing. Five years later I went again and this time I got it signed. I met her here, another aging hippie type. She liked to sing Aretha, looked like her, too. We were married a long time, still are I guess. A few years ago she signed on for some traveling dinner theater thing. I think the first road tour was *Dreamgirls*. Her Effie was irresistible, but I liked it here. She went. I stayed. We still see each other once a year when her show is in town. And when I say *see*, I mean *see*!"

Victor stared into his coffee, listening carefully to Johnny's story, then caught himself needing more. "Johnny, can I ask you a personal question?"

"A more personal question than *see*? I might not answer, but ask."

"Do you believe in God? I mean, after losing your first wife, then your second sort of, and third except once a year?"

"My answer might piss you off."

"I'm already pissed off."

"Of course I do. Where do you think I got my talent? This golden voice. It comes from God. Everything original comes from God, and the bad stuff is for a reason. We're not supposed to understand it, but it is."

"Your faith is that strong?"

"Brother V, did you ever write UNIX code?"

"Not exactly."

"You never wrote any code at all. You're a manager type, right? So all you do is scenario planning. You don't actually compile. You scenario planners believe you can out plan God, but you can't. UNIX programmers like me pray every time we compile, and when the program flies, we know God was there for us."

"Brother J, should you be drinking so early?"

"God makes this stuff, too. That's how it goes, really good and really bad. The thing is, marriage is good if it's good while you're in it. No regrets. Then if it doesn't work, you heal and love again. Like code. Version 2.0."

"Dark, Johnny."

"You asked me about God. I told you how it is for me. It is what it is. I don't know why that's hard for you. You make your own call on faith. Doesn't bother me, but somehow you got that talent. It didn't come from nowhere. It didn't come from nothing. You have to respect that. You want to tell me how you think you got in front of the Eagles?"

"It doesn't matter. I'll figure it out. What are you going to do if they close this place?"

"I'm going to hope that doesn't happen, and if it does then I'll sing somewhere else. So what, Global Harmonics has gotten pretty morbid? No one likes to come here anymore. No more live band karaoke. They can't pay the musicians. We sing with the machine. The joint is dying. That's what happens when companies go down. It's not just the company that suffers. You think you can help the new guys run it?"

"I doubt it. I don't think they're open to it. So much has happened. I don't think the place can heal."

"Like the kid who killed himself?"

"You know about that, too."

"Olano knows all. Got a lot of time on my hands. Sad, he was like a teenager, I think. Killing yourself for a company. It's like having a wife you love, only she doesn't love you back anymore, so you kill yourself rather than move on to another wife. How does that make sense?"

"It makes no sense. Right now I have to go see his friends. They all helped me try to save the company and it didn't work out. I don't know what to say to them."

"Doesn't matter what you say, matters that you're here. Matters that you cared enough to come here. I'm sure you got other things to do, other places to be. The Eagles, all that."

"We'll see. I'm glad I bumped into you. It's good to see a friendly face."

"Shareholder meeting is probably over."

"It probably is. They don't take long."

"You missed the whole thing."

"I got to hang out with you."

"Come back later tonight. We'll do a duet, Elton John and Elvis. We can trade off on harmony."

"We both work better alone."

"You're probably right. Good luck with the Eagles, and those kids."

"Good luck to you, Johnny. Don't stop rocking."

"Not a chance. I might even get married again."

"I don't doubt that. Remember, you are married."

"I don't forget much, kiddo."

With a final look over his shoulder at the karaoke machine, Victor left a few dollars on the bar and headed for the door. He looked at the stage where the band used to play. He looked at the microphone stand. He looked at the dance floor. The good times were good. He never appreciated them enough, never savored those forever moments. He wished he had tried that duet with Johnny when it would have mattered.

"V, some parting wisdom?"

"You bet, Johnny. What say the UNIX man?"

"Take the onramp. Move on."

"That simple, huh?"

"This show is dead. Forward out the door and onto the next song. Not here. The next tune is up for grabs."

Johnny Elvis Olano was a wise old drunk. Victor knew he was right. The next set of choices facing him weren't going to be any easier.

>> <<

Victor left his car in the parking lot and walked the half mile down the narrow road to the Scottsdale marsh landing. He wasn't feeling any stronger, but his head was clearer. Johnny had woken him up to something, made him feel wanted. Max and Clarence had already arrived. The scene reminded him of when they had crafted the perfect plan, only there had been one more of them there and a lot more hope.

"Selo, you missed the shareholder meeting," blurted out Max in lieu of a greeting.

"I know. I couldn't have changed anything. I don't like to be where I can't make a difference. How are you guys doing?"

It was a stupid question. They were a mess, same as he was. He wished he had something more inspired to say. Perfunctory chatter was never a great path with these guys. They didn't answer. They moved on.

"What are we going to tell his family if we find them?" asked Clarence.

"You're going to tell them that Juan was a hero, that he risked everything to save his friends' jobs," responded Victor.

Clarence was staring at his own feet. "A hero? He killed himself in the mud for no good reason."

"It was a good reason in his mind. He was confused, but he was courageous. His dedication was noble and overwhelmed him. It's awful. It's a tragedy. It shouldn't have happened, but it's my fault, not his and not yours."

Max fought back unrestrainable tears. "It's not your fault. It was in his head. He couldn't lose this job. He didn't think he'd get another chance, not a company this cool. It would be all downhill from here. Maybe he was right."

"He was not right. It was a place we worked. It was a job. We all have to move on. The two of you have to figure out the rest of your lives. You're young and I'm not that old. We can do other things."

Clarence gazed into the marsh. "Are you going to talk to that slime, McWhorter?"

"I was thinking about it. I talked to Darcy about it this morning. Then I bumped into an old friend and changed my mind."

Clarence had turned his head away from the wetlands, not yet making eye contact with Victor. "That's the right decision. McWhorter doesn't deserve us. So what happens now?"

"You're going to get severance checks and payout of your accrued vacation, plus all your stock is liquid. Take the money and start your own company."

"You think we can do that?" asked Max.

"I know you can do it or I wouldn't tell you to do it. So do it. Do you have any ideas?"

"No, but ideas are easy, there are thousands of them," said Max. "The hard part is doing it, making the idea into something. Almost no one can do that. We learned that from you."

"I'm glad you learned something from me. So you'll do it?"

"Do you think Darcy would throw in with us?"

"I think she'd be honored. You write the business plan. Email it to me and I'll take a look at it for you. A fresh start is what Juan would want for you."

"Make Juan proud," chanted Clarence. "Make Juan proud."

"He was already proud. He was proud of his friends. When's the memorial service?"

"Tomorrow," said Max. "Too bad you can't stay around."

"I can stay around. I haven't got anything planned."

"That's not what Darcy said," continued Max. "She said you have a gig at Madison Square Garden opening for the Eagles. You need to be at rehearsal."

"Darcy talks too much sometimes," said Victor.

"We'll stand in for you at the service," said Clarence. "Juan would be okay with that. Playing with that band, shredding, that's like coding. Juan would want you to be doing that."

"Coding is hard. Music is fun. Well, mostly it's fun."

"Coding used to be fun," said Max. "Maybe it will be again."

"It will be. Guys, you can do anything. I've seen you code miracles."

Clarence finally looked Victor in the eye. "Maybe we can do something together again someday, all of us. That would be fun."

"That would be fun," softly echoed Victor.

Max's mobile rang. He looked at the screen and lost another tear. "I think this is someone from Juan's family. We may have located them. I have to take this."

Max answered the call and stepped away toward the edge of the marsh, out of hearing range, leaving Victor alone with Clarence.

"I want to meet them," said Victor. "It would mean a lot to me for a bunch of reasons."

"You don't have time. You need to go to New York. We have this."

Now Victor stared into the marsh, beyond where Max was talking on the phone, imagining Juan making that awful decision to give up. "I'm not sure I belong there, Clarence."

"Be sure. Listen to your own words. We all have to move on."

Victor knew that Clarence was right. He didn't like the idea of leaving before Juan's life celebration, but he had no time if he wanted to make the gig in New York. He couldn't let down Torch and Synthia. He couldn't let himself down. Madison Square Garden was once in a lifetime. Max and Clarence would start over and take Darcy along on their new venture. That resonated with him, no matter how the tragic loss of Juan would forever haunt him. Their gathering at this swamp, their nights at the nearby karaoke club, the decomposing company up the road, all of it would cast shadows on the days and years ahead. Ghosts were eternal. Mistakes left scars. Open wounds could only be healed by new challenges, new horizons, forgiveness of inadequacies and failures. Time was imperfect, but if redirected to positive ends, it would mend some remorse.

Johnny and Darcy were also right. This song was over. The lyrics had to be retired. The melody had to be cast in mothballs. Victor wasn't at a fork in the road. He was at a stop sign gating a highway.

TRACK 13: WHAT'S THAT SMELL?

THE SIXTH AVENUE REHEARSAL HALL IN NEW YORK WAS NOT WHAT VICTOR EXPECTED. He may have read too many issues of Rolling Stone growing up, all those glossy pages of mega-switch sound boards and plush sectionals, crystal and chrome sound studios with gorgeous gawkers hanging around. The walk-up was a rat hole. The plumbing was old and exposed. The walls were undecorated. The marred wood floors had been worn by rolling equipment cases. The freight elevator was a fenced cage. There were no frothy cappuccinos or fruity mai tais, no M&Ms with hand-picked colors, not even a vending machine. Musical equipment was aplenty and he guessed the place was soundproofed, but beyond that it was a windowless box with a steel door and five flights of stairs to street level. The stench fit the decor. Body odor, algae, fungus, hard to tell. Rodents probably. No way the Eagles rehearsed in a dump like this. Second class road status was its own animal.

The rest of the band was waiting for Victor when he arrived, working on an all too familiar line-up extracted from timeless Set A. He hardly recognized Baker Bagley who had shaved off his beard. Sans the facial scrub, it was even harder to imagine him as a ballplayer.

Torch barely looked up from coiling his microphone cord. "Hey, lookie who made it to the job. The red-eye from San Fran do you in, Nowhere Man? We got a show to play this weekend, kind of a big one."

"I'm fine. I'm sorry I've been all over the place. A friend of mine, a kid I knew at work, he lost perspective and . . . it doesn't matter. I'm sorry I'm late. Yeah, I came straight from the airport. Let's play something."

"You should have been on the flight with us, but you had other business on your mind. You got convinced we need you more than you need us. That's just not right."

"Torch, we talked about this on the phone. I got here in time, okay?"

"No, not okay. Attitude is wrong. Consistency is disjointed. See, you think you're something special. You think this band's meteoric liftoff is all about you. I don't think so. None of us do. You were in the right place at the right time. That's it, not more."

Victor couldn't counter that. He knew Torch was right. It was a lucky break for all of them, but most of all for him. His presence a coincidence? Probably. His ability to claim otherwise? Not worth trying. He held his tongue. The loft felt cold to him, his skin clammy, his palms drawing moisture. His eyes were slowly watering, but he willed it to stop.

"Torch, this isn't helping," said Synthia.

"No, it's not helping. Little boy blue and the man in the moon is soft. Can't keep his head in the game when it matters. He doesn't realize we've been at this all our lives. No magic potions, no magic carpet rides. We worked for this. He showed up. The dots got connected on his shift, so damn what? Prizes show up after the work happens, long after the waiting room. He isn't the ride. He's along for the ride, unless he's not."

"I promise you I'm here 100%. I'm not going anywhere."

"Maybe you're not. Maybe you're not going on that stage. Who's to know?"

"Can we please figure out the set?" Thank God for Synthia with an S, trying to move them onto something productive. She wouldn't look at Victor. He had stepped on her trust as well. He had to get it back. He had to make her believe.

"I say we stick with Set A," said Baker Bagley. "We know it the best. Who gives a shit what we play. No one will be listening to us. They're here for the Eagles and we're here to push the lobby bar and give them more time to sell T-shirts. We have the gig. They aren't gonna fire us on the road."

"Hell they won't," said Phil-Phil. "A few days ago they fired the band that had our slot and gave it to us. They get to do what they want."

"Phil-Phil is right, this is a tryout," said Synthia. "We have to win the rest of the tour."

"Maybe Brother Nowhere has some thoughts on that. How about it, Knopfler-san, you got some funky new thinking to share?"

Victor said nothing. He knew Torch was baiting him. He also knew he had only one chance left to get back in the game.

"I asked you a question," continued Torch. "The Act wants to know what kind of change you got in mind next."

Victor had no choice. He had to respond. "Okay, here's the thing, I've been thinking about . . ." He couldn't get out the words before Torch cut him off.

"Thinking? You got too many issues to be thinking. You tell us what songs to play. You write nutty lyrics no one understands. You leave the band. You get dizzy under the lights. How do I know you won't pass out cold in front of twenty thousand people at Madison Square?"

"This is the bigs, rookie," coaxed Baker Bagley. "You can't collapse in The Show . . ."

"Sludge made bail," interrupted Phil-Phil. "Not enough beds at the inn so they booted him. How hard does this have to be?"

"Seriously?" said Synthia. "Victor's a pain in the ass, but he's not a drug dealer."

"I'm not going to pass out onstage. I've figured stuff out. I'm fine to go on."

"You talked to Sludge?" asked Baker Bagley.

"Maybe I did," said Phil-Phil.

"Maybe I did," repeated Torch. "I call a lot of people. I called Nowhere like twenty times in one night before he picked up. Maybe I went another way."

"He's here, let's rehearse," insisted Synthia. Victor must have connected with her, or maybe she felt sorry for him. It didn't matter. They needed to stop talking and play.

"Let me guess, something new?" Phil-Phil had never shown any warmth toward Victor, but now he was outright confrontational. He wanted Sludge. That was going to be a problem.

"I've been giving it some thought," said Victor. "If you're open to hearing it, I have an idea that might work."

"Lucky us, an idea that might work from Data Boy." Baker Bagley was on the bandwagon of doubt.

Phil-Phil threw his drumsticks against the wall. "You know what works? 'Funeral for a Friend' works. I played that behind Elton John. Doesn't mean shit here. You know what doesn't work? Getting fired from the gig because you're a flunkout loser. I did that, too. I don't know why you're here."

"You got a reason you should be here, Nowhere?" asked Torch.

"I told you, I let go of the past."

"No, I want to hear something that is gonna spike this gig," continued Torch. "Tell us what you think is going to work, maybe we take you back."

Victor took the risk that Torch was sincere, truly interested in his next idea, leaving the door to his return a crack open. "We have a lot of equity in the Mandalay and Greek sets. How about splitting the difference and pulling all the new material together? That energy is good. The songs are fresh. Our original has to be there in case there's a label guy in the house, which we know there will be. Our opening song has to complement the main act, surprise the crowd and win them over in a second, all at once. So I'm thinking . . . I don't know, you might or might not like this . . . You sure you want to hear this?"

"I hate it and you haven't even told us yet," said Torch. "What's the open?"

"'Don't Be Cruel.'"

"Do Elvis at Madison Square. Before the Eagles? You are an idiot."

"Cheap Trick did it. They killed."

"African American Elvis impersonator laughed off the most important stage on the planet—yeah, that's how I want to early retire."

"They'll never see Elvis coming. You'll own the arena."

Torch coiled more of the mic cord. "No, too much of a risk."

"The King is your sweet spot, vocal nirvana," argued Victor. "Take us to a place you know well and we've never been."

"He's right, it's brilliant," said Synthia.

"I hate Elvis," added Phil-Phil. "But I don't hate it when you do it."

"Your interpretation is unique." Baker Bagley grabbed his bass and played a few bars.

"Not worth the downside."

"Timbre, baby, timbre," rallied Victor. "You don't like that one, do 'All Shook Up.' Same idea."

"Nah, it won't work."

"It will work," contended Synthia. "How many people can pull off Elvis and not make it a tribute? They'll come alive if you sell it. You can sell it, Torch."

"No, it's the wrong direction. Another one."

The dark circles under Victor's eyes were impossible to hide. "I don't have another one."

"I do," said Torch. "'Burning Love.'"

Victor sprung back to life. "Really, you like this idea?"

"That's one's mine. Cheap Trick doesn't do that one. Let's try it."

"Right now? At this moment?"

"We're in rehearsal. Why would I say try it if I didn't want to try it? Try it means try it."

The band got the message and moved into place to try out the Elvis tune. Victor got the idea that Torch was beginning to forgive him for going sideways in LA, but the tension between them was on the edge of boiling over. On her way to the keyboards, Synthia stepped past Torch near the mic stand. She and Torch lowered their voices, but Victor overheard them.

"Did you really call Sludge?"

"You bet I did. Sludge is backup, in the on-deck circle in case we need him."

"Putting in Sludge would be a mistake. We have one chance to get this right."

"Trusting this dude is the mistake. I'll make the call when the time comes. Let's play Elvis, okay?"

Victor grabbed a freshly strung Gibson solid-body off a guitar stand and tried to play back "Burning Love" in his head. After the first time through it he would be fine. Could they trust him with the gig? He understood that was its own risk. He had to prove they could depend on him, but even he wasn't all that sure.

>> <<

Risk, always risk, the wise and the reckless. The opaque nights in Vegas loomed large. A short subway ride away was Wall Street, the high-stakes day game. The whole idea of gambling seemed strange to Victor, but not more so than investing. They were supposed to be different, that's what the text books said. Gambling was a game of chance with short-term results, often immediate, odds in favor of the house, way more losing than winning. Investing was a discipline with a daily clock but ultimately a winner's paradise of skill and strategy, odds in favor of the patient, still more losers than winners, but winners had more control if they stuck to a plan. Buy low, sell high, don't bet on whim—seemed reasonable enough.

Don't gamble. Invest. So how come they both had so many arcane rules allegedly steeped in mathematics? You could win a hand of blackjack with anything from a twelve to a twenty-one depending on what the dealer pulled. Pure chance, but you were supposed to hold a sixteen against a six showing because there were more tens in the deck than anything else forcing a bust. *Supposed to?* The pit rules were more explicit than those of the trading floor, a false advantage if ever one existed. On the exchanges, you could buy at an earnings multiple of 6 or 106. In either event, if the stock went up on noise, you won, but you were investing, not gambling, noise was supposed to be irrelevant. How come suckers could lose money buying at any price? That should never happen if transacting was a discipline, but it did without warning, massive unpredictable spreads every day. So much for hard lines of differentiation.

The hope of easy money was eternal, lotto lunacy. Fast bucks were enticing. Greed was academic. Anyone could convince themselves they understood the numbers well enough to compete. The depth of the scam was impossible to comprehend and yet it was as inexhaustible as it was inescapable. The few true winners needed discipline not to gamble and game to invest. The paradox gave and took all. To be in it was not to see it. To be outside was to leave money on the table or at least believe that was the consequence.

Victor loved playing music nightly at the Golden Nugget, but he couldn't have been happier to leave Las Vegas behind him. He had defied Katem, a gamble if ever there was one, and still appeared to be beating the odds. That didn't completely make sense to him, since the odds of the financial community were forever against him. As a longtime loser addicted to buying high-risk securities at impossibly inflated prices, he discovered time and again the odds always win in the end. Katem wasn't the kind of guy who would walk away from the table a loser. If he wasn't taking Victor down at the moment, he would try again. Vegas was a microcosm for risk. Bad risk went to the house eventually. To deny that was to set oneself up for a fall. Victor expected it was coming. He couldn't have envisioned when or where.

Many times at the Nugget, before a show, after a late night drink at the bar, following breakfast at the Claim Jumper, Victor thought about the odds, about going to the tables. Why not? Everyone else did it, almost everyone around him. Sometimes after the show in the wee hours he would see Baker Bagley and Phil-Phil at the craps tables giving away their split of the evening's cash in record time. They would leave the casino miserable at dawn, pledging never to do it again, but always doing it again. Then again, maybe everyone wasn't duped. He never saw Torch there, nor would he see Synthia forking over her income for a few minutes of head rush. They had too much to lose, too much to protect, too many obvious mistakes in their paths. They didn't need more problems.

Victor never went there, not even the proverbial single deck of blackjack. He had never done it. He had won out on that, followed Torch's warning. There were too many stupid IPOs in near memory, most of them cleverly disguised cons, shakedowns with bells ringing on TV. Too many of his hard-earned dollars obliterated in milliseconds of selloff with nothing to show for it. He knew he had been hooked. That was why he had nothing to his name. Betting on stocks may not have looked the same as betting on a deck of cards, but it wasn't investing. It was speculating on the absurd. This guy won today, that guy lost, but in the end most everyone was a loser. On his last day in Vegas, Victor passed the final test. He walked out past the tables, across the oxygen enhanced casino floor, and into the smoldering daylight. He had tested himself, but had he recovered? Had he been rehabilitated? He would never be sure. That's why they called it addiction.

After the rough rehearsal on Sixth Avenue, Victor took the subway downtown. The real casino floor, the place where he had dropped all of his money, was a place he had never been. Strangely enough, he had never been to New York, never visited Wall Street. It had always been a broadcast image on a screen, distant enough to be a fantasy. He needed to see it in person.

It was late afternoon when Victor arrived downtown. He walked to the front of the New York Stock Exchange and stood there in awe. What was it about this place? Why did it matter? Stocks could be traded in real time over computer networks. They didn't need a home, a marble shrine, but there he stood in front of the door to their encasement. Wall Street had become like Hollywood and Silicon Valley, more an idea than a place, but there was still Hollywood Boulevard with its Walk of Fame and there was still Sand Hill Road with its venture capital low-rises near Stanford. This was the New York Stock Exchange. It mattered as an icon. Its aura and physicality were definitive, its permanency presumptuous. It was all at once arena and tomb.

Did he want to see the bell? Sure, tourist of the moment, he wouldn't have minded seeing a smiling someone ring it, especially a wily entrepreneur surviving to IPO eminence. Too bad, that was hours ago. Come back tomorrow and enjoy the viewing gallery.

He wasn't a tourist in the truest sense. He was in New York for a business purpose distant from the financial world, yet he wanted to meet a trader and ask some prying questions. He wanted to understand what happened here, how what he did in Marin County more than two thousand miles away translated into money changing hands. Was there a connection beyond the commission or were they pit bosses like the guys in Vegas? Did they add value or simply make odds and take an override? What was a trader anyway? Why would someone do this every day? Why would they take his money without a care in the world and leave him with nothing? They loved nouveau con artists like Sangstrum and McWhorter, freewheeling swindlers like Katem who managed outposts that fed deal flow. Dealers and pit bosses or mathematically trained professionals—which was it?

Victor wandered in and out of the local bars nearby. He was out of place, lost in a maze of suits and ties mostly pulled loose for the day—banter, soft dealing, gossiping, shouting across beers and martinis as if the trading day were still on. They were young, most of him, like he used to be. The older ones, the bosses, the managing directors, had probably gone home, taken the train or their car services to Connecticut, to their kids' soccer games or maybe to Teterboro in New Jersey to take a private jet to West Palm overnight and return tomorrow for late breakfast. The young traders, the movers, the shakers, they were still around, working each other for information, working each other for leads and tips. It was a cacophony, not a lot different from the ding-ding-dinging casino floors. Slots were digitized, trading was digitized, but the analog activity painted the draining with authenticity. So few humans stole from each other, right? Make it look human and the neural vacuums would do the dirty work.

Victor felt his mobile buzz in his pocket. He looked at the screen and saw it was Synthia, her lovely name still giving him pause with an S. It actually looked right with the S because that was who she was, her identity beyond the norm. He didn't answer it. He wasn't ready. Rehearsal had been another debacle. Maybe Sludge was coming back. He didn't want to hear that. He was in a unique place, one he might not ever see again. The Eagles had it right, *this could be heaven or this could be hell*. He wasn't ready to decide.

He passed the brass bull on the street, much less symbolic in person than it appeared on TV. The tourists were snapping photos. Why? They could download a perfect photo from the Internet anytime as a souvenir, but they needed proof they were there. They weren't there. They were outsiders in perpetuity. Victor knew the commissions he paid helped underwrite the plated moldings, the towering white pillars, the billowing flags hanging overhead, plus most of the pricy cocktails being expensed. That used to be his money. He didn't need a picture of the bull.

He tried a few times to strike up a conversation with the players. They weren't interested. Maybe he was wearing the wrong clothes, no loosened tie, no stained armpits in his shirtsleeves. He wasn't one of them. Did they know that for sure? In Silicon Valley they play a game called "Billionaire or Bum" where people try to guess which one is the guy in the hoodie. Here their instincts mattered more. He got a "hi-ya" or a "enjoy your vacation" but little more.

He walked up and down the main block a few times and then had his fill. He wandered over to Battery Park, overlooking the choppy inlet. He could see to the Statue of Liberty, just barely through the rising fog on the harbor. He sat on a bench next to a guy about his age smoking a cigarette and pounding furiously on an Android handset. Wow, people outside of Las Vegas smoked cigarettes. He wore the Wall Street post-war day uniform, rumpled high-end suit and loosened tie. Maybe this guy could tell him something.

"You a trader?"

"That's an idiotic question." The words came with a smoking exhale.

Of course he was a trader. Victor must have hit a nerve.

"Sorry, didn't mean to interrupt your email." Victor backed down quickly. He knew he should get back to Midtown. He should check his messages and find out why Synthia had called.

"No, that's alright. I'm not a trader. I'm an analyst for a bank that covers the equities market, industrial equipment sector. Exciting stuff, huh?"

"High stress stuff. I'm from out of town."

"No shit, really? You can still make the last ferry to Liberty Island if you hustle."

"Nah, I'm good. I'm a musician. I have to get back to my bandmates soon. We have a big gig tomorrow."

"Yeah, what club? Tell me what kind of music. Maybe I'll drop by."

"It's sold out, but thanks for asking. You like working on Wall Street?"

"We get paid a lot, more than we should."

"What do you like best about it, when you're preparing a report on a company?"

"The immediacy, I guess. I'm considered a subject matter expert, an authority on a sliver of the whole shebang. My little upgrade or downgrade can mean a lot. I can write whatever I want, clean data or muddy. People who disagree sometimes call it a clowngrade, but they still pay attention. Why do you ask?"

"I'm trying to talk myself out of trading forever."

"Got bit by a nasty one, huh?"

"Not really, kind of got nibbled to death by a bunch of bad ones. I used to work for a hot tech company. They paid me mostly in stock. I gave it back the same way."

"Like a crack addict. Everyone thinks they're smarter than the market. No one is smarter than the market. Not me, not Warren Buffett. He's rich because he knows that. He studies, buys, and holds. The guys who trade, they get hooked, they never let go. Sounds like you know that."

"You always know it in your head, but you do dumb things. I've done a lot of dumb things."

"We all do. Let it go. Stop trading and move on."

"Yep, I'm thinking about it."

"I thought you said you were a musician, but you were in a tech company and you trade retail. Your story is confused."

"It's very confused. I'm not sure why I'm in New York except to play this gig. A friend of mine took his own life a few days ago. I need to do this because I said I would."

The analyst looked at him funny. New Yorkers knew a crackpot when they saw one. Deflection was an instinct. "Must be a good gig."

"It's a really good gig. I wish I had an extra ticket. I'd give it to you. I better get going. You've been very kind to let me bother you."

"What do you want to know, my friend, analyst to retail trader? I already told you how not to get shellacked. Buy the index, not the clowngrade, and you mostly won't get bludgeoned. You look like you want to know something else."

Victor thought about that. Yeah, that was the question: What did he come to Wall Street to know? "I want to know why what we have is not enough, why we bet it on the unknown."

"Beats me. When you do what I do and think people wager their money on my opinions, you know the game is screwed. Odds are stacked against little guys, but little guys who can't afford it and don't know the game come to the Coliseum to bet their lives away."

"Like a poker table."

"Just like a poker table, plus we have our own 24-7 television coverage on CNBC that makes it look like a sporting event, and the best newspaper in the country is named after our street address. So it seems legit. The pros take the money from the amateurs. Lightweights wallow pitifully in the losses. That's the way it always works and they still keep coming."

"Can I ask you a personal question?"

"Sounds like you're going to."

"If you had enough right now, what you needed to get by and be happy, would you take your chips off the table and call it a day?"

"No, I wouldn't."

"You don't even need to think about it?"

"No. I could tell you I might, but I wouldn't. No one here would. It's not for the reason you probably think."

"You probably think I think greed."

"Bingo, and that's wrong. It's a motivator, but it's not everything. Fear is everything. If I stop and don't accumulate more, someone will surprise me one day and take everything I have. They'll show up one day and take it. I won't know where they came from or why. They get you when you're not looking. That's how the big lions reign. They loom, they intimidate, they force their prey to expose themselves unsuspectingly, and then they strike and take the spoils."

"And you're the shill who sets them on edge."

"You got it. I write analyses to deflect obvious entry points. The pros slap you down and take what was yours when it's in a trough because you've had your fill. You think you're done, you've had enough pain. Then you have nothing and you have to start over. Starting over sucks."

"Winners don't walk away because it's a drug, and losers don't walk away because they don't know they're losers."

"That's how we're wired. No regrets, no apologies, I would keep fighting for more. So would everyone else around here. Keep everyone else guessing. Keep your prey on the open prairie. Seek more meat than you could ever eat even if it costs you your sanity."

Victor was silent.

"Did that answer your question?" asked the analyst.

"It did, it hit home in a way I can't quite articulate. The only thing missing was faith."

"I'm the wrong guy to ask about that, not when you see how my team makes sausage."

Victor got up to leave. He had his answer. He had no more questions. He would leave the analyst on the prairie, but not before being on the receiving end of an inquiry.

"Are you really a musician?"

"I think I am."

"Where's your gig?"

"Madison Square Garden."

"Sure it is."

"Thank you for the truth."

"You got it, musician friend. Don't tiptoe into conquered territory. Outsiders get creamed. Whatever opponent you confront, you have to fight for more. Otherwise they'll take what you have."

The analyst lit another cigarette and went back to pounding on his mobile. He and the analyst had never even told each other their names, kind of a New York encounter when he thought about it. Way better than a selfie with the bronze bull.

Victor took a final look at New York Harbor and then made his way from Battery Park back to the subway. He needed to get back to Midtown and get some rest before the big gig tomorrow. He badly needed some rest. He couldn't blow the gig. People he cared about were counting on him. He needed to make good on that promise. No more gambling.

>> <<

When Victor returned to his hotel room, he found Synthia at her keyboard wearing a set of headphones. She was always where she wanted to be. She hadn't left him a message on his mobile so it was a bit of a surprise to see her, though she usually emerged unannounced.

"How did you get in here?" he asked.

"I told them I was your wife. I can be convincing."

"You could be my wife, I guess."

"We'd have to start with a date. I'm old-fashioned. Maybe someday you'll ask."

"I'll take it under advisement. What are you really doing here?"

"You didn't answer my call."

"I was trying to figure out some stuff. Why didn't you leave a message?"

"I didn't need to leave a message. You knew it was me."

"Yeah, I'm sorry. I was down on Wall Street. I wanted to see what it was."

"What was it?"

"Not somewhere I want to be, but there's something about it I can't shake."

"I thought you were done pissing away your money."

"I don't have any money to piss away. Yeah, I'm over that. I should be happier with what I have, even though what I have is a mess. I should be nicer to people like you."

They stared at each other a moment. He didn't think he had opened a door, but maybe he had in a backhanded way.

"Vic, why hasn't something happened between us?"

He should have been expecting that at some point, but her challenge was too theoretical to grasp. He didn't have a good answer. He tried anyway. "It would piss off Torch."

"Right, like you're not already an expert at that."

Dumb answer. He wasn't ready for a relationship. What, after ten years, still not ready? Nope, not healed. Not looking forward. Not emotionally grounded. A tryst, yeah, that would be acceptable, possibly even enjoyable. It would be fantastic actually, but not with someone in the band, not a coworker where a breakup would be a disaster and he had been warned. Not warned, threatened. Risk avoidance, remember? No rolling the dice. Not with these table stakes.

He needed to imagine her looking awful, screaming at him in a breakup. That would kill the mood—see her as seething and spiteful, leaving him and blaming him for blowing it. It would all be his fault, always his fault. She knew he was damaged goods. Hell, he came from foster care, emancipated without promise from the unworkable system. How could she not get that? Look ugly, damn you, Synthia. Stop being so captivating, so enthralling, so beguiling. Call in the emergency airlift, escape before impact. Why did she have to smell that good? Vanilla, jasmine, almond, violet, all at once, really? Stop that. Forget to bathe. Wear old sweats. Stink yourself up. Protect the band. Don't go to a dangerous place risking everyone's future.

Victor sidestepped the threat with a tactical block, shifting their focus to the beast not in the room. "Is Torch bringing back Doc Sludge?"

"If he wanted Sludge back, he'd be here. He wants you onstage. That's why you're here. No other reason."

"Torch is negotiating?"

"You have to win it in his mind to make it yours. You sure you're ready for this gig?"

"I can do it. You?"

She nodded confidently, then pulled out some sheet music and set it on the piano cover. "I've been tweaking our song. I want to play you some changes in the modulation."

"Your song."

"Our song. You wrote the lyrics."

"I wrote those ages ago. That doesn't count. It's yours."

"I say it counts so it counts. Listen to the changes and tell me what you think."

Impossibly, she had made their song even better. She altered the intro and extended the bridge, then took up the range, made it her own, for her voice, her signature. No question it was going to be a hit, whatever that meant these days, but people would know the song and they would know the band for the song. They would be more than a cover band with their first hit in front of the Eagles crowd at Madison Square Garden. From Nothing was about to deliver its first charting single. All they had to do was play it as well as she composed it.

Victor was humming along. "This song is going to put the band on the map."

"Opening for the Eagles won't hurt. You know if we pass the test we're going to be on the road a few months, like thirty cities. Torch gave Petrumi hell about that tenement rehearsal hall. The promoter told him that was part of the test. They always haze newcomers to see how they handle the road. If the Eagles keep us on, he promises he'll do everything for us, make our travel arrangements, town car shuttles, set up our equipment. All we have to do is show up and play. If you break a string onstage, they'll bring you a new guitar. We've never had that, being treated like we mattered."

"You've waited a long time for star treatment."

"Baker Bagley calls it getting called up from the farm club to The Show. We have to add something measurable to the win or they'll send us back down."

"No pressure. You'll exceed their expectations."

"Vic, you're coming with us. You're a part of this band. Torch isn't going to boot you unless you give him a reason."

"I don't trust myself. I'm not as good at this as you are. Like Torch said, I'm inconsistent."

"Be in one place and you'll be fine. Focus on this and it will become yours."

That was weird how she said that. What was this? What was yours? Did she want a relationship with him? With *him*? Would she actually be intimate with him? Didn't she tell him not to piss off Torch? People thought he was complicated. She was complicated.

"No one has ever handed me a tuned guitar when I broke a string. Maybe I should try not to break a string, especially in front of twenty thousand people."

"Stop trying to figure out everything. I just wanted to play you the final version of the song, to make sure I hadn't screwed it up with the changes. You think it's ready for prime time?"

"It was ready before. It's better now. It's going to chart."

That was why she was here—to get the song right, to make "Playing" even better than it was, insurance to win air play. Whew, he was relieved. No relationship. No complications. No pissing off Torch. She was kidding before about something happening between them. Maybe he could stay in the band. Maybe Global Harmonics was behind him and all those conniving monstrosities were gone. His heartbeat was accelerating. She was so beautiful, so incomparably talented. He loved the back and forth on the Preston finale they played every night, going around on the solos. Friday they would play it at sound check, then Saturday in front of twenty thousand human beings. That could go somewhere. Could they go somewhere? Screw Torch and his rules. No, hold the line. Get rid of her. Get her out of that room!

"Charting would be cool. If it happens, we did it together. You look tired, Vic. Jet lag is getting you. Get some rest, big gig in the headlights. I should get some rest, too."

Fine, done, run. She was heading for the door. Complications in the rearview mirror. Band saved. Forge ahead. Forward, only forward.

If only she hadn't spoken again. "Like I said, if we're going to be on the road awhile, maybe something can develop between us. I've had worse ideas."

"Yeah, I've had worse ideas, too. Way worse. I mean, you think it could happen?" That was abysmal, but what else could he say?

"You never know, Vic. One of us has to make a move. Might have to be me. Maybe I'll surprise you one night when you least expect it."

"Yeah, Synthia, maybe. Yeah."

She waved goodbye whimsically and closed the door. No, that didn't happen. She didn't say that. He was hearing things. He was projecting what he wanted to hear onto her speech patterns. She was going to make a move on him when he least expected it on a thirty-city national tour opening for the Eagles? Bloody not possible.

Victor was exhausted. He needed to sleep. Badly.

TRACK 14: SING OR HIT THE CURVE BALL

IT WAS SOUND CHECK AT MADISON SQUARE GARDEN THE DAY BEFORE THE SHOW. Massive amounts of sound and lighting equipment were piled across the stage area, overflowing into the seats. Portable cranes hoisted intricate rigging overhead, enormous stretches of steel and aluminum framing. Victor looked around and saw enough Mac laptops to fill an Apple distribution center. An army of roadies was building a village meant to last a night and then move to another set of coordinates. Clipboards, hammers, power drills, forklifts—everything was flowing like a commercial construction site. From Nothing may have been the drag along act, but they were an included component of the logistics. A masterplan was being realized by a tight team that knew how. Being on tour with the Eagles was an exercise in the surreal.

The band had been told to stand and wait onstage, the five of them each on a taped mark. Torch was downstage center as always. Synthia with an S was behind him stage left. Baker Bagley was behind him stage right. Phil-Phil was sitting at the raised kit upstage center multiple body lengths above the others. Victor stood without a mic stand on the diagonal between Torch and Synthia, dropping back toward the elevated percussion platform. Each of them had a set list taped to the floor beside their marks. Their instruments and equipment had all been staged for them. The roadies moved at light speed, to the untrained eye randomly, but there was nothing random about it. Each element was synchronized every few minutes, the building crew playing out its own rhythm. After their sound check, the Eagles would be on the same stage for their sound check. It didn't seem possible.

They had made it from Vegas to LA to Madison Square in what seemed like record time, but other than for Victor, it was the proverbial result of years of working and waiting. Torch kept saying he always knew it was coming. The Philosopher King had willed opportunity into reality. Everything that would go live was controlled from the center of the auditorium floor, from the monster switchboard mixing the instrument levels and light cues, all flowing through the rows of high-end Macs twenty rows in front of them. At the Nugget they worked their own sound and lights. At Mandalay Bay they had one dedicated guy. Here it was NASA mission control. Even Torch seemed impressed in his own restrained way.

Victor felt lost. He stood further upstage, anxiously trying to sneak into the sidelines, looking for a place where he could hide in the shadows during showtime. He was out of place. His Les Paul was plugged in but the monitor amp facing him wasn't yet hot. He nervously practiced his scales up and down the fretboard. He needed to let off the anxiety pulsing through his nervous system. He knew he had to shake off his discomfort quickly. It didn't help matters any when a mangy, middle-aged guy in a biker's vest carrying a logo-stickered Fender Strat case entered the auditorium and made his way down front. His hair was stringy, his arms and neck a collage of faded warlord tattoos. Torch feebly waved to him and he half smiled. Baker Bagley did the same. So did Phil-Phil, clearly with more enthusiasm than the others. Synthia winced, looked away from him and made eye contact with Victor.

"Is that who I think it is?" Victor asked.

"Yeah, unless he's a nobody impersonator, it's Sludge," she answered.

"Insurance policy," interrupted Torch, overhearing them at close distance. "Hope we don't need him, but you freaked me out, Nowhere Man. This gig is too important to bet all-in."

Doc Sludge set his guitar case in the wide aisle and planted himself third row center, starting at Victor. Staring, just staring. Victor did his best to ignore him, but his best wasn't very good. He went back to playing scales. More scales.

"Give me sixteen live bars," sounded a baritone voice on the PA.

"Band ready?" prompted Torch.

They nodded. If they hadn't, Torch might have used his mic stand as a weapon. "Sister Syn, give us some sweet sound at Madison Square. Finale, Phil-Phil, on the beat."

Phil-Phil clicked four counts and Synthia hit the opening chords of "Nothing from Nothing." Perfectly amplified sound filled the arena from her fingertips, reverberating like a church pipe organ bouncing off the back wall. Phil-Phil and Baker Bagley were in perfect time. Victor stood ready, then missed his cue. He saw the dead stare from Torch and found the chord progression a half beat behind. Torch grabbed the mic and let go the lyrics:

Nothing from nothing leaves nothing

Sludge scrutinized Victor from the house seats and maniacally sneered like a werewolf in daylight. Victor could swear Torch was staring him down just as hard from the back of his head when the PA interrupted the song.

"Hold there, we're locking the levels. Stand by for rigging reset. I hope you guys know how hot it's going to be out there when the real lights come up. Going again right away."

It was all so matter of fact. The roadies had done it a million times. They would get them through it.

Torch got in Victor's face. "You missed. You gonna miss tomorrow night?"

"I'm not going to miss. I was distracted."

"Sludge is the backup plan. You're the plan if your head is in the game. Get it there."

The PA came live: "Again, please."

Phil-Phil clicked off another four count. Synthia opened harder this time, more explosive, invigorated by the cavernous echo. Phil-Phil and Baker Bagley joined on cue. Victor couldn't get his eyes off Sludge in the third row and was late again. Torch shook his head but sang through.

Nothing from nothing leaves nothing

The amps cut out and the PA stopped the band. "Hold again. Almost there on equalization. Then we go from the top, play the set straight through. Remember, the lights will be way hotter tomorrow, scorching . . ." BAM! They heard a crash of colliding objects behind the stage but saw nothing. Oops, someone was less than perfect, someone besides Victor. The PA was still live: "Damn, what's up with the rigging? Stand by while we see what's broken."

"That's why we have sound check, to root out all evil." Victor tried to lighten the mood.

"You missed twice," grilled Torch. "How can you not have that song locked by now?"

"It's a big room. I'm figuring out the acoustics. You've been at this a lot longer than I have. I can get there."

"You can or you can't. If you can't, I got you covered. Pay him no mind unless you'd rather be sitting where he is. He won't be late."

"I'll be fine. Shaking off a few nerves, that's all." Victor played another set of fast scales, more to convince himself than Torch.

As the technicians fiddled at the board, Baker Bagley took notice of Victor's uneasiness and took a few steps in his direction.

"Selo, you ever a hit a curve ball?"

It was a strange question. Victor answered as he continued to play his scales silently. "No, I wasn't much of an athlete. Never played baseball."

"A lot of people said the same thing about me. That's why I never got out of the minors. Couldn't hit the curve ball. I was an easy mark. Lights out."

"I'm guessing there's a point you want to make." Victor continued playing his scales.

"In the bigs, that's how the pitchers take you down. You think you know where the ball is coming, then at the last fraction of a second it breaks in another direction, but your swing is already in motion. The guy who can hit the curve ball, who can wait long enough to swing until he knows where the ball is gonna be, that's the guy who gets to stay on the team."

"Anticipate the unknown? That's not an easy thing to do, not consistently."

"It's not supposed to be easy. That's why so few people get paid to play baseball or music. In this racket, they throw you a lot of curve balls, too. No one cares if you're ready. There's always a guy waiting for your spot. Like Torch said, you can or you can't."

"You couldn't hit the curve ball. What did you do about it?"

"Couldn't fix my swing, so I learned to sing. Took up music, found out I was better at it. Perfect pitch, different game. So what if I'm only backup vocals, now I'm in the lineup as an everyday player. Changed my game so I can hit it when it comes, whatever they throw my way—Torch, the audience, the promoter—wherever the ball breaks, I'm ahead of it. If you can't hit what they throw at the plate, you're not standing where you should be. Don't swing blindly."

Baker Bagley stepped away, plucking a few bass notes. Victor tried to understand his analogy but wondered if Baker Bagley was messing with his head to open the door for Sludge.

The PA rang out again: "No one hurt. Loose casing. Trouble with an old ceiling mount. This structure is rusting away. Hold tight, they need to check the fuses. We're going dark for a moment."

The houselights went to blackness. Then the spinning overhead lights in front blinded them briefly and powered down. They were standing in total darkness, their eyes left to recover from the pulsating flash until they could see the outlines of each other in the shadows.

Without warning, an overhead spotlight fell to the stage and missed Torch by inches. KABAM! Torch jumped about eight feet, startled as if by cannon fire. The glass casing from above was crushed but didn't shatter. It didn't even put a dent in the floor. It was safety glass, no shards, but the weight alone was sufficient to annihilate a musician.

"You almost killed me," shouted Torch at the control board team.

"You're alive, stay cool," announced the PA.

"What if I had been Walsh?"

"We'd have gotten fired," shouted back a roadie from the floor.

Victor fought back a chuckle. He knew if he laughed he would be out and Sludge would be in. He was amazed to observe that even in the big leagues sometimes they blew it, a ton of steel here, a ton of glass there. Trust was a bigger deal than Victor imagined.

The house lights came up and the PA sounded: "We need a break on stage. Musicians back in fifteen, please. Do not be late. We have your set and the main act still to do."

Torch stormed off the stage and made his way toward Sludge. Phil-Phil tossed his drumsticks off the platform and followed Torch into the house seats. A team of roadies immediately appeared from the wings and began sweeping up the wreckage around Torch's mic stand. It was all business as usual.

"That was a hanging curve ball." Baker Bagley passed beside Victor and stepped offstage, joining Torch and Phil-Phil near Doc Sludge. The four of them exchanged high fives. Victor wasn't going anywhere near them. Neither was Synthia.

"If Torch says it's insurance then it's insurance," advised Synthia. "Go take a break, then come back and blow us away. Same as Vegas. Same as The Greek."

"Maybe I need insurance," said Victor.

"I'm your insurance," said Synthia. "All you have to do is play the songs."

Victor headed off the stage. When he turned to look back, Synthia wasn't there. She moved quickly.

Insurance, right. Yeah, insurance.

>> <<

Victor caught his breath and went exploring. He climbed the steep steps to the highest row of the upper deck all the way in the back of the arena, the furthest seats from the stage. He sat in the nosebleed section, staring at the stage setup, imagining himself playing there in about twenty-four hours. He could see small dots of the roadies cleaning up the mess of broken stuff. That meant from where he was, the audience during the show could barely see him. All he had to do was duck into the shadows. Their eyes would be on Torch, their focus on The Act as it was meant to be. There was comfort for him in obfuscation. That would be a win-win.

Then he looked up at the enormous, towering video monitors. They had come alive, a zillion high-definition kilowatts. At the moment they were hot on the roadies. He could see the wrenches in their hands, every pixel of their finger flesh. He could see the life scars on the backs of their hands working the wrenches. Tomorrow night the cameras would be on the band. They would be filled with close-up images of Torch. On the band's original tune they would project the image of Synthia with an S. Victor didn't want a close-up. He knew he wouldn't be invisible but he wanted minimal screen time. He hated the way he looked on camera but knew he couldn't escape it. There would only be five people on stage under all those lights and the camera would keep finding him despite his objections. He was barely a musician, not at all a celebrity, but he was going to be on the big screen. People would see him. If he made a mistake, people would tie the off-pitch notes to his playing. He wondered if the video cameras would zero in on his fingers when he soloed. Of course they would. That was the drill, pile on the pizzazz. This was how it went down at a rock concert in a major league arena.

Crap, he had never been on a video screen before. He never wanted to be on a video screen. Too much exposure was frightening. At The Greek the screens had only been used for the main act, not the warm-up act. Maybe they would do that here. No, not at these prices, not with a crowd four times The Greek's capacity. That's why they fired them up in sound check. This was the Eagles in New York City. From Nothing was part of the ticket. What was he thinking?

Victor started shaking, trying to clear it from his mind. He would get through it, but he already wished it was over, at least the first one. Get rid of the first one, survive the close-up, then if they were invited he would be fine for the rest of the tour. Sure he would, as long as no one he knew recognized him, as long as the video feed didn't make its way to the Internet. No mistakes. Ignore the cameras. Ignore the video screens. Yeah, sure he would.

He wasn't feeling well. Since the day he had met Maurice Sangstrum, the day he took over as CEO of Global Harmonics, Victor couldn't remember a day when he did feel well. It wasn't the beating in the back alley that had taken him down. It was the constant draining of disapproval, the abuse of authority, the manipulation of creativity for wealth and nothing more. All the negativity made him weak. All the anger made him ill.

Yet there was more to his undoing, more to why he felt so disconnected as he had ascended stair after stair above the arena floor to the rafters of Madison Square Garden. His aloneness was taking over again. He tried to remember back to the first time he realized he had no parents, no family. When was that? How had that happened? They left him in the birth ward of an underfunded community hospital and let the system have at him to fend for himself?

When did he know that? When he was three? Four? Five? When he woke up in a residential care facility that was more dormitory than home? When he found himself in a group home and knew his room was not his at all but a shared physical space in a county-owned housing project? When he woke up in his first single bed in a foster home and wondered who the pretend mom and dad were that let him stay there for cash? He remembered the stark walls of residential, the stupid posters on the group home walls with the brain dead slogans of hope, the packing up of all his clothes that came from donations in two rolling suitcases from the swap meet that traveled with him from one foster care home to another.

Despite the constant danger of those around him—the knife that could appear out of nowhere, the fist to the back of his head in a cafeteria line, the transformation of any wood or steel object into a bat or a club—he never learned to fight with his hands. He could defend himself from lightweight attacks by covering his face, he had learned that much as an instinctive response, but returning fire in a playground attack, that wasn't Victor. Maybe that's why he had taken the beating so well at Providence. He was used to getting beat up, but no matter how hard he tried as a kid, he wasn't threatening. He wasn't imposing or physical. One time in elementary school, he had thrown another kid who'd attacked him from behind into a shelf of clay pottery that had collapsed on his adversary and cracked open his skull. It was an accident more than an attack, a reflex reaction, but he had felt bad for hurting the other kid instead of proud for winning the fight. He didn't do it again. He preferred to fight with ideas, with learning and calculation. That also made him an outcast, though it gave him a future he never could have imagined.

He had survived all that—the fights, the transience, bouts of hunger, lonely birthdays and Christmas Eve emptiness—so much random distress, so little self-esteem, but a survivor who was wealthy for a minute and then back to nothing. Today he was at Madison Square Garden. He was fighting the only way he knew how: ducking, rerouting, retrenching, and rethinking without a stitch of help. Here he was in the thinning air of a hollow indoor stadium all by himself.

Forever by himself—that was the constant connecting past to present. He had survived another bout in the rough ring and tomorrow night he would play music on a professionally lit stage followed by one of the most successful bands in the world. They had their own strife, it was well-documented. So did Torch. So did Synthia. She could be his friend. She could take him forward if he could find a way to let her. He had found one career, blown it, lost it, then found another, which also would be taken from him. Everything would be taken from him. That was his destiny. That was determinism no matter how he fought it. That was God's choice.

Alone, surviving, yet alone. He would have wrapped himself in that pervasive thought except for the sound of an unnaturally familiar voice that caught him off guard.

"The cheap seats become you, Victor. You look right at home."

It wasn't the voice he expected. It was a male voice. It was the voice of Thomas Katem. Smarmy, unctuous, unrelenting. No, it couldn't be. It just couldn't be. He would never be free of these parasites. Global Harmonics was a life sentence beyond its meltdown.

"Are you stalking me?" asked Victor.

"Don't flatter yourself. I don't stalk. I get what I want."

"We're done with each other. I said no. I walked away. I left everything behind. Can't you let that sink in? Can't you let me play with the band and go destroy someone else's life for a better payday? Or did you get Petrumi to turn around and snuff me after all?"

"Petrumi did what was best for Petrumi, beyond my control. Walsh wanted your band. Torch said you came with the band. That's a done deal. I can't stop what's in motion. Petrumi and I are good. He invited me to the show. You'll see me in the front row tomorrow night, more for the Eagles than you, but putting a little heat on you is a fine bonus."

All Victor heard was that Torch had stood up for him and wanted him on the stage. He wasn't getting booted. Doc Sludge was a threat meant to motivate him. That was news enough.

"I'll be looking forward to seeing you out front, Katem. Don't worry, after what I've been through, I'm not going to flinch. I can stand the heat. This is my time."

"We'll see. The thing is, as far as our falling out in LA, you're not off the hook. You're not even a little bit off the hook."

"It's over. It's really over. McWhorter has the company. He's stripping it down. Sangstrum got his inside kickback and the world spins. One of my friends is dead. My others will move on. You need to move on. I need to move on. It's healthier if everyone moves on."

"I didn't get to where I am giving up that easily, Victor. Here's the deal: We've done a significant amount of homework with our lawyers. When you violated your NDA and intentionally tried to do harm to your own company, you broke fiduciary duty as an officer. You purposefully attempted to lower the value of your company out of spite. You didn't have a right to do that."

"I have a release in full from Sangstrum. You were there when he signed it. You witnessed it. I gave up all my interest in the company for zero liability."

"Yes, from the company you have zero liability. You're off the hook there, but you screwed your shareholders. One of those shareholders, however minority, was my client, MSE. They say you acted in your own interest. That made the stock they held valueless. They lost money because of you, so they can lead a class action lawsuit against you. Since you acted outside your agreement to protect the company, the company doesn't have to protect you and the insurance company holding the D&O and E&O policies don't have to protect you. You're on your own, Chuck Berry. It's MSE vs. you."

"MSE is going to bring a class action lawsuit against me because they didn't prevail as the buyer of Global Harmonics? What do you want? My guitar? My car? That's all I have. Why sue someone who has nothing?"

"It will make you unemployable. No one will want to touch you when you are getting yanked into court week after week for years to come. You'll have to leave the band and Petrumi assures me they will replace you if that's the case. I hear from good sources that your predecessor is suddenly available."

"All this is retribution? You want to hurt me because I didn't do things your way? This is a vendetta?"

"We have you in our gunsights. *Be Bop A Lula*."

Victor looked down at the video monitors and saw a crane hoist the broken boom that had almost killed Torch clear from the stage. These guys were remarkable. Fifteen minutes and they were back in business. The stage was back to ready.

"Band back for pre-check in ten, please," called out the public address system.

Victor rose to his feet. "Fine, destroy me. What do I care? At least I'll get to play once at Madison Square Garden. You can't take that away from me. Take the rest, whatever the rest is."

"This isn't a vendetta, Victor. It's a negotiation. You can go on the tour. All we need you to do is give one deposition testifying to Sangstrum and McWhorter's fraud. You won't even need to appear in court. Once we have the video deposition, we'll take it to McWhorter. He either sells us the company for pennies or does time. We'll absolve and shield you. It's that simple."

"It can't be that simple. Sangstrum said if I signed the release I was protected. Obviously I got swindled on that. If I give the depo, he'll sue me into oblivion."

"Not if he committed a criminal act. Whistleblower applies. I promise we can defend you and you don't even have to come back from the road. MSE's resources are virtually unlimited."

"You promise, they promise, everyone promises. It's all words that mean nothing. You guys never make peace. You make war until all that's left are ashes. I'm the ashes."

"This is clean, Victor, as clean as it gets. This is your final chess move. There's nothing bad in it for you. Do it our way and you're done. Have a nice life. Don't do it our way and you lose the band, the tour, probably the keyboard player."

"You're an asshole. You don't know anything about my life. Tell me why I should trust you after all the manipulation and lies."

"You're ungrateful, Victor. We've offered you the world. This is our last offer and there is no downside. You have a few days after opening night before the tour moves on. We can do the deposition in our attorney's office here in Manhattan. Do it and go on the road or don't do it and wait for your subpoena."

"We don't have the full tour yet. We have to play perfectly tomorrow to get that. I need to think about it, okay? Right now I need to get back to my post or Torch will replace me."

Katem handed Victor a thin envelope. "I think you're going to get the tour, so here's what you're agreeing to fulfill. Sign it and hand it back to me tomorrow night after the show. It's binding. If you back out, the damages are incalculable. You can't change your mind. You decide."

"I need to do some research, my own homework, make sure there is no downside, make sure they can't get me once and for all."

"I wouldn't lie to you, Victor. We have you completely covered. You give us what we need and you're done. You can move on. Think about it hard. I'll see you in the front row."

Victor turned and headed down the stairs to rejoin the band for sound check. This gig had to go right. That's all Victor could see ahead of him. Katem had thrown him the ugliest of curve balls on a full count. Swinging or looking? Sing or swing?

>> <<

The rest of the sound check was uneventful. The band got through the set. Torch calmed down and nailed the Elvis opener. Synthia delivered the new version of "Playing" to jaw dropping from the roadies. Doc Sludge continued to stare down Victor. Phil-Phil and Baker Bagley were Phil-Phil and Baker Bagley. The gig was going to be fine as long as Victor could stand on his feet.

The threat of Thomas Katem would rule the night and the following day until Victor reached a decision—that plus the text from Petrumi asking him to meet in the hotel lobby bar as soon as he got back from Madison Square Garden. Katem worked fast, no surprise there.

Give the deposition or not. That was what Victor had to decide. He knew never to make an important decision under emotional pressure, never in the moment. He thought back to his corporate experience. Never send an insulting, threatening email without letting it sit overnight. Never quit a job on the spot after an ugly fight with a supervisor. Never throw a laptop at a megalomaniac financier. Oh well, too late on that last one. How about don't make the same mistake twice? Yeah, he would settle for that.

Victor got back to the hotel in Midtown and found Petrumi waiting for him in the bar. He was as reptilian in person as he was on the accidental video call. Thin legs, tight jeans, black leather jacket, Brook Brothers starch white shirt and lemon yellow tie, gold oval wireframes. He must have liked to play the part. He was the part, a bit on the goofy side, standing alone at a high-top pub table several steps away from the crowd. No, this agent was no ordinary thinker.

"Is anything about music easy?" asked Victor.

"Music is the least of your problems," countered Petrumi. "You got my pal Katem horrifically upset. He's even mad at me and all I did was protect the band."

"You all lie with such ease. I have no idea who to believe."

"Believe yourself. Who else are you going to believe? Or maybe you want to ask me again about God. We could take a detour into epistemology, see where that takes us. Are you at all familiar with the work of Bertrand Russell?"

"Got it, Petrumi, we don't have the same hobby. Why did you defy Katem and put me back in the band? It wasn't just because Walsh wanted me. It wasn't even because Torch wanted me. You could have steered them both away from me with a single sentence."

"Easy question. Because you wanted it badly enough not to be a CEO and let Global Harmonics die. I don't see passion like that much. I wanted you to have your shot and I wanted the band to have its best shot."

"That simple, huh?"

"I'm really a simple guy. I book a lot of B acts like this one. This is as close as I've gotten to a breakthrough. When I heard Synthia play your original, I knew we could go somewhere. We could chart. Call me metaphysical, maybe I'm paranoid, but I don't like changes when something is working. Seen too many acts fall apart nuking the drummer or the bass player. Shouldn't matter, but it does."

Victor gazed at the bar. "I'm spent. I don't know what to do."

"I know that. That's why I asked to meet you. You want a drink?"

"Yeah, Vodka Gatorade."

"A man mentored by Torch. Hang out a second. Keep breathing."

Petrumi went to the bar, ordered, then stood there waiting as the bartender ducked away momentarily. Victor looked around. Nice place. Crowded. He was unknown to the public. He would be slightly less unknown after the gig. That was, if he made it to the gig. Petrumi returned with a draft beer for himself and a Vodka Gatorade for Victor.

"The bartender never made one of those before. He had to go to the sports shop and get a bottle of Gatorade to do it. Resourceful fellow."

"I could have had something else."

"You're almost famous, as they say. You should have what you want. You need what you need to be on your game. I don't judge. I navigate."

"I assume you have some advice for me?"

"I do and it isn't going to surprise you. You need to give the deposition for Katem. Like he told you, there is no downside."

"I keep hearing that. Wish I could believe it."

"Believe it. It's going to save your ass."

"Did you feed Doc Sludge back to Torch?"

Victor knew that came out awkwardly. Petrumi broke out laughing and took a long drink from his beer. Victor looked at him curiously, missing the joke.

"Of course I did. More navigation. Why?"

"I'm working through this no-downside thing."

"You didn't think that was a coincidence. Torch got worried when you disappeared in LA, asked me if I knew where Sludge was since he got out of the pen. I found him in an easy phone call. Insurance for Torch is insurance for me."

"But Torch wants me, not Sludge."

"Sure, if you're trouble-free. He knows Sludge isn't trouble-free and he likes the way you play. Mostly he likes that Walsh likes the way you play, but if you're a problem, we have a solution. So don't be a problem."

Victor had heard the words "no downside" so many times they had become impossible to believe. Petrumi was Katem's shill, that's all. He would say anything to get Victor to turn. This was a make-good sale. Katem had to be lying. Petrumi had to be lying. How could there be no downside?

"I don't believe there's no downside to scorching the earth under Sangstrum and McWhorter when it's all behind me," mused Victor.

"You probably thought that when you first walked out of that conference room and found yourself nearly beaten to death in a bar. Remember, the guys Katem plays with are way scarier than your guys. Those MSE guys wanted the deal badly enough to get Katem's attention. You're how they got his attention."

"You're saying if I don't give testimony, they're going to have me beaten up again?"

Petrumi took off his designer glasses and set them on the tabletop. "Of course I'm not saying that. You might be wearing a wire and that would be threatening you with bodily harm. I don't do that. I also know you're not wearing a wire. You're too frail for that, which I understand given your unconventional upbringing. I'm saying you need to pay attention to how you get out of this. Torch and I want you in the band. Synthia wants you in the band. There are a hundred bar bands where I can place Sludge. I need you to work with Katem and protect all of us. We're on the edge of a breakthrough, serious money, and we've waited a long time to be this close."

"I don't see who's protecting me, Petrumi. Guess I'm a product of my frail upbringing."

"You don't need protection. When you take out Sangstrum and McWhorter, they'll have nothing left to fight for and they will move on. That's how business works. When it's over, it's sunk cost. You don't sink more. Cost and time, same thing."

That's when the revelation hit Victor like a trainload of bricks: Sangstrum and McWhorter could hire the same guys who MSE hired to finish the job. Maybe this time they would kill him and blame MSE. No downside my ass. There was no way out. Don't give the depo, lose the band and get sued. Give the depo and probably get killed out of retribution, pure spite, to set an example for the next guy who came along and didn't play ball with them. At that point the band would have broken through and he wouldn't even qualify as a footnote in its success story. His grave might even enhance the legend with detox Sludge laughing his way back into the lineup. It was all downside as far as he could see.

Victor finished his drink in one long gulp.

"We good?" Petrumi returned his glasses to their rightful spot, masking his lizard face.

"I wish I could tell you. I still don't know."

"You know where I stand. You know where Katem stands."

"You've been clear. Don't think I haven't been appreciative. Katem told me I haven't been appreciative, but I am."

"You have a weird way of showing it, Victor. Every guy in my file would kill to be you right now. Think it through overnight. Give Katem your answer after the show. I'm keeping Sludge on a tight leash. Give me a reason to let him move on."

Petrumi abandoned his half-finished beer and lithely strolled out of the hotel bar onto Broadway. Victor briefly imagined the George Benson tune accompanying Petrumi's dance step stage exit, shades of Bob Fosse's *All That Jazz*, but the words stuck in his mind were "kill to be you." He downed the remains of Petrumi's beer, then went to the bar to order another drink. This one wouldn't require Gatorade. He guessed the bartender would appreciate skipping another trip to the sports shop. It wouldn't be the last drink he ordered that night.

TRACK 15: PLEASE DON'T HIT ME AGAIN

ON SATURDAY VICTOR WOKE UP AROUND 2:00 P.M. It was the housekeeper banging on the door that finally got him moving. He could not remember what time he went to bed or how many drinks he had. He vaguely remembered a number of random conversations with strangers the prior night about how much he hated Doc Sludge. He remembered telling someone how Sludge's tattoos made him look like a scary clown without a clown suit. He didn't remember much else.

With the long sleep—it had to be twelve hours at least—he felt surprisingly strong, his head unusually clear. He asked housekeeping to give him a half hour so he could shower, then grabbed a cup of coffee in the lobby and exited onto the bustling streets of Manhattan. He wasn't hungry. He went for a long walk up Sixth Avenue to Central Park South, a constant cold wind in his face more invigorating than annoying. He crossed the street into Central Park and continued walking until he reached the carved pond with the remote control sailboats. He sat on a bench there for a long time, watching the hobbyists skillfully maneuver the model vessels through the gusty breeze. After a while he had a New York pretzel, his entire food intake for the day. He noticed on one of the posted clocks it was already past 4:00 p.m., still giving him enough time to walk the mile and a half south to Madison Square Garden and be early for the gig.

He arrived at the arena before 5:00 p.m., presented his credentials as instructed at the side artists' entrance, and was led to the green room where he had left a change of clothing the day before. Nothing fancy, black jeans and a white linen shirt, he didn't want to stand out. He was the first in the band to arrive. Synthia texted him that the rest of the band was around the corner having an early dinner on Petrumi, but he still wasn't hungry and preferred the time alone. She said they would be there by 6:00 and would see him then. His adrenaline was pumping. He was ready.

Madison Square Garden is a one-of-a-kind venue. Victor knew that the same way every musician who made it there knew that. It can't be described in words, least of all by someone standing on its stage. For touring bands it is the pinnacle of stature, a rite of passage, what Carnegie Hall means to classical musicians. Playing MSG gives a band a different kind of bragging rights, a legitimacy that can stand up in any drunken argument. To play the storied Garden is to join the club.

A few months ago when Victor showed up, From Nothing was a talented but nearly invisible cover band in the Nevada dessert. Now, like Torch always knew, they were getting a real shot. Victor's bandmates arrived shortly and marveled at their surroundings. Finally they were in a green room stocked for royalty, an opulent holding area beside their launch pad. Somewhere nearby in an even more regal green room waited the Eagles, the actual Eagles, a legend that would follow them onstage. They had been asked to be there—requested, invited, escorted. They weren't stepping up to the next level. They were soaring into the stratosphere.

Ground control to Major Torch, you've really made the grade.

Bowie had been there so many times, his DNA was probably traceable in the paneling. When you played MSG, you were in historic company, living and otherwise.

Despite the luxurious enclave, for the next two hours Victor remained quiet. Torch, Synthia, Baker Bagley, Phil-Phil, even the glam lizard Petrumi were all enjoying a life high, laughing, foretelling, prognosticating, pumping each other up, but Victor kept to himself. He knew he was about to walk on the field for his own World Series and could blow it. Yep, that could really happen. As he listened to the crowd arriving and watched the seats fill to capacity on a video monitor, he knew there was no upside in obsessing about the potential downside ahead of him, yet that was all he could visualize. That was who he was. He had to get over it. He had to find confidence, belief, authenticity, satisfaction in his own assurance. He needed to find enough self-esteem to play through the set, dig for the fight within. Eye out for the curve ball. No going south on an unexpected move. An unexpected move was coming. Something weird had to be coming. It would be inconsistent for normalcy to prevail. Torch had willed a deep normalcy on the band that no longer applied. Nimbleness was survival. Focus was triumph.

"Playing." It was all about "Playing."

Their original song would put them on the map. It would rewrite their future, blaze a new path, ignite a rocket launch to the amazing uncharted unmet of success. Torch would get his wedding chapel, his industry retirement secured. Synthia's parents would be proud. Victor would have fulfilled his promise to them. That one song would deliver on every level.

It would or it could? That was up for grabs.

Petrumi announced it was almost time. Victor silently stepped out of the green room ahead of the others and made his way through the backstage corridors, up and down the winding staircases and alcoves to the floor level. He emerged from an obscured stairwell and found himself on a side ramp near the stage. From that vantage point he looked onstage and saw the band's instruments serenely lit in preshow, basked in flowing dry ice fog covering the platform to vent anticipation to the twenty thousand Eagles fans filing into the arena. So what if they were there to see the Eagles? First they were going to listen to From Nothing. Those were the rules. For once the rules worked in their favor.

Victor stood in the wings stage left waiting for the walk-on signal. He breathed repeatedly in a patterned sequence, clawing his way to courage, when he saw the unexpected emerging to ruin him on schedule. Standing in the wings stage right was Doc Sludge. He was smoking a joint with Phil-Phil, who had also arrived from the green room. On closer examination, Victor saw that Sludge was smoking it alone. Torch wouldn't tolerate Phil-Phil getting loaded before a show, especially this one. The Philosopher King had his rules. The Act made the law. Penalty for violation was rendered without appeal.

Victor tried to take his eyes off Sludge but found it impossible. How many tattoos could a human being absorb and still have functioning skin? Some of that ink in the hard to reach places must have been painful unless he was perpetually too anaesthetized to feel anything. Staring that closely at his legacy replacement sent his mind paddling upstream. Why would Torch do that to him? To get the best performance he could? To shake him up? As a payback? Nah, none of that. It was all business. Sludge was the insurance policy. If Victor had been more dependable, no insurance would have been necessary. In a peculiar way, he understood. He was a victim of his own uncertainty, his own ambivalence. His occasional dizzy spells didn't help things. He should have eaten something more than a pretzel. No matter, Victor would live with the insurance policy staring him down. He needed to ensure Torch wouldn't need to cash it in. They all had their power. Continuity was Victor's realm.

All of that would have made sense if the darkest threat afloat hadn't returned to tap him on the shoulder. That was Thomas Katem. There he was, command performance, well-dressed on the town, forever a banker, poised in the foreign outpost, the same stage left wing as Victor. It was to be expected. It couldn't be otherwise. Victor couldn't avoid him. He had to deal with the viper. He wished it didn't have to be now, but that was Katem's call, not his. Damn the insurance. Damn Doc Sludge. Damn Thomas Katem.

Victor needed to hold on, maintain composure, keep his head together. He had to get through the gig and then clean up his act. Too bad, it was what it was. With that crippling tap on the shoulder, he looked away from Sludge and into the sunken eyes of Katem.

"Big crowd out there, a night to remember," waxed Katem.

It wasn't enough that Katem had to be a power hungry asshole. He overly enjoyed the role of power hungry asshole. Calm, Victor needed to be calm. No sweat. No weak knees. Tear up the insurance policy. Handle the asshole.

"That it is." Victor's words were absent commitment. He would allow no telegraphing of intent.

"Petrumi said the two of you had a constructive chat last night."

"We talked. He's a smart guy. He got me here."

"I got you here, Victor. Do we have a deal?"

"I'm going onstage in a few minutes, Madison Square Garden. My mind is on that."

"I gave you the night to think about your future. This is opening night or closing night for you. I need to know which it is."

"Let's talk after the show, okay?" Victor saw one of the roadies holding his backup Les Paul and motioned for him to bring it over. He didn't need to see it but he needed to look engaged with something, anything to get his attention off Katem and Sludge. The roadie brought over the mahogany beauty, hand-carved maple top with mother of pearl fret inlays, finished in heritage cherry sunburst. Victor pretended to inspect the gold tuning heads.

"Victor, I'm not playing games tonight. You're going to tell me your intentions before you walk onto that stage. I'm setting the agenda. You're in or you're out."

Victor checked the six strings one at a time, nodded approval, and handed the guitar back to the roadie. "Katem, this is not right."

"That's a judgment call. I'm not looking for your values assessment. I'm looking for your capitulation. You testify for us or I no longer have an interest in you. What's your call?"

"Milk the cow, never feed her," muttered Victor.

"I don't know what that means."

"Same as it ever was." Victor thought David Byrne would appreciate the inclusion.

"You drink a lot again last night, Victor? Your head exploding with all this excitement?"

"You know what it means. You, Sangstrum, McWhorter—you invented it, your insider's club. Yeah, I thought about it a lot, all night. I'm a thoughtful guy. It's what I do—contemplate, argue with myself until I'm sick. It's not like I haven't taken what you said seriously. I've taken the offer very seriously. I've taken the threat even more seriously."

"You're a sensible fellow, Victor. I've always had a good feeling about you."

"Always, how about that?" Victor felt his knees shaking. He looked over and saw inkblot Sludge keen to pounce, plotting his return with Phil-Phil. That damn insurance policy was going to crush his soul.

"I like your independent streak," said Katem. "You haven't given me what I've needed yet, but maybe that's the way it was supposed to work out, storybook ending. We can still make that happen. The door is open."

Victor felt ill, nauseous, woozy. He looked out at the arena and saw it about 80% occupied. He was going onstage in minutes, but before that he had to tell Katem his answer. It couldn't be avoided. Katem stood between him and everything on the other side of his life. He wasn't stepping down or away. The obstacle required attention. The disease required treatment.

"You've always had a good feeling about me. Maybe you know me better than I know myself." Victor knew that sounded awkward. His mind was astray, distracted with assault. Across the proscenium he saw Torch approach Sludge, rip the joint from his mouth and snuff out the lit end with his fingers. He needed his insurance policy sober. That was Torch, always the leader, ahead of the pack. The Philosopher King was unswerving. His logic didn't disappoint.

"I know you, Victor. I know who you are. Do what's smart and we all get what we want. Everyone gets what's coming to him. That's how a good deal is constructed."

Victor took another breath, then exhaled his future in a string of four short declarations: "Katem, I need to be free. We have no deal. I don't trust you. I'm not going to do it your way."

Katem's eyes bulged on receipt of the blunt declarations. "Selo, you're dead in this world. Enjoy the gig. It's your last—the last pleasant moment of your worthless life."

There was no more posturing, no more negotiating. Katem walked off without another syllable. Victor had made his decision. He frantically looked down the corridors for a friendly face, for Synthia with an S. He needed to find her. He needed grounding. He needed air, to find a way back to a steady state. Where was she? Please, where was Synthia?

>> <<

The stage manager gave word it was ten minutes to curtain. Victor sat alone backstage. His head hurt, but at this point that was normal. The numbing pain came and went but never stopped returning. He was shivering, wildly off balance, cowering behind a scrim forty feet from a jubilant mob pounding booze before the opening act. Madison Square Garden could give anyone the shivers, especially a first-timer. His life had been threatened by Thomas Katem. He had no idea if it was a metaphor. He couldn't steady himself.

Where was Synthia? She had to be nearby. He needed her to be nearby.

Nine body lengths away Victor saw Don Henley reviewing logistics with a roadie. Yes, that Don Henley, the one and only untouchable, unreachable, unfathomable Don Henley. Victor had never even spoken with Joe Walsh. At least he knew that Walsh liked his playing. Henley would have no idea who he was. Could he talk to Henley? Of course not, that wasn't proper backstage etiquette for a Nowhere Man. The unwritten rules were clear, a nobody does not address a somebody. Star talent kept a distance for a reason, to stay focused on the work. Only an amateur would violate that sacred personal space. But wait, talking to Henley could make things better. It would give him confidence. It would prop up his pride. So do it. Why not? Walk over to Don Henley and say . . . what?

It didn't matter. There was no way he was going to do it. Even if they toured thirty cities together they would never exchange a single word. Yet if they did talk to each other, Victor imagined it might go like this:

"Don, you're Don?"

"Yes, would you like to call me something else?"

"No, that's your name. Why would I call you something else? Like Mr. Henley? That wouldn't sound right."

"Not unless we're at odds. Are you working the tour?"

"Yes Don, Mr. Henley, I'm with the opening act. I play guitar. Mr. Walsh brought us to your attention."

"Mr. Walsh, right, you're the Vegas export. Glad to have you along. Anything else you want to tell me?"

"Yes, I wanted to tell you, that last song on *Hotel California*, 'The Last Resort,' it's an unbelievable song. It means a lot to me."

"Yeah, that's a good one. We hardly ever play it live for some reason. Maybe we'll play it tonight."

"Unrehearsed like a bar band? You'd do that?"

"We might. I like to keep the band sharp."

"Yeah, me too. I do things like that. Mix it up so it's not rote."

"Why that song?"

"I had this girlfriend. The first time I met her I was singing that song with my band."

"Did I get a royalty?"

"The club was like sixty people."

"I was kidding. It was a joke."

"Right, sorry, I missed it. Funny, you've got an awesome sense of humor. Awesome, stupid word. Why did I say that? Great song. I think it's why, you know, she liked me."

"Awesome. Are you still together?"

"No. We should be, but I messed up."

"We all do."

Wait, that was wrong. What was Victor projecting on Don Henley? He was a superstar. He never messed up. Or did he? Of course he did. That's where the songs came from. Not from the happy, from the sad. "The Sad Café." "Wasted Time." "Lyin' Eyes." "Peaceful Easy Feeling." All losers. All about loss.

Why Claire? Why couldn't he get over her? Over a decade, it was ridiculous, insane. He had to let her go. He had to move on.

There was no more to pretend to say to Don Henley. It was all about Claire. It was always about Claire. She had been that moment in his life that mattered. She had been there to show him he could be more than a mistake, an accidental pregnancy left behind at the hospital to be someone else's problem. She had shown love to a foster kid, the first time in his life he felt love. It mattered. It really mattered. For an infinitesimally brief moment he mattered as a human being, a living person, a citizen of the world around him, but not anymore. How do you learn to love when you grow up not knowing what it is? God was nowhere for him. She couldn't save him. He couldn't be saved. He didn't want to be saved. Faith was lunacy. It wasn't for him.

Why Claire? Why, Why, Why?

It was music that had gotten him through the system. Music had gotten him through foster care. Headphones in group homes—that was his blessing, his respite. Listening internally every night, the outside world silenced by his earphones, that made the world livable, even occasionally safe. The songs, always the songs. That was his first love, his inviolable superhero power, the poetry of escape. It was survival, but it wasn't enough. The songs were about love, but what was love? Was it a word, a phony construct invented to manipulate him, another word for God? All that had left him alone in the system. The grey metal foster care facilities. The conflicted, paid off foster parents. The paint-peeling walls of the group homes. Constructs, not love. Exchanges of promises, but not love. Long awful years, but not love. He learned to listen, to play back what he heard in real time, but he never learned to love.

There was no human love until there was Claire. He played, he went to school, he got work, but she lifted him to humanity. He hardly ever smiled but found comfort because she helped him understand love. So what if they had only been together two years. Those two years made it possible for him to acknowledge connection, the ability to care about another life more than his contemptible own, the willingness to want joy for someone else without a defined expectation. No favors, no exploitation, no trading on privilege. She showed him he could be loved. Give, not get. He could do the same if he made that choice. Thrive in unity, not struggle alone. The evidence of potential was abundant. Then when he trusted the idea of love, his anger took it all from him. He chased success because it came without feeling, but love, no, that was too hard. He knew it, but he ran from it. He ran from it all the way from Los Angeles to San Francisco to Las Vegas to Madison Square Garden. He had everything and nothing all at once, but he didn't have Claire and he didn't have love. He never would. She made the world better and he didn't deserve better. It was all so clear. The truth hurt. He could never sustain what drove her day to day and then took her from his life. It was fate, and it wasn't meant to be. To hell with escape. To hell with faith.

He needed to play this set and then disappear forever. Somewhere, anywhere, but it had to be over. This all had to be over. No more pain. No more longing. No more blame. He couldn't let down Torch. He owed Torch that, but Torch had his insurance policy and always would ascend to the temple. Synthia? No, same as Claire, beyond his reach, beyond his scope.

Victor was the Nowhere Man. The Nowhere Man belonged Nowhere.

Synthia with an S found him sitting on the floorboards alone. She saw the tears running from his eyes. She knew he was afraid, terrified. She would never know why. He could never tell her. Her distance was her safety net, same as Torch's insurance policy. This was a business transaction for both of them. The band was their investment vehicle, their candle, their salvation. He was the problem and he would always be the problem. He couldn't heal, and she couldn't meet him in the middle without some kind of healing. She was smarter than she ever let on. That's why she had survived and he was still treading water. She had been elevated navigating the challenges in her path. He could only drown, the foul sea consuming him.

"Torch told me to come get you," she said. "It's time."

"Yep, it's time," echoed Victor.

She handed him a water bottle.

"Vodka Gatorade?" he asked.

"Try water with electrolytes, that's what you need. Quickly, we're going on."

Water with electrolytes. Yes, that was what he needed, fluid, anything to restore energy, replace the sweat. She knew what he needed. She always knew. He had gotten lucky. He was coming to believe that, but luck, ah luck—so ephemeral, so deceptive. Don't take the lure. Protect the flanks. Fall back and regroup. Playing the songs was all that mattered. He could play the songs. He had to play the songs. "Playing."

"Are you sure you can play?" she asked reluctantly.

"Torch ask you to find that out?"

"It's an important night for all of us. The Philosopher King needs to know all."

"I can play. Sludge isn't getting this. This is mine. I've earned it. I'm going on with The Act. Not Sludge. Me."

"You have earned it," she said. "Let's go work up the crowd and chart a hit."

Victor took another drink of water with electrolytes. He felt better. Sturdier, more assured—ready to put on a show, enact his part, carry that weight. He could do this. He was ready. He had no idea what was beyond the curtain call that night but he was ready to get that far.

He looked into Synthia's eyes and knew something was different. She was the same, but he was different. He had learned something from her, the belief that something good could happen to him if he let it. It would be taken from him because cruelty was a constant in his life. Kindness had to become accessible. Hope had to be found in tiny bursts, micro fragments. He would take what he could get. He would do something with it, something life-affirming. Then he would lose it all.

As Synthia helped Victor to his feet, Don Henley walked up to them. Impossibly, he had something to say to them.

"You the guitarist Walsh uncovered in Vegas? He says you're good. That's as strong an endorsement as they come. Not feeling great, huh?"

Crap, he really was talking to them. Don Henley was talking to them. He saw Victor losing it. Not good. Victor knew he needed to say something intelligent, most of all not upchuck his afternoon pretzel, but no words were coming to him. A minute ago he was scared. Now in the presence of a deity, he was immobilized.

"Walsh ever tell you he barfed on the stage manager the first time we played the Garden?"

"No, sir. I mean, no, Don. Yeah, Joe's been good to us. I'll be fine. I'm just a little, you know, overwhelmed by it all. It's like a miracle we're here. Otherworldly. Awesome."

"Yeah, it's amazing, hell of a fast climb."

"Vic is a serious Eagles fan." The interjection came from Synthia, once again saving his ass. "We picked him for a reason. Our band has come a long way. We've always been tight, but he helped us find our voice, our sound. Any words of wisdom before we go on?"

"Let go of the doubt. We picked you for a reason, too. If you didn't have the talent, you wouldn't be here. Just play the songs."

Henley walked off without further comment. What else could he say? "Have a good set"? Nah, that would be trite. "Just play the songs." That was as perfect as perfect could be. He was counting on them. He had made a solid bet.

Synthia with an S kissed Victor on the cheek for what seemed like an hour in all of two seconds. That meant something. She was worth it, all of the pain, all of the risk. They were going onstage together to chart a hit in front of an audience of twenty thousand.

Now it was real.

>> <<

The show would go on. Screw Katem and his punk ultimatum. Screw his menacing threat and arrogant self-importance. Screw Sangstrum and McWhorter and the layoff lists that wallpapered the halls at Global Harmonics. Screw all the overpaid lawyers who covered for their criminal greed. Screw the formula avarice that led Juan to take his own life. Of course the show would go on. It always went on. Victor had heard that so many times before. There was a reason. People bought tickets. People showed up. Showtime arrived and the talent took the stage, as simple a paradigm as any ever tested. The algorithm cared nothing for sorrow or disaffection. You were booked to perform, you were paid to perform, you performed. No more resistance.

If only Victor could come to terms with that clarity. He knew he was exposed. The company's demise was his fault. He had brought on the downfall of Global Harmonics and hidden out in a cover band that somehow made it to the bigtime. He didn't belong at Madison Square Garden. He didn't belong anywhere. That was why Torch called him the Nowhere Man. That was why Claire let him go. That was why he was an abandoned infant in the system whose parents never wanted to know what would become of him, a reject of normal order rightly set aside. That was why Sangstrum undermined him. That was why McWhorter had gone to war with him. That was why Katem had built an impermeable box around him. They did it because they could, because he was feeble, because the only constant in his life was that he was no good. His downfall was master-planned beyond the realm of human choice. Torch knew that. That's why Victor was backed by an insurance policy.

Victor's struggle would soon be over, but first the gig, just this gig. Don't self-defeat. Find your way back. Fight your way back. To hell with fatalism. If God wanted him to play the gig then he would find the will to play the gig. That would be his triumph. He would go out happy, whatever it meant to be happy. He had to hang on, bare and excluded and sliding into Katem's abyss. Playing once more would be his redemption.

He reached in his back pocket. Katem's no-downside letter was a folded-up scrap stashed in reserve. He hadn't signed it, but maybe he still could. He desperately wanted to stay with the band. He wanted to stay with Synthia and see where that would go. He wanted, he wanted, he wanted, but too damn bad. It was time to play the gig. That was all that mattered.

Synthia could see he was sweating uncontrollably. He wasn't even onstage and the lights remained low in readiness, but he was drenched below the neckline. She held his hand in the wings. He saw his lustrous guitar on the stand in the preshow light, a five-second walk from here to there. How hard could it be? He never wanted her to let go of his hand. He could stand there all night as long as she held his hand. Her touch was precious, daringly reinforcing, a connection to soul and spirit that conducted pure acceptance. His question about love, could there be love, there was an answer in her gift, a form and ideal buried in the shows but alive in her touch. She knew who he was. Confession be damned. She didn't care anymore than Claire where he grew up, how he grew up, all that he had missed in a normal family life. They were musicians. They could hold their own. He could hold his own. Yes, he could do that.

Not a minute later, Torch called the band together, his arms waving, his eyes alight. "Holy Mother of Invention, you're never gonna believe this. Joe Walsh grabbed me backstage. He wants to come out right before our finale and do 'Rocky Mountain Way' with us. Might stay onstage for the Preston tune."

Victor abruptly let go of Synthia's hand. "Walsh spoke to you?"

"Yes, that would be the part where he said he wanted to jam with us, help lift us into orbit. We never played 'Rocky Mountain Way,' but you know it, right, Nowhere?"

"Yeah, but not the leads. Those are tough. I'd need to listen again. Give me a few minutes to log onto Spotify. "

Torch's sightline remained at eye level. "No time for tutorials. Walsh is going to be standing in front of you. It's his song. Don't think you gotta worry about playing the leads."

Synthia took his hand again and whispered in his ear. "Steady rhythm, Vic. Strum if you have to. You can do it. You're a pro, part of us."

"I did it once with him at a Ringo All-Stars show," interjected Phil-Phil. "Ringo wasn't feeling well and needed cover."

"You played drums with Ringo?" challenged Baker Bagley.

"I played drums *for* Ringo. And Walsh. Both perfectionists who demand dependability."

Victor knew where that comment was directed and was about to respond when Torch waved his arms again, this time to silence them. "I can't believe this conversation five seconds before curtain.

Enough, no squabbling. We're going on. Our set, then Walsh. We ascend anew."

The lights went black. Synthia took Victor's hand again and guided him onstage in the dark. The massive audience on its feet was generous, welcoming, deafening. Torch was on his mark. Baker Bagley was on his mark. Phil-Phil was at the kit. Someone must have introduced them, but Victor couldn't hear the PA over the roar of the crowd. In a half hour Victor would be playing beside Joe Walsh, no stress there. Madison Square Garden, Joe Walsh, and a song he hadn't played since he was fifteen. Phil-Phil was right, perfectionists demanded dependability. Torch was right, too—there was no precision without polish. How could he pull off an untried song playing next to Joe Walsh?

Screw that as well. It was half an hour in the future, deal with it then. The opening song as agreed would be Elvis Presley's "Burning Love." It was an inside straight for Torch, unbeatable for his range. Torch had trusted Victor's concept but made his own selection. Victor had been right before and he would be right again. This would fire up the crowd.

The stage lights blazed with an intensity that made Vegas seem balmy. The electrical heat almost knocked Victor off his feet, his untucked linen shirt soaked beyond the worst of his night sweats. The rotating spots were blinding. He could see nothing ahead of him but the back of Torch's frame. Beyond that was thunder, the din of the assembled. Could they see he was dripping and blind? What did it matter? Power on.

Phil-Phil hit the backbeat. Victor came in flawlessly on the guitar lead with Baker Bagley and Synthia building a fortified wall of sound. Their music flowed geometrically into the headcount, sprawling waves of amplified notes pouring through the rows of ticked patrons. Torch stepped forward, taking the crowd for himself, owning the room no matter the scale. The Act did what he always did: He held them in the palm of his hand before his lips uttered a line. He met the first verse with boisterous definition and on the chorus he deftly let it go:

I'm just a hunk, a hunk of burning love
Just a hunk, a hunk of burning love

Moments into the Elvis opener, Torch leapt off the stage and was in the aisles of Madison Square, same as he was at the 24 Karat Club. The Philosopher King was having his way with the lyrics, no matter the simplicity, no matter the nonsense. The Act was always The Act, and The Act loved Madison Square Garden. He had been born to play Madison Square Garden. Victor had been right, never more right, the liftoff impact as explosive as predicted. The melody landed perfectly, a liquid oxygen Falcon rocket squarely targeting its landing pad floating in the sea. Passion, beat, soul—was there anything The Act couldn't pull off?

I'm just a hunk, a hunk of burning love
Just a hunk, a hunk of burning love

The lighting was hotter than Victor had imagined, ceaseless roasting, the stagehands' warnings hadn't done it justice. He looked up and saw the video screens alternating one band member to the next, mostly Torch, cut to Synthia, then Baker Bagley and Phil-Phil, back to Torch, then to Victor. Close-up on Victor. Extreme insert shot of Victor. He couldn't hide. The cameras were everywhere, high-def on the huge screens. Victor's face was the size of a summer cabin, his fingers in close-up the size of Sequoia branches shredding the fretboard.

The audience was unfaltering. Victor stepped into a dark spot and focused on the solo notes filling in for harmony. He couldn't duck the cameras but he could avoid the spotlight, retreating to safety in the shadows, though it was no cooler there. His hair was singed, but his fingers knew where to land on instinct. Feel it. Embrace it. Let it go. Don't be drained. He was beyond joy, but in the clamor he couldn't escape dizziness. Not enough air coming into his lungs, not enough blood flowing to his forehead. The weakness was back, the flaw, the overthrow. He fought the takedown of his being, but the internal assailant had returned masterfully regenerated. He looked to Synthia who smiled to give him strength, but his knees, his spine, his head—all at once they were pounding, reduced by thinner and thinner air.

I'm just a hunk, a hunk of burning love
Just a hunk, a hunk of burning love

Fight it. Don't let the knees buckle. For the love of God, Madison Square Garden, opening for the Eagles, Joe Walsh in the wings. Don Henley had spoken to him, damn near a conversation. Walsh was coming onstage for their finale. Victor heard Torch's voice echoing off the back wall but his fingers were going numb.

I'm just a hunk, a hunk of burning love

Just a hunk, a hunk of burning love

Hold on, don't lose it. Damn, he dropped his pick. He played with his fingers but he couldn't sustain the lead line. Maestro Synthia looked at him for musical direction but couldn't cover his part, not on this orchestration. Baker Bagley turned up the bass line but couldn't cover for him. The crew on the mixing board half a basketball court away couldn't cover for him. Torch was down front, maybe he couldn't hear the failure. Torch looked back. He could hear it. The front row could hear it. The back row and cheap seats could hear it. Later Phil-Phil would beat him to a pulp and he wouldn't fight back, same as Providence, same at the group homes and foster care. The beatings were a constant, blow after blow to every inch of his torso. He thought about the pain coming his way again as Torch kept pounding the lyrics.

I'm just a hunk, a hunk of burning love

Just a hunk, a hunk of burning love

The sound board took his sliders to zero. Synthia brought up the lead line on the keyboard—she must have recorded him and played back the sample. Baker Bagley improvised on top of her and carried the bass notes she left uncovered. Torch sang louder into the microphone exponentially amplifying his voice. Victor was wilting, his knees locking.

I'm just a hunk, a hunk of burning love

Just a hunk, a hunk of burning love

Victor could feel the vibrations but no longer hear the music. Under the blistering lights, on the gigantic video screens he saw himself growing weaker. He felt his knees buckle. He was not going to make it to play with Synthia on their original. No, he would miss "Playing." He couldn't hold it together any longer. He had failed as planned, failed as fate demanded. He hoped Doc Sludge was ready in the wings as his backup, that Torch could ride out his prophesied implosion. Cash in the insurance policy, the big show would have to continue without him.

Onstage, in front of twenty thousand people, Victor passed out cold.

SIDE FOUR: EP BONUS JAM SESSION

They call it paradise, I don't know why
You call someplace paradise, kiss it goodbye.

Eagles, "The Last Resort"

Victor awoke in a hospital bed. He was weak, groggy, sore, weary—ample words could not be assembled to describe his discomfort. He hurt all over, every limb, every appendage, as if someone had hit him again dozens of times over. More than anything his mind was muddled. It was a familiar feeling. Too familiar, too many unresolved arguments with himself lost, won, and then lost again. He did not like feeling this way. He never liked feeling this way.

In his head he heard the soft refrain from "The Battle of Evermore." Why was he hearing that? He was never a big fan of Led Zeppelin, but he knew the band from the database. The haunting chorus was impossible to forget:

Dance in the dark of night
Sing to the morning light

He wasn't hearing it in his head. It was the Muzak version being piped into the hospital through the mono speakers in the ceiling, presumably to comfort him. There were no lyrics. That was the London Philharmonic version. He knew that from the database as well. This was weird. He wanted the music to stop but he couldn't make it stop.

He pulled himself up in bed. The movement in his extremities throbbed something awful. Had he fallen off the raised platform when he relapsed? Tubes were stuck in what seemed to be every accessible vein beyond his bandages, tape, and masking. That made no sense. It was overkill. They were fleecing his health insurance, except he no longer had health insurance. Could his condition have been worse than he thought—something more severe incapacitating him? He felt light-headed but unusually hungry. His waistline felt narrow, reduced, free of everyday tension. Hospital pajamas, of course. He also must have lost a lot of fluid sweating in front of twenty thousand people. He was surrounded by a thin white pull curtain hanging on chain links from a loop of metal rail. It was a room for two, but the other bed was empty. Maybe there was a God, at least he was alone. That was gift enough to make him a believer. Small talk would be dreadful, painful to a point of self-impalement. Imagine the back and forth:

"Where were you last night, bud?"

"Madison Square Garden playing guitar on 'Burning Love' until I fainted."

"You play behind an Elvis impersonator?"

"Not exactly, a guy named Torch."

"That's your story? You sure you remember it right?"

"Would it sound better if I told you we were opening for the Eagles?"

"They have you on some serious meds, huh?"

"I'm not sure. Have you seen anyone suspicious around invoking the words 'dead in this world'?"

"It's a hospital. People die here all the time."

No conversation, thank you, Almighty Overseer. No small talk. No ghastly, insidious chitchat. No roommate, good. He was completely alone. He didn't expect Torch would be there, not after he destroyed the gig, but wouldn't Synthia have shown up after the show? When he collapsed Doc Sludge must have finished his shift, but how had the rest of the show gone? Was he out of the band for good? Even Katem couldn't work that quickly. No, Katem didn't matter. He had to be out of the band. There was no chance Torch would give him another chance, no chance in hell after he put the Elvis Chapel of Love at risk. No band. No Philosopher King at his bedside. No Synthia with an S to comfort him. Nothing but lifelines and blipping monitors. He was disoriented, isolated in public, sequestered for judgment. The blame was his. Right, like collapsing under the searing lights was his fault. Heat stroke, fatigue, chronic pain—bodies gave out. Human beings were fragile that way. A little empathy, perhaps? Just a little?

He needed information. Medical care check-in. No hospital personnel in sight. He reached to the side table for his iPhone and looked at the lock screen. The time stamp was a wakeup call all its own. It said September.

That was not possible. He must not have fully comprehended the moment. Either he broke his phone when his legs gave out underneath him or the signal synch needed a reboot.

He looked again at his mobile. Corrupted device, he broke it when he fell. The month was wrong. There was no way it could be September. How could he have been out cold half a year? He had passed out onstage under stress. The most it could have been was a night's sleep; if he was dehydrated, another day on top of that. Despite how he felt, he wasn't traumatized. It was another relapse from getting his head bashed in. The lock screen had reset and frozen.

You, yes you, stand still, laddy.

Pink Floyd mashup from Led Zeppelin, but only in his head. Something wasn't right. Then the strangest thought. What happened to the holidays? What happened to Thanksgiving and Christmas? It had been months since he left Global Harmonics. He had been in Vegas more than two months, then a week getting ready for The Greek, then the trip back to Marin and another week getting ready for New York. Surely the band would have played a big New Year's Eve gig, but no one had mentioned New Year's. No one in the band exchanged a gift or mentioned any celebrations, special dinners, no decorations, not even a *bah humbug!* How could that be?

On closer inspection, his iPhone did not appear broken. There were no cracks in the glass touchscreen and the clock app was ticking normally. Fine then, the network data feed was off. His head wasn't clear, but he was lucid enough to know hours from months. Why would it say September when he left Global Harmonics in September?

Don't panic. Examine surroundings. He looked across the room and out the window where his annoying roommate would have been if he had one. Outside in the sunlight he saw green forest. Forest in New York City? Why had they transported him out of the city? Where was he? How long had he been unconscious? Why so many cords attached to him, so many blips and bleeps and digitally rendered sine curves on the monitors? He had hit his head. People died that way in bathtubs all the time, but they usually drowned. Could he have knocked himself out with a blow to the skull? He reached to his forehead to check for blood. There was no wet blood. He must have hit something on the way down from the elevated boards to the concrete. There had to be brain damage. Why else would he be feeling so drugged?

He pushed the button on the steel armrest to call for an attendant. When a nurse arrived, he saw the insignia on her white coat: Marin General. Next to that was her name: Shirley Chen RN. He never knew how bleached a hospital could be. White coats, white curtains, white bandages. A little color would brighten things up—would no one consider that? Forget it, he was wandering again. Maybe he had passed out longer than he thought, a mini-coma triggered by his concussion. They shipped him from New York back to Marin while he was unconscious. Hmm, why would they risk transporting him while he was out cold except to fleece his medical insurance? They would have checked his records and seen that his coverage had expired before sending him air-evac. It made no sense.

Wait, it could make sense. Katem did this. Katem was at the helm pulling all the levers. He'd been in a coma and Katem had taken command of his life. Monster once, monster forever. Katem had taken him down. That drink of water before he went onstage was Katem's doing. He'd poisoned Victor, watched him collapse, then carted him off while Doc Sludge took his place. Petrumi was in Katem's pocket and would still get his commission. Victor should have listened to Petrumi and done it Katem's way. Katem was lethal. Now what would he do, figure out how to kill him in the hospital? He was capable of it. Could Victor change his mind and testify? Was it too late? He wasn't ruling it out.

"How are you feeling, Victor?" Nurse Chen was reviewing the chart she recovered from the foot of his bed.

"Awful, mostly confused." He sat as upright as he could get, which wasn't very upright.

"It's to be expected. That was some beating you took. You've been unconscious almost a week. Apologies if you're a little dizzy. We have you on some top-shelf narcotics for pain management."

"Can you turn off the Muzak, please?" he pleaded.

"No problem. Some of our patients find that it calms them. You have the volume dial there on the bedside console."

Victor saw the dial and ended the Led Zeppelin wake, or was it Pink Floyd? The Muzak ruined them both. Almost a week? What beating? The beating was half a year ago. Didn't she know he played Madison Square Garden last night and passed out onstage? Some sick-minded investment banker had him poisoned and then freighted back to Marin. Of course she knew. She had his chart with all the details. Was she on Katem's payroll, too, those top-shelf narcotics meant to finish him off? She had to come clean. If he was going to die under the watch of Nurse Chen, so be it, but have the decency to be honest about the mercy killing.

"Why did they send me here?" Victor noticed the sunlight shining brightly into the room through the window. Was God calling for him or messing with his mind? The ambiguity made him more anxious. He didn't need a divine gesture. He needed to know what Nurse Chen knew to survive Katem's finishing move. He wasn't going to make it easy for Katem. She needed to help him escape. It was only fair, except he couldn't pay her as much as Katem.

"It was the closest hospital to where the ambulance picked you up." She looked again at his chart. "Providence, that's a bar over near the marsh. Karaoke, right?"

It wasn't possible. He was coming back to consciousness from the night of the beating? No, not this nightmare, not after Sangstrum and McWhorter. He should have been in a hospital in New York, not Marin. He had to let it go. He had to wake up and figure out where he was, how the gig had ended, how to get Synthia with an S to come for him.

"You're early on the mend, but it's good to see your eyes open. Like I said, the drugs we had to administer aren't the ordinary brew. I wouldn't be surprised if your mind wandered to some faraway places. Let's get some more fluids in you and flush them out. Now that you're conscious, I'm going to bring the doctor in to do some tests."

"Where's Thomas Katem?" demanded Victor.

"I have no idea who that is. No mention of him on your chart. A woman named Darcy Alden has been here a few times to see how you're doing. She asked that we call her when you woke up. Is that okay?"

"What about Synthia? Torch?"

"No Cynthia Torch in the notes. Just Darcy Alden. If you'd rather we call your family we can do that."

"I don't have any family." Victor looked away from the sunlight.

"I'm sorry to hear that. It's going to take a while for your thinking to even out. Let me get the doctor and then you can decide if you want us to call Darcy. Okay?"

"Yeah, okay." There was nothing else he could say.

Nurse Chen left the room. Victor looked at his iPhone again. September, six days since Providence. He had been unconscious six days in Marin General. There had been no relapse. He remained in the shadow of karaoke night, the day he was fired, the day Sangstrum and McWhorter had taken him down, the day he had taken himself down.

No band. No Petrumi. No Vegas. No Torch. No Synthia. No Elvis Chapel of Love. No Greek. No Joe Walsh. No Eagles. No Madison Square Garden. No hit song about to chart.

No more lies. No more broken deals.

For that blink of an eye, Torch and Synthia were the two most important people in his life. He never got to say goodbye to them. His last words to them were . . . what? Synthia had no last words he could place. Think, think. Something about Joe Walsh coming onstage. Torch had declared the vision: "We ascend anew."

No, No, No! Something was wrong, the picture had been too vivid. There had to be root in the real world, something that triggered his imagination. Some part of it had to be real, a point of connection, a physical anchor that was meant to tell him something, meant to cause him to reach out and embrace the elements that hid the next invisible fork in the road. It had to be so.

Victor grabbed his iPhone and brought up the search box. He pounded in the words "From Nothing" and hit enter. On the screen appeared multiple references to the Billy Preston tune—videos, MP3 downloads, sheet music, the original record, multiple cover versions. There was no mention of Vegas, no mention of a lounge at the Golden Nugget. He searched the name "Synthia Hamada." The return query asked, "Did you mean Cynthia Hamada?" He clicked yes and up came the results, numerous women on Facebook and LinkedIn named Cynthia Hamada, even Cyndi Hamada. None of them were her, not even a close match.

There was no grounding, no tangible dream reference he could find. There was no way to lean on the joy of the adventure, no way to extract a chance at love or triumph. It was a story of his invention, an impassioned letter to himself, more loss, this time of something he never had.

Then he thought it through, beyond the smackdown. If none of it was true, he had much more to consider. The threats and walls were also gone. Without the dark came the light.

Did that mean Juan was alive?

Did that mean Claire never got married?

Did that mean Global Harmonics was a going concern?

Still there was no closure. Who was Thomas Katem? Who had beaten him? He was in a hospital bed, that much was real. Did Sangstrum do this to him? McWhorter? He was broke and unemployed. How would he pay the medical bills? Where would he go? What would he do next?

He couldn't make any sense of it. He grew suspicious, then contentious, then irate. Nurse Chen must have lied to him. That wasn't a normal IV. He had to be hydrated after six days of drip. She was sedating him. Thomas Katem would never relent. She wasn't going for the doctor. He wasn't supposed to regain consciousness. She was putting on the final touches where Thomas Katem had paid good money for her handiwork. He was being murdered in a hospital bed. People died there all the time. God had a wicked sense of humor and he was the punch line.

This was all a sick joke. He looked again at his iPhone. Six days. He was supposed to believe he was in a bed in Marin General and only beginning to heal. Maybe so, but had he fought his way back only so that she could pull the plug? Would the enduring argument with his own voice end here?

A dream you dream alone is only a dream. A dream you dream together is reality.

The words came into his mind through the haze. John, borrowing from Yoko. Why wasn't he still with us? Why did God need John Lennon more than we did?

He had no proof of God. Nurse Chen was putting him back to sleep for eternity. Her true motive was God's will. Fine then, bring on sleep again. Permanent sleep would be dreamless, so he hoped. No meditation in Technicolor, no false hope of resurgence. When his eyes opened again, if they opened, he would at last have proof of God.

Even if she wasn't a murderer, he had never been worse off. There was no more meaning in his epic tale. He had failed on all fronts. If he awoke in this world, he might learn what had happened to him, but he would never learn why. There was no why. If there had been a path to happiness, he would have found it. There was no redemption. He was born to the wrong parents at the wrong time in the wrong place. It happened and it left him weak, unable to find safety or acknowledge trust. His lingering antipathy would forever contain his escape. If that meant he couldn't fit in, then he couldn't fit in.

Instead he would revel in music, the sounds and memories that connected those flailing years. He would replay in his mind the dizzying melodies etched on a stone wall holding him in a pen of purgatory. He could never escape. Limbo was forever. Anguish was punishment human beings weren't meant to comprehend. Sins were shared. Retribution was select. It was time to get used to the reality of pain. It was time to retreat, to give up on understanding. Until then extended sleep would be a brief, dastardly, cosmic gift. God had determined it was to be so.

>> <<

When Victor awoke the second time, Darcy was next to his bed. He felt better. Whatever poison Nurse Chen had pumped into his body had not killed him. Maybe this was how Katem got him to talk, confess, testify. They could keep him healthy but numb, temporarily out of pain but defenseless while they closed their file and finished the paperwork. He remained confused, overwhelmed, confounded by the deception of his own consciousness. He was physically stronger but scarcely coherent.

That didn't mean they wouldn't kill him later. Puppeteer Katem hadn't gotten to him, not yet—the first Thomas Katem, the real, actual Thomas Katem in the bar, the once friendly guy with the warring posse. It was as if no time had passed at all. He looked at the iPhone for reassurance. Six days, yes, and a few hours, that's all, no more manipulation of the game clock. He tried to zero in on what was tangible and what was perceived. He didn't know what had happened. He only knew for certain what hadn't happened.

"I'm so glad you're awake," said Darcy. "We were really worried about you."

"I think I look worse than it is. I don't know, maybe not."

"You look like you fell off Mt. Everest in an avalanche."

"Thanks, that's reassuring."

"It should be. You survived. A few scars become a man. Builds character, they say. Looks like you lost a little weight."

"Not the ideal way to slim down, but hey, whatever it takes to get into shape. It doesn't bother you, the way I look?"

She winced, the seriousness in her expression undefinable. He knew she was on his side, but he probably did look like the Elephant Man. He was back in their shared world and her kindness was as deep as her diplomacy.

"What happened to the company?" he asked.

"McWhorter agreed to buy it. Sangstrum is already gone. Most of us expect to be laid off soon. Not much we can do about it."

It was going to be an afternoon of awkwardness and disappointment. No way around that. Tough times, but at least she was there. That was hope. "No, not much you can do about it."

"It was what you thought, Vic. The shareholder meeting to close the sale is in two weeks. McWhorter already announced another target he intends to buy on the cheap. That would make nine including us he's rolled up, eliminating about eight-ninths of the cost. I don't know where he goes with all that."

Something was resonant in one of her syllables, a single alto note aglow. The way she said his name was different. At least what he heard was different. Maybe he was listening differently. The rest of the ruins surrounding them were the same. Something had to be different. Some goodness of the vision had to survive.

"He sells to an idiot," said Victor. "He'll sell the whole thing on revenue momentum, only the buyer won't factor all the one-time charges—which aren't really one-time charges if you understand the business—and they'll get stuck holding the bag."

"Are there buyers that dumb?"

He tried to sit up straighter but it hurt too much. He put his head back on the pillow, hunting for symbols, connecting rays of bearing. "Let's say there are investment bankers that motivated. Yes, there are buyers that dumb. I'm sure McWhorter has a short list."

"Why wouldn't Sangstrum sell to the guy who will take out McWhorter?"

"More press attention at a bigger take out where he still would be underwater and get nothing. I'm sure Sangstrum is getting some kind of kickback from McWhorter. We'll never see it. I tried, but I couldn't get him to cough it up. I blew the whole thing going at him head on."

"We know you tried, Vic. These guys are pros. You can't stop them with guilt. If honesty meant anything to them, they'd be working stiffs like us."

"You're right. They never cared about a word I had to say. I don't know why I thought they would. I lacked finesse. Evidence who is in the hospital bed with multiple injuries. Do you know how I got here? Who beat me up?"

"No idea, but I saw you the next morning. It was scary, you looked . . . I didn't think you were going to make it. The hospital called the office and it got routed to me. I came over here."

"Broken but not entirely. Does the name Thomas Katem mean anything to you?"

"No, it's not familiar."

Victor looked across the room and saw his soiled shirt hanging on a laundry hook. Remember now, damn it. Interpret, piece together, attach. "Check my shirt pocket for his business card. He gave it to me right before he beat the crap out of me."

Darcy looked at Victor improbably and went to the shirt. She reached in the pocket and found the business card crumbled but intact.

"Why would he leave it behind?" she asked. "It could lead to an arrest."

"It can't be his real name, but he must have wanted to leave some way to find him. I need to find out who he is."

"I wonder if he's in your iPhone contacts." She searched the name on his iPhone. "Yeah, there's a guy named Thomas Katem listed. You must have met him sometime and one of us put it in there. No phone number or company but there's a Gmail account, matches the one on the card. Should I reach out to him?"

"I doubt if that's going to get you to him. Are Max, Clarence, and Juan around?"

"I haven't seen them at work since the board meeting but I can text them. I'm guessing they haven't gone far. Should I ask them to do a trace?"

"It would help me clear my mind, yeah. Tell them to be careful. If it's the same guy, he's not particularly friendly."

"I'll get them on it."

Darcy was always dependable. Detailed, loyal, impossible to underestimate. A few words of text and the gang would be on the job, no fail.

"I wish I could explain all this to you, what's in my head," said Victor. "I'm not sure I can explain it to myself."

"You're going to be okay, Vic. The hospital staff says you'll be fine. It will take a while. You have to figure out what you're going to do next."

"I have to let go of the anger."

"Kind of goes without saying. Global Harmonics is over. Kaput. Next."

"Right, next. If only I had some money."

"You've had money before. You'll have it again."

"Sure I will." He paused on that, then looked out the window and continued without looking at her directly. "Darcy, do you believe in God?"

"That's an unusual question for you."

"Sorry to put you on the spot, but it's stuck in my head."

"I'm a Jesuit, have been all my life, so yeah, I have faith. It gets me through things like this. I believe in a lot of things, like peace in the universe is something we need to find."

"Tell me how you believe in God when so many bad things happen."

"The Jesuits teach us about finding God in all things. I get that. It works for me."

She was channeling a familiar voice and didn't even know it. She never knew Claire. She only knew of Claire. Maybe she called her at some point without his knowing. Had Darcy and Claire traded notes on God, on his ambiguity about God, his fury in the abandonment God had decided for him?

"Finding God in all things—is that how it works? That's too simple."

"I wish it were, Vic, but it's not. Faith is not as easy an answer as most people think it is. It's not a cop out. It's a commitment to different kinds of questions. You see what you see, you have what you have. You can't unravel it, but you can apply it. You learn, you do your best to make it better. You see the miracle of time and know you are a part of it and it is a part of you."

"Like a really good song." He tried to laugh even slightly, but it hurt his neck.

"Or a bad one you don't play again. Either one teaches us something important, something useful, something that matters. You can pick the songs you hear, but not the ones you write. Those come from somewhere else."

"Stop it, you're making too much sense. I'm going to lose the argument."

"It's not an argument. It's presence, as natural as what you see out the window. We learn to look harder, and then slowly our eyes start to open to what we otherwise can't see. First our eyes, then our hearts. Sorry, I might be getting a little out there, but you opened the door. It's who I am. It might be who you are only you don't know yet. You don't have to decide. If it happens, it happens. If not, that's cool, too."

"Creation, the unexplainable inspiration of creativity, I guess that's as sufficient an argument as there is. At peace with the Philosopher King."

"Not sure I get that part."

"You wouldn't. It's part of The Act. When I've got some more energy, I'll explain."

"You don't have to explain, Vic. You have to be who you want to be and move forward."

Move forward. She had that right. Same as Claire, same as Synthia with an S, only Darcy was here and they weren't. That was reality. That he understood.

"How come I never asked you out?" mumbled Victor.

"That would be kind of weird since we worked together, don't you think?"

"Yeah, it would have been weird." Victor wasn't sure where to go from there. Where was forward? These things were never clear in his mind. Maybe they were never clear in anyone's mind. He had to try. That was part of letting go of the anger.

"We don't work together anymore, so maybe it's not that weird?" There it was. Presence. He hadn't opened the door, she had.

Maybe they both had. His head was spinning again as he saw that she was leaving. That wasn't what he had in mind. He needed to backpedal, or was he reading too much into her exit? She probably needed to think about it. Thinking about it would be a good thing, a considered decision, no regret that way. Turn back, don't go out the door. He was ready to take a real risk, an important risk, one that mattered. The soundtrack needed adjustment. Tune left, tune right. Find the right channel.

Oh won't you stay, just a little bit longer.

"Darcy, are you coming back later?"

She paused at the door. "I can."

"That would be awesome."

"I thought you hated that word. Never mind, I'll be back. I want to hear about the Philosopher King."

Victor nodded. As she reached for the doorknob, she hesitated again, seeming to remember something. She reached in her backpack and retrieved a rumpled sheet of paper.

"I almost forgot to give this to you. I found it in the bottom drawer of your desk when I was emptying out your office."

"I don't want any souvenirs, Darcy. I don't want anything that reminds me of that place."

"The paper is pretty old, but it looks like your handwriting, some lyrics. *Wishing the Eyes of Shakespeare.* I think it's good but I'm biased."

Victor looked at it and saw it was an early incarnation of his handwriting. He remembered putting it in that drawer so many years ago. He had found it in one of his boxes when he moved to the Bay Area. He remembered writing it for Claire—at least he thought he had written it for Claire. That's how he had remembered it and how she had remembered it. His eyes tracked to the bottom of the page and he saw that he had dated it. He was fifteen when he wrote it, ages before he met Claire. The words stayed with him.

"You take it," he said.

"Are you sure? It's kind of personal."

"If I want it back, I'll ask you for it."

Darcy smiled cautiously, as if she knew what he meant more than he did. Then she left.

Victor looked out the window and watched her drive away through the lofty redwoods in her lime green Prius. When she was long out of sight, he grabbed his iPhone and launched the LinkedIn app. He needed to be sure of something. He paused a moment, then looked up Claire Mathias. Her name was still the same. Maybe she wasn't married. He had to know.

He dialed her number, but before anyone answered, he disconnected the line.

He had to move on. He had to let go. The commitment to move forward fell upon him. If he was starting over, the promise had to be whole. Starting over was moving on. Starting over was letting go. Everything that mattered was ahead. He had to build it completely to ascend anew. It began from nothing.

>> <<

Two weeks later the crowd at Providence was a full house. If Live Band Karaoke was on the schedule, the world was back in its proper order.

Victor had been out of the hospital for three days. Timing being everything, he walked out the door commensurate with the termination of his insurance coverage. That made the prospect of a relapse pragmatically impossible, or at the very least someone else's financial problem. He had confessed to Nurse Chen and apologized for thinking the worst of her intentions in the fog of medication. She was glad to know he no longer thought of her as an assassin and suggested for a while that he "take it easy." Did she know she was borrowing from the Eagles? It hardly mattered but it made sense.

Johnny Olano was onstage, mostly sober. He had welcomed back Victor before launching into "All Shook Up." Now he was belting out "Don't Be Cruel." Victor thought later on he would ask Johnny if he ever performed an Elvis wedding. He didn't know Johnny that well but thought he might be good at it, make a little money to carry him through retirement.

Max, Clarence, and Juan entered the club and headed straight for Victor near the stage, where he waited for his spot in the line-up. The Tres Amigos—the Three Musketeers of Geekdom—remained an inseparable pack, once and always the algorithm valiant. Victor took comfort in that continuity.

"Damn, you look like an MMA victim," began Max. "Darcy said try not to look. You in pain?"

"You should have seen me two weeks ago when she did. I'm getting better. Most of this will heal."

Clarence stared at him like a scientist collecting data. "I doubt that. You have welts in your skull structure."

Juan tried not to look, but at least he had the good sense not to say anything to make it worse. "We were worried about you, amigo."

Victor knew he looked terrible, but he was ready to move onto something more important. "How's it feel to be out of there, done with Global Harmonics? Shareholder meeting was this morning, right?"

Max pulled Clarence back from inspecting Victor's face. "Yeah, we missed you there, Selo. Whole thing didn't take half an hour. Never thought I'd embrace unemployment, but it's better than grinding out more of the same for douche tyrants. I guess we're here to celebrate."

"I'm relieved," said Clarence. "Ready to write code again."

"I feel free," said Juan. "A little hungry, but free."

Victor glanced at Johnny, who was gaining momentum in the aisles, then looked back at his colleagues. "I'm sorry, I didn't think I belonged at the meeting. I'm still feeling incomplete. Any chance you were able to track down Thomas Katem? Is he the guy who beat me up?"

Max took a swig of his beer. "Yeah, we located him. The thing is, there is no Thomas Katem, not one that matches your description. It's an alias. He made it up."

"How do you know that?" asked Victor.

"He told us," blurted out Clarence.

"He talked to you? How do you know it was him if that's not his name? How did you get to him with an old email address?"

Max took the lead again. "That email bounced liked we expected, but for kicks we ran it through the archive at Global Harmonics. Server encryption took us about a minute to pierce."

Victor wasn't surprised but felt he had to act like he was. "Privacy laws not a problem?"

"They left the door open and we don't leave fingerprints. It's the twenty-first century. Privacy is a myth. We did a search and found his TKatem Gmail account matchup with a retail shareholder by the name of Louis Martini, which is a joke when you think about it, another alias. Louis voted his shares in a proxy once using that email to confirm, so we tracked his custodial account."

"Don't tell me you tapped his brokerage," asserted Victor.

"Tapped is a troubling word," said Clarence. "We accessed his client trading info and got his phone number, no big deal."

"So that's the guy who beat me up, Louis Martini, which is not his real name, a shareholder pretending to be a guy named Thomas Katem?"

Clarence looked again closely at Victor's wounded face. "Not exactly, but Louis hired the guys who beat you up and told one guy to use the name Thomas Katem. It was like Louis wanted you to contact him, so he had them plant the business card. We called the number."

"He had no problem talking to us, seemed to be expecting the call," said Juan.

Johnny Olano segued to one of his signature tunes, "Viva Las Vegas." Victor moved closer to the geek squad so he could hear better over the building vocals. "Okay, who is he?"

"You met him once before at an investor conference where you spoke," said Max. "He was impressed and told you his name was Thomas Katem."

"So that's how I got his name and email the first time and gave it to Darcy to put in my contacts, even if it was a lie. Why did he kick the crap out of me? Why so many guys? Why so brutal?"

"You sounded too good when you spoke," said Juan. "You always do."

"It was over a year ago," continued Max. "He loved your vision for the new product line. Our stock was down 50% so he went all-in. A year later the stock was down another 50% and he had a margin call. He lost everything, a butt load of cash."

"Blamed you for the company crapping out," interjected Clarence. "When he heard that McWhorter was taking it private at pennies on the dollar, he had no comeback. He was counting on you."

"How did he know what was happening on the inside?"

"Old friend of McWhorter, or so he said," explained Max. "McWhorter called him after you broke his jaw with the laptop and told him he had the deal and invited him in. He had no money to play. It set him off."

"The whole thing was revenge for something that wasn't my fault?"

Max took another swig of his beer. "Pure revenge. Does that seem strange to you? And it sort of was your fault, just not the way he thought."

"I got beat up and almost died for failing to deliver on a speech. A guy bets on me and loses because I couldn't get Sangstrum to support my product plans. Can we track him to an address, have someone go after him?"

Clarence downed his beer. "He said if you did, he would kill you. I'm not an expert on these things, but I'm thinking you should probably move on."

"Sounds like the right move," commented Juan. "Bodily safety is where I'd go."

Victor didn't know how to respond. The room would have gone quiet, save for the Elvis beat blaring from the speakers. Johnny Olano had the mic and was hitting it hard on his finale, "Burning Love." Juan stared quietly at Victor, who looked back at him with a sense of relief.

"Do you mind if I ask you a personal question?" continued Juan.

"Personal as in . . . ?"

"Like, a hypothetical situation. Like if I had a trace on all of Sangstrum's email accounts and knew he had a bank account in the Caribbean and there was a line of shell companies leading back to Sangstrum and $5 million had been passed to Sangstrum from McWhorter, is that something you'd want to know about?"

Max and Clarence smiled. They had trained Juan well.

"To tell you the truth, Juan, I wouldn't want to know."

"Really, no?"

"No, but I'm certain the IRS and the SEC would. Do you think you could accidentally leak record of the bank transfer to their whistleblower hotline without a direct trace back?"

"I think if Max and Clarence and I worked together on it, it could happen. Router paths aren't that hard to obscure, hypothetically speaking."

"Hypothetically speaking, I think that would be immensely gratifying," said Victor. "Won't fix anything, but at least it will cost Sangstrum most of his illegal spoils defending himself in court and probably ruin him in the press so he can't screw over anyone else. Cook us up a little pendejo pudding!"

"I like that," said Juan. "Where'd you come up with that, 'pendejo pudding'?"

"It came to me."

"What about McWhorter?" asked Max.

"That monstrosity is bulletproof, don't waste your time," said Victor. "Rumor has always been that he has designs on high political office. Campaign strip down should be punishment enough."

"We can always help the press with fact checking, exhume the latent tidbits," said Max. "Should we consider the case closed?"

"I think we're where we need to be for now. You guys are amazing. You should think about starting your own surveillance company. There's a lot of demand for legitimate counter-hacking. Global market opportunity, big bucks."

"Only if you're the CEO," said Max. "I'll bet I could get Bud Thacker to roll the angel round. He's done okay by us. He'd go again."

"Seriously?" laughed Victor.

"Mega-seriously," said Clarence. "What do we know about global market opportunities? We write code."

"You don't need a CEO and you don't need me, but I'm flattered you'd ask."

"Don't be flattered, this is business," said Max. "Thacker wouldn't bet big money without you. He knows what you can do. We know what you can do."

"If we're gonna write code, someone has to deal with the distractions," added Clarence. "You're the only stick figure we trust."

"I'm too old to do another startup. They're for young guys like you. I don't have it in me to try again."

"You're never too old to make something happen, boss. It's a blank canvas. That's as good as it gets. You can't get lower than zero. Let's build something."

Juan, it had to be Juan. Living, breathing, nineteen-year-old, probably illegal Juan. He had learned the culture. He was convincing. No way to argue with nowhere but up. It was tempting. He'd need to find the inner resolve. These guys might be the way back. Maybe. Just maybe.

"I'll think about it. You think about it, too. Fair enough?"

"Fair enough," said Max. "We're gonna get some more beers. We figure you're going to sing so we probably should get drunk."

Victor smiled. He knew his work wasn't close to done. It was beginning. Global Harmonics was dead. He wanted vindication but that wasn't possible. How could he be vindicated? Who could absolve him of guilt? The rules had changed too dramatically and being right was no more important than being without blame. Going forward was what counted, survival and rebirth. Redemption was an ideal, an unobtainable form as Plato would have it. Redemption was a path, not an outcome. A path had to be a continuum. It was as it should be. He was starting over again from nothing.

Johnny Olano stepped off the stage to warm applause. Victor beheld him with love and aspiration. He was envious, but in a gracious manner, more curious than longing. The applause for this old amateur was more than polite. It was enthusiastic. It was authentic. It was earned. Johnny had pulled off something few would achieve in a lifetime. He was appreciated and admired for who he was. He created joy even when he sang out of tune. His performances were as natural as the redwoods. That was enough to make anyone believe in God.

It was Victor's turn to take the mic. He had chosen his selection carefully.

"What are we doing, King Biscuit?" asked his old friend Leonard, the lead guitarist.

"You guys know 'Nothing from Nothing' by Billy Preston?"

"That's different, not exactly in your range. Haven't played it in a while, but we can probably make it work."

"Let's make it work."

As Victor took the stage, he saw Darcy enter the club. She was smiling again, her optimism reliably alight. He waved to her from the stage and she headed down front. He was pretty sure she was going to like the song. Afterward he would do what he should have done a long time ago. Her voice would help him change the question. He would no longer demand proof of the intangible, only reassurance that inspiration wouldn't abandon him. The inextinguishable was a privilege to be cherished, a gift to be respected, a mystery that overturned hope if unraveled.

The band came in strong, surely improvising on the unfamiliar but only Victor would know that. In a burst of uncontained energy, the lyrics flowed easily from his lips:

Nothing from nothing leaves nothing

You gotta have somethin' if you wanna be with me

Victor held the mic tightly. Applause bounced off the walls, a resounding reception. Though he'd never sung it before, somehow he knew all the words.

To hell with Madison Square Garden. Providence was a solid gig. The Nowhere Man was going somewhere.

Sing it. Live it. Hold it. Build it.

Dream on.

Timbre, baby, timbre.

Finis

ACKNOWLEDGEMENTS & LINER NOTES

This is my third book. There's something complete about a trilogy, even if the three books only hang together in loose themes. For me, that's reinvention.

As always, it begins with my darling wife, Shelley. I told her I would set aside the years necessary to write three books and then we'd see what happened. I tried to bail on all three. She held me accountable for my pledge. She's tough that way. You should be so lucky.

Also holding my fingers to the keyboard is my forever supportive editor, publisher, and friend, Lou Aronica. It's not natural for me to take on the seclusion necessary of a writer. Lou reminds me to do it as me, as a form of introspection rather than introversion, shutting out all noise, inner and exterior. Again, you should be so lucky.

You'll see my dad mentioned near the top of the page count here in the dedication. We shared business and music and comedy, but not technology, rock and roll, or perennial obsession with existential doubt. Back-to-back generations are tough, particularly with Type A volumes thundering down the path of the immigrant's legacy. We got there, somewhere. He told me to read Twain, choose words carefully, and make a reasonable attempt at being clear. I was able to read Twain faithfully. The rest is a work in progress. His words matter more than mine.

Harry Shahoian taught me about the day-to-day life of a working Vegas musician, the dynamics of an old-school no-cover lounge in the modern era, and what it means for a band to own a room hour after hour, night after night, week after week. Brendan Paul, who owns the world-famous Graceland Wedding Chapel on Las

Vegas Boulevard showed me how his Elvis Weddings surprise and delight devoted couples nine thousand times each year.

Scott Freiman, creator of the lecture series *Deconstructing the Beatles*, has taken me inside the music of the lads from Liverpool at depths I never knew were reachable, with or without a *Yellow Submarine*. Lisa Hickey at The Good Men Project teaches me something new about written ideas every single day. Gene Del Vecchio is always there for me in every moment of doubt. Kate Zentall is like having a second literary conscience from concept to semicolon.

My early draft readers not only offered me consequential feedback that made me work harder at tearing down the wall, but also reminded me how much friendship matters in getting over, around, and through every wall that can't be psychically eliminated. They also remind me that the art of literature is not so much what the author writes as the creative thinking it can ignite in the reader. Yeah, Lennon/McCartney and Dylan deserve credit for all the things we thought they meant whether or not they loaded their lyrics with secret meaning—we wouldn't have come up with our nutty interpretations except for listening, so it's a fair exchange. Deepest thanks to Philip Hopbell, Karen Nishimura, Bryan Yates, Jeff Sturges, Mark Lloyd, Sabrina Roblin, Paul Shitabata, Stephen Jay Schwartz, Wilson Milam, Jon Ochiai, Robert Blair, Brian Thomas, Julie Singer Chernoff, Beth Collins Ellard, Lance Groody, Ed Wolfman, Lee Ruttenberg, Barb Adams, Dan Sherlock, Robert Gonsalves, Bruce Friedricks, David Leibowitz, Annsley Strong, and Robert Burke Warren.

Others in the band on this tour include the usual suspects at The Story Plant. Aaron Brown makes all of us look better than we are with website excellence and online promotion. Nora Tamada, again my eagle-eye copyeditor, fixes every mistake I missed and then challenges me to inject that final sparkle into the phrasings that matter most; she is also a true champion of this tale and provided some last minute feedback that caused me to polish it once more.

All books begin somewhere, for me largely in the wandering mind, decades of processing symbolic references, and the percolation of reemerging images. I have always been enamored with song-cycles, those audacious and often imperfect bodies of music that attempt to tell a story or collectively express a formative theme. When I first purchased a VCR in the mid-1980s, there was no question how initially to put it to work. I unearthed a VHS copy of *The Wizard of Oz*, set the movie volume to silent and then let it roll against an amplified vinyl LP playback of Pink Floyd's *Dark Side of the Moon*. The drill back then was common knowledge, and while it was a bother to keep flipping over the record on the turntable every twenty or so minutes, the combined experience lived up the billing. It occurred to me then that the fusion of a concept album and dual-world allegory was a creative challenge worth investigating. While it took me thirty years to figure out how to go after that notion and then two years with my head down, the emotional journey I discovered in its core now at last begins to make sense to me.

I remember in high school seeing the lyrics to "Eleanor Rigby" in a poetry compilation and one enlightened teacher thanking the publisher for being so bold. I also remember another teacher reminding us that no matter what we might read to the contrary in *Rolling Stone*, Jim Morrison was not a poet. The moral of that story is that some people will open your eyes while others try to close them. When you are most impressionable, stand vigilant. A good idea does not cancel out a bad idea, and vice versa. Remember that.

A few days after I finished the first full rough draft of this novel, around the first day of summer in 2016, I happened upon one of those silly ten-question PlayBuzz quizzes on Facebook that posed the evaluation: "What Your Taste in Classic Rock Says About You." This one was posted by a community member called Ziggy Stardust. Some of the bands I clicked as preferences in the various questions included the Beatles, Eagles, Led Zeppelin, Fleetwood Mac, the Rolling Stones, Pink Floyd, and the Who. On my preference of how I most preferred to listen to music, I picked "live." I earned the descriptor "groupie." While I wasn't particularly flattered by that label, the extended description of "the me in music" rang proudly true:

> *You practically worship rock n' roll, whether by actually being a groupie or just being a dedicated fan. You are loyal when it comes to friends, lovers, and family, and wouldn't dare do anything to lose their trust. You*

> *get heartbroken easily, but quickly move on. Instead of sorrowing over it, you channel your feelings into creative works. As your favorite musicians, you are dedicated and passionate about what you love!*

I can live with that. I do live with that.

Sometimes I'm convinced there is a soundtrack to our lives, an endless set of songs playing in our heads behind our actions, encounters, and contemplations. Weird idea, huh? That would reduce our lives to the confines of an exaggerated movie, the high and low notes scored with bass and treble accents. When I hear myself thinking—which is more often than I would like—I give thanks to the composers and lyricists who messed with my mind and brought me into theirs. If you were one of those, consider yourself here acknowledged. That backbeat is as real as it gets. You suffering songsters make it happen.

Los Angeles, California
Spring 2018

DISCOGRAPHY

Many of the brief references, allusions, and quotations utilizing famous songs are embedded throughout the text. Below is additional attribution for excerpted lyrics appearing throughout the novel where spot notice might have interrupted story flow. Any mistakes or omissions here or throughout the novel are entirely unintentional with deepest apologies to the writers. The intended fair use inclusion of all these amazing words is honored with gracious thanks and lifelong appreciation from the author. The citations below were notated mid-2017 in *Wikipedia*.

Track 1

"Dream On," as performed by Aerosmith, written by Steven Tyler © 1973.

Track 2

"Hollywood Nights," as performed by Bob Seger and the Silver Bullet Band, written by Bob Seger © 1978.

"Take Me to the Pilot," as performed by Elton John, written by Elton John and Bernie Taupin © 1970.

Track 6

"Play That Funky Music," as performed by Wild Cherry, written by Rob Parissi © 1976.

"Devil With A Blue Dress," as performed by Mitch Ryder and the Detroit Wheels, written by Frederick "Shorty" Long and William "Mickey" Stevenson © 1964.

"Devil Inside," as performed by INXS, written by Andrew Farriss and Michael Hutchence © 1988.

"Goodbye to You," as performed by Scandal, written by Zack Smith © 1982.

"Will It Go Round In Circles," as performed by Billy Preston, written by Billy Preston and Bruce Fisher © 1972.

"Nothing from Nothing," as performed by Billy Preston, written by Billy Preston and Bruce Fisher © 1974.

Track 7

"Rock and Roll," as performed by Led Zeppelin, written by John Bonham, John Paul Jones, Jimmy Page, and Robert Plant © 1971.

"Sympathy for the Devil," as performed by the Rolling Stones, written by Mick Jagger and Keith Richards © 1968.

"Gimme Shelter," as performed by The Rolling Stones, written by Mick Jagger and Keith Richards © 1969.

"Miss You," as performed by The Rolling Stones, written by Mick Jagger and Keith Richards © 1977.

"A Hazy Shade of Winter," as performed by The Bangles, written by Paul Simon © 1966.

"Crazy on You," as performed by Heart, written by Ann Wilson and Nancy Wilson © 1976.

"Superstition," as performed by Stevie Wonder, written by Stevie Wonder © 1972.

Track 8

"I Gotta Feeling," as performed by The Black Eyed Peas, written by William Adams, Stacy Ferguson, Jamie Gomez, Pierre Guetta, Allan Lindo, and Frederic Riesterer © 2009.

"Roll With The Changes," as performed by REO Speedwagon, written by Kevin Cronin © 1977.

"Find Your Way Back," as performed by Jefferson Starship, written by Craig Chaquico © 1981.

"Twilight Zone," as performed by Golden Earring, written by George Kooymans © 1982.

"California Love," as performed by Tupac Shakur, written by Tupac Shakur, Andre Young, Woodrow Cunningham, Norman Durham, Mikel Hooks, Ronald Hudson, Christopher Stainton, Larry Troutman, and Roger Troutman © 1995.

"Heard It Through The Grapevine," as performed by Marvin Gaye, written by Norman Whitfield and Barrett Strong © 1968.

"While My Guitar Gently Weeps," as performed by The Beatles, written by George Harrison © 1968.

Track 10

"Let's Go Crazy," as performed by Prince and The Revolution, written by Prince © 1984.

"Nowhere Man," as performed by The Beatles, written by John Lennon and Paul McCartney © 1965.

"Sugar Sugar," as performed by The Archies, written by Jeff Barry and Andy Kim © 1969.

"Elevation," as performed by U2, written by Bono, Adam Clayton, The Edge, and Larry Mullen, Jr. © 2000.

"L.A. Woman," as performed by The Doors, written by John Densmore, Robby Krieger, Ray Manzarek, and Jim Morrison © 1971.

"In The City," as performed by Eagles, written by Joe Walsh and Barry De Vorzon © 1979.

Track 15

"Burning Love," as performed by Elvis Presley written by Dennis Linde © 1972.

EP Bonus Jam Session

"The Battle of Evermore," as performed by Led Zeppelin, written by Jimmy Page and Robert Plant © 1971.

ABOUT THE AUTHOR

Ken Goldstein advises start-ups and established corporations in technology, entertainment, media, and e-commerce. He is currently chairman of ThriftBooks Global, the worldwide largest online seller of used books, and The Good Men Project, an expansive digital content network offering perspectives on social issues in the twenty-first century, where he is a frequent contributor. He publishes the business blog CorporateIntel.us and speaks frequently on the topics of creativity, innovation, and high-performance teamwork.

Ken served as chief executive officer and chairman of the board of SHOP.COM, a market leader in developing creative new experiences for online consumer commerce through the convenience of OneCart®, its patented universal shopping cart. SHOP.COM was acquired by Market America, where Ken became a strategic advisor to the company's founders and senior management.

He previously served as executive vice president and managing director of Disney Online, the business unit of the Walt Disney Internet Group that produced the leading entertainment web destination for kids and families. Key achievements at Disney developed by his teams included launch of the first massively multiplayer online game for kids, *Toontown*, as well as FamilyFun.com, Movies.com, and the early broadband service Disney Connection.

Prior to Disney, Ken was vice president of entertainment at Broderbund Software and founding general manager of the company's Red Orb Entertainment division. Before the formation of Red Orb, he was responsible for all aspects of development on Broderbund's acclaimed *Carmen Sandiego* series. He also worked as a designer/

producer at Philips Interactive Media and Cinemaware Corporation, and for several years as a screenwriter and television executive.

Ken and his wife Shelley, who teaches English as a Second Language, make their home in Southern California, where he is active in local government and children's welfare issues. He has served on the boards of Hathaway-Sycamores Child and Family Services, the Make-A-Wish Foundation of Greater Los Angeles, and Full Circle Programs. He received his Bachelor of Arts degree from Yale University.

His first book, *This Is Rage: A Novel of Silicon Valley and Other Madness*, was published by The Story Plant in 2013. It was a Barnes & Noble bestseller and has been adapted by the author for podcast and stage production. His second book, *Endless Encores: Repeating Success Through People, Products, and Profits*, was published by The Story Plant in 2015. *From Nothing: A Novel of Technology, Bar Music, and Redemption* is his third book.

CPSIA information can be obtained
at www.ICGtesting.com
Printed in the USA
BVHW031154250919
559364BV00001B/23/P

9 781611